"ENOCH ALWA

Susan An

"ONE OF MY VERY FAVORITE AUTHORS!"
Julia Quinn

"RICHARD AND SAMANTHA MAKE AN EXPLOSIVE COMBINATION."
Kasey Michaels

"A FUNNY, FRISKY SERIES."
Publishers Weekly

"ENOCH FINDS THE RIGHT COMBINATION OF SEXY AND FUN FOR A FABULOUS READ."
Oakland Press

He tilted his head at her. "What?"

"Just taking you in," she said with a smiling sigh. "You look good with that sexy crazy bed hair and the stubble. Does it feel like we've known each other for a year?"

Richard shook his head, feeling his heart beating all the way out to his fingertips. "Sometimes it feels like a day. That first day. Electric."

"Yeah. Electric. We do have the sparks, don't we?"

As he came downstairs twenty minutes later, he hummed "Rule Britannia." That amusement stopped as the front bell rang. He paused on the landing while Reinaldo appeared to pull open the door. "Good morning, Detective," the housekeeper said, stepping back.

Homicide Detective Frank Castillo of the Palm Beach Police Department sauntered into the foyer, looked up to see Rick, and gave a half wave. "Good morning, Rick. Is Sam around?"

Another thing his life had become since he'd met Samantha Elizabeth Jellicoe—chock full of surprises.

By Suzanne Enoch

Contemporary Titles

A Touch of Minx
Billionaires Prefer Blondes
Don't Look Down
Flirting With Danger

Historical Titles

Twice the Temptation
Sins of a Duke
Something Sinful
An Invitation to Sin
Sin and Sensibility
England's Perfect Hero
London's Perfect Scoundrel
The Rake
A Matter of Scandal
Meet Me at Midnight
Reforming a Rake
Taming Rafe
By Love Undone
Stolen Kisses
Lady Rogue

SUZANNE
ENOCH

OF Minx

AVON
An Imprint of HarperCollins*Publishers*

AVON BOOKS
An Imprint of HarperCollins*Publishers*
10 East 53rd Street
New York, New York 10022-5299

ISBN: 978-0-06-087523-7
ISBN-10: 0-06-087523-2
www.avonromance.com

First Avon Books paperback printing: October 2007

Printed in the U.S.A.

10 9 8 7 6 5 4 3 2 1

Chapter 1

Palm Beach, Florida
Thursday, 11:28 p.m.

Samantha Jellicoe crouched between a full suit of sixteenth-century Prussian armor and a life-size terra cotta warrior from the tomb of Qin Shi Huang. Footsteps entered the dark hallway a few yards beyond her and she stilled, keeping her breathing slow and deep.

"I know you're here," the deep voice said in a slightly faded British accent. "You may as well give up now."

No friggin' way. If he had any idea where she was, he would have found her already. Richard Addison might be a high-powered billionaire, a great white shark in the world of business, but where creeping around in the dark was concerned, he was a rank amateur.

She, on the other hand, had gone professional well before her tenth birthday. Resisting the instinct to back deeper into the shadows as he approached, she took a breath and held it. Adrenaline pumped into her system, making her want to move, make a run for it. That, though, wasn't part of the plan.

"You'll never make it," Addison's voice taunted. "All I have to do is stand in front of the door, and you lose."

He paused, his bare feet shifting in a slow circle about a dozen feet from where she crouched behind good old Colonel Klink's shield. If he'd had a flashlight with him she would have been done for, but she knew him, knew that his pride would consider a flashlight to be cheating. She'd counted on that, and had made her plans with his large ego in mind.

"Okay, have it your way," he continued. "I just thought it might be less humiliating for you to give up than for me to find you."

That was probably true, but obviously his chances of finding her weren't all that he claimed they were. As soon as his footsteps resumed down a side hallway she moved, springing down one flight of stairs and dashing into the first door on the left. Technically she could already have been out of the house with a million plus in merchandise, but the Matisse and the fourteenth-century Turkish tapestry weren't on her list. Neither were any other of the hundred-odd other pieces of art and antiques inside the three-acre expanse of Solano Dorado.

Still working in the dark, Samantha walked to the far corner of the library and unlatched the window there. Normally the alarm would have gone off, but she knew for a fact that the whole system was down. She smiled as she slipped out the window and onto the two-inch-wide ledge running along the wall. Now *this* was fun.

Reaching back, she pushed the window closed again. She couldn't latch it, but unless he came in very close he would never know anyone had unlocked it. Since she also knew that the power was out for at least the next twenty minutes, she had the early October darkness working in her favor, too.

Edging sideways another six or seven feet with her back to the wall, she stopped as she came opposite one of the ubiquitous palm trees surrounding the mansion and the entire walled-in estate. This one stood about five feet in front of her, and climbed about sixty feet into the air. "Okay, Sam," she muttered, drew a breath, and pushed out from the ledge.

For a second she hung in the air before she smacked into the palm's trunk and wrapped her arms and legs around it. That would have hurt if she hadn't worn jeans and a long-sleeved shirt. Black, of course; not only was the dark color slimming, but it was the clothing of choice for disappearing into shadows. Sucking in another breath, she shimmied up the rough trunk until she was about four feet above the house's roof.

The roof here at the back of the house was flat and had a very nice skylight set into the ceiling of the room she needed to get into. Glancing over her shoulder to make sure she was lined up, she pushed off backward, twisting in midair to land on her hands and knees on the rooftop. Keeping her forward momentum going, she somersaulted and came up onto her feet.

Normally speed wasn't as important as stealth, but tonight she needed to get into Richard Addison's office before he tracked her down. And for an amateur, he had a pretty good nose for larceny. Of course she was a damned bloodhound, if she said so herself.

With another smile she crouched in front of the skylight and leaned over to peer into the dark office space below. Just because he'd announced that he would wait for her to show up outside the door didn't mean that he'd done so. The padlock he'd put on the skylight stopped her for about twelve seconds, most of that taken up by the time it took her to dig the paper clip out of her pocket.

Setting the lock aside, she unlatched the skylight and carefully shoved it open, gripping the edge to lean in head first. The large room with its conference table, desk, and sitting area at one end looked empty, and her Spider-Man senses weren't wigging out.

Pushing off with her feet, she flipped head over hands and landed in the middle of the room, bending her knees to cushion her landing and cut down on any sound. A small black box topped by a red bow sat on the desk, but after a glance and a quick wrestling match with her curiosity, she walked past it to the refrigerator set into the credenza and pulled out a Diet Coke. Deliberately she walked to the office door, leaned against the frame, and popped the soda tab.

A second later she heard the distinctive sound of a key sliding into a lock, and the door handle flipped down. "Surprise," she said, taking a swallow of soda.

The tall, black-haired Englishman stopped just inside the doorway and glared at her. Blue eyes darkened to black in the dimness, but she didn't need light to read his expression. *Annoyed.* Rick Addison didn't like to be bested.

"You used the skylight, didn't you?" he said, making the sentence a statement rather than a question.

"Yep."

"I padlocked it an hour ago."

"Hello," she returned, handing him the Diet Coke, "thief. Remember?"

"Retired thief." He took a drink and gave it back to her before he continued past her to the desk. "You didn't peek?"

"Nope. The thought never crossed my mind." Well, it had, but she hadn't given in, so that counted. "I wouldn't ruin your surprise."

When he faced her again, his mouth relaxed into a slight smile. "I was certain you'd attempt to get around me in the gallery hall."

"I went out through the library window. If I'da been a bomb, you would have been blowed up, slick."

Grabbing her by the front of the shirt, he yanked her up against him, bent his face down, and kissed her. Adrenaline flowed into arousal, and she kissed him back, pulling off her black leather gloves to tangle her bare fingers into his dark hair. A successful B and E was a lot like sex, and when she could actually combine the two, hoo baby.

"You smell like palm tree," he muttered, sweeping her legs out from under her and lowering her onto the gray carpeted floor.

"How do you think I got in here?"

Rick's hands paused on their trek up under her shirt. "You climbed up the palm tree?"

"It's the fastest way to go." She pulled his face down over hers again, yanking open the fly of his jeans with her free hand. She loved his body, the feel of his skin against hers. It amazed her that a guy who spent his days sitting at conference tables and computers and arguing over pieces of paper could have the body of a professional soccer player, but he did. And he knew how to use it, too.

He backed off a little again. "This was supposed to be fun, Samantha. Not you climbing up a tree and jumping onto a roof thirty feet in the air."

"That *is* fun, Brit. Quit stalling. I want my present." She shoved her hand down the front of his pants. "Mm, feels like you want to give it to me, too."

With a moan he settled onto his knees, balancing as he pulled her shirt off over her head. Her bra followed, landing somewhere beside the conference table. Rick slipped out of his own shirt before he lowered his head again, flicking his tongue across her nipples while his busy hands opened her black jeans and yanked them down to her knees. "Black thongs," he breathed, sliding a hand between the panties and her skin.

"Surprise again," she returned, shoving his pants and boxers down past his thighs and kicking her own jeans off the rest of the way. The man had a serious thing for her underwear, thankfully only when she was in it. She'd never enjoyed shopping at Victoria's Secret as much as she had since they'd met.

He kissed the base of her jaw, chuckling at her sigh. "You are so easy," he murmured, slipping his fingers under the band of her thongs and stripping them off her.

"What would *Entertainment Tonight* say if they knew you were doing it on your office floor when you have twenty bedrooms?"

Slowly he pushed forward, entering her. "They would say, 'That lucky Addison bloke,'" he breathed, "'having sex with the beautiful, gorgeous, funny, brilliant, multitalented Samantha Jellicoe.'"

"It can't be flattery," she moaned, laughing breathlessly, "because you've already got my underwear off."

"Talk later," he returned, nibbling on her ear as he thrust. "Sex now."

Like she was going to argue with that. Samantha lifted her hips in time with his humping, wrapping her ankles into his thighs. She loved when he was like this, too eager, too aroused to even think straight. And nothing got him hotter than a little B and E on her part—which made the whole encouraging and supporting her retirement from the game just a little problematic.

As her brain shut down she dug her fingers into his shoulders, arching her back and squealing as she came. "You feel so good when you come for me," Rick grunted, lowering his head against her neck and increasing his pace. A second later he shuddered, growling.

"So do you, Brit," she managed, every bone and muscle going loose and disconnected as he relaxed on top of her. Rick sex—there was nothing like it in the world.

He rolled them so that he lay underneath and she could sprawl across his chest to listen to the hard, fast beating of his heart. For somebody like her who'd spent most of her life looking over her shoulder, ready to fade into the shadows with a few seconds' notice, the safety and satisfaction Rick brought her was just . . . indescribable.

Overhead the lights blinked on, blinding after the gloom. The fax machine on the credenza beeped and whirred to life, and the computer on the desk played the first four notes of "Rule Britannia" to announce that it lived.

"Ah, my natural habitat," Rick murmured, twining strands of her hair loosely around his fingers. "The soothing sounds of technology."

"With all of the antiques and your Sir Galahad rep, I still picture you more as the Henry the Eighth type. You know, before he got fat and crazy and married all those girls."

"I'm not certain I like the comparison even with the exceptions," he returned, his British drawl amused, "but I'll live with it. So, my heart, do you know what today is?"

Of course she knew. Aside from her having a nearly photographic memory, he'd been hinting at it for the past two weeks. "I like to hear you tell it," she said, raising up to kiss his chin. "But first I think I should point out that with the lights on and the blinds open, your security patrol outside is probably—"

"Shit," he muttered, grabbing his jeans. "I thought you gave them the night off. I didn't know we were starring in *Nudity at Night*."

Samantha eyed him as she pulled his T-shirt over her naked body. "Sure. I disable the entire estate security system, so at the same time I send away the only guys between the big bad world and you."

"And me?" he repeated, standing and reaching down a hand to pull her to her feet. "I'll worry about me. I thought you put all these security upgrades in to protect my Matisse and the Remingtons and the—"

She stopped the recitation with a kiss. "I know what you own, Rick," she said against his mouth. "And I think I've mentioned before that those things are not why I'm here."

"But they are," he returned, lifting the small black box off his desk and taking her hand. "Because as I started to say before you pointed out that we were engaged in some naked performance art, today is our one-year anniversary."

Samantha grinned. "Technically it's in about two hours."

Still holding her hand, he led the way out of the office and up the stairs to the master bedroom suite they shared. He liked to touch her, and considering the occasion they were celebrating this evening, the contact was just as important to her. If things had gone just a little differently that night . . .

"You saved my life," he said on the tail end of her thoughts.

"I was trying to rob you."

"But you didn't have to tackle me right when the bomb went off," Rick countered, drawing her down onto the couch beside him in the large sitting area of the suite.

And at the time she'd wondered whether saving the life of a very wealthy, very influential witness hadn't been the stupidest thing she'd ever done. Even if that had turned out to be the case, though, and contrary to her father Martin Jellicoe's lifelong lesson that nothing was as important as looking out for number one, she didn't think she would have regretted it. "Yes, I did," she said. "Now give me my present. My other present."

Snorting, he handed her the box. Pretending that she wasn't just a little bit nervous about what might be inside, Samantha pulled the end of the ribbon to untie the bow. "It's not cursed or anything, is it?"

"I've learned my lesson about that." Leaning over, he kissed the base of her jaw. "This is voodoo priestess and witch doctor certified safe."

"Smart ass." With a quick breath she pulled off the lid. And froze.

A couple of months ago he'd given her a gorgeous diamond necklace and a matching pair of earrings, and with his budget and eye for beauty she'd expected something equally . . . jaw-dropping. The best and worst case scenarios had both centered around the gift being a ring. This, though—

"Well?" he prompted, his Caribbean-blue gaze on her face.

"It's a piece of paper," she said, her breath rattling free in her lungs again. It wasn't anything sparkly, thank God.

"So read it."

Setting the box aside, she slowly scanned the embossed lettering on the check-size document. "You do have a flair for the unexpected," she said a moment later, her voice shaking a little. Inside she shook a lot harder. Okay. Christ. It *was* a ring—practically—just not the round kind with a diamond.

"It's the best nursery in eastern Florida," he said proudly. "I did some research. And they'll work with you in person, on line, by phone, however you like. They can find any plant in the world, whatever you want."

She blinked. *Get with it, Sam.* "But this gift certificate's for a hundred thousand dollars," she said. "That's a lot of plants."

"You mentioned maybe wanting to do some hardscaping, too. They also contract for that. Change the pool, put in a volcano, whatever—"

"Whatever I want," she finished.

"Whatever you want." He took the fingers of her free hand and kissed them, feather-light. "I told you that the pool area was yours. It needs to be redone, and you said you've never had your own garden. I know you've been doing some sketches, and I just want you to know that I meant it."

She met his gaze. "So this is your subtle way of telling me to quit stalling and get to work. I have not been stalling, though. You asked me to design that whole gallery for your Devonshire estate, and it does open in two and a half months. We've spent the last three months in England. I oversaw that gemstone exhibit for four weeks. And I have a new business, and—"

"I know. It's a gift, Samantha—not a complaint. If you want something else, I'll—"

"It's amazing," she interrupted, swallowing down her own nerves. Taken for itself, it was a really nice gift. He knew she liked gardens, and he'd just paid for her to create the garden of her dreams. Just because a garden had roots, and roots were a whole metaphorical thing for someone who until the past year had lived most of her life on the move—either he didn't know that, or he did. She was pretty sure, though, that he did. He wanted her putting down roots, and right there with him. But it was still a nice gift. "You're amazing." Slowly she kissed him. "Thank you."

"You are entirely welcome. And now, I have *Godzilla, Mothra and King Ghidorah: Giant Monsters All-Out Attack*—which I have on good authority is the best of the second wave of Godzilla movies—all cued up on the DVD player, or we can go to bed and have more sex."

Samantha laughed. That was her Rick. He might scare the hell out of her, but he did know what she liked. "Don't you want your present?"

He nibbled on her ear, sliding one hand up under her borrowed shirt to cup her breast. "You gave me your present."

Yowsa. "That was not a present. That was . . . us."

One eyebrow lifting, he straightened. "Very well, then."

Pushing her shirt back down, she stood up and went to her dressing closet. Reaching up behind the door, she freed the manila envelope she'd taped there. He probably wouldn't have snooped, and so she probably hadn't needed to hide it, but some instincts died harder than others. She lived in—used to live in—a world where people took things from one another, and so she took extra steps to make sure that her things stayed safe. And apparently now "her things" included Rick and her one-year-of-knowing-you present for him.

"Here," she said, handing him the envelope as she sat down beside him again.

Half his attention still clearly on her, he opened the metal tabs and tilted the contents onto his lap. "'Off-Road Extreme,'" he read, picking up the top brochure. "What's this?"

"It's three days in the Rockies taking four-wheel-drive vehicles through mud and water and over dirt and rocks and probably small furry animals, and then going fishing in the afternoons," she returned, leaning against his arm. "Man stuff."

"With man cars?"

"You betcha." She pulled out the ticket information. "You can redeem it anytime over the next year."

"This is for two," he said, eyeing her. "You're going fishing and mud flinging with me?"

Samantha wrinkled her nose. Maybe she sympathized with the fish too much to ever enjoy that. The whole being tempted and deciding whether to take the bait or not. "Only if my life depended on it," she said aloud. "I thought you and Donner could go bond or something. But don't you dare tell him that I voluntarily included him."

All she needed was for Rick's closest friend, that Yale graduate lawyer, to find out that she'd bought something for him. She'd never live it down. The Boy Scout was impossible to be around as it was.

"Your secret is safe with me. I'll tell Tom I insisted that

someone go with me, and throwing his name out was your last recourse to escape the trip."

"I like it." She kissed him again.

He smiled. "Happy anniversary, Samantha Jellicoe. So, Godzilla, or sex?"

Samantha laughed. "How about both?"

"I like *that*. I get to be Godzilla."

"I guess that makes me Tokyo."

Chapter 2

Friday, 10:10 a.m.

"Yes, she suggested your name, so she wouldn't have to go." Richard Addison flipped the off-roading brochure across the wide desk of Tom Donner, senior partner in the law firm of Donner, Rhodes and Chritchenson. If Samantha was finally beginning to soften toward Tom, he had no intention of ruining that phenomenon by letting the attorney know it.

"Huh. Well, since you're going, I guess she wouldn't set up a death hunt thing on me," Tom commented in his deep Texas drawl. "Probably not, anyway."

"Come on, admit it. It looks fun."

"For something cooked up by Jellicoe, it does look pretty good." Donner read through the brochure before he handed it back. "I still can't believe that you two—and you, especially—are celebrating the night you met. One of your security guards died when that bomb went off. And she was there to rob you, remember?"

Richard clamped down on his abrupt annoyance. "I think we've reviewed your opinion of what happened. This is about a gift she gave me."

Tom held up his hands. "Fine. You know more about her than I do."

"That's right. I do."

"Speaking of presents," the attorney continued, clearly doing his best to ignore the hostility Richard wasn't even trying to disguise, "how did she like *yours*?"

That was a damned good question. "It went over quite well, thank you."

Clearing his throat, Tom sat back. "Maybe we should just worry about filing these incorporation documents, and leave the personal stuff out."

"What's that supposed to mean?"

"You said 'quite well,'" he answered in a very poor imitation of a British accent. "That's how people talk about trips to the doctor, Rick. But I'm not butting in. I know you don't like that. So look over the dates I set for estimated tax payments and your first profit audit. If they're okay, we can get this filed today."

Richard shook himself. Samantha had said she liked his gift, and he had no reason to doubt that. No, she hadn't been precisely gobsmacked, but then she was unpredictable. That was one of the things he loved most about his former cat burglar. If that hadn't been the case, he would have given her jewelry, and she would have oohed and aahed, and he would have gotten a tie clip or something. His nagging worry wasn't that he was pushing her, because he knew that he was, but that he was pushing a little too hard again.

"Or we can sit here and contemplate our navels," Tom continued. "You're the boss."

"Oh, shut up," Richard grumbled, leaning over the incorporation documents again. After a moment, though, he closed the folder.

"It's just a present, Rick." The attorney dug into his desk for a roll of Life Savers and popped one into his mouth. "A really expensive one, but I don't think either one of you care much about that."

"I want to buy her a ring, Tom."

Silence.

Taking a breath, Richard pushed to his feet and paced to the window. Samantha's office, Jellicoe Security, was just across the street. As far as he knew, she was over there complaining to her business partner, surrogate father, and former fence, Walter "Stoney" Barstone, that stupid old Rick had given her a gift certificate for plants in honor of the anniversary of their first meeting.

"A ring," Tom finally repeated, his voice cracking. "*The* ring?"

"An engagement ring," Richard clarified. "I want to ask Samantha to marry me."

"Rick, that's—I don't even know what to say."

"How about, 'Yee haw, she's a hell of a gal, and y'all are great together'?" Richard suggested in his best imitation of a Texas accent.

"Christ, I hope I don't actually sound like that. And *can* you marry her? I mean, even if she says yes, does she have a birth certificate? A country of origin? You can't have her dad give her away, even if he's not dead like he's supposed to be, because the last time the two of them got together they tried to rob the Metropolitan Museum of Art."

"You make her sound like a space alien. I'm certain she has a birth certificate somewhere. And while I don't think I need to remind you, she also thought her father was dead until six months ago, and she worked with both the NYPD and the FBI on the Met job."

"Okay, then ask her. Pop the question."

He wanted to—and that was what made everything so difficult. When he wanted something, he got it. Either he bought it, or he maneuvered the opposition until it was given to him. That was how he ran his life. Samantha, though, didn't follow anyone else's rules or protocols.

The diamond necklace he'd given her in June when they'd stayed at his country estate in England hadn't spooked her. In fact, she treasured it. But a necklace didn't have the same significance as a ring. And he still wasn't certain about her reaction to being offered a garden.

He'd granted her the pool garden nearly nine months ago, and she still hadn't bought a single plant for it. Yes, they'd been busy with other things, but unless he was seriously mistaken, she *was* stalling about the garden. And if she couldn't handle a garden, she definitely wouldn't be able to handle an engagement ring.

"I'm not asking your permission," he finally said. "I'm just telling you."

"And in response, I'm just saying holy crap."

"Thank you for clarifying. Do you think Katie would be willing to take Samantha to lunch?" he asked, putting his back to the window in order to see the largest of the framed photos Tom kept on his desk. The whole towheaded Donner family—Tom; his wife, Katie; and their three children.

"Probably," Tom returned. "But Katie's not going to turn around and tell you everything they talk about."

That would have been handy, though. "I'm aware of that. But Samantha doesn't seem to have any female friends, and I don't want her getting all of her advice from Walter Barstone." In fact, the only positive thing he had to say about Barstone was that he was a better father to her than Martin Jellicoe had ever been. If he hadn't been a high-level fence and Samantha's spiritual and practical advisor, Richard probably would have been more inclined to like him.

"No, you don't want that," Tom agreed.

"The only other female she's had conversation with is Patricia, and there is no way in hell that I want Samantha getting chummy with my ex-wife."

"Are you kidding me? Those two hate each other."

Personally, Richard thought it was more complicated than that, but he wasn't going to discuss the dynamics of Samantha and Patricia's apparent horrified fascination with one another. "And I have no problem with their animosity," he said when he realized Donner was still looking at him.

"I'll mention lunch to Katie, then, but I'm not going to tell her why. You can do that."

"Thank you."

"Yeah, don't thank me yet. She may find out that Jellicoe really has just been using you since day one. You said—"

"That's enough."

"No, I'm getting this one out. You said she was 'fine,' I think it was, with the nursery gift certificate. Not bowled over. That makes sense. What does a cat burglar really want with a garden?"

Richard leaned his spine against the window frame. As a rule he didn't explode when he got angry; he got even.

Only Samantha could push him past where he wanted to be. "I am going to say this one last time," he murmured, knowing he sounded cold and not caring. "I love Samantha Jellicoe. I trust her. In her way, she's the most honest person I've ever met. If you two don't like one another, that's fine. I'm not throwing her over for you and I'm not throwing you over for her. The end."

From Tom's expression he wanted to keep arguing. Richard waited. After fifteen or so years spent maneuvering through tough and frequently hostile negotiations and usually coming out on top, he'd become something of an expert at reading people. And Tom Donner was about to concede. A nicer, less competitive man would probably have spared his friend the humiliation by changing the subject, but Rick wanted to hear it.

"Okay," his friend finally said heavily. "If you want her to stay around, then ask her to. I don't think *I'll* be the problem."

"Bastard," Richard growled. He looked from the window to the paperwork on the attorney's desk. "Let's go," he said, heading for the door.

"Go where?" Tom stood.

"Golfing." He pulled open the door and stepped into the corridor.

"I can't go golfing. I have two meetings this afternoon."

"Cancel them. Your business is about my business, and I give you permission. In fact, I insist."

"We don't have a tee time reservation."

Richard pulled out his cell phone and dialed. "Robert Mayhill, please," he said when a pleasant female voice answered. "Robert? Rick Addison. Is there any way you can get my friend and me on the course in about forty minutes?"

"Of course, Mr. Addison. I'll see to it."

"Thank you." Snapping the phone closed, Richard pocketed it again. "Well?"

"Mayhill. Mar-a-Lago?"

"Where else?"

Tom sighed. "I'll have Shelly reschedule the meetings."

"Good."

"No," Samantha said with a sigh, setting aside the phone message. "I'll give them a call and recommend another company. Maybe DeSilva."

Her office secretary gazed at her wisely. "You've robbed Dr. and Mrs. Harkley."

She scowled. "You know, Aubrey, a gentleman wouldn't accuse a lady of such things."

Aubrey Pendleton stood and went to the conference room refrigerator to fetch her a Diet Coke. Tall and stately, his blond hair just going to gray, he looked exactly like what he was—a Southern gentleman, almost antebellum. "You are right, Miss Samantha," he drawled in his practically patented accent. "And I do apologize. Allow me to make that phone call. I've escorted Lydia Harkley to several social gatherings over the years, and I golf with Randall. We're good friends."

Apparently not good enough that he would inform them who'd in all likelihood stolen their Mayan crystal skull six years ago. But since previous to Samantha's acquaintance with him Aubrey had worked as a walker, a professional escort for the ladies of Palm Beach, he might view his friends the same way she tended to—a means to an end. "Thanks. I appreciate it."

The receptionist sat down again to lean his chin on both fists. "So tell me how Rick liked your present."

She grinned. "It was fab. He practically started drooling."

"Now didn't I tell you that men can be broken down into three components? Food, c—"

"Cars, and sex. Yes, you did. I would like to point out, though, that you suggested drag racing. *I* picked the off-roading."

"Yes, you did. I suppose I just have an affection for drag."

Samantha swatted him on the arm. "You are so bad."

"And don't you forget it."

In truth, while she remained fairly certain that Aubrey was gay, Rick said it was an act. Apparently a man who rebuilt the engine of his own '62 El Dorado had to be straight. She liked him either way—she had from the moment they'd met. And that was why when he'd just started showing up at the office, taking messages and helping her decorate and organize, she'd gone along with it. Stoney cut the paychecks, so she didn't even have any idea if and what they were paying Aubrey, but everybody seemed happy with the arrangement.

"Any other potential clients I can reject?" she asked, gazing at the folder in front of him.

"The art gallery in the Town Center at Boca Raton called. From what I could tell, all they seem to want is some sort of keyless entry system on the cheap."

She nodded. Going from cat burglar to security consulting and installation had seemed a good fit nine months ago when she'd started Jellicoe Security, but she hadn't realized she would have to factor in such a huge boredom quotient. "I'll stop by there this afternoon. Did they say whether they wanted keypad or thumbprint?"

"I don't think they have any idea at all."

"Okay." She sipped her soda, while Aubrey sat across

from her, his gray eyes still watching her. "What?" she finally prompted.

"You had one other phone call."

The thing about Southern gentlemen was that they tended to use the same warm tone whether they were discussing a bazillion-dollar lottery win or the death of dear old Aunt Mabel Sue. The only clue she had was the damned twinkle in his eyes, but that could just as easily have been from Viagra or something. "Are we going to play twenty questions, or are you going to tell me who called?"

"Dr. Joseph Viscanti."

A thrill of adrenaline rushed down her spine. Samantha stood up. "And you saved that for last? You son of a—"

"He said he would be out of his office until after one o'clock, Miss Samantha. Otherwise I would never have delayed telling you about his call."

Checking the clock on the microwave, she blew out her breath. Twenty more minutes. Normally she didn't jump even for the director of the Metropolitan Museum of Art, but Joseph Viscanti had made her a unique business proposition six months ago. One that so far hadn't panned out, but if he'd called . . . "Did he give you a hint what it might be about?" she asked.

"He did not. And believe me, I tried to get one."

"I'll give him a call, then." She shook out her shoulders. "Is that it?"

"Two—or maybe three—job requests in a week, three months before the winter season even starts, isn't bad at all, Miss Samantha."

"I know, I know. I guess I was just hoping for something more—"

"Exciting?"

"Interesting."

"Were you two talking about me?" came from the conference room doorway, and she grinned.

"Stoney. It's nearly quitting time, man. Why'd you even bother coming in?"

"Oh, don't you start that shit with me, honey," he rumbled, taking a bottled water out of the fridge and sitting beside her. "I have spent way more time in this damn office than you have."

Considering that she'd made him retire from his very lucrative career as a high-level fence, Stoney had definitely gone above and beyond the call of duty in helping her run a security business neither of them particularly liked. She patted his dark-skinned hand. "I apologize. You're the best."

"Thank you. That's all I wanted to hear. Now what's interesting?"

"Aubrey just gave me a message from Joseph Viscanti. I'm supposed to give him a call back this afternoon."

The big man frowned. "I'm going to tell you one more time, baby, working for museums to recover their stolen stuff is not the way to live a long life."

"Like stealing stuff is."

"At least you were well paid for your services then."

"You can't spend money if you're dead."

He jabbed a beefy finger into her shoulder. "That is my point."

"Yeah, well, it's my point, too."

They'd already debated whether it was less dangerous to take things in the first place or to try to get them back for the proper owners. She knew what worried Stoney, and the same thing bothered her; undoing a thief's work crossed a line she wouldn't be able to uncross. She became a white hat, and thanks to her high-profile life with Rick Addison, all the black hats knew where she lived.

On the other hand, she could get her adrenaline fix without too much worry over being forced to go into hiding or getting thrown into the slam. Of course, stealing from people who bought stolen goods had its own risks. But risk excited her.

As she refocused on Stoney, he was shaking his head at her. "I don't know about you, Sam," he muttered.

The reception phone rang, and Aubrey excused himself to answer it. Samantha edged closer to her former fence and current business partner. "What don't you know about me?"

"I still get calls from brokers. If you want to do some B and E, you could fly to Paris for the weekend, nab a Monet, and make a quarter million. You think the Met is going to pay you anything like that?"

"It's not about the money. It's about the rush. And about doing the right thing, of course."

"Of course." He shook his head. "You were crazy before, and this is not an improvement."

She took a drink of soda. "Sure it is."

"Why? The only difference is that the cops might not get called."

"You know, there's nothing that says I have to break in somewhere and steal things back. Maybe I do some research and then *I* call the cops."

Stoney snorted. "Who do you think you're talking to? You would never call the cops if you could pull and B and E instead."

"Maybe, and maybe not. But at least with me working

on the side of the good guys I get to have a really cool boyfriend."

"Great. Is that what it comes down to? You being as crazy as you can be and still get away with sleeping in the big house on the hill?"

"I am not having this conversation again. I'm a millionaire all on my own, Stoney. I could afford my own house on the hill, and yeah, I could keep up my old career—except that sooner or later my luck would have run out, and I would have ended up in jail or dead. I had a hell of a run, but I have no intention of ending up like Martin."

Her dad had kept working too long, taken one job too many, and had ended up in prison. And until six months ago she'd thought—they'd all thought—that he'd died there. However smug he pretended to be now, the younger version of Martin Jellicoe would never brag about making a deal with Interpol, even one he seemed to think he could manipulate.

"I'm just worried, honey, that now you're working with even less of a safety net. Because as long as you're with the English muffin, you can't slip away if something goes south. You're living in houses that have names, and everybody knows your address."

"The muffin is very nice, though."

"I know you think so."

Samantha leaned around to kiss him on the tip of his nose. "And I know you worry about what I'm doing. But I'm still going to call Viscanti back."

Stoney sat back, blowing out his breath. "Yeah, I figured that." Tightening the cap on his bottle of water, he stood. "Are you still sending Daltrey and Jaime out to pull the wiring for the Mallorey job?"

She nodded. "Gwyneth is throwing a charity thing next weekend, so we need to get it done before then." A charity thing that she and Rick were attending, so she needed to have the security system rewired or she'd never hear the end of it.

"You're insane, Sam," Stoney grumbled, pushing to his feet. "Really, really insane."

Probably. Maybe Rick thought so, too, and that was why he'd given her a gift certificate for plants for their anniversary thingy. "Thanks," she said aloud, following Stoney along the short corridor to her office. "I'll call Gwyneth."

"And sign those petty cash vouchers on your desk," he threw over his shoulder as he continued on to his own office. "I don't want to get nailed by the IRS like Capone."

Christ. Petty cash vouchers, employees, anniversary plants. Joseph Viscanti's call had better be interesting, or for her next trick she was going to start drinking.

"Miss Samantha?" her name echoed over the office intercom.

Man, she hated having her voice bounce off the walls. She leaned over the conference room phone and hit speaker. "What's up, Aubrey?"

"You have a call."

"Viscanti?"

"No. Female."

He was clearly holding something back. "Put it through." What the hell. Even if curiosity killed the cat, she still had a couple of lives left. "Sam Jellicoe."

"Aunt Sam?" a young voice asked.

She scowled. "Olivia?" Olivia Donner, the attorney's kid, was the only girl who considered her a relation, and that was only because of her so-called Uncle Rick. "Is everything okay?"

"No. Dad said you recover stolen treasu...

Great. Had somebody stolen the ten-year-... gum? "For museums and stuff, yes."

"Oh."

Samantha waited for a second, listening to the silence. Then she took a breath. "Is something of yours missing?"

"Not mine, exactly. My class just got a really great life-size anatomical man—you know, the one where his front comes off and you can see all of his internal organs and they detach? Somebody took it last night."

"That's too bad," Samantha supplied. "Did your principal call the police?"

"Yeah, but they don't care. And my teacher, Miss Barlow, was going to teach a unit on anatomy, and I want to be a doctor, but now we'll have to look at pictures or something instead of using Anatomy Man. It sucks."

"Wow. I'm sorry, honey. How about if I buy a new Anatomy Man for your class?"

"But somebody *stole* ours. Dad said he would buy a new one, too, and that whoever took it just has bad character, but it's not right, you know?"

Bad character, eh? Had Donner meant that little crack for her? "I'll tell you what, Livia. I'll ask around and see what I can come up with. Okay?"

"No. I want you to find it for us. I'll hire you."

Great. "We'll discuss that."

"Thanks, Aunt Sam. The anatomy unit starts Monday after next. And Anatomy Man's name is Clark. It's written across the back of his head." She giggled.

"Ah. Was that Miss Barlow's idea?"

"Yeah. She thinks he looks kind of like Superman—when he has his skull and his chest on and all his organs and bones in."

Miss Barlow needed a boyfriend. "I'll let you know if I find out anything. Bye, sweetie."

"Bye, Aunt Sam."

Well, if Joseph Viscanti didn't actually have a gig for her, at least she had Anatomy Man to find. Yes, a former thief's life was a glamorous one.

Chapter 3

Friday, 3:52 p.m.

When Richard reached the door with the plaque reading *Jellicoe Security*, he smiled. He always smiled at the sight of the tasteful embossed gold letters over the deep onyx background; he couldn't help himself. Samantha Elizabeth Jellicoe, his Sam, had gone straight. And while he knew she'd had myriad reasons for doing so, one of those reasons was him. And he'd never been happier to have influenced anyone into doing anything in his life.

"Good afternoon, Richard," Aubrey said from behind the reception desk as he walked into the office.

"Aubrey. Is Samantha available?"

Pendleton glanced down at the phone, then stood. "She's still on a call. I'll let her know you're here."

Giving a brief nod, Richard took a seat on one of the plush chairs in the reception area. Blue this month—Walter's source for furniture had apparently come through again. As far as he knew, Jellicoe Security changed furniture approximately every four to six weeks, and they'd never paid for a stick of it.

"Miss Samantha will be right with you," Aubrey drawled, resuming his seat.

"That's fine." He could go back into her office, but he tried to respect this space as her territory.

"So you liked your present?" the receptionist and former escort to the lonely females of Palm Beach asked offhandedly, pasting some sort of labels on a half-dozen manila files.

"Yes, I did. Samantha told you about it?"

"She asked my opinion. I actually thought either the weekend in Daytona or the diving with sharks would work, but—"

"But I'm still working on a way to combine those two," Samantha finished, pushing through the door separating the reception area from the offices. "I can get the scuba gear and the sharks, but I just can't figure out how to keep the driver compartments of the race cars filled with water."

Richard stood as she approached. When they were apart, he always imagined that she was taller and larger than she was—a match for her personality. In reality, though, when she wore flat shoes the top of her head didn't quite come to his chin. With her auburn hair softly framing her face and those deeper-than-the-ocean green eyes, she mesmerized him. "Hello," he said, smiling.

"Hi." Samantha slipped her arms around his shoulders, rose up on her toes, and kissed him.

She seemed to be vibrating almost on some sort of subatomic level. "What's going on?" he murmured against her mouth. It probably shouldn't, but seeing her that excited made him distinctly nervous.

"I got a job," she returned, flashing him a grin that lingered on her soft mouth. "Two jobs, actually."

Uh oh. "Considering the wide variety of work you've done in the past, may I ask whether this is legal or more . . . questionable employment?" he asked, glancing in Pendleton's direction.

Samantha kissed him again. "Both, hopefully."

"Samantha."

"Oh, don't worry about it," she said, releasing him and abruptly testy. "You're such a tight ass."

He caught her wrist before she could retreat from the reception area. "I know what excites you, Sam," he said in a low voice, "And I reserve the right to be concerned when you get all giggly over a job."

She pulled her arm free to jab him in the chest with a forefinger. "I do not get giggly," she retorted, jabbing in iambic pentameter. "Ever."

"Okay. Would you elaborate about this job—jobs? Just to satisfy my curiosity?"

"Maybe. If you buy me an ice cream."

"Done."

And somehow she'd maneuvered him into being the one trying to make amends. No one else in the world could do that to him. He simply didn't allow it. His question had been a legitimate one—even the above-board work she did seemed to include some element or other of danger or deception. Those were the jobs—the "gigs," as she called them—that she liked.

She headed for the main door and pushed it open. "I have my cell, Aubrey," she called over her shoulder.

"I'll love you forever if you bring me back a lemon sorbet," Pendleton returned.

A muscle in Richard's jaw twitched. "I told you he's not gay," he said as they walked to the elevators and began their descent to the lobby.

"He asked for a lemon sorbet, Brit. He's totally gay."

Rick still had considerable doubts about that, but since Samantha seemed to look at Aubrey Pendleton as some sort of eccentric uncle, he supposed the bloke's orientation didn't matter. But he was still correct—Pendleton was straight.

They headed down the street, Samantha fiddling with her pocket probably so he couldn't hold her hand. Richard swallowed his irritation; it would only egg her on. "Tom and I went golfing today," he said instead. "Nine holes at Mar-a-Lago."

She eyed him. "You mean you blew off work to go play?"

"Just for a couple of hours."

"Good for you."

"You're being sarcastic, aren't you?"

"No. All work doesn't make you a dull boy, but at the same time it's not like your empire's going to crumble if you relax once in a while."

Before he'd met Samantha, he'd never really realized that. Or more likely, it had just never occurred to him. Golf and skiing were for wooing reluctant partners or buyers, polo was for charity fund-raising. He enjoyed them, yes,

but he enjoyed them more when there was no point to them. "Is that why you gifted me with the man trip?"

Samantha grinned. "You betcha. Did you tell Donner?"

"I did. His only concern was that you might be sending him out on a death hunt, but he reckoned he'd be safe if I was along."

This time she laughed outright. "Just make sure he gets the special gold ticket."

Ah, a little insinuation of murder and mayhem, and she was back in good spirits again. He held the door of the ice cream shop open for her. "What's your news, then?"

At the sight of them, the young man behind the counter gulped audibly and sprinted for the back, from where he reemerged a moment later with a second employee in tow. "How can we help you?" he squeaked.

Samantha stepped forward. "A scoop of peppermint on a sugar cone for me," she said, "and one with almond praline for him."

He moved up behind her to kiss the top of her head. "Does this mean we're in a rut?" he murmured, sliding his arms around her waist.

"It means we know what we like," she returned in the same tone. "Now let go before I have to dump my ice cream onto your crotch."

Richard let her go, mainly because he knew she would do it. Apparently he was still on the outs in Jellicoe village. She'd relaxed in his presence to an astounding degree given her background, but she still had her touchy subjects with a very prickly fence around them. So did he, he supposed.

While Samantha took the cones and found a Formica table by the front window, he paid for the ices and retrieved

napkins. If they were going to discuss these new jobs of hers, he would have preferred a more private setting, which was probably why she'd decided to remain in the shop. Was everything a power play between them, or did he merely read it that way? He liked the way she kept him constantly on his toes, but just holding hands and relaxing once in a while would be nice, too.

"All right," he said, sitting opposite her and taking his ice, "you have your bribe. What are these new jobs you're not giggly about?"

Samantha took a long, deliberate lick of peppermint ice. "I got a phone call from Olivia Donner."

"Tom's Livia?"

"Yes, Uncle Rick. Someone took Clark the anatomical man from her classroom right before she could begin her predoctoral studies. She wants me to look into it."

Richard snorted. "And you agreed?"

"Could you tell her no, Mr. Forty Boxes of Girl Scout Cookies?"

"Point taken. What's the other job?"

"My second call was from Joseph Viscanti at the Met."

Now came the trouble. "Ah. An item retrieval for the museum?"

"Yep. He's giving me another shot."

Though he kept his expression calm, inwardly Richard flinched. She'd done only one of those previously, and the trail had petered out well before she'd tracked the painting down. Though he'd commiserated with Samantha's disappointment, he'd actually been relieved that she hadn't gotten close enough to try a retrieval. Very relieved. "Do you have any details yet?" he asked aloud.

"Do you remember about ten years ago when the Met

hosted that traveling Japanese cultural exhibit? *The Samurai*, it was called."

"I remember," he said, going to work on his almond praline. No sense letting it go to waste just because he was a little worried. "But you were what, fifteen?"

"Hey, burglary is my life," she returned, then flashed her quicksilver smile as he lifted an eyebrow. "*Was* my life. Anyway, I was in Italy at the time, but I remember reading about it."

"Is that your way of informing me that you had nothing to do with whatever you're going to tell me happened to the exhibit?"

"Aside from the fact that I never hit a museum, I wouldn't take a job now to retrieve an item I'd stolen then. That would be both wrong and really weird."

Ah, her unique code of honor again. "So what happened? I don't remember hearing about a theft."

"They didn't actually know there'd been one at the time. According to Viscanti, the exhibit went great, they packed it up for the next stop in Chicago, and when it loaded onto the transport trucks they were two crates short. The armor and both ceremonial swords of Minamoto Yoritomo."

"Wow. He's the founder of the Kamekura shogunate, isn't he? The first shogun."

"You and your war guys," she chuckled. "The pieces are nearly a thousand years old."

Rick frowned. "Why did Joseph give you this job now? The statute of limitations had to have run out three years ago."

She nodded. "Apparently the Japanese are accepting applications and bids from museums wanting to host the return engagement of the exhibit, and they're rejecting the

Met because of the theft. Viscanti says they made it pretty clear that the only way for the Met to redeem its honor and be acceptable again for any traveling exhibit from Japan is for them to produce the armor and swords."

"Which is where you come in."

"If possible. He doesn't seem to hold out much hope, but I think he figured he didn't have anything to lose by giving this a shot."

Richard realized he was letting his ice melt after all, and he licked almond praline off his knuckles. No, Joseph Viscanti didn't have anything to lose, but Samantha Jellicoe did.

Adjusting her mom purse, her harried expression, and the piece of paper with school letterhead she'd snagged from the trash, Samantha walked up to the front of J. C. Thomas Elementary School, bypassing the wheelchair ramp in favor of the steps. A security guard met her just inside the doorway. "May I help you?" he asked.

"I certainly hope so," she snapped, clutching the paper harder. "My daughter's teacher asked me to 'stop by,'" she pretended to read, "as if I can just take off from work on a whim."

He gave a sympathetic nod. "School hours are hard when both parents work full—"

"*Both* parents?" she snapped back at him. "That would be a miracle. I would appreciate if you would stop insulting me and tell me where I can find Miss Barlow's class."

His face reddened. "Sure. Fourth classroom down on the west side—to the right."

She stuffed the paper into her purse and stalked off. "Thank you."

The kids were all gone, but she hoped it was early enough that Miss Barlow would still be inside her fifth grade class-

room. If not, she would take a look around for any clues. Okay, she felt like a goof, but Livia had asked, and she didn't want to lie and say she'd checked things out when she hadn't.

Most of the school was under one roof, joined by long hallways and a central auditorium. Friendly drawings of big-headed friends and family and rainbows and elephants lined the walls. She'd been to a couple of different elementary schools when Martin settled them somewhere to scout a job and Stoney bullied him into enrolling her, but it still looked and smelled foreign—like cookies and washable paint.

The door to Livia's classroom stood open, and a slim, dark-haired woman with an actual teacherly bun on the back of her head stood in front of a blackboard writing out lessons. "Miss Barlow?"

The woman jumped, putting a hand to her heart as she turned around. "My goodness, you startled me. Yes, I'm Simone Barlow."

"Hi. I'm Sam Jellicoe. I'm kind of Olivia Donner's honorary aunt. She—"

"You're Samantha Jellicoe," Miss Barlow repeated, her brown eyes widening. "Rick Addison is your—"

"My good friend," Samantha interrupted, though a little bit of her was curious to see how the teacher would describe her relationship with Rick.

"Yes, yes. Your good friend. What may I do for you, Miss Jellicoe?"

"Call me Sam. Livia told me that your anatomical man went missing, and she asked if I'd check into it."

"But I thought you did security inspections and installations."

Miss Barlow seemed to be a member of the Rick Addison fan club—or at least of Rick's Chicks, the online version. "I do, mostly. I also work with museums to track down missing or stolen artifacts. Livia thought I might be able to help here. Do you have a police report?"

"Yes. Principal Horner gave me a copy of it. Would you like a photocopy?"

"That would be great."

The teacher went to her desk and pulled some papers out of the wire basket labeled *For Miss Barlow* in pretty, flowery letters. "I'll be right back. Olivia's desk is over here." She pointed at the seat in the front row, second from the left.

"Thanks. No hurry."

As soon as Miss Barlow left, Samantha took out her digital camera and snapped photos going around the room. Then she walked back to the door and took a look at it. It had a lock, as did the one at the other end of the room. The second one stopped her for a second.

When she looked at the frame, she immediately noticed a tiny patch of sticky residue right above and another one directly below the latch plate. Someone had put a piece of tape across it to keep the door from catching and locking. If the classroom doors had been fitted with dead bolts it never would have worked, but these were interior doors, and the lock mechanism was part of the knob itself.

Hm. Somebody with access to the doors while they were open or unlocked, which meant during the day. An inside job, then, and planned in advance.

Just to be sure she wasn't jumping to conclusions, she checked the windows that lined the far wall. Rows of sprouting lima beans and tomato plants and crazy-painted ceramic pots crowded the shallow sill. No spilled dirt, no broken art projects, no footprints or smears—the thief or thieves hadn't come through this way.

"Here you are," Miss Barlow said, returning to the room and walking up to hand her two sheets of paper. "I had the feeling that taking down the report was as far as the police would go."

"You're probably right. Anatomy Man would be pretty low on their priority list."

The teacher sighed. "I understand that. We had a very exciting interactive unit planned. It's . . . it's aggravating."

"Aren't some of your parents willing to replace him?"

"Yes, though I don't think they realize that Anatomy Man is a very precise life-size model shared by six classrooms. We purchased him just a month ago, and he cost the school nearly three thousand dollars."

"Wow." Samantha folded the papers in half. "Thanks for the report. I'll see what I can do."

"Thank you. If you could recover it, this would be a terrific lesson for the kids about consequences and doing the right thing."

Gosh, maybe if she'd had a couple of those lessons, she wouldn't have fallen into a life of crime. "Livia said the unit starts a week from Monday?"

"Yes, though I'll have to switch it with the unit on electricity if Anatomy Man isn't returned. I had the whole three weeks planned out to coordinate with a hands-on experience. The kids retain so much more that way." She briskly restacked the police report, then slammed it back into the in-box. "Besides wasting *my* time to rewrite the lessons, it just . . . makes me very angry."

Another lesson in seeing the aftermath of a theft from the perspective of a victim. No wonder she never used to socialize with marks. Samantha forced a smile. "I'll see what I can do."

"Thank you, Miss Jellicoe. Sam."

"Don't mention it." *Please don't mention it.* Sam Jellicoe, elementary school sleuth. She'd never live it down. Even worse, every thief in the country would start hitting all the places where she'd done security work, because obviously she'd fallen on hard times.

The next step would be to get a list of people with access to the classroom during the day, though that list would probably include every single student, teacher, and janitor who attended or worked at J.C. Thomas Elementary School. Maybe Olivia would be able to help her out with that. That would have to wait until tomorrow, though, because she had a real job to get to work on—rare Japanese armor and samurai swords. Something she could actually put on her résumé.

Samantha hummed to herself as she sat beneath the windows of Solano Dorado's library. The morning sun felt warm on her back as she flipped through one of Rick's books on antiques. She didn't consider herself particularly skilled at singing, but nobody except for the marble busts of DaVinci and Aristotle had to suffer through it, and they couldn't complain.

Japanese history, the whole honor versus death thing, fascinated her, and she took her time looking at the various photographs in the book. That was one of the things her father, Martin, hadn't gotten about her—when she contracted to steal something, she tried to learn everything she could about it first. As far as Martin was concerned, a theft was nothing more than a business transaction, and the item itself didn't matter.

But she liked to learn the age and provenance of items, liked to know what she was holding in her hands and what it meant in the course of history. And apparently now this interest extended to items she meant to return to their proper owners as well as those she relocated to other interested parties.

"Gardening ideas?" Rick asked, indicating the book across her lap as he strolled into the room. He carried his cell phone in his hand; his chief assistant, John Stillwell, was in Los Angeles working on a plan to make Addisco the main subcontractor in an LAX computer upgrade project.

She shook her head. "Samurai and shogun armor," she replied. "Some of these pieces are amazing. You don't have any books on Japanese history, do you?"

"Probably. Check the list on the computer."

He sounded a little sour, but she ignored it. She liked this part of a theft, and he wasn't going to spoil it for her. "Okay."

Rick nodded. "Have you gotten the packet from the Met?"

"Not yet. Sometime today, though, according to Viscanti."

"So you're just doing some advance research."

Again she heard something in his tone that said he wasn't happy about something, but if he wasn't going to say, then she wasn't going to ask. "Can't be too thorough, I guess."

"Perhaps you can make time to talk about your garden plans at brunch tomorrow."

"Sure."

His phone rang, and he glanced down at the display. "Then I'll leave you to it," he said, vanishing down the hallway again.

As he left the library, Reinaldo, the head housekeeper, came in, a thick manila envelope in his hands. "Good morning, Miss Sam," he said in his light Cuban accent. "This just arrived for you."

She took the bulky envelope from him. "Thanks, Reinaldo."

"Of course. May I get you a fresh Diet Coke?"

"That would be great." All of Rick's employees knew she liked Diet Coke and detested coffee. There had probably been a memo or something.

Once he'd gone to fetch her soda, she took a moment to enjoy the abrupt feeling of anticipation, then opened the envelope from the Metropolitan Museum of Art. Joseph Viscanti had enclosed a letter restating the circumstances of the theft, not very helpful but at least pretty concise.

He'd also included some crime scene photos, the police report, the book of the samurai exhibit, and a CD of the surveillance videos taken the night the theft had likely occurred. It actually amazed her how little the Met and the cops knew about what had happened.

Viscanti wanted her to figure out who'd pulled the job, where the loot had gone, and where it was now. Well, actually he only cared about the last bit, but she needed to know all of it if she meant to solve it. And she did mean to solve it. Otherwise Viscanti and the other museums who respected his opinion would figure it wasn't worth the trouble to hire her to recover their missing goodies, and she'd be back to security inspections and upgrades and finding elementary school property full time. And she really didn't like doing that.

The last—and only other—job Viscanti had asked her to take a look at had gone exactly nowhere. A small, portable urn, no surveillance, no prints, no signs at all. Probably some very lucky small-time hood. This theft didn't look any more promising, but it hadn't been luck that enabled somebody to get away with the goods; to manage a full suit of shogun armor and two priceless swords, all belonging to the same guy and packed in different crates, somebody had known what they were doing—and they'd been paid well to do it.

A low skitter of adrenaline flowed into her muscles as she settled at the library work table. Finding out where something had got to and retrieving it wasn't as flat-out-hair-raising as a straight-up theft, but it was close. And to-day, close was good enough.

Chapter 4

Saturday, 12:15 p.m.

"Remind them that I own Computech," Richard said, shifting the cell phone from his left to his right ear. "Zellman likes the Computech system, and anyone else offering to install software from my company is a glorified middleman."

"Right," the crisp, upper-crust London accent of John Stillwell replied. "I've already pointed out that you can provide the hardware from ACG at near cost; hopefully the Computech connection will put us over the top."

Rick grinned at the enthusiasm in his chief assistant's voice. Hiring Stillwell six months ago was one of the most brilliant decisions he'd ever made. If not for John he would be in Los Angeles himself right now, instead of looking forward to a foliage discussion with Samantha in the morning.

"You have a break tomorrow, yes?" he continued.

"Yes. I thought I might get a head start on the Burei-Halfin merger and look through the—"

"John, take the day for yourself," he interrupted. "Go to the beach or a movie studio or something." Samantha was always teasing him about being more sympathetic toward his minions, as she called them. "Be a tourist. On my dime, of course."

"Are you certain, Rick?"

"Tomorrow's Sunday. Relax a bit. I intend to."

For a moment, all he could hear was silence. "Well, you know, I've actually always wanted to go to Disneyland."

Rick grinned. "Go to Disneyland, then. And any luck on that other item?"

"It's on its way to Florida. You should have it Monday morning."

"Excellent. Have fun tomorrow."

"I will, Rick. Thank you."

He closed the phone and sat back. Though he didn't believe in premature celebrations, the LAX job seemed to be in the bag, as it were. And once he had LAX, O'Hare and La Guardia and a dozen other of the larger facilities would likely follow suit. The idea of taking on airports and their accompanying responsibility had given him pause, but when he considered it, he would trust his own products and personnel over anyone else's.

With a deep breath he straightened and pulled his computer keyboard into easy reach. Reinaldo had delivered Samantha's package to her, so for once he knew what she was up to. So two dozen e-mails waited for him to answer, and then he could do one of the rarest things in his large repertoire and relax for the next day and a half.

A knock came at the half-open office door, and he looked up. "Did you solve your mystery already?" he asked, smiling as Samantha walked into the room with her usual grace and dropped into the chair opposite his desk.

"Totally," she replied. "And I figured out Jimmy Hoffa and the Man in the Iron Mask on the way here from the library."

"Well done. Let me finish these e-mails, then, and let's fly down to Nassau and have dinner at Montagu Gardens. They prepare a wonderful lobster."

"In the Bahamas."

"Well, yes."

She snorted. "You are so smooth. I'm actually here to pick your brain about Japanese antiquities. But since you're busy, I think I'll go talk to Livia Donner about Anatomy Man and then go for a run. Will you have time after?"

"I will." He refused to let her see that his heart lifted whenever she asked for his aid, assistance, advice, or knowledge about anything. He didn't want her using it against him.

"Cool. And maybe I'll let you have your way with me while I'm all hot and sweaty." She gave an exaggerated scowl, clearly amused at herself. "Or maybe in the shower. That might be more fun for you."

"I'll manage either way," he commented, finally giving in and grinning. "Thanks for being so thoughtful, though."

Samantha pushed to her feet. "Oh, you know me. I aim to please."

Richard refrained from commenting on that, instead watching her backside sway as she left the room. He needed to go for a run himself, but he would settle for an hour in the weight room down in the basement later—unless Samantha had been serious about sex when she returned. At thirty-five years of age, a round or two with her could fairly well satisfy his exercise requirements for the day.

Besides, it was the weekend, and though taking any time off was still a novelty for him, he was attempting to become accustomed to it. One of the things his ex-wife, Patricia Addison-Wallis, had complained about during their divorce had been that he worked from the moment his eyes opened in the morning until he closed them at night. Considering that he'd discovered her in bed with his friend and former college roommate, Peter Wallis, he didn't have much sympathy for her complaints, but he'd learned the lesson. He would not put his work before his relationship ever again. And certainly not when that relationship was with Samantha Jellicoe.

He was halfway through the e-mails when his cell phone rang again. As he checked the caller ID, Richard frowned. "Walter?" he said, hitting the talk button.

"Rick," Walter Barstone's voice returned. "I tried Sam's number, but she didn't answer."

"She was going to take a run," Richard said, standing. Except when it came to Samantha's well-being, he and Walter weren't anything close to being allies, or friends. Walter had practically raised Samantha, had been her mentor and her fence for the high-end items she stole. And Barstone would have been completely content to see her away from her new life and back into her old one. "Is something wrong?"

"No. Could you have her call me when she shows up?"

"Not if you don't tell me why."

"Mm hm." In the ensuing silence Rick could practically hear the wily old wheels turning in Walter's brain. "Okay.

Gwyneth Mallorey wants Sam to be there when they mount the security cameras at the house, to make sure they don't mess up the 'aesthetics' of the place. According to Mrs. Mallorey, if Sam's working for her, she'd better show up."

"Gwyneth Mallorey?" Rick repeated, frowning.

"That's right. You wanted to know, so now you can tell Sam the good news. Bye."

"Walt—"

With a click the line went dead.

"Bloody hell," Richard muttered. Yes, he knew that if Samantha did anything behind his back it would be with Walter. And no, he didn't like that Barstone knew more about her than he did, or probably ever would. Hence his wanting to be in on any exchanges of information between them.

Neither, though, did he want to be in the position of having to tell Samantha that one of her clients was throwing a tantrum and expected the president of Jellicoe Security to be at her beck and call. And next week they were to attend a charity dinner at the Malloreys' house. *Dammit.* He could buy and sell the Malloreys, and Sam was now in the position of being subservient to them.

Perhaps her objections to security work *were* about more than boredom and routine, and setting herself up for a fall with her former thieving compatriots. Now it was about *his* life, and her place among *his* acquaintances and business partners. Rick Addison's live-in girlfriend who installed security cameras.

It definitely made her work for the museum look better. Those jobs, though, also had the potential to be much more dangerous to her physical well-being than the security work. None of it was just about her ego alone any longer, because it involved him, as well.

So was he willing to allow her to put herself in danger

in order for him to avoid being the security guard's boyfriend? Or was it even his call to make? The logical part of him, as well as the one that knew Samantha, said no. The part that remembered he was Richard Addison, the fourteenth Marquis of Rawley and a man who'd worked hard to be where he was and to be thought of in the manner he was, said yes.

Still chewing on how he was going to tell her about Gwyneth's latest demands without causing an argument or looking like he was interfering in one of her jobs, he sat down again to finish his correspondence. One thing at a time. And damn Walter. Samantha wasn't the only former lawbreaker who had some skill at manipulating the people around her.

Thankfully Richard knew a little something about negotiation himself. He just hoped he knew enough.

Tom Donner opened the door when Samantha rang the front bell. "Hi," she said, keeping her expression cool and confident. "Nice shirt." Either he'd been working on a car, or somebody had run over him with a lawnmower.

"Thanks. What do you want?" he returned.

"Is Olivia home?"

"You're kidding me, right?" He put a hand on the door frame, the bear guarding his den from what—the cat, she supposed.

"No. She called me. I'm helping her with something."

His eyes narrowed. "Anatomy Man?"

She nodded. "That's confidential, between me and my client," she said aloud.

He blew out his breath. "Okay. She's in the living room with some of her friends."

Samantha slipped past him and strolled into the living

room. Though she and Rick and the Donners had shared more than a couple of outings and dinners, she'd actually been inside their house only once before. Luckily she remembered the layout, because she wasn't about to ask Donner where the living room was.

"Hi, Livia," she said with a smile.

Two girls were seated on the couch, and another two on the floor in front of them, all of them laughing over a video game where the goal was apparently to dress up and get a date to the prom. The tallest of them, blue-eyed and with cropped blonde hair, stood up and came over to hug her. "Aunt Sam! Did you find it already?"

"Not yet. I wanted to ask you a couple of questions. Are your friends in your class, too?"

She nodded. "Everybody, this is Sam Jellicoe. She's like a private detective. Aunt Sam, this is Tiffany, and Emma, and Haley."

"Hi, guys," Samantha said, giving them a half wave. Her and kids. It was like confronting Martians. She'd never even been a kid, really. Pocket-picking lessons had started the week after her mom had kicked Martin out and he'd taken her along with him.

"Are you really dating Rick Addison?" the darkest-haired of the girls, Emma, asked.

"I am."

"Awesome."

"Pause the game, Haley," Livia instructed. "We need to pay Sam, and then she's going to help get Anatomy Man back."

Great. Now she could rob piggy banks. "You don't need to pay me. We'll call it a family courtesy."

"Are you sure? We have twenty dollars each."

Eighty bucks. And she'd taken Monets with less hesitation. "I'll add up my expenses at the end," she hedged, not wanting to insult them, "but I'm pretty sure I've got it covered. So tell me what you know about Clark."

"Miss Barlow was so pissed," Haley observed, hitting a button on the cordless game controller. "And then Principal Horner came in and yelled at her right in front of the class."

"He didn't yell at her," Olivia countered. "But he wasn't happy, either."

"I'm glad it's gone," Tiffany said, swishing her long blonde hair. "That Anatomy Man was so gross. And the boys kept peeling his chest off and pulling out his guts."

"So he was pretty realistic-looking, huh?"

"Too realistic. I'm just glad it didn't have a winkie."

"Hi, Sam."

She looked over her shoulder as the middle Donner offspring, Mike, crossed the edge of the living room, two other boys behind him. "Mike. How are you?"

"Good. Is Uncle Rick here?"

"No, just me."

"She's investigating Anatomy Man," Olivia offered. "We hired her."

"Oh." He gave a half grimace as the boys bunched to a stop. "Well, good luck. Livi, tell Dad that I'm going to David's for dinner."

"You tell him, Mike."

"Can't. We're already late." He yanked on the nearest boy's arm. "Let's go."

The other boy gawked at her. "She—"

"See you later, Sam."

Samantha waved. "Bye, Mike."

She turned back around as the boys left the room. *Hm.* Interesting. After a second she realized that the girls were all giggling about the boys, and she shook herself. "What grade is Mike in?"

"Tenth. He's a sophomore."

"So he doesn't go to your school."

Olivia shook her head. "No. He goes to Leonard High School."

"How far is that from your school?"

"It's right across the street."

"The high school kids are supposed to stay off our campus," Tiffany put in, "but they always walk across the baseball field at lunchtime and stuff."

So she could add the entire population of Leonard High School to her list of suspects. She'd had to scam a security guard to reach Miss Barlow's classroom. A kid would probably have an easier time of it, especially during school hours, and especially if maybe he had a sibling on campus. The question was, would a teenager have the nerve to make off with Anatomy Man in broad daylight? Or could they have gotten into the main building at night after taping the classroom door open? Whatever the answer was, she had the abrupt feeling that Mike Donner knew something about it.

"Aunt Sam, do you want to play Prom with us?"

She looked at the television screen, where the game waited to resume, then at the fresh faces of the four ten-year-old girls looking at her. "Sure. I'll play for a couple of minutes." She still needed to go for her run, but these kids kind of fascinated her. They seemed so . . . innocent, something she'd never been. And maybe they'd say something that could help her unravel the mystery of Clark the Anatomy Man.

* * *

Rick came into the bedroom as Samantha finished stripping off her clothes. She was glad he'd opted out of immediate post-run sex; not only was she pretty sure she was stinky, but after five miles along the shore of Lake Worth she felt pooped. Not much more clearheaded, but definitely pooped.

"You're very shiny," he said in his smooth British accent.

She laughed between her subsiding huffs and puffs. "What I am is sweaty. Stand back; I may be lethal."

"I've never doubted that." He gestured her toward the bathroom. "I have some information for you. Do you want it pre- or post-shower?"

"Is it life-threatening?" she asked, wondering if any other couples regularly started their twenty questions games by asking that. Probably not. Trying to level out her breathing, Samantha turned on the shower.

"No, not life-threatening," he answered, hopping backward onto the counter as she tested the water and then stepped inside. *Ahh.* Showers were why humans qualified as civilized.

"Well, that's a nice change, isn't it?" She dumped shampoo onto her palm and went to work on her hair. "Hey, can we skip the Bahamas tonight? I ran across Hans when I came into the house, and he mentioned something about spaghetti. I love his spaghetti." And she also wanted to drive by Livia's school and see how hard it would be for an amateur to sneak in after hours.

"I would never presume to separate a woman from her pasta."

She chuckled again. This was much better than when he'd been testy earlier. Not that she didn't enjoy arguing with him, but she liked to know what they were fighting about. And tomorrow she'd promised to show him her garden sketches. Yipes. "Okay, what's the information?" she asked, before a panic attack could hit.

Rick's figure shifted outside the frosted glass of the shower wall. "It can wait. I'm fantasizing right now."

"Come in here and say that." Sex would distract her. Sex with Rick would distract anybody.

"In all fairness, my love," his deep voice drawled, "if we have sex and then I tell you the news, you'll be mad at me twice over."

That did not sound good. Samantha wiped shampoo off her face and leaned out of the door. "Then stop fantasizing and tell me, or I'll be mad at you a half-dozen more times just for the hell of it."

Rick gazed at her for a moment. "Walter called me looking for you. Gwyneth Mallorey wants you to be there when they install the cameras at her house, to make certain the walls don't get damaged."

Great. More fun for Jellicoe. "Okay. Why is this making me mad? Because Stoney told you? That's between him and me." And Stoney *would* hear about it. She didn't call Rick's ex to give Patty tidbits about Rick's business dealings.

His eyebrows drew together. "It makes you mad because she's treating you like a lay person."

"She hired me. I work for her." Samantha blinked away a water droplet and tried to think like Rick. "You don't like that she's ordering me around, so you figure I won't like it, either. Right?"

"Partially. Good enough." He stood again, and pulled his gray T-shirt off over his head. "No reason to hold off on the sex, then."

Samantha pushed her palm against his bare chest as he

approached, keeping him at arm's length. "No way, Brit. What's bugging you?" He was wearing his you're-not-the-boss-of-me face, so she went over it again herself. "Let's see. Rick hears that some woman is trying to order me around. Being a knight in shining armor for real, he doesn't like that I answer to anybody but him."

"That is not the—"

"Hush. I'm being you. Samantha and I are a couple," she went on, assuming his accent, "and treating her badly equals treating me badly. If Sam's a servant, I'm a servant. And wait a minute, I'm much better than these blighters. I could swat them like bugs." From his darkening expression, she was on to something. "You think that she put me in a position that makes you look bad, don't you?"

"I never said any such thing."

"But you thought it, didn't you?" Fucking wonderful. Work she didn't particularly like but that he considered safe was acceptable to him, except that he didn't like when she contracted with people who moved in his circle. Removing her hand, Samantha retreated into the shower.

"Samantha."

"Gee, it must suck to be you," she continued, going back to washing her hair. "All powerful and stuck with somebody who drags you down. It's even funnier when you think that if I used my ill-gotten gains I could buy and sell some of these people, too."

He yanked the shower door open again. "No, I don't like it when some wife of a wholesale refrigerator manufacturer thinks she can make herself feel more important by asking ridiculous things of you." Rick unfastened his belt and jeans and shoved them down, kicking out of them. "You're with me, and you're doing security work to ease your conscience and my blood pressure."

"My conscience is just fine, thank you very much."

"My blood pressure, then."

Rick stepped into the shower, closed the door behind him, and grabbed both sides of her face. Kissing her hard, he pressed her back against the far wall. His blood pressure seemed pretty good, because it was obviously all heading away from his brain. Samantha moaned as his palms grazed her slick breasts and then came around for more.

He trailed his mouth down her chin to her throat, where he licked and nibbled until her legs felt ready to give out. Every time she tried to touch him, slide her palms down his chest, he elbowed her hands out of the way. God, it frustrated the hell out of her when he did that, making sex all about her, mainly because she liked the knowledge that she drove him as crazy as he drove her.

His mouth closed over her left breast, his tongue teasing at her nipple. "Rick," she rasped, "you had me at 'blood pressure.' Stop fooling around."

When he chuckled, the sound reverberated into her chest. The sensation practically gave her an orgasm right there. And then he slid a hand down her belly, through her curls, and curved a finger up inside her. She gasped, throwing her head back and nearly braining herself on the toiletry shelf in the corner.

"Sorry," he murmured, turning his attention to her other breast. "I forget my own power sometimes."

"You lying British bastard," she growled, finally pushing past his arms to slide her hands around his shoulders. She dug in with the pads of her fingers, holding him close against her, skin to skin, warm water cascading over both of them.

"I want you, Sam," he said, pushing against her hold to

raise his head and take her mouth again. "I always want you."

"There's probably something wrong with us," she panted in agreement, shifting to tangle her fingers through his damp black hair. He'd let it grow out a little; not enough to be considered shaggy, but stylishly so that the ends brushed the collar of his suit jacket. She liked it like that. A lot.

Rick swept his hands down her back, cupped her bottom, and lifted her up. Samantha laughed again, sweeping her legs around his hips and locking her ankles as he shoved her against the shower wall again, impaling her with his cock. God, she loved when he did that, like he couldn't stand the delay of foreplay and teasing and just wanted her.

"I don't know about something being wrong with us," Rick returned, beginning his rhythmic humping. "Everything feels pretty damned good to me."

"I have to agree with that." Breathing hard, losing the power of speech, Samantha leaned her damp cheek against Rick's and kissed his ear as she held on to him. Slowly she drew tighter and tighter, reveling in the feel of his body against hers, inside hers, until with a half shriek she came.

"There you go," he breathed, lowering his head to her shoulder and thrusting faster. A minute later he gave a deep groan and convulsed against her.

"And there you go," she said, kissing him again.

Slowly he lowered her feet back to the floor. Sliding his arms around her, he held her close. Samantha smiled, listening to the hard beat of his heart against hers. This was it—the thing. The warmth and safety Rick gave to her. The thing she'd never had until she'd met him, and now didn't think she could breathe without. Whatever the thing was that she provided him—and she still wasn't entirely certain what it was—she knew very well how she felt about Rick Addison.

"I love you," she murmured, kissing his shoulder.

"I love you."

"And now I have to get dressed and go see Gwyneth Mallorey."

With obvious reluctance he released her to wash the remaining suds out of her hair. "To quit?" he suggested.

"To tell her that my being there will cost her an additional thousand bucks, and then to stand there while my guys install her security cameras."

"Mm hm. That's good, but maybe you shouldn't work for people we socialize with."

"Then I'll have to take more jobs from Stinky Pete the Sausage Man and Bob the Builder." Eyeing him, she shut off the water and led the way out of the shower. "My ego's okay with this, Rick. If yours isn't, that's not my problem."

"I know. I'm just trying to figure out how I'm going to respond when Gwyneth stands up and publicly compliments your work in assembling her security system."

Samantha frowned as she picked up a towel and tossed him a second one. "Say that you hope my system works as well for her as her husband's refrigerator has worked for us."

His sensuous lips twitched. "That might serve."

"You work for a living too, you know. Somebody could just as easily compliment their plumbing joists from Kingdom Fittings, and you'd have to say thank you."

"It's not the same thing."

"Yes, it is. And I'm good at what I do. So stop worrying about how you'll look around me, or stop being around me." She wrapped the towel around her hair and headed for the bedroom. "Besides, don't forget that one day it might not be about security alarms. One day Detective Frank Castillo might come by with handcuffs and arrest me for stealing a Klimt or a Monet. You'd be better off spending some time thinking about how you'd respond to that."

He took her elbow. "Don't even jest about it."

"I'm not jesting. If you're worried about PR, Rick, I'm not the best choice for you to have around. I thought you would have realized that by now."

Chapter 5

Saturday, 2:18 p.m.

Richard released Samantha's arm and watched as she pulled on a lacy blue bra and a matching thong. She was absolutely correct about her work and his work, and it simply wasn't like him to lose sight of the larger picture, as it were. She was gainfully employed, and he was complaining that the jobs weren't as lofty as he'd like. *Idiot*. A few months ago he'd been worried that she would reject any gainful employment at all for a quick, exciting, and illegal job somewhere. *Bloody muggins*.

"You're the perfect choice for me," he said aloud. "I apologize."

She glanced over at him. "I'm not perfect," she said smoothly, stepping into a pair of jeans, "but I am kinda cool. Don't worry about it. You were wrong; I was right. I rule the kingdom."

Richard snorted. "You had something you wanted to ask me about Japanese antiquities?"

"Mm hm. Put your clothes on, first. You're very distracting with just that towel on."

Obviously he hadn't fumbled badly enough to make her angry, though that was pure and simple good luck on his part. If he was looking for signs that she still had her doubts about their relationship, he wasn't finding any. Richard gave a slow smile as he exchanged the towel for boxers and jeans. Rather, if he was looking for signs that she meant to stay with him, he was finding them. And that was a very fortunate thing as far as he was concerned.

"Better?" he asked, fastening his pants.

Samantha gave a quicksilver grin. "Not necessarily. But I'd like to have our conversation in your armor gallery. Can we do it after dinner?"

"Certainly. Do you want me to keep you company at the Malloreys'?"

"I don't think so. You just don't know what to do with yourself when you don't have work, do you? It's called relaxing. Taking it easy. Call Donner. Maybe there's a ball game you can attend or something. Or golf those other nine holes you missed yesterday."

"Are you trying to get rid of me?" he asked, collecting his gray T-shirt.

"Let's just say that I don't want you sharing your opinion of Gwyneth Mallorey with her until after I get paid. Whoever said words can never hurt me obviously never had an argument with you."

That seemed like a compliment, although she probably hadn't meant it as one. "Very well. I'll call Tom and keep myself occupied. Perhaps Mike is playing ball today."

"He's not. He's having dinner at his friend David's house."

Richard paused. "And how do you know that?"

"I'm looking for Anatomy Man, remember? I had to go talk to my client." She glanced at him as she glided on her deodorant. "Mike's a good kid, isn't he?"

"Yes. Why?"

Samantha shrugged. "Just a question. I don't know kids very well."

"The Donner kids certainly like you."

"I didn't say I didn't like them. I said I don't get them."

That made sense, given her so-called upbringing. "Ah. Any clues so far?"

"It's too early to tell."

Samantha went into her walk-in closet and reappeared a moment later pulling on a yellow blouse and a black dress jacket. Christ, this was strange, her going off to meet a client and him scrambling to keep himself occupied. She was right again. He needed to learn how to relax a little. Of course, enjoying the moment was considerably easier when she was present to enjoy it with him, but he could cope for an afternoon. He'd use it as a character-building exercise.

Tucking in her blouse, Samantha lifted up on her tiptoes to kiss him softly on the mouth. "I'll be back in a couple of hours. Don't do anything I wouldn't do."

He grinned. "That doesn't eliminate much. Good luck with Gwyneth Mallorey."

"Luck's for schmucks, but thanks."

Richard walked her down to the garage and held open

the door of her blue Bentley for her. He'd given her the car a year ago, and had offered to purchase her a new one since then, but she'd turned him down. Apparently the Bentley was the first car she'd ever actually owned legitimately, and she didn't want to give it up, even for a new model.

As soon as she left, he pulled out his cell phone and hit one of the speed dials. After two rings the line clicked open. "Hey, Rick," Tom's voice came. "I don't know where Jellicoe is, if that's what you're calling about."

"It's not."

"Oh. Okay. Problems with the LAX negotiations?"

"No, everything's fine. What are you up to right now?"

"Hold on a sec." Dimly on the open line he heard what sounded like a radio deejay. "Okay, what's up?"

Richard held the phone away from his ear for a second to look at it. "Nothing. What are you doing right now?"

"I'm regluing the leg on a barstool," Tom finally answered. "No more WWE wrestling for Mike this month. Now do I get to ask what you're doing?"

"Absolutely nothing."

"Really? Where's Jellicoe, since she's not here?"

"Meeting a client. So Katie's at home, is she?" Richard continued, ignoring the sudden accelerated beating of his heart. Why not do this today? He'd been wanting to for weeks, and Samantha had told him to go enjoy himself. This wasn't what she would have had in mind, but now that the idea had occurred to him, it seemed like a bloody fine plan.

"Katie's here. Mike's at his friend David's, Livia went to her friend Tiffany's house, and Chris is at Yale. Anything else?"

"Might I speak to your wife?" Reminding himself that Tom was his closest friend and that as an attorney he was obsessed with minute details, he took a breath and counted to five.

"Okay, but now I have to go back into the house. Hold on."

"Good God," Rick muttered.

"I heard that," came back to him. "Here she is."

"Who am I talking to?" Katie Donner's voice came in her charming Southern accent. "Rick? Hi, Rick."

"Katie. I was wondering if you had a few hours this afternoon to help me out with something."

"Sure. What do you need?"

"I need you to come with me."

Silence. "With Sam?"

"She's busy elsewhere. Might I pick you up in twenty minutes?"

"Um, okay. What should I tell Tom?"

"That we're going somewhere I won't disclose to you until you get in the car with me."

"Hold on a sec." Even with her hand over the speaker he could make out "secret" and "sex" and "rendezvous" as she translated the conversation to her husband. If the Donners hadn't been high school sweethearts, and if he hadn't known the two of them for a little over ten years, even the joking implication would have made him uncomfortable. As it was, he grinned and shook his head.

"Tom wants to know if he can come," Katie finally said, her voice amused.

Bloody wonderful. "Only if he swears to keep his opinion on any and all related subjects to himself."

She relayed the information again. "He agrees. Am I supposed to abide by the same demands?"

Rick popped open the lockbox on the garage wall and

pulled out the keys to his green Jaguar. "Absolutely not. I *want* your opinion. See you in twenty."

"We'll be ready. And don't worry, I'll make Tom change his shirt first."

He didn't want to know what Donner might have been wearing to prompt that comment. Instead he debated whether he should change his destination now that Tom had invited himself along. Turning him down would have been simple, but however much he publicly disagreed with his friend's assessment of Samantha and her character, Donner's was the only voice of reason he had where she was concerned.

"Do you want me to drive you, sir?" his driver, Ben, said from the near corner of the garage where he was stacking clean rags in a cabinet.

That would definitely be more convenient, but it would also mean a witness in the household—another member of the staff who'd been charmed by Samantha almost from the moment she'd arrived at Solano Dorado. "I'll manage, Ben. Thank you."

Twenty minutes later he pulled into the Donners' driveway in front of their nice two-story house in the West Palm Beach suburbs. Middle- to upper-class families lived everywhere here, with their two or three children and pets. They even had block parties at least twice a year. Domesticity. He hadn't used to think much of the condition, until recently. Until Samantha. Now, though, seeing the trio of helmeted children riding their bikes up the street actually made him feel warm and fuzzy. Odd, that.

A few seconds later Katie and Tom emerged, and Tom squeezed his long legs into the back seat so his wife could sit up front.

"Okay, do we get to know where we're going now?" Tom asked as they headed toward I–95 south and Bal Harbour.

"Yes. We're going to Harry Winston."

He felt the seat jolt as Tom straightened. "Harry Winston?" the attorney repeated, his voice squeaking. "The jewelers?"

"Yes. To look at rings."

Samantha sat at Stoney's Formica-topped kitchen table, her head propped in her arms, and watched his sliding-eyes cat clock tick off the minutes. In front of the counter a few feet away Stoney paced, his phone to his ear and his expression, well . . . stony.

"You're a real piece of work, Merrado," he grumbled. "I told you I'd pay you for a good lead. Those are directions, not a lead. And I don't need your help to go there." Swearing under his breath, he hung up the phone.

She lifted her head. "Directions?"

"On where I can stuff my—well, you get the picture."

"Shit," Samantha muttered. "These people used to fall all over themselves to work with us."

"You don't exactly top the list in *Thief of the Month* magazine anymore, honey. You helped put Veittsreig and his crew in jail. Fences don't make money when their acquirers are in prison."

"Even scary, gun-toting acquirers who tried to feed me a bullet?"

"Even those. We aren't a discriminating bunch, really."

She sent him a grim smile. "You are. Now, anyway."

"Yep." He frowned. "And so are they, now, since nobody wants to talk to me anymore. Not about new thefts, or old ones, or which rich black hat is collecting what."

"So nothing on who's collected samurai artifacts in the past, present, or future."

"Nope."

"What do *you* know, then? I've commissioned for pieces like that. So did Martin, back in the day."

Stoney cleared his throat. "There were a couple of regulars. It's been a while, though. Since my memory's not as good as yours, I'll have to look through my files."

"Need any help?"

"Not even you get to know where I keep my client files."

"You don't trust me?" She put a hand over her heart. "Me?"

"I don't trust that you'll never use anything you see against somebody we worked for. You remember everything you see and hear, Sam. So if you don't look in the first place, I won't have to worry about some of those really scary guys you stole for getting a visit from you and taking the opportunity to blow your head off. Or my head off, since you live behind big walls and I don't."

Frowning, she pushed to her feet. "So this is for my own good?"

"And mine."

She could probably argue him into giving her a look, but he had a point. She'd turned down security jobs for people she'd robbed in the past, and she already knew a few unsavory things about some of Rick's business and social acquaintances, things he had no idea about. Maybe ignorance would at least save her from a sleepless night once in a while. "Okay. I'll see you Monday, then. But call me if you think of anything."

"I will."

Blowing him a kiss, she left the nondescript house perched at the edge of Pompano Beach and climbed back into her really out-of-place Bentley. Halfway back to Solano Dorado she detoured to one of the chain bookstores to pick up a handful of magazines devoted to showcasing the interior designs of the rich and famous. Stoney might not have any leads about who collected samurai artifacts, but with any luck she could narrow it down herself.

Most people didn't just randomly collect. They collected things they liked—Impressionist art, Greek pottery, Renaissance sculpture. A fan of Picasso probably wouldn't be moved to commission for the theft of a thousand-year-old set of Japanese armor and samurai swords. And anybody who *could* commission for that would be the kind of person who could afford the cool stuff that landed them in interior design magazines.

It was a long shot, but hey, she lived by long shots. Back at the estate she keyed the front gate open and drove up the long, winding drive amid the swaying palm trees. Even with all of the traveling they'd done over the past year, her business was here in Palm Beach, and she and Rick had spent enough time in Florida that he would have to pay a substantial tax penalty.

She probably would, too, if the government ever found out about any of her income other than that from Jellicoe Security. Her Milan retirement fund, savings from all of her burglaries and other various bad deeds, lay safely in a numbered account in Switzerland. Though she'd been dipping into it in order to set up her business, she wasn't volunteering any information about it to anyone.

Ben Hinnock met her just inside the garage and took charge of the Bentley for her. Despite the number of cars in the bat cave, as she'd begun calling the stadium-size car storage facility, every one of them had its place. "Ben, what time did Rick leave?" she asked, noting the absence of the Jag.

"At about two-forty," the driver returned.

"Thanks." He and Tom had probably gone golfing again. Personally she didn't see the point of hitting a little ball around a park unless there was loot in the holes, but Rick enjoyed it. And he'd taken her advice to go have some fun.

Smiling, she headed upstairs to change out of her business clothes. And then she went up to the third floor and the long art gallery there. Long, floor-length windows lined one side of the hall, while suits of armor stood on the far side, other war-related artifacts scattered among them.

This was where she and Rick had first met. Of course she'd been trying to rob him at the time, and he'd returned home early from a trip to Stuttgart in time to get himself involved in an explosion and a triple-cross that had nearly killed both of them. "Ah, the good old days," she murmured, grinning.

A large part of the gallery had been replaced after the explosion, and several of Rick's pieces had been damaged or destroyed. Anyone coming for a first look wouldn't have any idea—not only did Rick have enough antiques and pieces of art to keep several houses full, but he had very sharp taste about what looked good where.

She sat cross-legged on the floor beside a suit of samurai armor and looked through the magazines. A couple of the houses in the layouts featured Japanese and other Far Eastern decor, but she knew enough about the items she saw in the photos to eliminate all of them. People showed off their best stuff for a photo shoot, and while she didn't expect to see the Yoritomo armor, there wasn't anything close to that monetary value.

"Damn." Okay, no suspects, but at least she had six non-suspects. That was a help, dull and mundane as finding it out was.

"How was the camera installation?"

She jumped, looking up as Rick topped the stairs. Her breath always caught when she first got a look at him—if she'd been the girly, giggly type it would have been flat-out embarrassing. Wherever he'd been, he still wore the jeans and gray T-shirt with a black open shirt over that, a pair of sockless loafers on his feet. "Lucrative," she returned, standing up to grin at him. "When I told Gwyneth that my appearance would cost her an extra grand, she was too snooty to turn me down, so I stood there for two hours and ate her cashews."

Rick chuckled. "You still want spaghetti, though, I assume?"

"That's a different stomach." She slid a hand around his waist. "What did you do this afternoon, stud muffin?"

He closed his arm over her shoulders and drew her closer to kiss the top of her head. "More golf."

"Did Donner lose?"

"Yes."

"Excellent."

"Any leads on the school or the armor thefts?"

"Some ideas on the school. And I know a couple of collectors who *didn't* take the armor."

After a moment Rick let her loose and walked over to one of his two prime suits of samurai armor. He'd gotten pretty good at letting her go before she started to get squirrelly about it, but she'd been working at stuff, too, at touching him before he had to reach out to her. She and Martin had left her mom when she'd been five. She didn't remember anything about unconditional acceptance before then, and after that her job had been to learn everything she could to be good at what she did. Better than Martin, eventually. Rick was a whole new chapter; hell, a whole new life.

"The armor Joseph wants you to look for is from the late Heian period," he said, half to himself. "This is about three hundred years later, from the middle Muromachi period."

She nodded, strolling over to join him. "Viscanti sent me the exhibit book and a couple of photos. How much do these things weigh?"

"About sixty pounds. It's mostly metal and leather. Samurai fought from horseback then, and the saddle supported some of the armor's weight."

Samantha grinned again. "Look at you, knowing all kinds of stuff about ancient Japan. Way to go, Brit."

"I collect what I like," he said with a shrug.

"That's kind of what I wanted to ask you about," she said, running a finger down the overlapping plates of steel that would have protected a samurai's upper arm while he shot arrows at people. "People collect what they like. Do you know of anybody else who likes warrior stuff? Japanese in particular?"

He lifted an eyebrow. "So now we're suspecting my acquaintances?"

"Your acquaintances have money. Somebody wanted the armor and swords of Japan's first shogun. That's not a random snatch-and-run. This is somebody who places a lot of importance on this stuff."

"Mm hm. Let's discuss it over dinner, shall we? And then I'll show you my sword."

With a chuckle she looped her arm through his, guiding him back toward the main staircase. "I've seen your sword. Very impressive."

"Saucy," he returned. At the top of the stairs he pulled

her to a stop, took her chin in his fingers, and leaned down to kiss her softly on the mouth.

Her toes practically curled. "What was that for?" she asked, after she cleared her throat.

Blue eyes regarded her. "Because I love you."

"I love you, too."

He smiled. "Good. I am very charming."

"And full of it. Take me to the spaghetti, or lose me forever."

Well, he'd put one past her, which didn't happen often. Tom had agreed to admit to a loss on the golf course, and if anyone asked her, Katie had spent the afternoon at home relaxing. Now all he needed to do was wait for Harry Winston to call and tell him that the ring he'd commissioned was ready, and hope that the company valued him enough as a customer that they wouldn't leak any information to the press about Rick Addison ordering a custom-made five-million-dollar diamond ring. And then he needed to decide how and when. How and when, and whether proposing to her would destroy what they'd managed to find over the past year.

"What are we watching tonight?" she asked, walking into the spacious sitting area of their master bedroom suite and holding a bowl of popcorn and two sodas cradled in her arms.

"Something in honor of your latest gig, as you call it."

"*Godzilla: Tokyo S.O.S.*?" she suggested, plopping herself onto the couch.

Richard shook his head. "*The Seven Samurai.*"

"Kurosawa? You rock."

Grabbing up the remote, he sank back beside her. "I've been thinking about what you said regarding collections and collectors," he said as he turned on the plasma television and the DVD player. "What if the thief was just some fan of *Shogun* and happened to grab two crates that coincidentally both had Yoritomo items in them?"

"According to Viscanti the crates were on two separate pallets. Whoever took them would've had to find them on the bills of lading and then locate each box in a stack with nineteen others."

"Very well. A professional, and therefore probably hired for those particular items."

Samantha tossed a piece of popcorn in the air and caught it in her mouth. "So who do you know besides you who collects samurai stuff? Somebody here in the States."

Richard helped himself to a handful of the popped kernels. "Tell me again why you think it's somebody I might know?"

"Ten years ago the exhibit had stops in Tokyo, Hamburg, Paris, London, New York, Chicago, and San Francisco," she returned, snuggling against his shoulder. "The stuff went missing in New York, which to me says that's when somebody decided they couldn't live without it —so that's where they got a good look at it. So East Coast residence and rich is my guess."

Remarkable. "I suppose I could be considered a suspect, then," he mused.

She shook her head. "I've already cleared you," she said between mouthfuls. "Only one thief allowed in the house."

"Oh, so there are rules now?"

"Ha ha, funny man. Who else collects?"

It was a good question. He did know most of the legitimate collectors around, mostly because he'd bid against them on items. Japanese collectibles had a small but fierce following—his two pieces of armor and half dozen daitu and wakizashi swords had mostly been to round out his ancient warrior collection, but there were people who collected nothing else.

"Okay," he mused, ticking off the names on his fingers, "Ron Mosley collects, and—"

"Not Mosley," she interrupted. "I saw his spread in *Fabulous Homes*. He doesn't own anything even close to the value of that armor."

"Okay. There's Yvette and August Picault, Gabriel Toombs, and Pascale Hasan."

Beneath his arm, Samantha stiffened a little. "Gabriel Toombs and the Picaults both have houses here in Palm Beach."

"Yes, they do. And we all have townhouses in Manhattan. And I'm certain there are a couple of others."

"Don't get all high-and-mighty on me. You'd be surprised how many of your acquaintances have sent work my way. In my old line of work, that is."

"Close to the same number you've stolen from?"

"Probably," she returned, surprisingly without heat. "Somebody wants something, somebody else loses something. It kind of has to work that way."

He gazed at her profile. In those clothes, in this house, she looked like she belonged here. She blended in anywhere; that was part of why she was—had been—so successful. But in this setting it would have been easy to forget that until a year ago she'd been a high-class cat burglar and had made an exceptional living at it.

"Have you worked for or against anybody I just mentioned?"

"Toombs," she returned after a moment. "He wanted a

Japanese war horse's bridle, of all things. I tracked one down for him and made fifty grand."

Alarm sped his heart. "So he knows you're a thief?"

"No. He knows that Stoney's a procurement agent."

"*Was* a procurement agent, now retired."

"Well, now working in security. Like me." With a sigh she sank back again. "Looks like I'll be checking out Toombs."

"Checking him out legally," he said carefully.

"Mm hm."

"Samantha, Toombs acquires weapons because he thinks he's some sort of Spartacus reincarnation or the Japanese equivalent thereof."

He felt her shoulders shake as she laughed silently. "'Spartacus'?"

"It was the first name that came to mind."

"I don't know if I'd admit to that, Sparky. Maybe he thinks he's the reincarnation of Minamoto Yoritomo."

"Which doesn't say much for his mental stabil—"

"Look, I'm going with what I know. Toombs spends most of his time here in Palm Beach. If he's got the armor, he'll have it here with him so he can admire it. Whoever has it, it's going to be where they spend the most time. That's just . . . human nature, I guess. You don't take that huge a risk and spend that much money without being able to enjoy the results."

"So thieves are predictable?"

"Everybody's predictable, once you learn their habits. Except for you, of course."

He gave a half grin. "You're just trying to flatter me, now."

"Is it working?"

"It always works. Sam—"

"Shh," she interrupted, holding the popcorn bowl up for him. "I like this part."

Richard ate popcorn and watched the movie with her. Only later did it occur to him that she'd never actually given her word to do her investigating legally. She had good instincts, but she also had a very deep craving for danger and excitement. Until he knew which Sam would win out, he needed to keep an eye on her—something that wasn't easy even under the best of circumstances. Thankfully he enjoyed a challenge.

When Samantha opened her eyes to look at the clock beside the bed, the time read nearly three o'clock in the morning. Stifling a groan, she slowly and silently rolled out of bed, grabbed up her emergency clothes from under the night stand, and slipped into the bathroom to dress in the dark. That done, she leaned back into the sleeping area to see Rick on his back, his chest moving slowly up and down, his face relaxed. So far, so good.

Given that it was the weekend, she could probably go by Olivia's school any time she wanted. With the climate of suspicion right now concerning people who hung around elementary schools, though, middle of the night seemed better.

Halfway out the suite's door, though, she paused. If Rick woke up to find her gone he would freak, and while there were instances that were worth the trouble, this really wasn't one of them. "Shit," she muttered, and went back into the bedroom.

"Rick," she murmured, putting a hand on his shoulder.

He woke up with a start. "What?" he asked, sitting up in an explosion of sheets. "What's wrong?"

"Nothing. I'm going to look around Olivia's school, just to see how easy it would be for a hack to get in."

Rick rubbed a hand across his eyes. "I thought you said it was probably an inside job."

"It probably is. I'm just going to confirm that."

"Hold on. I'll go with you."

"No, you won't. This is the easiest thing I've done in a year, even with being retired. I'll be back in like half an hour." Samantha leaned over and kissed him on the forehead.

For a second he looked at her, and she wondered whether he would demand that he go along anyway, either because he was Sir Galahad and needed to protect her, or because he didn't trust her judgment or abilities. Finally, though, he lay back again. "Don't blow up anything, then."

"I won't." Probably not, anyway.

Chapter 6

Sunday, 8:22 a.m.

When Richard awoke in the morning Samantha was asleep beside him. For several minutes he lay there with his head resting on his crooked arm and watched her sleep, her auburn hair half obscuring her face and one hand curled into her pillow. Had he ever sat and just gazed at Patricia like that? He couldn't recall doing so; more likely he'd been too focused on the day's schedule to think of lazing about anywhere.

If not for Samantha, he would probably be doing the same thing today. She'd brought his world to a grinding halt and then had sent it off in an entirely new direction.

The ride scared the bloody hell out of him, but he was definitely enjoying it. Last night she'd gone out hunting for clues to help a ten-year-old, and with the same zeal that she pursued four million dollars' worth of missing Japanese antiquities. Remarkable.

Silently he climbed out of bed and dressed, then went into his office to check his e-mail and faxes and to call Hans downstairs and make certain breakfast would be served out by the pool at nine o'clock. If Samantha backed out of their garden discussion, it wasn't going to be because *he'd* forgotten and made other arrangements.

When he headed down to the pool Reinaldo was setting one of the tables for breakfast, so he took a stroll around the perimeter of the rough slate patio area, taking in the well-manicured native-Florida plants interspersed with boulders in the substantial grounds, all of it set up to leave the pool private from the other areas of the estate.

He'd bought Solano Dorado, nearly ninety years old and one of the Palm Beach estates designed by the famous Addison Mizner, seven years earlier. Since then he'd done some major renovations, changes that *Architectural Digest* seemed to universally approve, but while he'd had the pool itself resurfaced, he hadn't touched the surrounding landscaping.

Once Samantha had arrived and confessed that she'd never had a garden, he'd given it to her. And nine months later, it still hadn't been touched. She'd brought clothes into the house, her *Godzilla* movies, and various toiletry items. Other than that, she hadn't seemed to own much of a personal nature. Before their meeting she'd been pretending to be the niece of a deceased homeowner in Pompano Beach and had been basically squatting on the property until she'd been forced to flee.

She'd moved in with him, though she could probably pack up all of her belongings in ten minutes. She even kept a folded set of clothes under the night stand in case of emergency, and in the closet a backpack with spare cash, skeleton keys, and various other items cat burglars probably found useful when they had to make a run for it.

Richard wanted to see her work on the garden, put her bloody clothes in a drawer, and unpack that backpack. Then he would know that she meant to stick around, and then maybe he could stop worrying that she would be able to vanish into the night where he would never find her.

"Good morning, stud muffin," she drawled from halfway down one of the two flights of stairs that descended into the pool area. Her arms were crammed with books and pads of paper, which he automatically went forward to take from her.

"Good morning," he said, kissing her. "You remembered our date."

"Like I'd want to hear about it if I forgot."

"Diet Coke, Miss Sam?" Reinaldo asked. "And coffee, Mr. Rick?"

"Yes, thank you," he returned, as Samantha gave the housekeeper a thumbs-up. "How was the school?" he asked after Reinaldo left.

"Locked up tight. Easy to get into for most jobbers, even hacks, but a hack wouldn't take Anatomy Man and leave the computers and cables and shit. It had to be a kid."

"How will you figure out which kid?"

"I have a couple of ideas. Don't worry; I'll keep you posted." Samantha took a deep breath. "It's nice this morning," she noted, taking a seat at the table. "Just think, if we were in England we'd be wearing woollies or jumpers or whatever you call them, and instead we get short sleeves and flip-flops."

He put the stack of magazines and papers on the table between them. "Yes, but in a few months we could have a white Christmas in Devon. You won't see that here unless a cargo plane dumps a shipment of cocaine."

Samantha snorted. "You are so cynical. Which is why I'm giving you one last chance to take back your garden here before I mess it up and offend Jorge and Ignacio and Joe."

Richard hadn't even known those were his gardeners' names. "I'll risk it," he said. "I want to see what you come up with."

"Okay, you asked for it." As Reinaldo reappeared with a rolling tray holding their drinks and two plates of pancakes, she pulled one of the magazines out of the stack and opened it. "I was thinking of something like this, only with big pieces of Mediterranean-style pottery and fake Greek ruins scattered around instead of the fallen tree thing. Then it would coordinate with the style of the house."

For something she'd put off for nine months, she seemed completely at ease with finally discussing it. It could be an act, but at least she'd truly been thinking about it. With a smile he couldn't help, Rick leaned forward to look at the photos. "I like it."

"You're not just saying that?"

"I wouldn't do that."

She gazed at him critically for a moment. "Okay. I suppose not. Look at these sketches I made, then. I'm thinking a lot of green foliage, and mostly reds and yellows for the flowers, with a sprinkling of white to tie in with the Greek pillars."

"Amazing." *Finally*. Now only half a hundred steps to

go, and he'd give himself a fifty-fifty chance of not sending her screaming for the hills when he produced a ring for her finger.

"No, *Toombs*," Samantha said, exaggerating her pronunciation as she swiveled in the newest of her succession of office chairs. "This would be much easier if you'd let me take a look at the files myself."

"Not for me, it wouldn't be," Stoney returned, the sound of rattling papers in the background. "I'll take another look."

"It was in March of '03," she said, clenching her office phone in her hand. "I can't believe you don't remember."

"What was the combination of Captain Kirk's safe?"

She grimaced. "There wasn't one. That's an urban legend. His safe had buttons that weren't numbered."

"That proves you're a freak, and that you shouldn't be allowed to question any normal person's memory. I'll call you."

"Why are you stalling me?" she asked, frowning.

"I'm not."

"Yes, you are."

"Jeez, Sam, I can't think why I have concerns about giving you my client information just because people you go up against tend to get arrested or dead."

Samantha frowned at the phone. "You're picking the money guys over me? We're family."

"Yeah, well, maybe family shouldn't screw shit up like you are."

"Sto—"

The phone clicked off. With a sigh Samantha hung the phone up again. Man, he was testy. And mean. The Kirk answer wasn't all that impressive; he should have asked her about the combination to the gold safe in the remake of *The Italian Job*. She loved that movie.

Her phone buzzed, and she jumped about a foot. "Holy heart attack, Batman." Hitting the intercom button, she leaned forward over the telephone. "What is it, Aubrey?"

"You don't have to be so close to the phone, Miss Samantha," his soft drawl returned. "It makes that pretty voice of yours all fuzzy. And you have a call on line two."

Okay, so she didn't know speakerphone etiquette. "Who is it?" she asked, sitting back again and hoping it wasn't Olivia Donner. She needed to look into a few more things before she relayed any information on that subject.

"That's better. It's Dr. Joseph Viscanti."

Great. "Thanks." Picking up the receiver, she hit the blinking red button. "Joseph. What can I do for you?"

"You received the package I sent you?" the director of the Metropolitan Museum of Art asked in his mild librarian voice.

"Yes, it came Saturday afternoon."

"Good, good." His voice trailed into silence.

"What's up?" she ventured after ten or so seconds.

"Ah. Any leads yet?"

"A couple of ideas, but it's too soon for leads." Especially any she would share. She was way too close to being a black hat herself to start throwing around names of potentially guilty people. As it was, she was going to have to be *really* sure before she repeated anything to anybody.

"Very good. You'll keep me posted, yes?"

Samantha frowned. "Sure. Is something wrong?"

"Wrong? No, no. It's just that, well, if we can't produce the stolen items by the end of business the Wednesday after next, the exhibition will accept the proposal from the Smithsonian. New York will be bypassed entirely."

"So you're giving me ten days? After ten years?"

"Technically you've already had two days."

"That was the weekend. You might have let me know how close time was to expiring when you first called me."

"I was afraid you'd turn me down if I did." He cleared his throat. "And the museum board—my board—suddenly remembered after ten years that we should have been pushing all along to find the armor and swords, and now it's my fault that we haven't, even though I was working for the Guggenheim back when this happened."

"So it's not just winning the exhibit that you're worried about," she said. It would have been nice if he'd mentioned his job would be on the line before he'd sent her the information, not to mention the damn deadline. Christ. She'd spent most of Saturday looking for Anatomy Man, and yesterday making lists of plants. Okay, she'd eliminated a few potential suspects, but still.

"None of that is your problem, Sam," Viscanti returned. "I just wanted to know if you'd—"

"You just made it my problem, Joseph. That's why you called. Next time, I'd appreciate having all the information up front."

"Sam, are you—"

"I'll keep in touch." She hung up the phone. "Dammit." Pushing to her feet, she headed for the back of the reception area. Rick was trying to widen the number of suspects rather than narrowing it, Stoney couldn't or wouldn't come up with the files she wanted, and now she had a deadline. "Aubrey, you're a man about town," she said, leaning on a credenza.

He spun in his chair to face her. "Indeed I am, honeybee."

"Do you know Gabriel Toombs?"

"Wild Bill? Yes, I do."

Wild Bill? Obviously this was going to take a few minutes. She hopped up to sit on the oak credenza. Last week's furniture had been black Masonite. "Okay, 'Wild Bill'?"

"Toombs. Tombstone. Wild Bill Hickok."

"Is that like the six-degrees-of-Kevin-Bacon thing? Does he really call himself Wild Bill?"

"He started it, and insisted that the rest of us go along." He took off his telephone earpiece. "Might one ask why you're suddenly making inquiries about Wild Bill Toombs?"

Samantha regarded him for a minute. She generally figured people out pretty fast, and she liked and trusted Aubrey as much as she did anyone. He'd known the upper-crust residents of Palm Beach a lot longer than she had, though, and a lot longer than he'd known her. Still, he seemed almost as cynical about them as she was—maybe because they'd both been in the position of working for them *and* walking among them as equals.

"Have you ever seen his collection of Japanese artifacts?" she asked.

"He loves to show them off. Rumor has it that he had a custom set of samurai armor and swords made for himself."

Hm. *Made, or stolen?* "Does he wear it?" she asked aloud.

"At the annual masked ball for the past two years. In private, I don't really know."

Which would put its debut right about when the statute of limitations on the Morimoto armor expired. Would a collector really wear nine-hundred-year-old armor, though? Maybe one who made everyone call him Wild Bill Toombs would. "If I showed you a photo of some armor, could you tell me if it's a match?"

"Are we embarking on a caper?" Aubrey asked with a grin, sitting forward.

"We might be."

He clapped his hands together. "I do love your capers, Miss Samantha."

She loved them, too, which she supposed was part of what made Rick nervous—except that in a way he got off on the danger stuff just as much as she did. At least he'd let her case the school unaccompanied. "I'll get the photos."

When she returned from her office to reception, Aubrey had cleared all of the messages and mail off the reception desk, and he'd produced a magnifying glass from a drawer. "I'm ready," he said.

"Boy, you don't do anything halfway," Samantha noted, grinning as she flicked a finger at the rounded glass. "Where did you get that, from the Sherlock Holmes Investigation Kit?"

"I'll have you know that on occasion some of the gifts I receive from my lady friends are best viewed through a magnifying lens. Though I have recently acquired a pair of night vision binoculars and a black ski mask, just in case. A gentleman does try to be prepared."

Next he'd want to come along on a B and E. "Here you go," she said, spreading out the half-dozen photos Viscanti had provided for her. "Does it look familiar?"

He looked at each photo, then swung the glass over and examined them again. Samantha resisted the urge to tap her foot; at least he was taking it seriously.

Finally he straightened. "I'm not sure," he said slowly, his drawl deepening. "The colors look right, but I haven't seen Wild Bill's in person since the party in January."

"But the colors are the same."

"I think so. I couldn't in all honesty swear to it, Miss Samantha."

Damn. "Okay. Thanks for looking."

"I'm sorry I couldn't be more helpful." He pursed his lips. "You know, maybe there is something I can do for you." He picked up his earpiece again and dialed the phone.

"Aubrey, what are you—"

"Wild Bill? Howdy, sir. It's Aubrey. You wouldn't happen to be free for lunch, would you? I still owe you a meal at the Sailfish Club. Care to collect?" He paused, then gave Samantha a broad grin and a thumbs-up. "Noon? And do you mind if I bring along a friend?" Another pause. "Yes, a female friend, and definitely easy on the eyes."

Samantha blew out her breath. Under the circumstances she would have preferred breaking into Toombs's house to having lunch with him, but Rick wanted her to do this legally. She supposed this kind of qualified. And maybe she could find out enough to make a B and E go more efficiently—or at best she supposed it could clear him. With eight days to solve this, the fewer suspects, the better.

Aubrey clicked off the call and faced her again. "We're on, Miss Samantha. He does like the ladies, so perhaps that peach-colored Halston, if I might suggest? Oh, wait, what in the world am I thinking? You can't wear peach to the Sailfish Club in October. What about that amethyst chiffon Vera Wang you have?"

"You are not supposed to know my wardrobe better than I do," she joked, hopping to the floor. "Are you going to drive?"

"Are you going to let me drive the Bentley?"

"Sure."

"Then be back here at about eleven-thirty. I'll call for reservations."

"It's a date, Aubrey. Thanks."

"Anything for you, Miss Samantha."

She went back to her office to retrieve her purse and the

rest of the Met file, then headed out to the elevator and down to the parking garage. As she climbed into the Bentley, her cell phone rang in the James Bond theme. Samantha smiled as she flipped it open. "Hello, Bond."

"You know, I thought once they premiered a blonde Bond you'd stop calling me that," Rick returned, his voice amused.

"Not a chance. You're way more Bondy than Bond, anyway."

"What does that even mean?"

"You know, the cool cars, the suave clothes, the women fawning all over you, the—"

"I don't have women fawning all over me."

"All over your photos and your fan website, then. And there's me, of course. Oh, and weren't you Britain's Sexiest Bachelor two years ago?"

"Who the devil told you that? No one's ever supposed to mention that to me again."

Samantha laughed. "I ordered a back issue of the magazine on eBay."

"Bloody wonderful."

"It cost me eighteen dollars. What's up?" she asked, starting the car.

"I'm at Tom's office. I just wanted to let you know that Katie's probably going to call and invite you to lunch."

Dammit. "Today?"

"Yes. Is that a problem?"

Now she had to do a quick debate with herself and decide how much she wanted Rick to know about what she was doing. On the surface there was nothing wrong with having lunch with anybody, but he knew she suspected Toombs, and he would think the worst and try to invite himself along, and that would just be awkward. "Aubrey's taking me to lunch today," she said by way of compromise. "It's for Boss's Day or something."

"That's next week."

Wow. There was actually a Boss's Day? "Maybe I can get him and Stoney to take me out twice, then," she returned. "If Katie calls I'll see if I can schedule lunch for tomorrow or something."

"Okay. Thanks."

"'Thanks'?" she repeated. "Why are you thanking me? Why am I going to lunch with Katie Donner?"

"Because we've been back in Palm Beach for three weeks and she likes you. And she's my best friend's wife. So thank you for making an effort to get to know her better."

"As long as Donner's not joining us, I have no problem in the world with Katie. *She's* nice. And maybe she has a theory about Anatomy Man."

"I'll call you later," he said. "Have a good lunch, boss."

"You, too."

Tom Donner's office was right across the street from hers, and she had to restrain herself from waving out the Bentley's window as she drove by. While it felt like Rick had at least half an eye on her all the time, he was probably too busy with his mega-empire to accomplish that. And she supposed that she couldn't blame him for trying to keep track of her—and at least he cared enough to annoy her with his concern.

She agreed with Aubrey's suggestion that she wear the Vera Wang dress. Blending in was always key when she worked, not being noticed as she cased a house or a party. She couldn't wear jeans to the Sailfish Club and expect to blend in. The clothes were the easy part, though. She had to figure out how to approach Gabriel "Wild Bill" Toombs, and how to make the most of this little encounter.

Maybe she should wear a kimono; that would be a good way to start up a conversation about all things Japanese. She could order sushi, she supposed, though raw fish was something for which she'd never developed a fondness.

Technically she could flat out ask Toombs if he had the armor and the swords, and he could show them to her, because the statute of limitations had run out. He could host a party for Joseph Viscanti and wear the armor and nobody could do anything about it.

And therefore she wouldn't be *asking* for the return of Minamoto's armor. He had no incentive to give it to her. On the other hand, if it went missing from his house, he'd be an idiot to call the cops and let everybody know he'd been robbed of his stolen property. All she needed was confirmation that he had the Met items. After that, she had until next Wednesday to figure out how to get them back to Viscanti.

"So she doesn't suspect anything?"

Richard returned to his seat across from Tom Donner's desk. "No. And I don't want her to, so watch your mouth."

"Okay, don't shoot me, but are you keeping this a secret because you're afraid she'll freak, or because you might come to your senses and change your mind?"

"Fuck you, Tom."

"That's not really an answer."

No, it wasn't, and he wasn't going to grace it with one. "All I'm going to say is that you were one hundred percent behind my asking Patricia to marry me, and we all know how that turned out," he said stiffly, picking up his copy of the contract they'd been reviewing and flipping the page.

"And yet your odds were better then. What does that say?"

Richard dropped the contract onto the desk again and stood. "As I recall," he snapped, "you were included in this only after you agreed to keep your bloody opinion to yourself. E-mail me your recommendations for the buyout clause, and the property value assessments for Ridgemont." Reining in his fraying temper as best he could, Rick went to the door and pulled it open. "Otherwise, don't bother me." Because every tense muscle wanted to slam the door hard enough to rattle the windows, he closed it quietly.

He did value Tom's friendship. Greatly. And being in a position where everyone agreed with everything he said and did, having someone he could count on to give him an honest opinion was vital. But whatever happened between him and Samantha was going to be because of Rick Addison and Sam Jellicoe—not because someone else stepped into the middle of the mess and frigged about with it.

In the elevator he pulled out his BlackBerry and checked his schedule. Because of the anniversary of Sam's acquaintance he'd intentionally made this a light week, though now he was beginning to regret that. He needed to call John Stillwell in Los Angeles, and his secretary at the main office in London. The Tokyo meeting wasn't for two and a half weeks, but he had several reports to look over before then

He paused as the elevator opened into the lobby. Tokyo. However he privately felt about Samantha working for the Met, the more safely she could conclude the venture, the better. Richard paged through his list of local phone numbers. Gabriel Toombs wasn't there, but the Picaults were.

Before he could take the time to reconsider, he dialed their number. "August?" he asked as a deep male voice answered the phone. "This is Rick Addison."

"Ah, Rick. *Bonjour.*"

"*Bonjour,* August. *Comment allez vous?*"

"*Bien, bien.* What can I do for you?"

"I am looking for a good set of Hina dolls for the daughter of a friend," he improvised. Olivia Donner did collect dolls, so the tale even made sense. "The ones made during the 1920s, preferably. I was wondering if you and Yvette would join me for lunch and tell me what you know about the market."

"Hold on for a moment."

As he waited, Richard accessed the BlackBerry's list of local restaurant phone numbers. There wasn't one where he couldn't get a table on very short notice, but he knew Yvette Picault had a weakness for seafood.

"Rick, what did you have in mind?"

"How about the Sailfish Club?"

He waited while August relayed that information. "Yvette and I would be delighted. What time should we meet you?"

"Does noon work for you?"

"Might we make it half past?"

"Certainly. I'll see you there."

As soon as he clicked off the phone call he dialed again, this time the Sailfish Club. In two minutes he had a table with a view overlooking Lake Worth and set for twelve-thirty sharp. That had been easy enough. Now all he needed to do was come up with a reasonable way to mention samurai armor and Minamoto Yoritomo. Perhaps he could claim to be hosting a charity dinner with an ancient Japan theme.

Samantha wouldn't like it very much if he suddenly sprang the idea of a party on her, but she would probably go along with it. In addition, a party might be a good place to make a certain public announcement.

His palms abruptly sweaty, he blew out his breath as he

made his way to the parking garage and his Barracuda. The whole scenario shouldn't have been difficult; he loved Samantha, he wanted to spend the rest of his life with her, and he wanted to give her the security of knowing all of that, and knowing that he would always have her back, as it were.

Because he was the Marquis of Rawley, a member of the British aristocracy, matters became a little more complicated. Inheritance rules were sticky, and approvals of a marriage had to come from traditional places and required official decrees. If she only trusted him enough to say yes, he would take care of the rest of it.

He wasn't afraid of taking chances; some of his most lucrative deals had been made because of pure bravado. The thought of making a mistake and because of that losing Samantha, however, frightened the shit out of him. Probably because, unlike a business deal, this one mattered.

Chapter 7

Monday, 11:59 a.m.

"Is that him?" Samantha asked, angling her chin toward the double open doors of the Sailfish Club's restaurant.

"That's him." Aubrey straightened his tasteful gray tie—a conservative choice for him. "So for the caper you're a Japanese antiques aficionado?"

"Shh. Yes. And it's not a caper. It's an investigation."

Technically this wasn't even an investigation as much as it was a poor excuse for a lunch. But Aubrey could call it whatever he wanted as long as he kept offering his help. She wished she'd had a little more time to prepare for meeting Gabriel Toombs, but hey, she worked off-the-cuff often enough to be pretty comfortable with it. At this moment, Toombs was nothing more than a potential mark. All she needed to discover was whether this mark had her target items in his possession.

Gabriel Toombs wore a black silk jacket and a string tie, the cut probably as Steven Seagal as he could get and still pass the jacket and tie dress code of the Club. As he stopped in front of them Aubrey didn't offer his hand. Instead he clamped his hands to his sides and bowed deeply while Toombs mirrored the gesture.

"Wild Bill, please allow me to introduce the exceedingly charming Samantha Jellicoe," Aubrey drawled, gesturing at her. "Miss Samantha, Wild Bill Toombs."

Samantha inclined her head in a more conservative version of a bow of respect. "Mr. Toombs," she said with a slight smile, lowering her head just a little. If Toombs was being the stereotypical American being a Japanese guy, she'd be the demure female he would probably feel the most comfortable around.

"Please call me Wild Bill," he said, gazing at her, and gestured for the maitre d'.

No smile, no display of emotion at all. Samantha kept an eye on him as they were led to their table in the middle of the large room. For the first time she wondered if he had any idea who she was—and then she had to stifle a laugh, because before she'd met Rick, nobody knew who she was unless she wanted them to. Now she was in magazines and featured on nightly entertainment shows, photographed leaving restaurants and entering movie premieres.

Aubrey held out her chair for her, and she sat. Already she was receiving looks from other diners; whether Wild Bill knew she and Rick Addison were an item or not, most of Palm Beach's elite did by now.

"Thank you for allowing me to tag along," she said as the men sat at either elbow. "When Aubrey said he was going to call you, I couldn't resist asking if I might join you."

"And why is that, Miss Jellicoe?" Toombs asked, looking straight at her again.

Oh, my God, he totally thinks he's an Akira Kurosawa movie samurai, Samantha thought, keeping her expression demure and pleasant. "You collect Japanese antiques," she ventured, hoping she wasn't being too direct. "Rick has some, but I keep wishing he would acquire more. There's something about the pure warrior look of the swords and armor that nothing else in the world can touch."

"Ah. A kindred spirit. Do you follow the Japanese antiquities market, then?" He gestured the waiter for an iced tea. Aubrey wanted a margarita, while Samantha stifled a grimace and went with the iced tea, too. Apparently they were keeping themselves pure. No carbonation or sugar substitutes. Crap.

"I try to."

"*Nihongo ga dekimasu ka?*"

"*Nihongo ga sukoshi dekimasu,*" she returned, glad she was able to pass the test part of their lunch program.

"I'm impressed."

"When I enjoy something, I try to learn as much about it as I can."

He nodded. "As do I."

The reply had an edge to it; did he know about her? Stoney always kept as much distance between himself and a contractor as possible, and even more between the money man and her. It protected everybody, and it made it possible for her to be sitting in the Sailfish Club restaurant among the buyers and the marks today.

Still, she knew that she'd once pulled a job for him, and

with her old dad's numero uno lesson of protecting oneself emblazoned across the backs of her eyelids, she was going to have to be cautious around this guy. Especially if he happened to know that Walter Barstone was her current business partner. Throwing Rick's name around could prove to be a valuable distraction, and not for the first time. How Rick would feel about that, she didn't intend to ask.

"Did I tell you," Aubrey put in before she could do more than open her mouth, "why it is I owe Wild Bill this very expensive lunch?"

Thank you, Aubrey. "No, you didn't. I was just happy to be included."

"Well, despite my erroneous belief to the contrary, our Mr. Toombs here is a very fine racquetball player. I had the temerity to challenge him, and he went on to wipe the floor with me."

"It's a matter of discipline and dedication," Toombs said in the same expressionless monotone he'd used since he walked through the door.

"I have it on good authority that Aubrey's a heck of a player," she decided, sitting a little forward and touching the back of Toombs's hand. "I think you could add 'skilled' to your list of racquetball abilities, Wild Bill."

His dark eyes assessed her again. "Very kind of you, Miss Jellicoe."

"Please, call me Samantha. All of my friends do." And Samantha sounded more regal than Sam. And if he knew that she generally went by Sam, he should understand and appreciate that she was trying to impress him. Everything meant something. Even flattery.

For the first time his lips curved a little. "Samantha it shall be, then."

Even with the smile he looked like a sleek shark, clothed

in black from his shoes to his slicked-back hair. She would have loved to see him in business competition against Rick; he probably wouldn't look nearly as well-manicured at the end of the day. Rick had been known to make grown men cry like babies.

"What are you going to order?" she asked, perusing the menu and ready to weep herself at the predominance of yucky seafood items. Ah, well. She could eat fish for a good cause. Hell, she'd even drink coffee if she couldn't avoid it. She wouldn't like it, but she would do it.

"The lobster Florentine, I believe. And you, Samantha?"

"I'll follow your lead," she returned with another smile.

Aubrey's gaze lifted beyond her shoulder, and his perfectly tanned face paled. Before she could ask him whether he was choking on an ice cube, a pair of warm hands touched her shoulders and then settled there. She jumped about a foot. "What—"

"Apparently we both have the same taste," Rick's cultured British accent drawled. As she craned her neck to look up at him, he leaned down to kiss her on the cheek. "Apologies for startling you."

Shit. Shit, shit, shit. "Great minds," she offered, kissing him back. Good as he was at covering his expression, she could read him like a book. The Marquis of Rawley was royally pissed off. "You know Gabriel Toombs, don't you? Wild Bill, Rick Addison."

She heard the click of camera phones around them as, shifting his right arm from her shoulder, Rick shook hands with Toombs. "Of course I know Mr. Toombs," he said. "Have you three met the Picaults? Yvette and August, may I present Mr. Gabriel Toombs, Mr. Aubrey Pendleton, and Miss Samantha Jellicoe?"

Beyond his shoulder stood a couple in their mid-fifties,

well-dressed but still managing to look a little . . . hippie-like. His dark, graying hair was in a ponytail, while hers was even blacker than Rick's, tightly curled and hanging loose past her shoulders.

Toombs stood and bowed. "August," he said, "Yvette. We appear to have gathered together all the major Japanese antiquities collectors living on the East Coast."

Oh, good. At least now they all realized it. Samantha began to feel faint. Rick would never believe it, though, if she feigned passing out and left the mess for him to handle. "We're—"

"I owed Wild Bill lunch," Aubrey interrupted, standing to shake hands with Mr. Picault and kiss Mrs. Picault's knuckles, "and didn't want to leave Miss Samantha alone at the office. That would be far too ungentlemanly."

"And you are always a gentleman," August Pendleton finished in a light French accent, smiling.

"Indeed, I am. Would you care to join us?"

"We couldn't impose," Yvette said, her accent a little heavier—but more cultured—than her husband's. The money probably came from her side of the family, then.

"It would be no imposition," Wild Bill stated, signaling the waiter to join a second table to theirs. "Samantha has been asking me about my collection. Perhaps all of us together might satisfy her curiosity."

"A grand idea," Rick said with an easy smile, his left hand still gripping her shoulder hard enough to bruise. "Though I suspect that Samantha was going to try to find those Hina dolls for Livia before I could manage it."

Hina dolls. "It's only fair," she ventured, mentally crossing her fingers that she was following the hint he'd shoved at her. "You've been a Donner family favorite for better than ten years. I have some catching up to do."

Richard wasn't certain how much of a favorite he was with at least one of the Donners right now, but he would deal with that later. He took the seat beside her, while Yvette ended across from him and August at the head of the table opposite Aubrey. A gentleman escort, a thief, and the three most avid collectors of Japanese antiques on the East Coast. And him. Life was very strange, sometimes. And much more often since he'd met Samantha.

The waiter appeared to take the drink and lunch order of the three late arrivals, while Samantha smiled and chatted and played the novice in awe of the professionals and looking for any information they would be so gracious as to share with her. Thankfully Hina dolls originated at the same time as Minamoto Yoritomo's armor, during the Heian period. That was the reason he'd chosen them—a flanking maneuver in order to acquire the information he wanted. *They* wanted, he amended with a sideways glance at Samantha.

"Do you know why Hina dolls are always royalty or members of the royal court, rather than samurai?" she asked.

Of course she would know about Hina dolls. They weren't as exciting or lucrative as diamonds or rare paintings, but some of them were worth hundreds of thousands of yen. Right up her alley, as it were.

"The dolls are traditionally put on display, nationally in Japan, in fact, on Girls' Day," Yvette said conversationally. "I suppose samurai are too warlike for such a celebration."

Toombs shook his head. "Girls' Day is a recent idea," he said in his absurd Kwai Chang Caine monotone. Didn't the poof realize that Caine was Chinese? Well, half Chinese, though admitting that he knew the plot of *Kung Fu* would have Samantha calling him a geek. "The dolls," Toombs continued, "have been around for much longer than the festival." He fixed his gaze on Samantha. "Your question is an astute one, and warrants further investigation."

She grinned, lowering her lashes. "You're very kind to say so, Wild Bill."

"The little girl you mentioned doesn't want a samurai doll, does she?" August Picault asked.

Since he was the one who'd brought up Olivia Donner, Richard supposed that he needed to be the one to field that question. "No, I don't think so. But she's quite a collector," he said. "Eventually I think she would like to acquire a complete set, including the miniature accessories—altars and cabinets, and things."

"I suppose it's one thing to be able to duplicate silk clothing and furniture in miniature," Samantha put in, "and another to create miniature leather or metal armor plating. Maybe that's why samurai armor's never been attempted. I've seen the two suits of samurai armor that Rick owns, and they're pretty intricate even at full size."

"Two sets of armor?" Toombs repeated, lifting an eyebrow. "What time period?"

"One is Muromachi, and the other, early Edo," Richard returned with an easy smile he didn't feel. This wasn't about his things. "My interest was in acquisition of armor and weapons from around the world at various periods. Russian, Greek, Aztec, whoever had culturally traditional armies at the time."

"I've seen photographs of some of the items in your collection," Yvette stated, smiling again. "Quite impressive."

"I can probably get Rick to show you his, if you'll show me yours," Samantha said with an excited breath.

"Certainly I would be honored," Toombs and his bloody foolish nickname returned. "If Rick is amenable."

"Yes, we would be thrilled to see your collection," Yvette added.

Richard clenched his jaw, smiling around it. "It would be my pleasure."

After that their lunch arrived, and they spent the next forty minutes chatting about the perils and thrills of collecting, and the respective value of Hina dolls depending on where and when they'd been made. Samantha managed to get an invitation to view Toombs's collection on Thursday. The Picaults decided to hold a small house party on Sunday, and extended invitations to everyone at the table.

That was well and good, but Richard did not like the way Toombs spent most of the meal talking just to Samantha, or that she'd scheduled her tour of his collection even after Rick pointed out that he had a video conference scheduled for the same time. He gave himself several pats on the back for not throwing punches right there at the Sailfish Club, but he wanted to—not necessarily because he was worried over Samantha's safety, which he was, but because Toombs thought he could poach another man's woman and didn't hesitate to do so in front of said man.

He paid for lunch over Aubrey Pendleton's well-choreographed protests. As they went their separate ways in the parking lot, he cupped Samantha's elbow. "Aubrey, would you mind taking the Bentley back to the office?" he asked coolly.

Pendleton looked at Samantha. "Which gentleman will you give the honor of escorting you, Miss Samantha?" he drawled.

If Pendleton wanted a fight, Richard would have been happy to accommodate him. On the other hand, he had to give the bloke credit for looking out for Samantha's well-being. He could respect a gentleman, even when the fellow stood against him.

"It's okay, Aubrey," Samantha said, moving around to the passenger door of the Barracuda as Richard pulled it open for her. "I'll see you back at the office in a little while."

Inclining his head, the walker slid behind the wheel of the Bentley and drove off. Smart fellow. "Shall we?" Rick gestured her to climb into the car, and then closed the door behind her.

"I wish you wouldn't do that," she grumbled, pulling on her seat belt as he sat down behind the wheel.

"Do what?" he asked, starting the car. "Open the door for you?"

"I know you can't help that, Galahad," she retorted. "No, I mean I wish you wouldn't act like you're my dad and you caught me breaking curfew or something. Because I'm pretty sure I never had a curfew."

"I have no desire to be Martin Jellicoe," he muttered as they roared into the street. Her father was, as far as he could determine, the very last person he ever wanted back in her life. "You didn't need to lie to me about whom you were dining with."

She folded her arms across her pert tits. "And when did you decide to lunch with the Picaults, Lord Hypocritical?"

"After I stalked out of Tom's office and you said you were celebrating Boss's Day. I thought perhaps I could lend a hand."

Samantha lowered her arms again. "Back the bus up there, Brit. You did what?"

Richard blew out his breath. *Bloody hell.* "We're talking about lunch."

"You're talking about lunch. I'm talking about why you

stalked out of Donner's office," she insisted. "What were you arguing about? Me, right? I thought I'd been pretty normal and humdrum lately."

"You are never humdrum," he retorted, seeking about for an excuse to argue with Tom that didn't include the questioning of his wisdom in purchasing her an engagement ring. "And it was business. I think he feels a little threatened now that I've hired John Stillwell to help represent my interests."

"Well, Donner's stupid, then. He knows how loyal you are to your friends, and that you have way more than enough business to keep ten Donners busy—even though the idea of more than one of him really scares me."

"Multiple Toms?" Richard went along with the meandering tale, even though it had nothing to do with Samantha and her insistence on putting herself in potential danger for a paycheck. It explained the argument with Tom, and that was what he needed.

She gave an exaggerated shudder. "Yipes. That'll give me nightmares. What were *you* mad about, though? You're the one who stalked out, you said."

Sometimes Samantha's overlarge share of intelligence and perceptiveness could be a pain in the arse. "His assumptions, I suppose. Now about Toombs. Next time you decide to go to lunch with a possibly dangerous man, will you please tell me first?"

"I had Aubrey with me."

"And what would Aubrey do if push came to shove, anecdote him to death?"

"Fine. I'll try to remember to tell you first," she conceded with obvious reluctance. "As long as the same goes for you."

"Deal."

As they drove along, he could feel her gaze still on him. He tried to ignore it, but ignoring Samantha was like ignoring sunlight.

"What?" he finally demanded.

"You need to go slap Donner on the butt or whatever you guys do to solve arguments."

"I'll manage my own friendships, thank you very much. And you don't even like Tom. You should be pleased that we've had a difference of opinion."

"I thought so, too," she returned slowly, "but I'm not. Except for Stoney, I never really had friends until I met you. I like having you as a friend. Friends are cool, and important. And I would guess that best friends, people who tell you things nobody else would, are pretty rare."

As they stopped for a red light, Rick leaned over and kissed her. "Tom is a very good friend," he murmured. "You are my best friend. And a very unusual and fascinating woman, Samantha Elizabeth Jellicoe."

She kissed him back, smiling. "And don't you forget it. Besides, I'm working for Olivia, and if you and Tom are fighting, I'll never get in to see her."

"Are you so certain that's a bad thing? You've been worried about your reputation. I would assume, then, that you don't want it spread about that you're helping a ten-year-old find Anatomy Man."

"Clark the Anatomy Man."

Richard lifted an eyebrow. "He has a name?"

"Apparently Livia's teacher, Miss Barlow, thinks he looks like Clark Kent."

"I find myself fascinated."

"If I find him, I'll bring him by and introduce you. You superheroes should all know each other, anyway."

"Speaking of which," he said, unable to help his abrupt

smile, "I had John Stillwell track down an item for me during his Los Angeles trip."

"A bottle of Botox?"

"It's behind your seat. Another anniversary present, I suppose."

"Okay," she said slowly, and undid her seat belt to lean around behind her seat. "Oh . . . my . . . God." She giggled. Actually giggled, as she freed the clear-plastic fronted box.

"He roars, and walks with the remote control."

Samantha settled the two feet of boxed Godzilla onto her lap, refastening her seat belt. "He roars?"

"There are some mini frightened Tokyo residents taped to the inside of the box. And the background forms into a skyscraper he can knock over."

"You got me a Godzilla, you handsome devil, you." She stretched over and kissed him soundly on the cheek. "Thank you!"

"My pleasure." He laughed as she pulled the monster out of the box and made him roar while they drove back to Worth Avenue. He probably could have forgone the hundred-thousand-dollar nursery gift certificate and just gotten the toy, and she would have been as happy. Happier, because Godzilla could travel, and the garden couldn't.

Chapter 8

Monday, 9:49 p.m.

"I'll be back in a moment, Ben," Rick said, opening the door of the stretch Mercedes S600 as soon as it came to a stop at the curb. Calling first probably would have been a good idea, but he still wasn't certain what he would say, and direct confrontation yielded much more interesting and telling results, anyway.

A few seconds after he rang the Donners' doorbell the porch light flipped on, and he heard the muffled voice of fifteen-year-old Mike calling out his identity, followed by the more distant reply of Tom. The Donners had best not leave him standing there on the bloody porch.

As he was beginning to debate whether ringing a second time would be a show of weakness, the door opened. "What?" Tom asked, leaning against the frame and blocking him from entering the house.

"Get a jacket," Richard returned in the same tone.

"Why?"

"We're going out."

Tom looked at him for a minute, then reached back to grab a denim jacket from behind the door. "I'm going out," he called over his shoulder.

"Don't kill anybody," Katie's voice came.

"You told her?" Richard asked, leading the way to the car.

"I told her we had a difference of opinion. Did you tell Jellicoe?"

"Kind of. I didn't think she needed to know the details."

"I bet she's pissed that you're here, then."

As Richard pulled open the rear door of the Mercedes, he paused. "She made me come, actually," he said conversationally. "Apparently close friends who speak their minds are rare and wondrous and to be treasured beyond all reasonable expectation. And I'm supposed to slap your arse, but I assume that's an American thing and we can forgo it."

"Okay," Tom returned warily, climbing into the limo. "Where are we going, then?"

"A place we can get drunk without making the cover of the *Inquirer* tomorrow."

"I'm all for that."

"I thought so. Just keep in mind that I'm here because Samantha refused to have sex with me until we made up." Well, she hadn't precisely said that, but he understood the significance of the sweatshirt and ponytail and the thick book on Japanese history across her lap.

"After I get some beers in me I'll think about it."

"Fair enough."

"And if I'm getting drunk, I'm probably going to be late getting to the office tomorrow," Tom added, sliding over to give Richard room.

"Shut up before you make me slap your arse."

"You'll have to get a lot of beer in me before that."

"Don't you know it."

Samantha reached for the television remote and switched the channel to *CSI: Miami*. Their forensics was a little ahead of the reality curve, and that Horatio guy drove her nuts with his monotone and the hands-on-his-hips thing, but she liked the problem-solving approach.

As she turned the page of the book she'd been perusing, the house phone rang. She looked at the caller ID. The Donners' home number. Maybe that meant that Donner and Rick had made up already. She presumed that was why Katie hadn't called her about lunch—if their men were on the outs, they probably wouldn't be eating together. Of course it could also be Livia, asking for an update on her case.

She picked up the receiver. "Hello?"

"Hi, Sam. It's Kate Donner."

"Hi, Katie," she returned, a little relieved that she didn't have to tell the little girl that she hadn't already located Anatomy Man. "Rick showed up over there, then? You haven't called the cops on him, have you?"

Katie chuckled. "No. They went off in the limo together, I assume to go drinking and play pool."

With a small sigh, Samantha smiled. However she felt about Donner, Rick liked having him around, and that meant the lawyer needed to be around. "Good."

"So I was wondering if you might be free for lunch tomorrow."

"Sure. Café l'Europe?"

"Ah, calzone. With real cheese. Do you want to meet, or should I pick you up?"

Katie sounded like she was ready to go right then. "I'll be at the office, so let's just meet there," Samantha said, her smile deepening. "What time's good for you?"

"How about noon? That'll give me time afterward to go grocery shopping before the kids get home. I'll make the reservations."

"I'll see you tomorrow, then."

Samantha hung up the phone and sat back on the deep couch. So tomorrow she would be having lunch with a stay-at-home soccer mom. *Huh.* She could add that to the list of things she'd never expected to do. Hell, she'd never expected to have to make a list at all until she'd met Rick.

She stretched out her bare toes. It might be fun to have a pair of bunny slippers. They were pink and frivolous, and somebody who lived in the shadows and who had to be ready to leave with one minute's notice and kept all her essential belongings in a backpack stuffed in the closet didn't have room for them. Didn't have a life where they fit.

Samantha shook herself. *Focus, Jellicoe.* Enough about the stupid bunny slippers. First things first. And the first thing was Yoritomo's armor. As she'd thought, Ron Mosley didn't qualify as a suspect. He hadn't even started collecting until about five years ago when he'd inherited a ton of money from an uncle. Rick's other non–Palm Beach suggestion, Pascale Hasan, could have afforded the armor, but according to the Internet and the few sources who still spoke to her, Hasan's obsession was with the silk and geishas, not samurai.

Considering the theft had been ten years ago, it surprised her that after a couple of long hours on the computer she could eliminate the number of people she had. Rich people tended to have their whereabouts well-publicized, their comings and goings well-documented, and she stuck by her theory that the buyer had seen the display, probably in New York, at which time they'd decided to acquire it. Whoever she could confirm had never seen the exhibit at any of its stops was out of the running.

In her book that left her with the hippies or Gabriel "Wild Bill" Toombs. She'd worked for Toombs once, though Stoney still hadn't called her back with the details. If Toombs had had anything to do with the Met job, at least one other guy had worked for him, too—since she didn't rob museums. And there might be others, if theft had become his favored method of collecting Japanese antiques. Since her sources were drying up and probably wishing her dead, she needed to find new ones.

Mentally adding another entry to her notebook of weirdness, she picked up the phone again and dialed. Two rings later she heard a familiar gravelly voice. "Castillo."

"Hi, Frank. It's Sam Jellicoe."

"Sam. I heard you were back in Palm Beach. Is this social, or do I need to call the coroner?"

She grinned. "You're such a cop."

"Yep." The homicide detective was silent for a moment, but Samantha could practically hear him running a finger across his thick, graying mustache. "What's up?"

She figuratively crossed her fingers. "Well, I know you're the homicide go-to guy, but is there any way you could find out information about a robbery?"

"Rick didn't get hit again," his voice returned, sharper. "I would have heard about that."

"No, this is more like a hypothetical theft, taking place sometime between now and the past seven years." The PD probably didn't keep records past then, anyway.

Castillo snorted. "Seven years' worth of thefts? Can you narrow that down? You know, days of the week, alphabetical order, anything like that?"

She ignored his mouthing off, willing to take the sarcasm as long as he would help her out. "I can give you a name, to see if there's anything connected to it. Three names, actually."

He grumbled something that didn't sound very nice. "I am not your damn snitch, Sam."

"I know that. We're two professionals sharing information."

"Mm hm. One, *I'm* the professional, and two, sharing means you give something back to me."

"Something like helping you solve Charles Kunz's murder, maybe? Or—"

"Okay, okay." Beneath the sound of his sigh, Samantha heard his ever-present notepad opening. "Give me the damn names."

"Gabriel Toombs, and August and Yvette Picault."

"Are you fucking kidding me, Sam? Should I add Trump to the list? You're talking about pillars of the community."

"Hey, the Sodom and Gomorrah people were pillars of their community, too. Pillars don't mean anything."

"Pillars mean money, and that means it's better not to piss them off. I'm going to have to be careful with this.

If one of their attorneys gets wind of this and thinks the PBPD is investigating them, then I'm stuck writing parking tickets out on Worth Avenue."

Samantha blew out her breath. "I hate lawyers."

"You and me both. I'll call you in a couple of days, because I have real, actual crime to investigate."

"I need it by the weekend, Frank."

"Fuck. You and Rick are buying a whole table's worth of tickets to the next police charity dinner. Two tables' worth."

He hung up the phone before she could reply to that; evidently he thought the tickets were a sure thing—which they were. Things were lining up okay, but after sitting on the damn file for ten years, Viscanti and the Met could have given her a little more time to solve the theft. She might be Cat Woman, but she wasn't Superman. That honor went to Clark the Anatomy Man.

For the next hour she read up on samurai armor and swords, comparing the book's photos with the ones Viscanti had sent her from the Met. She needed to be able to recognize them if she saw the items in person. The armor with its red and orange coloring would be pretty easy, but the daitu and wakizashi swords were very typical of the period, rare as anything that old was. They had the folded steel blades, and hilts made of wood and wrapped in stingray skin and silk. The scabbards were lacquered and inlaid with copper symbols for faith and good fortune—they would be distinctive, once she knew what to look for. Chances were that once she saw any of it, she would have to move fast.

When she checked the clock it was eleven-thirty, *Letterman* was starting, and Rick was still out bonding with the lawyer. Stretching, she stood up and went to bed. Maybe Katie could give her some gardening tips before she had to call Piskford Nurseries, and she could start a whole new chapter in her notebook of the unexpected. At the least, she needed to know when she could corner Mike Donner without his friends or his parents finding out about it.

She awoke with a start as cold feet touched her calves. "Christ, Rick," she muttered, parting her knees and closing them again around his feet. "I'm glad we don't live in North Dakota. You're going to give me frostbite."

He chuckled against the back of her hair. "If we lived in North Dakota, I would have worn socks."

"Well, that's something, anyway." She craned her neck around to eye him leaning there with his head resting on his crooked arm. "Are you and Yale okay? Did you scratch your crotches and spit and make up?"

"I thought I was supposed to swat him on the rump. This is very complicated."

Samantha turned on her back to face him. "Are you guys okay?" she repeated.

"Yes, we're okay." He leaned down and kissed her on the tip of her nose. "Thank you for pushing me to talk to him."

"You're welcome." Good. Good for Rick, and good for her that she wouldn't be blamed for breaking up a friendship. She slid her hands up his bare chest and kissed him back softly. "Wanna fool around?"

Rick returned the kiss. "Ordinarily, yes," he murmured, curving a strand of her hair behind her ear, "but I had about a half-dozen beers and something Tom called a 'Texas Scorpion,' and I can barely keep my eyes open."

"Okay. I'd be kind of mad if you fell asleep in the middle." She settled back onto her pillow and closed her eyes. "Good night."

"Did Katie ever call you?"

Pushing back the foggy sleepiness that still clogged her brain, Samantha opened her eyes again. "She did. We're going to lunch tomorrow. Today. It's today, right? Tuesday?"

"Several hours into it. Where are you eating?"

She frowned. "If you're so interested, why don't you come along?"

"No, thanks. I was just curious."

"Well, stop it. You're making me cranky."

"Okay."

Shutting her eyes again, she sighed. The fact that she hadn't awakened until Rick's cold feet had attacked her said a great deal about how comfortable she'd become in this house, and with him. And tonight she didn't even want to beat herself up for having blunted instincts. Rick had several times risked his life and his reputation for her. If there was one place she should be able to sleep safe and sound, it was here.

"Are the kids coming?"

Samantha opened one eye. "What?"

He moved a breath closer. "Are Olivia and Mike going to have lunch with you?" he clarified.

"No. They have school, doofus. Go to sleep."

"I like Tom's kids."

With a growl Samantha pushed upright and slung her pillow across his head. "For a sleepy drunk guy you're pretty pesky," she snapped, not sure whether she was more amused or annoyed at him.

"I'm fairly spry, too." He grabbed the pillow away and swung it at her.

She blocked the blow with her arm, and climbed up on her knees to tackle him flat onto the bed. "Go to sleep!" she demanded, laughing as she pinned his shoulders.

Rick knocked her arms out from under her and spun

them around so that she lay on her back looking up at him and his glittering blue eyes. Slowly he settled his weight down on her and kissed her again. "Do you think our kids would be as pretty as Tom's?"

"Prettier," she answered, sliding her arms around his shoulders. "They would have two good-looking parents. Livia, Mike, and Chris are just lucky they take after Katie and not Yale. Don't tell them I said that. Except for Donner. You can tell *him*."

"I think I'll save that for later." He slipped off of her and pulled her close until her back rested against his chest. "Do you ever think about it?"

"Oh, for crying out loud," she muttered, screwing her eyes shut. "Think about what?"

"About what our kids would look like. How many there would be, how many boys and how many girls. Things like that."

"I don't know. Sometimes I wonder, I guess." She tucked the sheets up under her chin. "Me and babies is scary. I never even babysat."

His fingers wrapped into hers. "You're working with Livia. You two seem to get along like a house afire."

"She's interesting. She thinks she's really wise, but she's so . . . innocent. You know what I mean?"

"I know what you mean. Maybe we should borrow a baby."

"Let's give Angelina Jolie a call. She's probably got some spares."

"I love you, Yank."

Finally he sounded sleepy. "I love you, Brit."

Richard felt Samantha in his arms relax and drift back to sleep. That had gone more smoothly than he'd expected. The idea of babies—of her having babies—had to scare her half to death. At least the thought had crossed her mind. At least she hadn't laughed at him and dismissed the notion.

Richard shook himself. He was getting *way* ahead of the matters at hand. The ring hadn't even been finished yet. And if he proposed and she turned him down, he had no idea what would happen. He wasn't losing her; he knew that. He persuaded people to do things all the time, so surely he could convince her that marrying him would be a good idea. A very good idea. The only idea he really wanted to contemplate.

He awoke to the sound of "Raindrops Keep Falling on My Head" coming from Samantha's cell phone. "Sam?"

"Sorry," she yelled from the direction of the bathroom, over the sound of the shower. "Can you get it?"

Reaching across to her side of the bed and trying to ignore the dull pounding in his skull, Richard picked up the phone and flipped it open. "*Hola*, Walter," he said.

"Oh. Hi, Rick," the former fence's voice came. "Are you answering Sam's phone now?"

Richard narrowed his eyes. "She's in the shower."

"Still, does she know you're taking her private phone ca—"

"Yes," he interrupted sharply. "Is there something I can do for you?"

"I just wanted to let her know I won't be coming in to the office today. I have a couple of errands to run. She can reach me on my cell if she needs to get hold of me."

Glancing toward the half-open bathroom door, Richard slid to the edge of the bed. "All animosity aside, is everything well, Walter?"

"Yeah, yeah. Everything's fine."

"Is there some coded message I need to give Samantha to convince her that I'm not lying about that?" he pursued.

Barstone cleared his throat. "Just tell her the peas are boiling, and I'll give her a call tomorrow. And . . . tell her to be careful."

The line clicked dead. Slowly Richard snapped the phone closed again. Something was off—hinky, as Samantha would say—but he didn't know what, precisely. Walter Barstone did travel, but according to Sam not nearly as much as he had when he was on the job. Was he working again, fencing for someone other than Samantha?

God, he hoped not. Because she needed Walter in her life, and if the former fence was back in business, they would need to be separated. Which would make him the villain of the piece, he supposed, for looking out for her best interests. And his own, of course.

"That was Stoney, wasn't it?" she asked, walking into the room wearing nothing but a towel around her hair. "Did he finally look up that stupid information for me?"

Good glory. "He didn't say."

She bent down, toweling her hair off. "What did he say, then?"

"He'll be out of the office today, running some errands."

Samantha straightened again, her whole stance alert. "What kind of errands?"

"He didn't say." Richard held up a hand before she could interrupt with another question. "I'm supposed to tell you that the peas are boiling. And I expect you to tell me what the devil that means."

"It means they need salt," she said absently, pulling her blue bathrobe off the back of a chair and shrugging into it. "Shaking. He's trying to shake something loose."

That sounded better than Barstone accepting and redistributing stolen property again, anyway. "What's he trying to shake loose?"

"I don't know. I asked him to look for his file on Toombs, and I feel like he's been stonewalling me since then."

"He said you could reach him on his cell phone if you needed to," he offered.

"That would make me a wuss. Dammit."

"He also said you should be careful."

Samantha stilled for a second. "That doesn't sound good. For him or for me."

"I think Walter can take care of himself, my love," Richard said, trying to untangle his left foot from the blankets. "I'm more worried about you. Why don't you come here and kiss me?"

She wrinkled her nose. "I'm squeaky clean and freshly brushed. You're morning-after-six-beers guy."

"Message understood," he returned with a grin, standing. "Shower and toothpaste. Are you staying for breakfast?"

Samantha looked at him for a long moment. "Sure."

He tilted his head at her. "What?"

"Just taking you in," she said with a smiling sigh. "You look good with that sexy crazy bed hair and the stubble. Does it feel like we've known each other for a year?"

Richard shook his head, feeling his heart beating all the way out to his fingertips. "Sometimes it feels like a day. That first day. Electric."

"Yeah. Electric. We do have the sparks, don't we?"

And the hills were alive with the sound of music. "We're an entire electrical storm."

Nothing made a bloke feel more satisfied and proud than knowing that the woman he loved, loved him. And to think when they'd first met, she hadn't trusted him enough to give him her last name. If he'd been a man with less patience, he would have given up in frustration months ago. But he'd known immediately what he wanted, and luckily her own stubborn path had led her in the same direction.

As he came downstairs twenty minutes later, he hummed "Rule Britannia." That amusement stopped as the front bell rang. He paused on the landing while Reinaldo appeared to pull open the door. "Good morning, Detective," the housekeeper said, stepping back.

Homicide Detective Frank Castillo of the Palm Beach Police Department sauntered into the foyer, looked up to see Rick, and gave a half wave. "Good morning, Rick. Is Sam around?"

Another thing his life had become since he'd met Samantha Elizabeth Jellicoe—chock full of surprises.

Chapter 9

Tuesday, 8:25 a.m.

Samantha shoveled strawberries and melon slices from the bowl on the sideboard and onto her plate. Toombs or the Picaults. However many suspects she named, it kept coming back to them. Both had enough money to afford it, both had been in New York sometime during the exhibit's six-week stop there, both resided on the East Coast, both collected Japanese antiquities. And at least as importantly, she *knew* Toombs had willingly acquired at least one piece of his collection illegally.

Maybe Stoney had a lead or a theory of his own, but whatever he was doing, he didn't seem to want to talk about it. And so she had to ask her own questions, do her own research. She had seven more days to find Yoritomo's armor. That, together with her social schedule—lunch today, the Toombs tour on Thursday, the Mallorey charity thing on Saturday, and the Picaults' dinner on Sunday—wasn't going to be easy. It was a good thing she liked a challenge.

"Samantha, you have a visitor," Rick said without preamble, entering the breakfast room.

She faced the door as he passed her, slowing to kiss her on the cheek. "Who is it?"

"Me," Detective Frank Castillo said, stopping in the doorway. "Surprise."

Her adrenaline went into overdrive, and she stood up. Even though they got along pretty well, even though she'd called him for help last night, seeing a cop in the house, in her territory, was just wrong. "Surprise, yourself," she said. "Is anybody I know dead or something?"

"Who am I now, the Grim Reaper?"

"I don't know; you tell me."

"Nobody's dead—that I know of."

"Good. Want some breakfast?"

"Sure."

As she retook her seat at the table, Frank walked over to the well-stocked sideboard and started selecting a mound of food. Apparently nobody else knew how to feed the guy. Rick chose scrambled eggs and toast, sitting to her right at the head of the table. "Do you know why he's here?" he mouthed, touching her fingers.

Samantha shook her head. "Well, maybe," she muttered, not wanting to tell—or get caught telling—a flat out lie.

Rick lifted an eyebrow. "'Maybe'?"

"Frank," she went on in a louder voice, "when I called

you last night you said you'd get back to me in a couple of days. Did something happen?"

The detective sat across from her. "About two hours after you called, Gabriel Toombs ran a test on his estate alarm system," he said around a mouthful of waffle. "On every sensor. His alarm company had to notify the PD because we get an automated signal when the system activates."

"Two questions," Rick put in, waiting until he'd chewed and swallowed to speak. "What did you ask Frank about Toombs, and don't the larger estates test their alarms on a regular basis?"

Samantha snorted. She couldn't help herself. "They *should* test them, but they don't. Once that little green light goes on for the first time, most people figure they're invulnerable for life. You've always tested your system regularly, which at least makes you a challenge." She glanced at Frank's interested expression. *Great, Sam. Incriminate yourself.* "A challenge to bad people who might want to rob you, I mean."

"Toombs actually hasn't run a test in nearly five years," Castillo agreed. "After you mentioned his name, I checked for any current events stats on the PD computer. Your question was about whether Toombs or the Picaults had ever been suspected in any kind of theft, but this was something." He leaned forward on his elbows. "And since you know stuff, is there anything I should pass on to my friends in Robbery?"

"Man, I thought you were here to give me something useful, not to ask *me* for clues."

"Sam, you know something. Cough it up."

She spread her arms. "I don't. I'm doing some research into the whereabouts of some items that have been missing for three years past the statute of limitations. If you guys have anything on Toombs or the Picaults it might give me an idea where to look." Well, she had a pretty good idea, but he might be able to confirm it.

"You can't break in to steal something back," Frank said, his expression hardening.

"Ooh, thanks for the scoop, Frank. I don't do B and E's, remember? I'm just looking around for clues."

"Right."

Samantha straightened, looking the detective straight in the eye. "Are you accusing me of something? Do I need to call a lawyer?"

Frank blew out his breath. "No. Your methods might be . . . unorthodox, but you've helped me and the PD out of jams a couple of times. Just make sure you don't go past looking. Leave the rest to the cops and the lawyers."

"Don't worry about that," she said, answering without committing herself to anything. *Always have a way out*, Martin had always said. And she pretty much always did, for everything except her relationship with Rick.

"So that's it? You came by to tell me that Wild Bill Toombs tested his alarm system?"

"And I figured it was about breakfast time. A cop's got to eat."

"Eat all you want, as long as you promise to look into Toombs and the Picaults like you said you would."

"I will, I will. I promise. Could I get some coffee?"

Rick signaled Reinaldo at the edge of the room, and the housekeeper made a silent exit. The house had more than a dozen people working in and around it—chef, maids, driver, gardeners, pool maintenance, security, plumbers, electricians. But Samantha had noticed that she tended to have dealings with the same small group, and she thought that was probably on purpose. Rick wanted her to be comfortable, and he saw to it in ways that he'd never mention, and that most people would probably never notice. But she noticed. That was kind of her specialty, noticing things.

Speaking of noticing things . . . "Are you sure there's nothing else?" she pursued. "You could have told me all this over the phone, Danishes or not."

"You are a very persistent woman," Castillo grunted. "All I'm saying is that you're not the only party who's ever asked questions about Gabriel Toombs. He's shown up on a couple of suspect lists for thefts over the years, but nobody's officially accused him of anything. No evidence."

"You did do some digging already, you big tease," Samantha said with a grin. "Thefts from where?"

"I don't know, yet. FBI-sized. But suspected only. No proof. And you didn't hear that from me." He shoveled in another mouthful.

"Like I want anybody to know that I have breakfast with cops." She leaned forward on her elbows. "Is this anything that a robbery detective in New York, say, might know more about?"

"You mean that cop who arrested you in March? Sam Gorstein?"

"I was cleared of any wrongdoing, thank you very much," she said stiffly. Jeez, get nabbed once and nobody let you forget it. "Do you think Gorstein might be able to help me out?"

Castillo shrugged. "I can't speak for the NYPD. All I will say is that if the only thing you have to repay me for my information is breakfast and some help nine months ago, you don't have much to offer a guy in another state."

Except for the feeling that that guy might be a little sweet on her. She glanced at Rick, who'd been following the conversation but uncharacteristically staying pretty much out of it. "Well, I guess I'm stuck with you then, Frank," she said, sitting back again. "Anything else you can find out would be great."

"Yes, I know. If you weren't so helpful about boosting my arrest and conviction ratio, I'd probably be less inclined." Reinaldo appeared with a coffee carafe, and the detective paused to fill his cup and add way too much sugar for an ordinary citizen. Built-up cop immunity, she guessed. Finally he took a long swallow, closed his eyes, and smiled. "Now *that* is good coffee."

"It's a Brazilian-Jamaican hybrid," Rick finally contributed. "I'll send the station a couple of pounds of it."

"Well, you'll never be getting another speeding ticket." Snorting and obviously amused at his cop humor, Frank took another drink. "Hey, how's that pool garden going? I did offer that blue turtle my uncle painted for me, but I guess you went with the gnomes."

"I've been a little late getting started on it," Samantha answered, avoiding Rick's gaze. She had other things to take care of at the moment. Things a lot less scary and root bound. "I'm making out a list right now of plants I want to order."

"Cool. Invite me to the grand unveiling."

She forced a smile. "I will."

For the next twenty minutes they chatted about the differences between fall in Palm Beach, Florida, and Devonshire, England, until Frank finally finished eating and decided to head back to the station. Rick stood beside her just inside the front doorway as the detective and his brown, late-model Taurus rolled down the drive to the street.

"You called him last night?" Rick asked, as he closed the door again.

"Just looking for anything obvious. Viscanti's really worried about losing this exhibit to the Smithsonian. He's only got until next Wednesday to produce the armor."

"That really isn't your problem."

"I know, I know." It felt like it was, though. She hadn't known about the time constraints when she'd taken the job, but it was part of the gig now. If she couldn't deliver on time, then as far as she was concerned she'd blown the contract.

"When you go sightseeing at Wild Bill's on Thursday, take Aubrey with you."

"Aubrey? You're the one who didn't think he was manly enough to protect me during lunch at the Sailfish Club."

"You're not going alone, Samantha."

"Rick—"

"You can make this a fight if you want to, but I'm not giving in on something that just makes good sense."

She took a breath, holding back her irritation at being dictated to. She was in a partnership now, even at the moments when it would be handier to be flying solo, even when sometimes she wondered how long it would last—and so she needed to adjust her game plan accordingly. "Okay, okay. Sheesh. I'll ask him to come with me."

"If he can't join you, then reschedule for when *I* can."

"Toombs can't be all suave and macho and show his stuff off to a naive admirer when you're there."

"Then you'd best hope Aubrey can join you on Thursday."

Samantha stuck her tongue out at him. "Fine, tough guy," she said, heading for the garage and her car. "You'll have to remind me to call Patty next week and wish her a happy thirtieth birthday."

"You don't need to torture me with my ex-wife," he commented, following her. "This is about your safety."

"If I have to deal with the consequences of my past mistakes, bub, so do you. See you later."

"Have a nice lunch with Katie. By the by, I'm flying to New York. I'll be home tonight."

Her heart lurched, and she stopped midway to the Bentley. "When did this happen? Just now, because you're mad at me?"

"No, and I'm not mad at you. Apparently after I left Tom's office yesterday afternoon he got a call from Showler and DeWitt. That office building next to mine may be going up for sale. I want to take a closer look at it before I decide whether to make a bid, and I thought I'd meet with my staff there in Manhattan if I have time."

"Make time," she said, walking back up to him. "You have a perfectly nice townhouse in Manhattan."

With a half smile Rick slid an arm around her waist, pulling her up against him. "Yes, I recall it. We spent several weeks there this past spring."

"So don't think you have to rush there and be back in time to keep me out of trouble. That's not your job."

He looked like he wanted to argue with that, but she leaned up on her tiptoes and kissed him, fighting against her surprise that her first instinct had been to blow off the armor and anatomy model hunt and offer to go with him. *Way to lose the killer instinct, Sam.*

"My wanting to rush back isn't because I worry about you getting into trouble," he murmured, letting his fingers drift across her cheek in a way that made her shiver. "It's because I'm crazy about you, and I don't like to spend the night away from you."

"Keep talking like that and I'll let you have your way with me when you get back. Which will be tomorrow, so you don't have to rush through building inspections and meetings like a crazy man."

He smiled again, kissing her deep and hot and slow. "Okay. I'll call you this evening."

Samantha chuckled, pretending that she thought he was sappy and that she wasn't really thinking that he was the best thing that had happened to her in her entire life. "Okay," she whispered. "But no phone sex. I prefer the real thing."

"You and me both, Yank."

After Samantha left for the office, Richard called the Palm Beach airport to have his pilot push back their return flight to tomorrow. Then he phoned his New York office to confirm meetings, schedule another one for Wednesday morning, and let Wilder at the townhouse know he would be spending the night. He packed a small overnight bag and dropped some contracts that needed his review into a briefcase.

It was funny; if this had been four years earlier and his conversation had been with Patricia—if he'd remembered to tell her in person and not by phone call from the jet—she would have wanted to know whether he'd be back for the party at the Malloreys' and that would have been it. No heart-stopping kisses, no mention of nighttime phone calls or making love. And once he'd walked out the door he wouldn't have thought about her until he walked back into the house. God, how times—and he—had changed.

His mobile phone rang as he slid into the back seat of the stretched S600 and Ben closed the door for him. He grinned as he looked at the caller ID. "Yes, my love?"

"I just checked Manhattan weather on the Net," Samantha's voice returned. "You do realize it's forty degrees colder there than it is here and that you're going to freeze your British patootie off."

"I have my coat."

"Okay. And if you have time, would you bring me back a couple of those peppermint brownies? But don't let Hans know that I like André's brownies better than his."

"Your secret is safe with me." And since he couldn't imagine that the chefs from his New York and Palm Beach residences ever conversed about brownie recipes, their secrets were probably safe from each other, as well. "I'll put them in a shirt box or something."

"Thanks, James Bond. Before you know it you'll be ready to smuggle fruits and vegetables across state lines." She snorted, obviously finding herself hilarious. "I love you. Be careful."

"I love you, too. Don't commit any federal offenses while I'm gone."

"No promises. Ta."

"Ta."

She'd said it first again, something she did only rarely. And there he was, rich, powerful, influential, and those three single-syllable words from her could lift his feet off the floor, give his heart happy palpitations, and make him feel like a genuine superhero.

And as a superhero, there was one more thing he could see to while he was in New York. Before he put his phone away he opened it again, scrolled through his saved phone numbers—which after having witnessed two of his phones destroyed over the past six months he now backed up onto his laptop—and found the one he wanted.

"Gorstein," came the terse voice on the other end.

"Detective. This is Rick Addison. Do you have a moment?"

"I have about one moment. What can I do for you, Addison?"

"I'll be in Manhattan this afternoon, and I wondered if you would be able to meet with me for fifteen or twenty minutes today or tomorrow."

"Is Ms. J in trouble again?"

He couldn't blame anybody for thinking that—she did have a way of finding mayhem. "No. She's doing some research. Since I'll be there, I thought I might see if I can lend her some assistance."

"Is this a home thing, or an office thing?"

"The police station would probably be the most useful place to meet."

"Okay." Gorstein flipped through some papers. "How about . . . eight tomorrow morning, right here?"

"I'll see you then. Thank you, Detective."

Good. Both Gabriel Toombs and the Picaults had homes in New York in addition to the mansions in Palm Beach, and Gorstein's odds of finding anything useful were as good as Castillo's. And before Samantha went to visit Wild Bill's house, with Aubrey Pendleton in tow or not, he wanted all of the information he could get his hands on. And he had no problem at all with throwing around his considerable influence to get what he wanted and needed to protect Samantha.

Chapter 10

Tuesday, 12:03 p.m.

Samantha pulled around the corner from Café l'Europe so she could park the Bentley herself. Valet parking was cool and all, but she preferred knowing where her own car and the keys were.

Katie Donner arrived just as she walked up to the front door of the restaurant. For a second she wondered whether they would do the fashionable Palm Beach double miss-kiss, but the petite blond gave her a sound hug and a peck on the cheek.

"Thanks for not being a ten- or a fifteen-year-old or an attorney," she said in her soft Texas accent, grinning. "Though they can all be pretty much the same thing."

"I'm not going to argue with that," Samantha returned, nodding as one of the hosts held the door open for them, "but I'll add British guy to the list."

"Reservations for Donner," Katie told the maitre d', who immediately summoned a waiter to seat them close to the window in the main dining room.

Samantha heard the whispers as she took the seat facing the entrance—apparently she had been attached to Rick Addison long enough that she was her own tourist attraction. Most of these people, though, were locals, tanned and rich and with too much time on their hands. However much it still bothered her to be stared at, to them she presented a confident smile and the attitude that she absolutely belonged there.

After a year it wasn't even the instinct to blend so much anymore as the thought that as long as she and Rick were together, she *did* belong there. Hell, she probably had as much money secreted away as some of these people did, anyway, and she had her own reservations about whether they'd been any more honest in acquiring their wealth than she had been. She'd definitely helped some of these people express their dark sides, whether they knew she was the one who'd done the acquiring of loot for them, or not.

"Hi, I'm Sean, and I'll be your server. May I get you something to drink?" the waiter asked.

"An iced tea for me," Katie said, opening the menu.

"A Diet Coke for me."

"No wine for you lovely ladies? Perhaps a nice Chardonnay?"

"We're both driving, but thanks," Katie commented, before Samantha could.

"Very good. I will give you a few moments to peruse the menu."

Samantha's gaze met Katie's, and they both laughed. "'Peruse'? Mr. Sean thinks he's hot stuff."

Katie chuckled. "It's a good thing for him that the food tastes so good."

Once they'd received their drinks and Katie ordered the calzone while Samantha decided on the chicken fettuccine, the waiter left them alone. Katie sipped her iced tea, her light blue eyes taking in the restaurant's decorations and the other diners. Considering that Katie was probably the most together, confident, and secure woman she knew, Sam's Spider-sense began to tingle. Katie was hesitating about something. Whether it was personal or had something to do with Anatomy Man or Rick and Yale's fight, she didn't know yet—but she would find out.

"Are you going to come stay at Rawley Park for the gallery opening in December?" she began, taking a piece of bread from the basket on the table.

"The kids are excited about it," Katie answered. "And Christmas in England sounds very . . . romantic."

"But?" Samantha prompted, hiding her abrupt irritation that Rick's closest friends might not show up to celebrate the opening of the Devonshire gallery. Rick had devoted the entire south wing of his ancestral mansion to showcase the rare artworks and antiques he and his forefathers had acquired, and the last year to renovations and selections. And he was doing it on his own dime, just because it was the right thing to do.

"It's kind of silly, I guess," Katie said, "but I really hate flying. It terrifies me."

Samantha blinked. She'd expected some lame excuse or other, but Katie's cheeks reddened and her gaze lowered. She was genuinely embarrassed. "I don't like it much, either," she admitted, "but mostly because once you go up, there's no exit until you land again."

Katie leaned forward. "Is that because of the thief thing?" she whispered. "Like the plane's a cage or a prison or something?"

So being a cat burglar was a "thing" now, like psoriasis? She shook herself. "I think it's about being in control. And if you can't spend five hours on a plane, Rick will understand."

"Yes, I know, but I want to go. I want to share the experience with my kids. And I don't want them to get all crazy about flying just because I am." She sighed. "When I married Tom, I never thought about being a mom. I had the worst crush on Pierce Brosnan from *Remington Steele*. Oh, boy, did I ever want to be Laura Holt."

Samantha snorted. "That's funny. I always figured *I* was Remington Steele." Shaking her head, she sipped at her soda. "I guess that makes Rick Laura Holt with an accent. Don't tell him I said that, though. He thinks he's James Bond."

"Do you think about kids, Sam? I don't mean for next week, but do you think about it?"

Okay, kids were apparently the theme of the week. "Not really," she answered. "My mom kicked us out when I was five, and I haven't heard from or seen her since. All I know about her is that her name's not Jellicoe. I guess I don't want to be in the position of being that person who hates her husband and kid so much that getting rid of them is the best solution—and yes, I know I probably need to see Dr. Phil or something about my screwy life, but what the heck. I had a terrible couple of role models."

"Yes, you did." Katie sat back again as Sean the waiter

brought their lunches by. "But you shouldn't judge your future by your past."

"You sound like Rick. But the mistakes I've made are the kind that other people care about." She hadn't even considered them mistakes until she'd met Rick and realized that the marks from whom she'd stolen were flesh and blood people and not just money and artworks and a B and E challenge.

"You know, we've never really talked about this before," Katie said in a low, confidential murmur, "but you weren't just a pickpocket, were you?"

Twirling her fettuccine onto her fork, Samantha shook her head. "Depending on who you asked, I was one of the top two or three cat burglars in the world." Or the top *one*, according to Stoney, but that sounded too much like bragging.

"And you stopped because of Rick?"

"I'd pretty much stopped before I met Rick, except for a really interesting gig now and then. I just had the feeling that things were going to catch up with me, sooner rather than later. But meeting Rick definitely gave me some . . . incentive I didn't have before." She looked down, knowing she was smiling and unable to help herself. *Sappy much, Sam*?

"Rick said your dad didn't think much of you retiring."

"Martin? Considering that he played dead for three years and didn't bother to tell me either that he was alive or that he was working with Interpol, I don't think much of what he thinks." It was way more complicated than that, but this was not the time or the place for *that* conversation.

"So you don't regret it? Retiring from that life, I mean."

Samantha eyed her lunch companion. "You're not secretly working for the *Inquirer*, are you?"

"I doubt they would hire me if they've heard my opinion of some of their articles about Rick." Katie stirred the artful pile of steamed veggies on her plate and then went back to the calzone. "I don't mean to pry. It's just that your life seems so much more . . . exciting than mine. I spend my days figuring out how many candy bars Livia has to sell to earn the spinning glow light, and whether I can attend the SPERM lunch and still make Mike's baseball game."

SPERM—the Society for the Protection of the Environment and Range of Manatees—and Samantha's favorite cause once she'd heard their acronym. She'd even given them a check once in the course of investigating a theft. But the thing about Mike's baseball game gave her an opening. "Does Mike have practice every day? It seems like he's always at a game or at practice."

"No, though it does seem that way sometimes," Katie said with a laugh. "He's got the whole afternoon off today, so he and his friends are going to, yes, go play baseball. I'll bet you've never been to a baseball game, have you?"

"No, I haven't." Though she might, this afternoon.

"And I've never been to a crime scene."

Samantha started to say something sympathetic about how Katie's life was more wholesome, but a pair of figures taking seats across the room caught her attention. August and Yvette Picault, the French collectors of Japanese antiques, apparently liked Italian food.

"What is it?" Katie asked, starting to turn around.

"Don't look," Samantha said sharply.

Katie immediately froze and returned to staring at her plate. "Oh, my. What's going on?"

"Two people I'm investigating just showed up here. The Picaults. Do you know them?"

"We've attended a couple of charity events together, but I don't think Tom and I travel enough to make it into their circle."

She didn't sound offended or even upset. Samantha had never been excluded from any event or circle she chose to attend or join, because she made sure that she fit in. Being stuck in a particular place and in a particular life—that seemed foreign. Weird. But perfectly normal for Kate Donner.

Kate Donner—who apparently wanted a little more excitement in her life. "Let's get out of here," Samantha said, motioning for the waiter. It might make her miss her chance to talk with Mike away from the Donners' house, but samurai armor trumped Anatomy Man.

"What? We've—"

"The Picaults are out of their house. I'm investigating something they might have acquired illegally. I need to take a quick look around and maybe eliminate them from my list of suspects." Her list was pretty much focused on Kwai Chang Toombs now, but much as she trusted her gut, she preferred fact to feeling.

"You mean break in?" Katie whispered, setting her fork down with a clatter. "Us?"

"I need a wheel man. Someone to keep watch. What do you think?" The waiter arrived, nodding politely. "Our bill, please."

"Is something not to your taste, mademoiselle?"

"Just a Bill Blass emergency," she returned, gesturing at an imaginary blemish on her dark gray blouse.

"Right away, then."

"You're serious, aren't you?" Katie continued as he hurried off, her tanned skin growing pale.

"I am, but I'm not going to drag you into anything you don't want to do. I'll manage on my—"

"Let's get going," she interrupted. "I have to be back in time to pick Livia up from school."

Well, this was going to be interesting.

"Ready?" Samantha asked, pushing open the passenger door of Katie's Lexus.

"Are you sure you want to trust me with this?" Katie returned, her ex-Texas drawl shaking a little. "I'm not exactly a professional wheel man or anything. I feel like my heart's going to explode or I'm going to throw up. Or both."

Samantha grinned. The old adrenaline rush. She could definitely sympathize with that sensation, though personally she liked—craved, even—the rattling of her muscles, the hyper-aware feeling of invincibility poised on the edge between fight and flight. *Hoo,baby.* "All you have to do is watch to see whether anybody pulls up to the gate. If they do, ring my cell, which is on vibrate, and I'll head back out again."

"But what if they notice me here?"

Katie obviously needed a little reassurance. "If they do, tell them your husband just called you to say he made reservations for a vacation in Morocco, and you were so excited you had to pull over before you wrecked the car."

"And they'll see me on the phone and not be suspicious. You're very good at this, aren't you?"

Sam shrugged. "I try. But I'd better get moving. I don't know how long it'll take them to eat their pasta, or if they're going somewhere else after or not. So are you ready?"

Katie took a deep breath. "Yes. I'm ready."

With a last, encouraging smile, Samantha closed the car

door. Once traffic cleared, she climbed onto the roof of the Lexus and from there hopped to the top of the fence. She wasn't in any kind of B and E uniform, but at least she'd worn slacks. Otherwise she would have had to do this in her thongs.

With a forward roll she flipped off the wall and landed on her feet just inside the well-manicured grounds of the Picaults' Palm Beach house. Rick wouldn't like this, because not even she could put enough spin on this to make it seem legal, but he was in New York by now. And if Toombs didn't have the armor, the Picaults did. So there she was. An opportunity to look into things firsthand—with relatively little risk involved.

No exterior cameras—apparently the Picaults lived in fairy-tale land where nobody tried to take anybody else's shit. If the windows hadn't been wired, she probably would have turned around in disgust and gone home.

As far as she'd been able to figure out, there were three classes of people: the cautious, paranoid ones determined to keep what they owned, stole, or otherwise acquired; the stupid, naive ones who figured everybody was as honest as they were; and the arrogant, self-centered ones who took what they wanted and thought nobody else was smart enough to stop them. Oh, and the fourth group—the ones who moved outside everybody else's boundaries and did what they wanted.

To the Picaults' credit, the windows and door were wired—nothing special, but at least they'd taken that one step. A pair of gardeners worked at the far side of the house, though, and through one of the windows at the side of the front door she spied an older lady dressed in a maid's uniform and carrying folded sheets. Half the upstairs windows were open, probably to catch the nice early afternoon breeze.

"Simple Simon," she murmured, shifting a patio chair close to the wall. In one fluid motion she stepped from the seat onto its back, and then pushed off to grab onto the low, overhanging eave with both hands. From there she levered herself onto the roof, walked carefully up the Spanish tiles, and then pulled off the window screen and stepped into the upstairs master bedroom.

The decor was definitely pre–World War Japanese, though it seemed to encompass anything and everything before the twentieth century. The hallway outside the bedroom had been fitted with ebony racks holding more than two dozen daitu swords of various eras and styles, though she didn't see anything as old and rare as the Minamoto blades would be.

She checked another two rooms. The couple did have a very refined taste, and even with the varying ages and styles of the collection, all of the pieces harmonized well with one another. Rick would probably like seeing some of this stuff when they visited legitimately on Sunday.

The shivering buzz of her cell phone actually startled her. She generally went into and got out of places all on her own. With a quick breath she ducked into a bathroom and pulled the phone from her pocket. The incoming number was Katie's. She pushed talk. "What?" she whispered.

"They just pulled through the gates," Katie said in a shaking, excited whisper. "Get out of the house!"

"I'm on my way," Samantha replied tersely, closing the phone and jamming it back into her pocket.

Crap. She hadn't completely eliminated the Picaults, but their security and their decor definitely didn't scream "thief" at her. Darting up the hallway again ahead of a testy discussion coming up the stairs behind her in French about who was allowed to drive the Mercedes, Samantha slipped back into the master bedroom and out the window again. It took only a second to pop the screen back into place.

That done, she edged back down the adobe-style roof, swung by her hands out over the air for a moment, then dropped to the ground. Quickly she moved the patio chair back where it belonged, and ducked behind it as one of the gardeners came around to plug in an extension cord. As soon as he disappeared past the corner again she sprinted for the wall, pushed up it with her toes, and scrambled over the top.

Katie's Lexus was parked just a few feet behind her. Once the way was clear she jumped to the ground, dusted off her blouse and slacks, and strolled to the passenger door, where she climbed in.

"Okay," she said, sitting back and pulling on her seat belt. "What time do the kids get out of school?"

"The, um . . . two-thirty for Livia, and three-fifteen for Mike."

"Do you want to get a soda, then, or do you need to go grocery shopping?"

"I, um . . . groceries, I think," Katie said, starting the sedan and pulling a little abruptly into the street.

"Just drop me back off at the restaurant, and I'll get my car." Samantha glanced at her driver, who seemed to be looking everywhere at once. "Everything's fine, Katie," she said in her calmest, easiest-going tone. All she needed was for Donner's wife to get them in a wreck. She'd *never* be able to explain that. "I'm working for the Metropolitan Museum of Art, just doing some research."

"Yes, but you broke and entered, and I helped you."

Great. Apparently she'd broken her one female friend, as well. "Technically I was just leaning *way* in to look through some open windows," she decided. "I didn't touch anything, and I didn't see anything suspicious. I'm sorry. I shouldn't have asked you to do this."

"I wouldn't have agreed to come along if I hadn't wanted to." They stopped for a red light, and Katie faced her. "You did this all the time. It would give me a coronary, but you like it. I can tell. Was today because you needed evidence, or because you . . . wanted to climb over somebody else's walls?"

Pretty astute for a soccer mom, Samantha thought, though she didn't say that out loud. Instead she shrugged. "I picked security and art recovery for a second career, I guess to try and keep what I liked most about my first career. So to answer your question, I could have spent a week looking into any legal investigations on the Picaults, or I could spend twenty minutes and climb over their wall—and I like wall climbing. Fast and practical. And fun."

"Well, 'fun' is a matter of opinion, but I think I understand."

"So if I promise not to take you out for any more B and E's, you won't be afraid to go to lunch with me again?"

"If you don't think I'm too boring to spend your time with."

Samantha snorted. "What I do might be scary to you, but believe me, Katie, what you do every day terrifies me."

Katie laughed, visibly relaxing. "Well, since I did come to one of your B and E's, now you have to come to one of Mike's baseball games. Fair is fair."

"I might just do that." And sooner than Katie realized.

* * *

Her best chance to get a look at Toombs's stuff was to wait for the guided tour on Thursday, but Samantha wasn't going to sit on her hands until then. With about an hour remaining before Mike Donner got out of Leonard High School, she drove home to take another look at the manila folder of paperwork Miss Barlow had given her and the list of "suspicious characters" from Livia and her friends.

The list consisted of fifth and sixth grade boys, who were all apparently evil except for Lance Miller, who was very hot. She grinned as she settled into a chair at the wide library table. There was also one teacher on the list, the art instructor who came by the school twice weekly. Miss Marina wore very short skirts, it seemed, and always had the cutest boys, including Lance Miller, sit in the front of the class so she could sit on the edge of the teacher's desk and show off her legs.

The same logic that told her that an adult crook would have taken items more valuable and more easily resalable than Anatomy Man also said that a female teacher might risk her career for an actual teenage boy, but not for a gender-neutral, parent-approved hunk of plastic and latex. No, this had the fingerprints of a kid or kids all over it.

She pulled out the police report. Officer James Kennedy seemed to have come to the same conclusions, noting that nothing was broken, no locks forced, and no other items missing. His final statement, "PRANK," echoed her own.

Both Donner and she had offered to replace Anatomy Man, but she understood the lesson Miss Barlow and Principal Horner were trying to deliver, annoyed by the theft or not: Stealing was bad. Buying a new model might make teaching anatomy easier, but that whole life lessons thing was more complicated than that.

"I have a Diet Coke for you, Miss Sam," Reinaldo said, walking into the library with the can sitting on a tray and accompanied by a chilled glass filled with ice.

"You rock, Reinaldo," she said with a grin, sitting back as he placed the items at her elbow. "And you read minds, don't you?"

"I try," he said, smiling back at her as he tucked the tray beneath his arm and vanished again.

The can was ice cold, so she popped the tab and took a long drink straight. Nothing else in the folder seemed helpful, so she went over to the computer in the corner and logged onto the Internet. Once she'd called up Google, she typed in "Anatomy Man" and the manufacturer. A couple of places offered him for sale, including eBay. When she checked that out, though, the seller was in Nebraska. Probably not Miss Barlow's Clark, then.

She did enlarge the photo, though. Anatomy Man stood six feet tall, had no winkie, but did possess male nipples and washboard abs. His skin peeled off in sections, allowing for the exposure of muscles and arteries and veins, and those were pliable to expose organs and bones and the brain for study and removal. If she squinted she guessed he did look Superman-like—in a vacuous, expressionless kind of way.

At least now she'd recognize him if she ran across him. Checking the time down in the corner of the monitor, she logged off, snagged the folder and her soda, and headed for the garage. The parents of Leonard High School students were mostly upper-middle class, but a Bentley was beyond the reach of most of them. Most of Rick's cars, in fact, would be über-conspicuous there. Pursing her lips, she decided on the silver '05 Ford Explorer, what Rick called his "incognito" car.

Driving the SUV felt like driving a bus at first, but she settled into it as she headed across the bridge toward suburbia. Samantha arrived in front of Leonard High just as the final bell rang, and she pulled onto a crowded side street where she had a pretty good view of the whole front of the school.

Katie and her gunmetal blue Lexus were already there, stopped in front of the elementary school across the street. The ensuing tangle of cars—mostly SUVs like hers—and kids gave her a whole new appreciation for soccer moms. She wasn't sure she'd even be able to pick her own offspring out of the crowd, because whole herds of the kids, especially the girls, seemed to be clones of one another. Same hair styles, same clothes, same backpacks, same shoes even. "Yipes," she muttered, adjusting her side-view mirror to keep Katie's Lexus in sight.

After a couple of minutes she spotted towheaded Mike and the same two friends he'd been with on Saturday. The boys jogged to Katie's car and piled in. Once the Lexus pulled into traffic, Samantha moved in two cars behind them. It might have been simpler if she'd known where Mike would be playing ball, but she still couldn't come up with a logical reason for her to be asking that.

The car stopped at a park about a mile from the Donners' house, and the boys climbed out again. After pulling a bag that looked like it held bats and gloves out of the trunk, Mike waved to Katie, and she drove off. Samantha put the Explorer into park and shut it off. The trick would be to talk to Mike without making him look like a snitch in front of his friends—if he did actually know anything and that nervous twitch she'd seen hadn't been just a teenage thing.

Once the Lexus turned the corner, Mike and his friends

hefted their backpacks and the bat bag and headed across the park—away from the baseball diamond. *Hm.* Samantha started the SUV again and kept pace with them on the street.

Two more kids of about the same age waited for them at the far edge of the park. The five of them, talking among themselves and obviously in a hurry, trotted down the street in the direction of a strip mall bordered by a fast food place with a hardware store and a couple of empty-looking warehouse buildings behind them.

Well, this was getting interesting. The boys didn't look like they were heading for the burger joint, but they clearly had something in mind. She pulled the SUV up in front of a dry cleaner's at the near end of the strip mall, waiting to see where they would go.

Her cell phone vibrated, making her jump. "Christ," she mumbled, pulling it from her pocket and flipping it open. The office number. "Jellicoe," she said, her gaze still on the kids.

"Miss Samantha," Aubrey said, "I have Gwyneth Mallorey on the other line. She says that she wants her whole alarm system removed because she can't stand the sound of the door entry chime."

The boys disappeared around the back of the second warehouse. "Dammit. Doesn't she know she can program the chime for any sound she wants?"

"Apparently not. I tried to tell her that, but she doesn't want to hear it from me."

Still cursing under her breath, Samantha climbed out of the Explorer. "Tell her I'll be at her house in fifteen—no, twenty—minutes, and I'll show her how to program all of the tones."

"Will do." He paused. "Did I interrupt something?"

"No. I was just doing some research."

She closed the phone and pocketed it. Before she went anywhere, she needed to make sure Mike wasn't meeting up with drug dealers or anything. Wow. Her, feeling protective over other peoples' kids. Shaking off the sensation that this was really weird, she stopped at the corner of the dry cleaner's to watch as the boys passed her. "You do have the camcorder this time," Mike was commenting to the skinny kid beside him.

"I have the camcorder. And it's got this cool fish-eye focus we can try out."

"Whoa, that'll be freaky," a third boy put in as they continued down the alleyway.

"Especially with you on camera, Evan."

"Oh, shut up!"

"You shut up!"

"No, you shut up!"

With a half grin that echoed their laughing, Samantha retreated to the car again. She practically read peoples' faces and voices for a living, and these boys weren't nervous or apprehensive about anything. And even though she hadn't quite figured out where they were going, neither had this been a waste of her time. She knew now that Mike Donner lied. He'd lied about his plans and his whereabouts to his mother, and maybe he was keeping a couple of other secrets, as well.

She headed back to the Explorer and left the strip mall. Back to her other job now. She was working on so many of them that it was getting hard to tell them apart.

Chapter 11

Wednesday, 8:01 a.m.

Richard had the taxi drop him off outside the Manhattan police precinct station. Used as he was to being responsible for billions of dollars, for making life-altering decisions, for buying and selling what amounted to his and others' lives on a fairly regular basis, walking alone into a police station made him a little nervous.

It hadn't been that way before Samantha—one place was as good a battlefield as any other. But Samantha had altered his perspective about a great many things—not the least of which was his own vulnerability. His personal safety, his possessions, and most of all his heart, could all be gotten to in ways he would never have previously expected.

Light flashed just to his right. Only years of familiarity enabled him not to flinch and to keep the cool, slightly bored expression on his face. Reporters and bloody tabloid photographers. They crawled around the public areas of police stations like cockroaches.

"Mr. Addison!" one of them called out, starting a rush in his direction. "Why are you here?"

"Are you here because of Miss Jellicoe's arrest in March?"

"Rick, look this way!"

He ignored all of them as he shouldered his way through the door and into the interior of the station. The cop faces inside were on the whole more difficult to read, but he understood the looks. They were curious, suspicious, and some of them were not happy at all to see him—a sentiment he returned. Five months ago the officers from this precinct had arrested Samantha, and though they'd been following procedure, though they'd been proven wrong and she'd been the one to help them prevent a robbery at the Metropolitan Museum of Art, he would not forget them driving her away from him in the back of a police car. Ever.

"I have an appointment to see Detective Gorstein this morning," he told the officer at the front desk.

The officer nodded, picking up a phone and putting a hand over his other ear against the considerable noise around him. A second later he hung up again. "He'll be right with you, Mr. Addison. You can wait here, or take a seat on one of the benches over there."

Richard looked where he indicated. "I'll wait here, thank you." He already felt like he needed to check his pockets to make certain he still had his wallet and his phone.

A minute or two later, Sam Gorstein approached through another doorway. "I didn't expect you to be on time," he said, proffering his hand. "Welcome back to New York, Mr. Addison."

"Thank you." Richard shook his hand, taking in the tasteful, understated gray suit and the quality black shoes with the scuffs on the toes as he did so. "And thank you for taking the time to see me."

"Mm hm. Like I wouldn't be directing traffic if I'd turned you down. My desk, or somewhere more private?"

Richard wasn't asking for anything illegal, but neither did he care to have his personal business overheard and speculated about—especially when his business on this occasion was also Samantha's. "Private."

"I thought so. This way."

They headed into a small interrogation room, where Richard shrugged out of his overcoat and set it over the back of a chair. His own suit was black with gray pinstriping, worn more in honor of his nine-thirty meeting at his office than because of this little conference. Considering that his attire probably cost four or five times as much as the detective's, however, he wasn't above indulging in a little one-upmanship when the opportunity arose.

"Do you want coffee or something?" Gorstein asked, taking the opposite seat.

If he did, he'd probably have to go get it himself. "No, thank you."

"Okay. What can I do for you then, Mr. Addison? And how's Ms. J? Staying out of trouble?"

Ah, the other reason he was less than fond of Sam Gorstein. Unless he was greatly mistaken, this Sam liked his Sam, and he didn't like that one bloody little bit. "She's well. She's actually the reason I'm here."

The detective cracked a grin. "Why am I not surprised?"

"It's completely aboveboard, I assure you. She's looking into an old theft, one the Met experienced a decade ago and would like to keep quiet. I wondered if you've ever run across the names Gabriel Toombs or August and Yvette Picault while you were investigating any of your higher-profile art or antique thefts. Japanese items in particular." The Met theft had been ten years ago, but as Samantha had pointed out, and demonstrated, crime was a habit. If they'd strayed once, they'd probably done so numerous times. And Gorstein was in the business of solving robberies.

"Do I look like Huggy Bear or something?"

Richard frowned. "Beg pardon?"

"Right. You're English."

The detective made that sound like an insult. There were some who found his accent sexy. "And?" Richard prompted.

"And I'm not some snitch you two get to go to when you need information."

"I look on it more as an opportunity for mutual benefit. Samantha locates a stolen item, and you perhaps get to stop someone who buys very expensive stolen property. She has assisted you before."

"I still have the feeling that I'd be solving a lot of very expensive crimes if I locked up Ms. J again."

Thanks to a great deal of self-control, Richard kept his hands from clenching. "As I believe we've explained, Samantha's only connection to theft is her father. And you had him in your custody."

"Yeah, until the Feds and Interpol stepped in."

"Since we both have other things to do, let's save the reminiscing for another time, shall we?"

"Fine by me. Anything actually within departmental regulations I can do for you, then?"

People didn't refuse Richard very often, and he didn't like it one bloody bit when it happened. Neither did he make a habit of accepting an answer other than the one he wanted. "So because the statute of limitations has expired, you're not interested. I understand," he said brusquely. "If Samantha doesn't find the things by next Wednesday, the Met—your Met—will lose a very prestigious traveling exhibit to the Smithsonian. Just be sure *you* understand that." He pushed to his feet, picking up his coat.

"Toombs and Picault," Gorstein said from behind him. "How long will you be in town?"

"I'm leaving at one o'clock today."

The detective sighed heavily. "Spell them out for me, and I'll look into it. Give me your cell number, and I'll call you before you leave."

Richard nodded. Sometimes it was fairly easy to get people to do what he wanted, particularly when what he wanted happened to be the right thing to do. "It was nice to see you again, Detective."

"I'll bet."

When Samantha woke up, she was sprawled across Rick's side of the bed. Apparently her subconscious didn't like having him gone even when her conscious mind thought it was kind of cool to have the run of the place once in a while.

Rubbing a hand across her face, she sat up. Nearly nine o'clock in the morning. Regular-people hours was still proving to be the hardest thing to adjust to in the legit life—in the old days things didn't start to get interesting until after midnight. At times she'd been nearly nocturnal. Now, though, she had an office where people expected to be able to contact her during daylight hours, and most of the people around her only caught the beginning of *Leno* or *Letterman*, and were fast asleep by the end.

Rolling out of bed, she threw on some sweats and went down to the gym in the basement. Working out was more fun when Rick was down there, too, and she could compete with him, but she managed to lift weights and do the stupid StairMaster thing for nearly an hour.

When she went back upstairs to shower, Reinaldo had set out a muffin and a chilled Diet Coke on the coffee table in the master bedroom suite. Ah, it was good to be the queen. After she showered and sat down to eat, she checked her cell phone for messages. Nothing.

"Dammit, Stoney," she muttered, and punched his mobile number. It rang once before the automated operator came on the line to say that the phone she was dialing was unavailable. So much for him being reachable if she wanted to call him. She tried again, this time dialing his house in Pompano Beach. The phone rang six times and then his female, Cuban-accented answering machine picked up.

Blowing out her breath and muttering to herself, Samantha next dialed her office. "Jellicoe Security, we're here to help," came Aubrey's smooth voice.

"You're a better employee than I am," she said with a half smile, flipping on the plasma TV to catch the morning news.

"I like being here. During the season I don't even get going until nightfall. Daytime is interesting."

"I know what you mean. I'll be there in about an hour."

"No hurry. Daltrey checked in to say he should be finished this afternoon, and Ortiz is bringing in his notes at about the same time."

"Nothing new from the Malloreys?"

"Not a peep. I guess Gwyneth liked whatever you did last night."

"I switched over her entry tone to Westminster Cathedral bells."

"Very nice."

"Glad to see my business runs better with me just out setting door chimes."

"Nonsense, Miss Samantha. A business is supposed to run well even when the boss is out of the country. At least that's what's supposed to happen when you hire people who know what they're doing."

Those employees knew what they were doing mostly because they'd done time for it previously. That was between her and the guys she hired to do the installations, though. And she and Stoney put them through hell first, to make sure this wasn't their way of getting back into the old business.

"Thanks. I'll bring lunch," she said, and hung up.

Since work didn't need her for anything urgent, Mike Donner was at school, and she had until tomorrow for the Toombs house tour, she spent an hour at the computer looking up everything public or otherwise she could find about old Wild Bill. Then she pulled on her shoes and went to collect the Bentley. Stoney might not be home, but that wouldn't stop her from visiting his place and trying to figure out where he'd gone. In her line of work people vanished for one of two reasons: either they were on the run, or they were caught or killed. If this was a third one, she wanted to know what it was.

Stoney's red '93 Chevy pickup wasn't in his driveway or in his garage, which she took to be a good sign. On the outside his small, slightly shabby house fit right into the

Pompano Beach neighborhood. On the inside, from the sliding-eyes cat clock in the kitchen to the classic 1950s radio console and actual tube television in the living room, it was pure Stoney. His idea of cool antiques ran to the *I Love Lucy* era.

He'd never given her a key, but they both knew that she'd never needed one. She picked his lock in about eight seconds and walked in. At least he had an answering machine, but the only message on it was the one she'd left last evening. Which could mean either that everybody else he knew was aware that he was out of town, or that he was picking up his messages from somewhere else.

Grumbling, Samantha opened his refrigerator. A couple of beers and two slices of pizza, plus half a head of lettuce and every low-calorie salad dressing known to man. Tomatoes, cauliflower, melon—if he didn't get back soon, his refrigerator was going to turn into a serious hazmat situation.

His toothbrush and stuff were still in the bathroom, but as far as she knew Stoney had an emergency bag just like she did—everything he'd need for a quick, clean getaway neatly packed inside. Just in case.

She hadn't expected to find a clue; after all, they were in the same business, and she wouldn't have left one. But it wasn't like him to vanish without at least a coded message to let her know he was okay. They'd been family since she could remember, and when Martin had proved to be a royal fuckup of a father, Stoney had been the one to step in for her.

His younger brother Delroy lived in New York, but he had a nice bakery business going. Calling him would only make him worry, so she'd delay that for as long as possible.

"Okay, Stoney," she muttered, stacking the pieces of mail from behind his door and setting them on the Formica kitchen table, "this is your gig. But whatever you're trying to shake loose, you'd better check in soon. I have enough things I'm hunting for right now without adding you to the list." Especially since he was supposed to be helping her with information on Toombs.

As she closed and locked his door again, she could admit that with her two main guys both gone, she felt a little off her game. Sure she could manage on her own, and frequently did so, but Stoney was her sounding board for ideas and theories. As for Rick . . . Well, he was everything else and then some more. And she was just crazy about him.

Once the house was buttoned up again she walked the half block to where she'd parked the Bentley. As she started to pull away from the curb, a metallic blue Volvo 750 passed her heading in the opposite direction. The car looked vaguely familiar, and as it pulled into Stoney's driveway and the petite brunette in the power business suit got out, she frowned. Kim Stacey, real estate agent extraordinaire, and Stoney's squeeze for the last couple of months.

Slowly she backed the Bentley until she was just a house away from Stoney's. As she unrolled the passenger window she could hear Kim pounding on the front door and yelling. "Walter! Are you in there? Walter, if you can hear me and you've had a stroke or something and can't talk, pound twice on the floor and I'll call 911."

Great. So Stoney hadn't even told the girl he was kind of dating where he'd gone. The nice, straitlaced Samantha with a security business partner missing and nothing to hide would have gotten back out of the car so she could commiserate with the girlfriend and they could call the cops together.

She wasn't straitlaced. Samantha put the car in gear and drove off, making the first right turn she could to get out of sight of the house. Then she dialed Stoney's cell phone again. Still nothing—not even the choice of leaving a message, probably because the techno-dummy didn't know how to set up an account.

If the cops were going to bust in they would find nothing but neatly stacked mail, which would probably make them figure one of his neighbors was watching the house for him. She couldn't leave a message on his home machine other than the one she had last night—which purposely didn't have anything weird in it.

Shit. The day had started out okay, but it was definitely going downhill.

Her opinion didn't change when she got to the office. "Hey," she greeted Aubrey, putting a turkey club sandwich and fries down in front of him. "And an iced tea," she finished, pulling it from the holder and handing over a straw.

He popped the plastic lid and looked inside. "You even added a lemon slice, you darlin' you."

"I know what my men like. Anything exciting?"

"Tom Donner called. No message, but he asked you to call him back at your earliest convenience."

She stopped just past the reception door. "Did he really say 'earliest convenience,' or are you cleaning it up?"

"Well, the actual quote was 'when she gets her ass into the office,' but a gentleman wouldn't repeat such things unless specifically requested to do so."

Samantha chuckled. "Gotcha."

Once she'd seated herself in her office and pulled out her Chinese chicken salad, she called Donner's office. "Donner, Rhodes and Chritchenson," the pert receptionist drawled after one ring.

"Donner, please. It's Jellicoe, returning his call."

"One moment, Miss Jellicoe."

Mozart's *Eine kleine Nachtmusik* reverberated through the line until it clicked open again. "Are you in your office?"

"Yes." She frowned. That was even less friendly than usual. "Is something wro—"

The line clicked dead and then returned to the dial tone.

"He's not going to get a Christmas present, if he keeps that up," she muttered, hanging up the phone. And if Rick had asked Donner to call and keep an eye on her, he wasn't getting a present tonight when he got back from New York. Which was a damned shame, because she really wanted him to get this one—her in nothing but a bow.

Six bites of salad later, she heard the outside office door open, followed by Aubrey's voice and then Donner's deeper one. She stiffened as he appeared at her office door. "I knew I rented this office too close to yours," she said, finishing her bite but keeping the plastic fork in her hand. It wasn't exactly lethal, but it would damn sure hurt.

He reached behind him to slam her door closed just as Aubrey reached it. "Did you, or did you not, take my wife on a burglary yesterday?" he snarled, all six-foot-plus of former Texan trying to intimidate her.

Samantha stood up. She might be five-foot-four, but she didn't intimidate. And she didn't like to be yelled at on her own turf. "I did not."

"Okay, so you didn't steal anything. You know what I mean, dammit."

"And if you're so sure you know the answer, why are you asking me?" she shot back.

Her door rattled. "Do you need assistance, Miss Samantha?"

"I'm fine, Aubrey. As you were."

Donner's gaze didn't leave her face. "I asked you a question."

"And I answered it."

"Are you going to dance around this all day?"

"You're the lawyer. Make me talk."

"You had lunch together. Which car did you take afterward?"

"You know what I think, Mr. Lawyer? I think you don't know anything, but you have some weird hunch, and you're trying to confirm what you want to hear. And I'm not saying anything one way or the other. Draw your own conclusions. I'm not a rat."

"You're not a rat. You're a cat, but they're both animals in my book."

"Ooh, very nice. I bet you worked on that one for a while. But being nasty isn't gonna make me spill anything."

"So you admit there's something to spill."

"I admit that you think there's something to spill."

"Dammit, Jellicoe, I should kick your ass."

"You should give it a try."

"Why won't you answer me?"

She folded her arms. "Because I don't want to."

Cursing under his breath, he stalked over to her window and pulled the blinds open. His own gleaming office building stood just across Worth Avenue, and he glared at it for a long moment. "Let's try this again. What did you and Katie do yesterday?"

"That's better. You're not accusing me of anything, anyway. Tell me why you want to know, and maybe—*maybe*—I'll tell you."

Donner muttered something to himself, then faced her. "Katie and I have three kids. Chris is twenty, for Christ's sake." His tanned face reddened. "I guess my point is that we've been having . . . we've been intimate for a lot of years."

"Yipes. And you're telling me this because?"

"Because last night she . . ." He cleared his throat. "I can't believe I'm saying this to you."

She was beginning to suspect what he was about to tell her, and she couldn't quite believe it, either. "So don't."

"Last night was the craziest, wildest night we've ever had," he fumbled in a rush. "She—she rocked my world, Jellicoe."

Samantha couldn't have stopped her grin for a million bucks. "And you have a problem with that?"

"It depends. Rick said that your theft thing is kind of a high for him. A sexual high."

"He actually told you that?" Samantha asked, lifting both eyebrows.

"Not exactly in those words, but yeah."

Great. Now *she* was embarrassed. "So you figured that because your wife was more into you than usual, something must be wrong? That's lame, even for a Boy Scout like you."

He shook his head. "You're not going to tell me, are you? She wouldn't say anything, either. But I *know* you were up to something. Just . . . was she in any danger yesterday? Other than the usual driving-around-in-Palm-Beach danger?"

"No. I wouldn't do that, and I hope you know that by now."

"I don't get you, Jellicoe. Rick's dancing around like you're going to break when he gives—" Donner swallowed. "But you stand up to me like you've got balls of granite."

She cocked her head sideways. "I've been shot, Donner. Being yelled at by a Boy Scout from Yale doesn't shiver my timbers. So whatever Katie and I did yesterday was our business, two girls on the town."

"Shit."

"But if you want another night like last night, tell her I said we'll have to do it again sometime. And you're welcome."

"One of these days, Jellicoe, you're going to give me a straight answer."

"Doubtful," she returned, walking to her door and pulling it open for him. "Because you're too straight to take on somebody as crooked as me. Have a nice day."

Once Donner left she returned to her desk and sat down again. And then she pushed her chair back and laughed.

Chapter 12

Wednesday, 4:18 p.m.

"Is she home?" Richard asked as Reinaldo pulled open the double front doors of Solano Dorado.

"Upstairs, Mr. Rick, in the suite. Hans has hamburgers and potato salad on the menu for tonight, if that is acceptable."

"Samantha's choice?"

Reinaldo cracked a grin. "You guessed it."

"That's fine. About seven?"

"I'll tell him."

Upstairs in the master suite he dropped his travel bag and briefcase onto the floor. "I'm home," he called, then noticed the trailing end of a wide red ribbon over the back of the couch.

A small card was attached to the end of it. Pulling it from its envelope, he unfolded it. "'Follow me,'" he read aloud. That was all it said.

He walked around the couch. The ribbon coiled and twisted loosely over an armchair, around the base of a floor lamp, and then flowed into the bedroom past the half-closed door. "It had best be you in here," he said with a smile as he slowly pushed the inner door open, "or I'm going to embarrass myself."

Silence. But he could feel her in there, her excitement, the warmth of her presence. His smile deepening, Richard stepped into the room.

His jaw dropped. "Wow."

It was the only sound he could choke out. All the blood left his brain and headed south.

Samantha stood, one leg bent and slightly in front of the other, one hand on the ornately carved bedpost and the other at her side. In between she wore nothing—nothing but that red ribbon, looped once around her hips and once across her breasts and back over her shoulder to the floor again. If this was Christmas, he'd obviously been a very good lad.

"What—" He cleared his throat. "What did I do to merit this present?"

"I believe," she said, her voice husky with suppressed excitement, "that this is the one-year anniversary of the first time you unwrapped me." She flicked her fingers toward the bed. "And right there, too, as I recall."

So it was. Three days after they'd met. Three very eventful, unforgettable days that had been followed by three hundred and sixty-five more. Shrugging out of his jacket, he dumped it to the floor. When he reached her, he slid his hands around her bare waist and leaned down to kiss her upturned mouth.

Chuckling against his lips, Samantha worked her fingers into the knot of his tie and tugged it open. "I thought about wearing pink thongs, but this seemed more fun. I know you like when I wear red."

"It's definitely working for me."

"I can see that." She skimmed a hand down the front of his trousers, then went to work on his shirt buttons. At the same time he slipped the ribbon down her shoulder and watched it float gracefully to the floor.

Drawing his fingers across her breasts, he listened with deep satisfaction to her sharp intake of breath. Whatever he'd accomplished in New York, whatever the news Gorstein had given him, it all could keep until later. She'd set this up for him, waited for him to come home, initiated this little party. She could be aggressive and demanding and proactive, but when it came to private matters between the two of them, he was the one who generally led the way. Not this afternoon, though.

He gently pushed her back against the bedpost, deepening his kiss, letting the feel of her skin beneath his hands flow into him. Some of his favorite nights were when they climbed into bed together and simply fell asleep, but nothing was better than sex with a revved-up Samantha. Nothing.

Once she'd stripped off his shirt and belt, he undid his pants himself and kicked them and his shoes off. He couldn't imagine that he looked very studly with his black dress socks on, so he sat on the edge of the bed and pulled them off, as well.

Samantha leaned over him as he yanked off the second one, pushing him flat on his back and crawling up to kiss him before she sank down to run her tongue across his nipples. Then she moved lower. As she took his cock in her soft mouth, his eyes rolled back in his head. *Good God.*

"Come here," he growled when he couldn't stand her enthusiastic bobbing any longer, pulling her up along him again and twisting to put her beneath him.

He kissed her mouth, her jaw, her throat, and trailed his lips down to her breasts, sucking and licking and trying to hold himself in check against the sounds of her moans of pleasure. Reaching down, he lowered one hand between her thighs. Teasing her folds apart, he slipped a finger inside her.

She bucked, gasping. "How do you always make me feel like that?"

Richard lifted his head for a moment. "That would be a trade secret. Kind of a James Bond thing."

She wrapped her fingers into his hair as he returned his attention to her tits. "You are so full of—"

He curled his finger, pressing against her. Samantha jumped, yanking hard on his hair. "See?" he murmured.

"Okay, okay. I give. Quit teasing and give me the main course."

"Not yet. I'm still snacking."

Richard trailed his mouth down her body, kissing her flat belly and the insides of her thighs and then moving in again with his fingers and his tongue. Her hard breathing, the writhing and the keening sounds she made drove him half mad, and he slid up over her again.

He parted her knees with his and slowly buried his cock inside her. She gave a shuddering sigh that nearly made him come right then. Holding his breath, he fought to gain back some control before he started moving on her and in her.

She wrapped her arms around his shoulders, meeting his gaze squarely as he pumped his hips against hers. "God, you feel good," she panted.

"So do you."

"Mm. Try this." With a quick, hard twist she rolled them both, putting him on his back with her on top.

"This is nice, too," he grunted, as she lifted up and down on him, arching her back and putting her palms flat on his chest for leverage. He tightened his grip on her hips, thrusting up to meet her downward strokes. Sex with a woman who knew what she wanted and who had excellent muscular toning and control. Yes, he'd been a very good lad.

She moved faster, harder, deeper, until she squealed, spasming. With a last push he joined her, pulling her face down for a kiss as he surged up into her.

"Holy smokes." Breathing hard, Samantha settled in against his shoulder, curving her arm across his chest and tangling her legs with his. "And welcome back, in case I forgot to tell you," she murmured.

So there she was, Miss Slip Into the Night Without Regrets, smiling happily and relaxed enough to doze off in her fella's embrace. Times had definitely changed, and nothing pointed out that fact more than the way she felt just touching this tall, lean Brit who ate lesser beings for lunch on a regular basis.

"Thank you," he returned. "That was almost enough to convince me to leave and return more often."

"'Almost'?"

"The only thing holding me back was the realization that I'd be dead after a week."

She laughed. "You and me both."

Rick shifted a little, moving his hand to entwine his fingers with hers. "I love you, you know."

"I know. I love you, too." For a minute she debated telling him about her little spat with Donner earlier, but that would just spoil the mood. Besides, she was pretty sure she'd be the one to come out looking evil for taking Katie Donner to the scene of a break-in. "Did you like the building?"

"I did. My people are putting together a bid."

"If you don't watch it, you're going to have all of downtown Metropolis under your control. I'll have to start calling you Lex Luthor or something."

"Oh, please. Luthor was bald. Trump can be Luthor." He kissed her hair. "How goes the search for Anatomy Man?"

"There's somebody I want to talk to, but that probably won't happen until the weekend." With Mike's sports and homework schedule, he was nearly as hard to get to as a piece of artwork she was trying to steal.

"It's good that you have a lead. By the way, Tom called me this afternoon."

Fuck. "Did you fire him?"

"No. He was actually concerned that he might have said something to you that he shouldn't have."

She started to give him a flip answer, but his tone was a little off. Whatever this was, it was serious. She lifted her head to look him in the face, at the same time running her earlier bout with the lawyer through her mind. Nearly photographic memory or not, nothing had particularly stuck in her craw at the time. Except . . . "He fumbled around about you giving me something," she said. "If you're going to give me a present, I'll pretend I don't know anything about it."

"Ah. So you wouldn't mind another present?"

Samantha pushed herself up onto one elbow. "The diamond necklace and the earrings were very nice. And the garden. And Godzilla totally freaked out Reinaldo. It was great." She grinned. "I never would have guessed that Reinaldo screams like a girl. But you never have to give me anything," she continued, figuring he wanted a serious answer. "You know that. I'm here for you, not because of the decor."

"One of these days very soon I'm going to ask you to marry me, Samantha."

She chuckled. "Oh, you talk big, mister. How was New York? Did you see anybody famous? Relatively speaking of course, since you've been on the cover of *Time* and nearly everybody else pales in comparison."

For a second he didn't say anything. "I saw Detective Gorstein, as a matter of fact," he finally contributed.

"Gorstein? What did he want?"

"Actually, I approached him."

"Oh, really? And why is that?" She sat up to look down at him.

"I wanted to know if the NYPD had any useful information about Toombs or the Picaults."

So he was stepping into her gig again. "You figured I needed the help, I suppose?"

"I thought that since I was there, I would ask. You did mention getting in touch with him. I'm assuming you have a problem with that?"

"You know I have a problem with that." She slid off the bed and grabbed her robe. "Dammit, Rick, you can't keep riding in and mowing over everything in sight."

"Actually, I probably can." He stood and made his way, naked and very sexy, into his walk-in closet. "Do you want to know what he said?"

If she said no, he probably wouldn't tell her. She hated the way he manipulated everything so that now she had to ask him for information that technically belonged to her.

"Fuck you." She grabbed her bra and green T-shirt and panties from the chest where she'd left them and pulled them back on.

Snatching up her jeans, she stalked into the sitting area of the master suite. Jamming her feet into the legs, she hopped to the balcony door and went outside. Down below in the pool area the lights flickered on, bathing the pool and patio in a soft white glow.

Dangerous or not to stay ignorant, she wasn't going to play that game. He was the one who'd stepped out of line this time, not her. She sat in one of the patio chairs facing away from the house and folded her arms across her chest. And to think, ten minutes ago she'd been completely satisfied.

A couple of minutes later she heard him come down the stairs and take a seat beside her. A cold can of soda touched her elbow, and she reached back to pick it up and pop the top. "Jerk," she said.

"Perhaps I should have unbuttoned immediately," he drawled, from his tone more than a little pissed off, himself, "but I took into consideration the fact that I had to make an appointment and walked into the police station at eight o'clock this morning. I imagine there will be some speculation about that on *E.T.* tonight."

"Did you tell Gorstein why you were asking questions? Because I don't think the Met wants to spread around the news that their security from time to time apparently sucks." Resolutely she kept turned away from him, her gaze on the area she was supposed to be re-landscaping. At least he hadn't brought that up again. Yet.

"Don't you think I know how to ask questions by now?"

"I think you're a billionaire whose conversations people tend to remember and repeat because they're going to end up in a book someday—*The Wit and Wisdom of Richard Addison*."

"The only thing I mentioned to Gorstein is that his failure to cooperate with me could cause the museum to lose out on a prestigious exhibit."

Not bad. "Okay. What did he say?"

"First turn around and face me. Your back is lovely, but I prefer gazing into your eyes."

"And you *still* have to be in charge," she retorted, even though she did twist her chair around to face him. She preferred seeing the face of the person she was arguing with, herself. "Happy?"

"Indescribably so." Rick reached over, brushing her fingers as they clenched around the soda can. "Toombs showed up on two watch lists after items went missing elsewhere, but nothing more than that. One of those items was an antique samurai war bridle, by the way. That nearly gave me a stroke."

She ignored his commentary in favor of the facts. "What was the other?"

"A fifteenth-century shogun battle flag."

"That follows. I'll keep an eye out for bridles and battle flags tomorrow. How about the Picaults?" Just because she hadn't found anything during her piecemeal run through their upstairs didn't mean they weren't guilty of something. And from what she'd been seeing and hearing, nobody had a more extensive collection of Japanese antiques outside of Japan—with the possible exception of Toombs.

"They had a break-in at their Manhattan townhouse about three years ago. Apparently most of their Japanese items are here, and only some cash and jewelry went missing." Blue eyes gazed at her, one eyebrow lifting in question.

"What? It wasn't me, if that's what you're implying."

She hadn't broken in to any of the Picaults' houses until yesterday. And she hadn't taken anything, then.

"Just mild curiosity." He took a drink of the beer he'd brought out for himself. "Care to share whether you've come up with anything?"

"Not really." She took a breath. "From what I've been able to find and figure out, it's Toombs. Or the Picaults. Palm Beach must be a vortex of evil, since they're all in town right now so I can't just stroll in and take a look around. But what do I know? I can't even find Stoney."

Rick sat forward. "Beg pardon?"

"His cell phone's turned off, and there's no sign of him at his house. His girlfriend doesn't know where he is, either."

"This isn't typical, I assume?"

She shook her head. "Even when we had to lie low, we still could get hold of each other. If he doesn't call me in the next day or two I'll place an ad in the *New York Times* to clue him in that I'm looking for him."

"Why would he disappear?"

Even though she knew Rick didn't like Stoney, she could hear the genuine concern in his voice—for her, if not for the missing fence. "Could be anything. Somebody we've riled in the past showed up, or he got a job offer, or—"

"He's retired."

She shrugged. "I thought so, but who knows? And he did warn me to be careful."

He took her fingers again, this time squeezing and not letting go. "He'll show up."

"Right now I'm more annoyed than worried. If he hasn't at least called me by the end of the week, that'll switch around."

"What about Walter's files?"

"I have no idea where he keeps them."

Rick blinked. "*You* have no idea. You."

"It's a fence thing. He had other guys who'd contract with him or bring him stuff to fence. Just like every once in a while I'd go through another broker. Everybody protects their own sources. Even cops do that."

"It appears that even after a year I'm still learning things about the dark side."

She shot him a smile. "That's me, Darth Sam."

"But you're not worried. Really."

"Not yet. Really." Okay, maybe she was a little worried, but in the big, bad world that she and Stoney inhabited—used to inhabit—vanishing for two or three days was nothing. She'd give him more time before she started turning things over—but then he'd better show up.

Reinaldo appeared at the side of the patio. "Dinner is ready," he announced.

"Thank you." Rick stood and walked around the table to hold her chair for her as she stood, still being Sir Galahad even when they were fighting. "Your primary suspect for the samurai thefts is definitely Toombs, yes?" he murmured, taking her hand as they followed Reinaldo into the house.

"He fits. And he's kind of weird."

"Don't go to his house tomorrow, then."

She took a breath. "I'm going to his house, Rick. If he's guilty I need to know, and soon. If not, I need to know that, too. And if he is innocent I don't want to hear the rumors that you didn't let me go see his collection. We travel in the same circles now, remember?"

His grip tightened. "Aubrey is going with you, yes?"

She nodded. "Aubrey is coming with me." She needed somebody to distract Toombs while she snooped, after all.

"If it's not Gabriel Toombs, what do you do?" Rick pursued. He always wanted to know the answer to everything, which made him a good and shrewd businessman, but could really annoy somebody who lived by her wits and instincts like she did.

"I'll look at the Picaults more closely and re-review the Met security disk to see if there's anything I missed the first three times I went over it, even though after ten years it's not good for much more than a laugh at the hair styles. I've got five days, or this case gets closed for the second time."

Rick looked at her for a minute. Neither of them said it, but they both knew that this was the second job Viscanti had sent her way. If she couldn't find the armor and swords this time, she probably wouldn't be getting any more work from the Met. Or from any other museum, if they had any sense. And then it would be back to straight security setups. Rick might prefer that for her, but she didn't. Not at all.

Chapter 13

Thursday, 10:12 a.m.

"What the devil happened to client-lawyer confidentiality, Tom?" Richard asked, setting his folder on the conference room table.

"Uh oh. You didn't say anything to her, did you?" Tom Donner reached into the small refrigerator under the credenza for a chilled bottle of water.

"Me? I'm not the problem. For God's sake, she remembers everything. So what do you do? You go and tell her that I have a present for her?"

"That was not exactly what I said. And besides, she didn't know what I meant."

Clearly she hadn't, Richard agreed, since when he'd told her that he meant to propose she'd made it into a joke. Not a good sign in itself, but probably better than her screaming and locking herself in a closet or stabbing him or something. "Very well. Don't mention it to her again."

"Okay, okay. Just keep me out of it."

"I am fucking attempting to."

"Fine."

"Fine." He knew what he intended to do, and his only hesitation was that he didn't know what her answer would be. As a businessman he saw that as a problem—one he badly wanted to resolve.

Tom cleared his throat. "What about a prenup?"

"Dammit, Donner, shut—"

"I know you said she doesn't care about your money," the attorney pushed, "but you've got a shitload of it. Two or three shitloads. And U.S. laws are—"

"I haven't even asked her yet. A prenup is not my concern at the moment." He drew a breath. The last thing he needed right now was this kind of distraction with a four-continent meeting about to begin. "Where's Beeling?" he asked. "The conference starts in fifteen minutes. It would be nice if we knew for certain we could log in."

Tom checked his watch. "He'll be here in two minutes. Or I can do it—I had Mike go over it step by step with me last night."

Richard eyed his friend. "Your fifteen-year-old."

"Yeah. Scary, huh? And at the risk of getting yelled at again, Jellicoe seems pretty happy. Why push things at all?"

He'd thought about that, about just letting things stay as they were until before they'd realized it, he and Samantha had grown old together. But there were parts of their current arrangement that he didn't like—the way he had that fear in the back of his mind that one day she would just leave, that something would either catch up to her or she would decide she'd find more excitement elsewhere and vanish.

He'd also considered this life from her point of view, or as closely as he could; a marriage to him could offer her a lifetime of safety and security, could let her relax as she'd begun to do over the past months. She'd have a place that was hers.

And then there was the third reason. He wanted children. Because of the old British inheritance laws, and because of the fact that deep down he was in fact a rather traditional fellow, he wanted to be married to their mother. And he wanted their mother to be Samantha.

His desk phone buzzed, making him jump. He hit the speaker. "Addison."

"Mr. Rick, Jim Beeling is here," Reinaldo said.

"Send him up to the conference room, please. And we could use some coffee."

"Right away."

Resolutely he put his dilemma about Samantha out of his head. This conference, if it went well, would set him up in partnerships with three burgeoning not-for-profit organizations working toward providing tools, materials, and education over four continents. It would cost him millions, but in the long run could work toward improving world economy—which could make him millions more. And it felt good, which was a nice change from some of his other, more profitable, ventures.

As he took a seat at the conference table, he checked his own watch. Samantha was at the Jellicoe Security office, where she'd be for the next hour or so. After that, she and Aubrey would be visiting Gabriel Toombs, and he would still be in this seat.

"Rick?"

"What?"

Tom frowned at him. "I asked whether you want me to see if Katie'll do the lunch thing with Jellicoe again."

"That might be a good idea." He fiddled with the pad of paper in front of him. "Am I mistaken, or are you offering to help me resolve something regarding Samantha?"

The attorney shifted. "You made it pretty clear that I could put up or shut up where you and she are concerned."

"So I did." Even with that in mind, Tom's offer seemed out of character. "You're 'putting up,' then."

"Yeah. I guess so."

"Did Katie say anything to you about how Tuesday went? Or did she say whether she had anything she'd be willing to tell me about?"

Tom's face actually reddened. "All she said is that she likes Sam, and that she had the impression that Sam likes you. A lot. I don't know whether she'd tell you more than that or not. Those two are kind of cagey."

Their liking each other wasn't the problem. There were other issues that were a great deal more complicated and troubling that needed resolution. The bitch of all this was that if he took a step to change the dynamic of his and Samantha's relationship, he was forcing her to take a step as well, and he didn't know whether it would be toward him or away. And that worried him more than setting up a twenty-million-dollar charity program. It worried him more than anything else he could imagine.

* * *

"I just want to be sure you know what you could be getting into." Samantha hopped onto the reception desk beside the office phone.

"I've been to Wild Bill's estate before," Aubrey drawled from his usual chair at the desk. "Never for a private tour, but for one or two seasonal parties."

"For charity?"

"Nearly all of them are, but I don't recall specifically. Is that a clue?"

She smiled at his enthusiastic tone, even though it worried her a little. This wasn't like having an amateur park down the street and call her if a car drove up, or her following a bunch of teenagers to a burger stand; this would mean bringing a novice into the house of somebody she *knew* had acquired at least one antique illegally, and who likely had more. And they were going specifically to look for things Toombs might not want them to see. "I'm more curious about his character," she returned. "Everything means something."

"This is so exciting. I brought gloves."

"Leave them here. That would be just a little suspicious, don't you think?"

"What about fingerprints?"

"He's inviting us in. We're supposed to leave fingerprints."

Aubrey blew out his breath. "I obviously have a great deal to learn about this clandestine stolen-item recovery business."

Samantha folded her legs Indian style. "You have another business, Aubrey. And the unattended ladies of Palm Beach won't ask for your escort if they don't trust you. So are you sure you want to get involved with this? At the least, somebody's gonna get mad. At the worst, we're talking handcuffs and bad booking photos and press coverage." There were even worse things than that, but she was trying to be realistic, not scare him to death.

He touched her knee with one finger, then backed off again. "I've been a walker for twelve years now. Between January and March I doubt I eat a single meal alone. Some of the ladies I escort are very nice, very kind, and very smart. But I could sit down at this moment and write out every conversation I'm likely to have over the entirety of next season. There are never any surprises, and every event might as well be scripted. I wouldn't have started working for you if I didn't want something different. And this is definitely different."

"Different is one thing. Dangerous is another. Just because you want one doesn't mean you have to accept the other. I'm giving you a chance to back out, Aubrey, with no blame on anybody." Yes, she'd promised Rick she'd take Aubrey with her, but if the walker decided he didn't want to put his safety on the line, she'd work solo. It would be far from the first time for that.

"I am a Southern gentleman, Miss Samantha. As such, I would never abandon a lady about to step into danger. Even potential, hypothetical danger." He flashed his perfect teeth in a grin. "And as we've discussed previously, though some of my clients are very pleasant, others—and their friends—never let me forget that I provide a service, like a caterer, and that that is the only reason I'm allowed to attend events."

She looked at him for a minute. Really looked at him. Age-wise she would put him in his late fifties, tanned with blond hair just going to silver, and in great physical condition. From their frequent conversations she knew he had a better formal education than she did, and that he was fairly well-traveled and had a wide range of sophisticated interests. What he'd done previous to twelve years ago, she had no clue.

He played up being gay, though he'd never come right out and said what his sexual preference might be. Rick claimed he was faking his orientation to avoid tension with the husbands of some of the wives he escorted. She wasn't so sure, though at the moment all of his usual affectations were missing.

"Wow," she said finally. "So you really don't have a problem with taking some of these guys down a few notches."

"No, I really don't."

"You've socialized with Toombs."

Gray eyes met hers steadily. "I really don't have a problem with this," he repeated.

She checked the time on the reception phone. "Okay, then. Let's go."

Aubrey switched the phones to the away feature, locked up the office, and followed her down to the parking garage to collect the Bentley. Reluctantly she let him drive again; chances were that Toombs would watch them pull into the drive, and her respectful, semi-submissive female schtick had gotten her this far.

She'd put on tan slacks with a short-sleeved pink knit top, a pale green shirt open over it to modestly cover her arms, and flat tan sandals. It had all been chosen as carefully as Rick chose his suits and ties, though her outfit had to serve two purposes. She had to look fresh and demure, and she had to be able to move quickly and silently with a second's notice. In her pants pockets she carried two paper clips and a rubber band, with a strip of duct tape wound around the inside bottom of her left pant leg. The dark side of MacGyver, as Stoney said.

Unlike Rick's Solano Dorado, which lay right on Lake Worth in the very most exclusive part of Palm Beach, Gabriel Toombs's house didn't have a name or an ocean view, though it was right on the edge of a golf course. It was still nice by just about anybody's standards, but Samantha approached it as she did any job, looking for faults, blind spots, windows obscured by vegetation—anything that could be used to her advantage. Maybe it was a cynical way to look at things, but so far it had kept her alive.

As Aubrey put the car in park at the top of the half-circular drive, Samantha took a breath. Adrenaline flowed into her muscles, heightening her awareness of her surroundings and goosing her heartbeat. *Be cool, Sam*, she reminded herself. This was a visit to see some artifacts in which she had an interest, and she had to be as nonaggressive as possible. After all, she'd once stolen something for this guy, and even though he very probably didn't have the slightest idea that it was her, there was no way in hell she wanted to come across as a cat burglar–type personality.

She'd discovered that people who stole things, or who commissioned for items to be stolen, rarely did so only once. Addiction or a loosening of a certain morality or whatever it was, if they got away with it that first time, they did it again. Toombs had acquired one item that didn't belong to him. To her that made it logical that he would have more. And he did love his antique Japanese shit.

"Ready, my dear?" Aubrey asked, offering his arm as he came around to the passenger side of the Bentley.

"Yep. Just play it cool, and follow my lead."

"Ten-four."

Samantha stifled a quick grin as they climbed the trio of shallow steps up to the front door. At least Aubrey wasn't complaining about being roped into something he didn't want to do.

The door opened as they reached it. "Good afternoon," Gabriel Toombs said, bowing from the hips.

"Good afternoon," she returned. "And thank you again for inviting me. I hope you don't mind that I brought Aubrey with me; he knew the way and offered to drive."

"I thought he might join you," Toombs returned, stepping back so they could follow him inside. "Aubrey, as he likes to say, is a gentleman. And a gentleman wouldn't send a lady unescorted into a man's home."

Certainly not in the nineteenth century, anyway, but Samantha refrained from commenting about that. Instead she smiled, inclining her head in as close to a bow as she could manage without looking like she was mocking him. "You are a very gracious host."

"I try to be, but I would be more flattered if you called me gracious at the end of your visit."

She'd be more interested in calling him guilty, but that would have to wait for proof. "I'm anxious to see your collection," she said aloud.

"Then please come with me. Aubrey?"

"Don't mind me, Wild Bill," her receptionist said. "I'm just an interested bystander."

Toombs led them through the foyer toward the large sitting area at the back of the house. "I've tried to keep the entire house thematically pure," he said, stopping before a half-size sculpture of a samurai on horseback, "so that my treasures are noticeable without standing out."

"I feel as though I've walked into the Japanese Imperial Palace," Samantha said agreeably, wondering silently if he forced his maids to dress as geishas or something.

"That is precisely the feeling I wanted to evoke," Toombs agreed, smiling a little and then quickly putting his Mr. Spock face back on. "I had the feeling you would see the truth of it."

For a second she wondered whether he'd ever actually been to Japan, or whether he was basing his appearance and demeanor solely on *The Seven Samurai* and *Black Rain*. But then again, someone like Toombs wouldn't want to look stupid, and if he collected all of this without even having visited the country, he would look both stupid and weird. Weirder.

"I've divided the house into sections," Wild Bill continued, stopping in front of a well-displayed cabinet at the edge of the foyer, the case filled with teacups and pots and pestles. "Hearth, politics, religion, and war." He gazed at her. "I'm afraid I have very few Hina dolls, though one or two of them might be of interest to you."

"My interest in Hina dolls is on behalf of the girl who collects them," she returned with a warm smile, resisting the urge to demand that they head right for the war section. "My own interests are a bit broader. I'd love to see the entire house."

He bowed his head. "Then you shall."

Toombs led them from room to room, explaining the intricacies and cultural or historical importance of various pieces in his collection. While she'd started out thinking Wild Bill was an odd eccentric, it didn't take long for Samantha to be underwhelmed by the overall theme. It wasn't that his things were less than impressive—some of them would be worth a fortune on either the legitimate or the black market.

Rather, he seemed to view everything the same way. If it was Japanese, he revered it. Even collectors of modern pop culture knew that different items had different value. A 1978 Han Solo mint in its bubble pack was worth way more than a 1995 version in the same condition. And yet here the only criterion to make it into a display cabinet seemed to be that it was traditionally Japanese and in use before WWII.

If a thief came in here for a quick grab-and-run without knowing anything about Japanese antiques, it would be a crap shoot. She had enough experience to know what to look for, and because of the sheer quantity of items it was still a little confusing. Maybe that was his best defense, though; have so much stuff that because of time considerations at least some of the better-quality items were bound to get missed.

"These are arquebus," he said, gesturing at a dozen wall-mounted guns. "All of them work; I had the matchlocks repaired where necessary to meet the specifications of the Sengoku period when they were made."

"Impressive," Aubrey said, leaning in to look at one of the weapons more closely. "These are the front loaders with the balls and ramrods, right?" He straightened to send Samantha an amused glance.

"Yes. All of the accouterments are in the glass cases there. I even have some of the original match cord, though after all this time it would probably go up in smoke before you could light the powder with it."

"Do you have any of the gun powder?" Aubrey pursued.

She hoped he wasn't planning on setting the place on fire

as a distraction or something. No way did she want that, and especially not before she'd found what she'd come looking for.

"Yes. Two of the powder pouches are full. I like to take the arquebus out and fire each of them once a year. It is what they were made to do."

As he said that last bit, he looked straight at Samantha. Her Spider-sense was tingling, but at the moment it seemed to be more because the guy creeped her out than because any danger was coming her way.

"How do you protect all of this?" Aubrey asked. "I'd hate for somebody to break in and then run me through with one of my own samurai swords."

"Are you about to recommend Jellicoe Security for my security needs?"

"Not at all," Samantha broke in. "I'm here because I'm fascinated, not to do business."

"In that case, if anybody ever tried to break in here, I think it would be very interesting," Toombs returned, his gaze on the wall of swords opposite the projectile-firing weapons. "Using a daitu sword is an art. Someone who studies that art is much more equipped to. . . deal with trouble than someone who thinks of it as a pointy stick."

All that bravado would only work if he was home to defend his territory, but Samantha refrained from pointing that out to him—especially if she was going to be the one doing the breaking in. "I love the way you've displayed the swords," she said aloud. "You see them as weapons, but also as works of art."

"Very perceptive, Samantha." He smiled again. "One more room to go, if you'll follow me."

Toombs led them farther down the hallway to a large circular room in the far corner of the house's second floor. Windows rimmed half the circle, while battle flags covered the walls of the other half, including one flag that pretty closely matched the description of the one from Gorstein's report. That, though, wasn't her problem or her concern. In the middle of the room on metal framework stands stood five full suits of samurai armor. *Bingo.*

"These are my pride and joy," he said. "The flags match the period of the armor—they might have been employed in battle together. I like to think that they were."

Covering her accelerated heartbeat, Samantha moved forward. Whatever Gorstein might have on his watch list, she frankly didn't care about battle flags. Not today. She was there to find a suit of armor.

As she walked the perimeter of the room, studying the armor, she compared it to the image she carried in her head of the one belonging to Minamoto Yoritomo, the first shogun. "What period are these?" she asked.

"The one in the center is Kamakura, the two closest to the window are both Azuchi-Momoyama, and the other two are Edo."

The Kamakura would be the oldest, but still a couple of decades short of the Heian period and Yoritomo. The armor was similar to the shogun's, but it obviously wasn't the one she was looking for. And given what she'd been discovering about Toombs's character, she didn't think he would lie to make a piece seem less valuable than it was.

She and Aubrey looked for another couple of minutes, until Toombs offered them lunch. "That's very kind of you," she said, imagining platters of raw fish and steamed rice and trying not to hurl, "but we have a client coming by the office in about an hour."

"I understand. I'll show you out, then."

They left the turret room, passing by a closed door directly to the right. From her look at the outside of the house, that would have been another turret room. "What's in there?" she asked.

"I'm doing renovations in there," he said, gesturing again to guide her toward the stairs. "Nothing inside but planks and paint cans, I'm afraid."

Hm. If she hadn't been pretending to be quiet and demure, she would have been saying, "Liar, liar, pants on fire." As they walked past the door she moved behind Aubrey, tapping him on the arm and angling her chin toward Toombs.

He glanced at the door, then nodded. "You know, Wild Bill," he said aloud, "I've been practicing my raquetball skills."

"Are you asking for a rematch?"

Once the walker blocked Toombs's view of her, Samantha reached out and pushed down the door handle. Locked.

It looked like she would be returning to Wild Bill Toombs's house after visiting hours. Hopefully while he was away and not guarding the doorway with one of his half a hundred samurai swords.

Chapter 14

Thursday, 3:28 p.m.

Richard sat back, rotating his shoulders. Video conferences had their own difficulties, and he remained unconvinced that the convenience of being able to sit in his own office in his own house outweighed them.

His cellular phone buzzed, and he pulled it from his belt and flipped it open. A text message from Samantha waited for his review, and he called it up on screen. "'M home,'" he read. "'R U free?'"

"Five minutes, ladies and gentlemen," he said, interrupting the latest argument, this one over supply priority between ANDFA—A New Day for Africa—and the Humanity Project. He pushed to his feet. "May I get you anything, Tom, Jim?"

"I'm good," Tom said.

Jim Beeling, sitting opposite them and off camera, gave a thumbs up. Assuming that meant the technician was in agreement with Tom's statement, Richard left the conference room and closed the door behind him. Then he dialed Samantha's number. A few seconds later the James Bond theme began playing faintly from the direction of the stairs. Before she could pick up he closed his phone and headed that way.

"Hi," he said, as she topped the stairs in front of him.

"Hi. Are you finished?"

"Just taking a break. How was your tour?" He kept his voice easy and relaxed, hoping he didn't look as relieved as he felt. Whether Gabriel Toombs had stolen the samurai armor she was after or not, Richard didn't like him. Sixth sense, male rivalry, whatever it was, he was just glad Samantha was out of the man's house in one piece.

"Interesting," she returned. "If he'd pare it down to what was really rare and precious and not just old and Japanese, he'd have a pretty nice collection."

As she spoke, Richard watched her face. "So you didn't see Minamoto's armor, I take it?"

She blew out her breath, neither her stance nor her expression giving much away, even to him. "No, I didn't. There was a familiar-seeming samurai battle flag, but none of the swords or armor I'm looking for were in sight. Neither was the bridle I took for him, though. There was one pretty big room he wouldn't let us into, and that he had locked. He lives alone, with a pair of housekeepers who come in twice a week. Thursday's not one of their days to work there."

"So who locks a door when they're the only one home, unless they're paranoid about something inside?"

"You're good," she said with a brief smile, her mind still clearly on her tour. "He puts on this really calm, collected, über-controlled demeanor, and I'm not sure he even realizes what kind of vibe a locked door puts out."

"Not to a former thief, anyway."

"Yep."

"Did he give any reason for not letting you in?"

"He said he was renovating the room."

"Hm."

This time she flashed her grin at him. "That's exactly what I said."

"He's definitely your suspect, then."

"I don't think locking a door in his own house would get him arrested or anything, but something hinky's going on. I'd put my own money on that."

And she meant to figure out what the hinky thing was. She didn't say that aloud, but he knew it all the same. He'd known her for a year, and he wasn't stupid, by any means. "And what happens if he catches you breaking into his house after he gave you a personal tour?"

From the quick flattening of her lips, she realized that she'd been figured out. Good. If she understood that he knew what she was likely to do under given circumstances, it might save him a great deal of worry.

"Well?" he prompted.

"Smart ass," she said easily. "*Satsujin*, I would guess."

"Murder? You think he would try to kill you?" *Christ*.

"He actually mentioned that if anybody ever tried to take

his things, he would go after them with a daitu. He's apparently been trained in samurai swordsmanship." She took a step closer and fiddled with his tie. "But that would mean catching me, which won't happen."

So much for sparing him some worry. Richard wanted to grab her, and he clenched his fists to keep from moving. "One way to be certain it won't happen is for you to call the police instead of breaking in."

She gave his tie a last tug and released it. "I can't do that, because the statute of limitations has expired and there's nothing the cops can do."

"Samantha—"

"No. I didn't have to tell you anything about today, but I know you were worried, and I'm trying to do what's right and not keep secrets. Sure I could call Viscanti and tell him I found the guy, but the fact is, I'm still not sure. *I* can think he has the pieces, and I can look into it, but I can't go around accusing people without proof. I can't."

"I understand that. But do you really think Joseph Viscanti expects you to go in with guns blazing and take back the museum's property? Especially since the armor and swords technically belong to whoever's had them for the last ten years?"

"I don't know what he expects. But somebody saying, 'Oh, yeah, I know where your stuff is, now pay me' doesn't seem like it would satisfy anybody."

"Perhaps you should call him and find out precisely what he does expect. Especially since breaking and entering is illegal."

Samantha narrowed her eyes. "How about if I verify that Minamoto's stuff is in that room, and I'll take it from there? Figuratively take it, I mean."

"Why don't I believe that?"

His office door down the hallway opened. "Rick, ANDFA is ready to let the Humanity Project take on the overall supervision," Tom said.

"Right." Richard backed away from Samantha, reluctant to turn away from her in case she decided his exit meant that he'd given in. "I assume you won't be doing anything questionable while it's still daylight?"

She shrugged. "Probably not. I need to check out a couple of other things, anyway."

"I'm trusting you," he said, knowing that wasn't sufficient and hoping she would accept it until he had time to put together a more compelling argument. At least one of them hadn't thought this all the way through, and he had the growing suspicion that it was he.

Samantha blew out her breath as Rick vanished back into his office. What the hell was she supposed to do with something like "I'm trusting you"? Sit in a chair with her hands folded until he was free to chaperone her around the city? Fuck that.

She pulled out her phone and dialed the Donner residence. A couple of rings later, Olivia picked up. "Donner house," she said.

"Hi, Livia. It's Sam."

"Aunt Sam! Do you have any news for me? Our unit starts next week, and it's going to be *so* lame without Anatomy Man."

"I have a few leads, honey, but I need to check a couple more things out first. In the meantime, is Mike there? I have a baseball question for him."

"Hold on a sec." The sound became muffled, but Samantha could still make out the screech of "Mike!"

Great. She'd been hoping he would be out, and that

Olivia would volunteer the information of where he might be. Now what?

"Sam?" Mike's voice came. "What's up?"

"Not much. I'm still trying to find that anatomy model for Olivia's class," she improvised. "I was just wondering if maybe somebody you know had mentioned anything about it."

"You think it was kids?"

"That's my guess," she said truthfully. "A prank or something. Somebody serious about stealing from the school would have taken computers or television monitors or something. Not just Anatomy Man."

"Wow. You're pretty good at finding stuff then, aren't you?"

"I try. Have you heard anything?"

"Not really."

She heard the lie in his voice, the hitch of his words, the shift in volume as he lowered his head to answer her. It was kind of reassuring, really; if he'd been hardcore, he wouldn't have been as nervous or guilty as he obviously felt. "Okay. If you hear anything, would you give me a call? You don't have to reveal any sources or anything. I just want to get it back in time for Livia's unit."

"It might show up on its own or something. You know, if it was a prank, maybe."

"Well, that would make things a lot easier." On everybody, though she didn't say that aloud. The school might want somebody to punish, but that wasn't her problem. A ten-year-old had asked her to get a model back. And so she would. "Thanks, Mike. I'll talk to you later."

"Bye, Sam."

Okay, did that mean that the Clark the Anatomy Man

problem would take care of itself? That would be nice, but she didn't have much time to wait and see whether Mike's conscience or Jiminy Cricket or whatever it was would be his guide. A day. Tomorrow was Friday, so she could give him one day. And then she'd have to hunt him down and scare the location out of him—which she really didn't want to do, because he was a kid.

Kids had this aura around them that everything was okay and they were bulletproof, and she didn't want to dispel that from Mike Donner. She only wished she'd had one of those auras when she'd been young. The idea of wrecking somebody else's felt . . . icky.

For a second longer she glared at Rick's closed office door, then headed for the library. Rick had offered to have one of the upstairs sitting rooms or bedrooms made into a home office for her, but she had an office just two miles or so away, and according to at least one of her coworkers—currently missing—she didn't spend enough time there as it was. The library worked just as well, and she liked the tall windows and the big work table.

She snagged a couple of sheets of graph paper from a cabinet there and sat at the table to sketch a layout of Gabriel Toombs's house as she remembered it. It wouldn't be as slick as an actual blueprint, but since she had a deadline of next Wednesday to find the armor and swords, she didn't have time to scam—or even legitimately request—one from the Palm Beach city planning offices.

Mainly she wanted to figure out the best way to get into that room—and to be able to carry out sixty pounds of ancient armor and two very old samurai swords, if they happened to be in there. Much as she hated to admit it, she could probably use some help on this one. Which could be a problem if Rick's "I'm trusting you" was any indication.

Stoney could probably be wrangled into volunteering, except that he *still* hadn't called her, e-mailed her, faxed her, or left her a coded message in the *Palm Beach Post* or the *New York Times*. She'd said she wouldn't start worrying until Friday, but that was a big fat lie. It was strange, but in the old days when she was busy pulling jobs and ducking the heat from the authorities, any of her allies disappearing for a couple of days wasn't a big deal. Now, when things around her were calmer, when she wasn't so focused on her own safety, she worried about Stoney's. And Rick's. And that of a few select other people.

Her cell phone rang to the tune of Darth Vader's theme. The Jellicoe Security office. Frowning, she pulled it free and hit the talk button. "Jellicoe."

"Miss Samantha," Aubrey's low drawl came. "We just received a fax from Ortiz with his notes from the Glass house review. You said you wanted to know when they arrived."

"How do they look?"

"Like about ten thousand dollars' worth of work."

In the good old days she would have sneezed at a ten-grand job. "Cool. Has he called?"

"Yes. He told Cynthia we'd have an estimate for her tomorrow."

"Okay. I'll be there in about twenty minutes."

"I'll be here, hoping you're bringing a mocha frappaccino with you."

Samantha snorted. "Deal, if you'll look at the sketches I'm doing of Toombs's house."

"Why, I'd be delighted."

She dumped the phone back into her jeans pocket and

rolled up the graph paper. On the way out to the garage she found Reinaldo and told him where she'd be in case Rick had doubts about his stupid trusting-her statement.

A block down the street from her office she stopped in front of the always-busy Starbucks. Because of her own intense dislike of coffee she'd been reluctant to learn the nuances of ordering the stuff, but with Starbucks becoming the center of most peoples' universe, the knowledge had already come in handy a couple of times. She requested a tall mocha frap, ignoring the looks and the mumblings of "It's Samantha Jellicoe" from the other customers and the kids behind the counter.

As she hopped back into the Bentley, a jet black Miata rolled by and made a right at the next corner. With all the traffic on Worth Avenue she wasn't sure why she'd focused on that car, except that it was very shiny and it had driven past her pretty slowly. Convertible Miatas were pretty common in the environs of Palm Beach, even though they didn't have the show-off sticker price of a good Mercedes or a Jag or a Bentley.

She parked in the three-story garage next to her office building and went up the elevator to the Jellicoe Security suite in the far corner of the third floor. "Hi," she said, walking into reception and handing over the cup of so-called coffee.

"You are a diamond, Miss Samantha," Aubrey said with a smile, closing his eyes as he took a sip.

"Thanks. Where's the fax?"

"On your desk."

It took her twenty minutes to plug the specifications Ortiz had sent into the contract macro she and Aubrey had set up, customize where necessary, and print out two hard copies for Ortiz to pick up in the morning. That done, she stuffed them into a folder and brought it and the graph paper up front to Aubrey.

"How close was I?" he asked, filing the folder and then clearing off his desk as she unrolled the graph paper.

"Ten thousand, two hundred, and eighty-six dollars," she returned, "and I'll probably knock off the two eighty-six when she wants a discount for being a fellow member of SPERM."

"I've often thought I should join the Manatee Society," Aubrey said with a chuckle.

"The lunches are nice, and I do like the acronym."

"My thoughts exactly." He sat forward in his chair. "What do we have here? You did this by hand?"

"It's a hobby."

"I see." Aubrey glanced from the drawing to her. "Wow. What do you need from me?"

"I've never seen the back of his house. Do you remember anything specific? Patio, pool, lawn furniture, flamingos?"

"He has a pool, and a veranda that curves all along the back of the house about out to here," he said, brushing a finger along her drawing.

"What about trees and shrubs?"

Aubrey looked up at her. "Are you going to break in?" he whispered. "I thought you didn't see what you were looking for."

"I didn't. I also didn't see what was in that one room. I need to take a look."

"What if the things aren't there?"

If they weren't, she was back to looking at the Picaults, and she'd have to admit that her instincts were so far off that any wealthy collectors of Japanese antiquities who lived in the eastern half of the United States were just as likely to have the armor. In other words, she was screwed and the Met was screwed and her future in item retrieval was screwed. "I guess I'll face that if it happens," she said aloud.

He unexpectedly took her hand, squeezing her fingers in his larger ones. "I've known Wild Bill a lot longer than you have, Samantha," he said in a tone more serious than she'd heard him use before. "There's a reason why when he suggested that everybody call him Wild Bill, we all did. His money comes from the two construction companies he inherited from his father. And the rumor is that he inherited his father's associates, as well."

Samantha frowned. "The mob?"

"The mob, some pushy labor union guys—whoever they are, people just don't cross him."

"Why didn't you tell me any of this before?"

"Before your visit was a legitimate one, and I was with you."

"Seriously, Aubrey, do you think you could . . ." She trailed off as he pulled his free hand out of his pocket, revealing a small, shiny, chrome-plated handgun. "Jeez. You had that with you?"

"A gentleman always looks after the lady in his company," he said in his soft drawl. "I may not know how you go about your business, but I know mine."

Samantha took a second to reassess the way she looked at Aubrey Pendleton. It would actually take longer than a second, but nobody got to catch her flat-footed—or at least looking that way. "So how often do you carry that around?" she asked, gesturing at his pocket as he slipped the pistol back inside.

"There are occasions." He smiled. "Usually I rely on my charm and good manners."

She snorted. Okay, there were things about him that she hadn't realized, but nothing here made her want to change her initial opinion of him. "Both also lethal," she commented.

He inclined his head. "Thank you, my dear. Do you go in tonight?"

"I'm not sure yet." That kind of depended on Rick, and she didn't want to admit that out loud. Or even to herself, really. Answering to somebody else, being accountable to them—whatever Dr. Phil might call it, she didn't like it. "Stoney's still supposed to get a little more background on Toombs for me, and I'm kind of hanging back for that."

"Speaking of Walter, he seems to be absent again today."

"Yeah, I figure he's out sowing his wild oats somewhere."

"Miss Kim's been calling. I've been telling her that he had to make an unexpected trip to New York to see his brother."

She hadn't realized that Aubrey knew about Delroy. "That's nice of you," she said, smiling. "Unless Stoney's trying to dump her—which would make him a big chicken, so I'm all for the making excuses thing and letting him face the music himself when he gets back."

"So what's next?"

Leaning in to sketch the layout of the terrace and the pool in Toombs's backyard according to his recollections, Samantha took a deep breath. "Well, I've got a couple of pots on the stove, and now I need to see what starts boiling first." And hope she had a mitt handy so she wouldn't get burned.

Chapter 15

Thursday, 8:24 p.m.

"That was a good dinner," Samantha said, wrapping her hand around Richard's arm and leaning into him as they left Chez Jean-Pierre and walked back to the Jaguar. "Did you know they had all of those Dali and Picasso reproductions on the walls?"

Of course she would know they were all reproductions. "I did. I thought you might appreciate them."

"You betcha. I liked the chicken breast more, though."

He kissed her hair. Whatever was running through that agile mind of hers, she seemed to be making an effort not to argue, and so for the moment he would be patient about it. "Are you sure you don't want me to go back for more of the chocolate profiteroles? I could feed them to you in bed."

"That might be messy. And if I ate any more of those I'd be too hefty to get *out* of bed."

He pulled the passenger door open for her, but she didn't move to get into the car. When he looked at her, Samantha's gaze was down the street. "What?" he asked.

"Do you know anybody who drives a shiny new black Miata?"

"Not off hand. Why?"

"I swear that's the third time I've seen it today."

"This is a rather small community, especially in the off-season, and especially on the island here. There are only so many places a car can go in town."

She rolled her shoulders. "Right. Okay. Take me home. And it's your turn to choose a movie."

"Excellent. *The Guns of Navarone*."

"You're such a guy," she said, chuckling.

He didn't know whether that was a compliment or not, but since she was smiling and she'd worn a gorgeous burgundy Vera Wang dress, he let it pass. They pulled out onto County Road, heading for Solano Dorado. "Does this mean you're staying home for the evening?" he asked, keeping his gaze on the road.

"I haven't decided yet," she returned, fiddling with the CD player in the dashboard. "Aubrey's supposed to call and let me know if Toombs is going to the Mallorey thing on Saturday. If he is, that would be a better night to get in. If he's not attending, then the sooner the better."

"So nothing I said is going to make any difference to you."

"Rick, knock it off."

"I don't want to knock it off. We live together. If you're going to break the law, I think I deserve a heads up."

She faced him, folding her arms across her chest. "Heads up, Brit. In the next couple of days I'm going to be breaking into Gabriel Toombs's house."

"What if *I* call Viscanti and tell him you've located the probable location of his property, and tell him to proceed however he chooses?"

For a long second she sat there, silent. "If you did that," she finally said, her voice clipped, "I would leave."

He pulled over and slammed the Jag into park. "Just like that?" he demanded, glaring at her set expression. "No discussion, no argument? If I did something to try to keep you safe, you would just leave? That's ridiculous."

"I'm not going to argue about this. You know it's not about keeping me safe. Something like just taking every decision away from me—I can't even—Fuck this." She hit her seat belt release and shoved open the door. "I can't believe you threatened me with that," she said quietly, her voice shaking. Then she got out of the car and slammed the door behind her.

For a second Richard sat there. *Christ.* He was used to the bluff and bravado method of negotiation, but she had said it so . . . matter-of-factly. Like she meant it. And she hadn't tried to argue. She hadn't even wanted to argue. She'd just walked away. People didn't walk away from him. Especially not Samantha.

He climbed out of the car and slammed the door shut. She was thirty feet in front of him, walking quickly in her burgundy heels down the sidewalk. "Samantha."

"Get back in the car," she said, not slowing. "I'm walking home. I need to think."

More than anything else, the even tone of her voice

bothered him. Bothered him—hell, it frightened him. Cars driving along the street were slowing down; in a couple of seconds cell phones would be snapping photos and taking videos. The spat would probably make the evening news, and then the entertainment shows tomorrow. He could pay attention to that, be annoyed by the unanticipated publicity, or he could take care of the very large problem at hand. Because he had the feeling that if he waited until she got home, gave her time to think over whatever she was considering, things would get much worse.

"Am I wrong to be worried about you putting yourself in danger for a paycheck you don't even need?" he asked, striding after her.

"It's not about the fucking paycheck," she snapped, not slowing. "And you know it, slick."

He heard anger in her voice this time. That and the name-calling was good. He could work with, understand, her emotions better than her version of logical assessment. "I don't want you to get arrested and sent to prison, especially not for the sake of a museum exhibit."

"That stuff *belongs* in the museum—not in Wild Bill Toombs's spare bedroom. I accepted the job, and I'm going to make it right."

Richard caught up and clutched her shoulder, turning her around to face him. "You can't make every job a crusade."

Samantha jabbed a finger into his chest. "*You* can't decide which jobs are important to me. And you don't get to decide what I do for a living or to try to go around me to shut me down. If *you* can't live with it, then we can't live together."

Just barely he resisted the sudden urge—need—to grab her and keep her there, keep her in his life. "That's somewhat drastic, don't you think?" he managed, his tone harder than he would have wished. "We should be able to reach a compromise."

"A compromise? What the hell do you think I've been doing for the past twelve months? I was making over two million dollars a year before we met. Now I'm installing security cameras. I have a damn office with a coffeemaker. What's your compromise, Rick?"

He opened his mouth to respond, but everything he might say would only make things worse. *When put in a weaker position, change the subject and attack.* "You haven't compromised as much as you claim."

"Excuse me?"

"You put on a good show," he returned, "but every time we argue you get ready to leave. No roots at all. Especially not in the bloody garden I gave you."

"The—I've been busy."

"If I don't get to decide what you do for a living, you don't get to blame me for it, either. You could have left me a year ago. I asked you to design the gallery wing at Rawley Park, but the security business was your idea."

"I couldn't keep doing what I was doing and be around you."

"No, you couldn't." Tentatively he reached out to brush a strand of her hair back behind her ear. "And I'm very glad you decided you wanted to be around me. I'd like to be able to count on you being around me for a very long time to come. When the decisions you make threaten that, yes it worries me, and yes it makes me angry. But the decisions are yours. That's my compromise, I suppose."

Samantha eyed him, her expression beneath the street lights still not giving much away. "You could probably convince a penguin to buy a tuxedo, couldn't you?"

"I don't know. I've never tried. But if you're implying

that I'm trying to force you to accept something you don't want or need, I have to disagree. I think I'm good for you. I *know* you're good for me."

She turned her back on him again, took a step away, and stopped. Richard didn't move. As he'd said, and however much he disliked it, the decision was hers. Even so, he couldn't help holding his breath as he watched her.

Her shoulders rose and fell as she took a deep breath. Then she faced him, stepped up, and tangled her hands into his hair to pull his face down and kiss him.

Richard closed his eyes for a second as he kissed her back, tasting chocolate faintly on her lips. A couple of months ago they'd fought, and Samantha had slashed his tires and fled England for Palm Beach. He'd known even as he'd followed her across the Atlantic, though, that they would make up. That fight had been frustration more than anything else. Tonight, however—this fight scared him. Not a good sign, considering the item he would be picking up from Harry Winston this weekend.

"May we go home?" he asked quietly, running his fingers along her cheeks.

"Yes. But I'm still thinking. And I'm still mad."

And he was still worried.

As they pulled up in front of Solano Dorado, Samantha's cell phone rang to the tune of "Somewhere Over the Rainbow." With a sideways glance at Rick she pulled the phone from her purse. "Hi, Aubrey."

"Miss Samantha. I made a few discreet inquiries, and Wild Bill will be attending the Mallorey soiree on Saturday."

"You'll be there too, right?"

"Most definitely."

"Thanks, Aubrey. I'll see you in the morning."

"Good evening, fair lady."

She hung up, and Ben appeared from the direction of the garage to open her car door for her. Rick usually beat the driver to the punch, but not tonight. Instead he went up the shallow granite steps to the front door as Reinaldo opened it.

Whatever the hell had gotten into him over the past couple of days, she didn't like it. First the "I'm trusting you" shit, like he was warning her to behave herself. Now tonight he'd apparently decided he needed to step in and remove temptation from her weak little fingers.

As she thought about it, it pissed her off all over again. Especially when she wasn't even convinced that breaking into the house of a known receiver of stolen goods in search of more stolen treasures was the wrong thing to do. At the top of the steps she brushed past him and went inside.

"Hans is just closing up the kitchen," Reinaldo said in his light Cuban accent. "Can I get you some coffee or cocoa, or a soda?"

"We're fine," Rick answered before she could. "Good night, Reinaldo."

The housekeeper nodded, backing out again. "Good night, boss, Miss Sam."

"Rude much?" she commented over her shoulder, heading upstairs.

"I take it that we're still arguing."

"That ramrod goes straight up your British ass when you get mad, doesn't it?" She could feel the angry heat coming off him as he climbed the stairs behind her. "What the hell are you mad at, anyway?" she continued. "You gave me the garden. That means it's mine, and I get to work on it if and when I damn well want to."

"I'm mad because you threatened to leave," he retorted,

surprising her. "Again. And because, yes, I suddenly realized that you still haven't even made a single bloody phone call about the pool garden, and now because I know what your first instinct still is, and that as soon as we get to the bedroom you're going into your closet and get that idiotic emergency backpack and then walk out."

"Wow, you've got me all figured out." At the top of the stairs she turned around and faced him. "You want a compromise?" she demanded, realizing even as she spoke that chickening out of this relationship would be *much* easier than staying. "I'll call the nursery in the morning and have somebody come out and look at my plans and start ordering materials. Then I'll go with you to the Mallorey party on Saturday. And then you will back the hell off and let me do my job for the Met as I see fit."

Dark blue eyes glared at her. "I don't like it."

That stopped her for a second. So she'd found it—his breaking point. She'd always figured it would happen sooner or later. Leaving wasn't her first instinct any longer, but this wasn't just an argument. This was about him trying to pull her entire new life out from under her. And for a second she was glad that she was so furious with him, because later it was going to really, really hurt.

"Okay," she finally said.

He took a step closer. "Okay, what?"

"Okay, I can't be what you want and still be what I want. So I guess you get to be right one more time. I'll go get my idiotic backpack and then I'll call a cab and you will never—*never*—see me again. Then you won't have to compro—"

"I said I didn't like it," he interrupted. "Not that I couldn't accept it."

She blinked. "What?" There was nothing like careening

down a road with no brakes and then slamming into a pile of pillows.

Rick shook his head. "Generally I don't like to tell an opponent my weaknesses, but you're not precisely an opponent. You're my weakness, in fact."

"I make you weak. Give me a break."

"Don't threaten me with leaving again." His fingers clenched and unclenched, and then he walked around her and into the bedroom.

If this was another of his negotiating tactics, it was a good one. He'd managed to undercut her entire tirade. "It wasn't a threat," she said, stalking after him. "I meant it."

"I know you meant it." His butt vanished into her walk-in closet. "And I hope you realize by now that I'm apparently willing to let you put yourself in danger in order to keep you around. Make whatever demands you want and threaten to leave if you don't get your way, and I'll give in."

"It's not like that. You were being a total jerk. And what are you doing in there?" She stopped just outside the closet door.

He appeared again, her emergency backpack in his hands. "According to television and the movies, when couples fight and one of them decides to stalk out, they have to go around and collect the pieces of their lives that they've entwined with their significant other." Unzipping the bag, he pulled out a roll of duct tape and a toothbrush. "They don't keep a pack ready and waiting to leave at any bloody moment."

"Stop that."

Ignoring her, he stalked into the bathroom and put the toothbrush into the medicine cabinet beside the one she used daily. Then, still holding the pack, he went to the balcony door, opened it, and tossed the duct tape down into the pool. He reached into the backpack again and came up with her spare jogging shoes, which got tossed back into her closet along with the T-shirt, jeans, pair of underwear and socks she kept in reserve.

The cash he dumped into her nightstand, along with the small coil of copper wire and the flashlight. The disposable cell phone went into the waste basket.

"Don't make me kick your ass, Addison," she warned, though in truth she felt more surprised than angry. Rick lost control so rarely, and this was a doozy.

Returning to the bed, he turned the backpack upside down and dumped the remaining bits—fake passport and driver's license, paper clips, pen, pad of paper, tube of lipstick—onto the coverlet before sweeping it all into the waste basket. Then he unzipped the small outer pocket and pulled out the Swiss army knife she kept in there, though how he'd known about it, she had no idea. He opened it, and proceeded to slash the backpack to shreds before he threw it away, sent the knife into the night stand, and slammed it shut. "There."

Feeling like her jaw was hanging open, Samantha stared at him. That pack—a pack—had been part of her life since she and Martin had left her mother. For the ensuing twenty years she'd kept one ready, and had made good use of it on more than one occasion. And Rick in his gray Armani suit and black and gray tie had just trashed it. Not just trashed it, but demolished it.

"You threw my duct tape into the pool," she said, focusing on the most obvious offense.

"I didn't want to walk it down to the utility room."

Her gaze went to the crumpled, ripped blue pack sticking out of the mahogany waste basket. "This wouldn't stop me if I wanted to go."

"I know that." He blew out his breath. "Now it just won't be as easy." Rick dusted his hands off on his slacks and walked up to her. "Do you want to leave?"

"You tried to step all over my—"

"You're backtracking," he cut in. "We had an argument, and I gave in. Do you want to leave?"

"Your way of giving in looks kind of like you conceding one point and then demolishing my stuff."

"Do you—"

"No, I don't want to leave. Of course I don't want to leave."

"Good." He touched her wrists with his fingers, sliding his hands around slowly to embrace her.

"But," she continued, unwilling to let him believe that by trashing her stuff he'd erased every reservation she'd ever had, "if we aren't compatible, I'm thinking we should figure that out now."

"We're compatible," he said, backing away a little to meet her gaze. "Stubborn and arrogant and independent, but compatible."

"You're that sure?"

"It's hearts and minds, Samantha. What my heart wants, my mind will bend, fold, and mutilate in order for me to have. We may not be there yet, but I have no intention of letting you walk out of here."

He spoke softly, but she heard the steel in his voice. For a second she wondered what he would have done if she had actually seriously tried to leave. Not just throw a fit and stalk out for a day or two, as she'd done before, but leave for good.

His blue eyes studied her face, trying to figure out what she was thinking. Rick Addison was a man who could buy and sell most of the world, and he knew how to get what he wanted. He *expected* to get what he wanted. Man, she must frustrate him, just like he frustrated her. She'd spent her life maneuvering and manipulating, seeing every other person as a mark to be taken advantage of or an enemy or an ally to be dealt with accordingly. He saw through all of her shit. She'd been more honest with him than she had anyone else in her life, with the possible exception of Stoney—wherever the hell he was.

"Have you noticed that our fights are getting more serious?" she finally asked, moving her arms to break his grip.

"That's because we're getting more serious. The stakes are higher." She felt his gaze on her as she headed toward the balcony door that overlooked the pool area. "Air?"

"I'm going to fish the duct tape out of the pool before it clogs the filter," she said, pushing open the door and stepping onto the small balcony. Then she stopped and looked back into the suite. "You've had more experience with the whole relationship thing than I have," she said, taking a dig at his nasty, failed ex-marriage even though she knew she should probably shut up and leave fairly okay alone, "but once in a while, instead of the logic thing and attacking or negotiating your way into coming out ahead, you might just try apologizing."

"Mm hm. Maybe next time."

Samantha blew out her breath as she descended the red stone stairs. Leaving, staying, offended, worried, hurt—arguing with Rick was tough. She'd pulled jobs that left her less mentally and physically tired. Her dad, Martin, wouldn't have gotten why she'd bothered to stay and fight—after all, he'd taken himself and her and left their house without even looking back. Look out for number one, and get rid of anything that might get in the way of that. That was the first and most important rule of survival in Martin's thief world. And once she'd met Rick, that was the first rule she'd begun to chip away at.

Obviously she still had some more work to do. Rick kept pushing at her, but he wasn't Mr. Perfect, either. Too many people asked how high when he said jump, and he'd gotten used to that.

She found the pool net and managed to fish out the roll of duct tape from the deep end without getting chlorinated water all over her dress. Then she sat at one of the tables surrounded by the low area lights, and listened to the sound of the nearby ocean. Man, she felt wiped out. And angry as she'd been, more than anything else she'd wanted a reason not to leave. Even Rick demolishing her emergency backpack hadn't freaked her out like she'd thought it would.

She stayed by the pool for nearly an hour, until her bare legs and arms began to goose pimple in the light ocean breeze. Rick hadn't come down to see what she was doing, and she had to give him credit for that. At least he'd realized that she needed a little space, a breather without him analyzing and countering everything she did or didn't say.

Back upstairs, only the lights outside her dressing closet and in the bathroom were on, and the bedroom door was half closed. She relaxed a little bit more as she changed into loose shorts and a T-shirt. No more confrontations tonight then, hopefully. If Rick had been up waiting for her she probably would have opted to sleep on the couch or in one of the guest rooms. He'd more than likely realized that, too.

Once she'd brushed her teeth and tidied the bathroom, she slipped into the bedroom. Rick lay in bed, and in the dark she couldn't tell whether he was still awake or not. Silently she slipped into bed and curled onto her side, her back to him.

As she settled in, Rick moved closer, slipping an arm across her waist and fitting her back against his chest. "Sorry," he whispered into her hair.

Samantha nodded; if she'd said anything out loud, she would have started blubbering. And she never cried. Not even from relief.

Chapter 16

Friday, 12:18 p.m.

"I don't want to interfere," Richard said, hefting his notebook computer under his arm.

"So don't interfere. You can still join us." Samantha finished tying her hair back in a perky ponytail. She looked the image of what she was no doubt trying to project—the wealthy, competent mistress of a large, wealthy estate.

"But it's *your* anniversary present."

"If you don't want to sit in, then don't," she returned, slipping into her deck shoes, sockless to go with her blue capri pants and snug white T-shirt spattered with pastel butterflies. "Spying out the library windows, though, will just make you look creepy."

"Not mysterious and eccentric?" he asked with a slight grin. He'd taken the whole morning very carefully, trying to avoid any mention of the blow-up from last night. He didn't care for a repeat of that.

Apparently, neither did she. In fact, she seemed more at ease today than he could remember—though that might very well be wishful thinking on his part. At the least he'd expected her to go out to purchase a replacement backpack, but she hadn't even glanced at the full waste basket.

"Not so much. It's your house, Rick. If the nursery guy or I suggest something that you don't like, you get to say so."

He was actually more interested in just seeing how the meeting went. She acted a good game, but faced with an actual landscaping expert, he didn't know how she would react. "How about if I let you get started, then wander by?"

Samantha chuckled, picking up the phone next to her as the house intercom buzzed. "Hi, Reinaldo. Okay, show them to the pool, if you don't mind. Thanks." She hung up. "We must be important," she said, a half smile still on her face as she looked over at Richard. "Piskford Nurseries sent three people, including Burt Piskford."

"They know how much money you have to spend." Taking her fingers, he tugged her up against him and kissed her. Perhaps they'd made up, but he preferred proof. As she sank against him, her lips warm and soft against his, he finally felt relieved. She couldn't fake that. Probably.

Laughing again, she pulled free of his grip. "I'll make sure they know that. Wander by at your leisure."

With three of them for her to deal with, he'd be wandering by sooner rather than later. This was supposed to be fun for her, not another challenge of courage and willpower—though she did seem to like those sorts of challenges.

Samantha rolled up her plans, picked up her books, and with another quick kiss left the library. As soon as he was certain she wouldn't turn around and walk back in to catch him, he set aside the computer and went to the window.

Standing alongside the wall so hopefully no one from outside would be able to see him, he settled in to look down at the pool area. Creepy or eccentric, he wanted to know how Samantha fared, and whether or not she needed him for backup or for decoration. Either one would suffice today, as far as he was concerned.

His cellular rang, making him jump. If that was Samantha commenting on his spying, he was going to have to give up his stealth activities as pitiful beyond comprehension. "Addison," he said as he flipped it open.

"Mr. Addison. I didn't realize this was a direct line," a cultured female voice with a hint of Southern drawl said.

"It is," he returned, ready to hang up and have the number blocked if someone was going to try to sell him a subscription to something.

"This is Joanna at Harry Winston. Your ring is ready for you to pick up, or we can have it delivered if you prefer th—"

"I'll come get it," he interrupted, his heart pounding.

"Of course. And you'll have final approval, naturally, but if I might say so, Mr. Addison, it's . . . quite lovely."

"Thank you. I'll be by in the next day or so."

He wanted to go immediately, just to be sure he had it in his hands, but he was being supportive at the moment. Once he had it on him, he wasn't entirely certain how to go about giving it to Samantha, anyway. Judging from last night, they still had some serious issues to work through. Whether that had been the biggest hurdle or worse was still to come, he didn't know yet. The question was whether he was willing to wait to find out, or take the plunge and demand an answer immediately—and risk the consequences.

Rick was probably more anxious about the pool area planning meeting than she was, Samantha reflected as she spread her sketches across one of the patio tables. He thought she was nervous about making a mistake or looking like she didn't know what she was doing in front of Burt Piskford, because that kind of thing would bother *him.*

As for her, however, the tough part had been the decision to put down her literal and metaphorical roots. After that, everything else garden-wise was pretty much a piece of cake.

"Changing the size and configuration of the pool will be the hardest part," Benjamin Alvaro, Piskford's number two guy, said as he made some notes on a clipboard. "Are you sure you wouldn't prefer a resurfacing to match the new sandstone?"

Samantha lowered her sunglasses a little to look at him. "This is a rectangular pool," she said smoothly, playing the sophisticated socialite to the hilt. "I don't think coloring the walls tan will make it look like a natural rock grotto, do you?"

"I just want you to realize what a mess it's going to be. And changing out the pool will add at least four weeks to the project."

"We won't be here through most of November and December, anyway. I'd rather have it look nice than be finished quickly."

"Who did you consult in putting together this list of

plants, if you don't mind my asking?" Alma Rivera, the nursery's head plant consultant, asked.

"Why, is something wrong with the selections?" Samantha returned. All right, maybe they'd struck a nerve. She'd worked hard on that list.

"No, this is terrific," Alma said quickly, smiling.

"Then I did it myself."

"You have a very fine eye." Alma was obviously better at the soft sell than Alvaro. "Most people pick plants by color, but these are all growers for this climate. The only thing I would recommend is adding a half dozen Gaillardia Fanfare. The red and yellow blossoms are gorgeous and Mediterranean-looking, and it blooms for most of the year."

"Sounds good."

"Great," Piskford finally put in, obviously waiting until his minions had done all the preliminary work. "I guess all that's left now is setting the price." His gaze lifted past her. "Mr. Addison. Thank you again for choosing Piskford Nurseries, sir."

A warm hand slid around Samantha's waist. "You have a grand reputation," Rick said, "which seemed to be a good match with Miss Jellicoe's plans."

He'd lasted lurking up in the library window a lot longer than she'd expected. "We were just getting to the price for all this," she informed him, wondering not for the first time if he had a radar for negotiation stuff.

"Ah, my favorite part. The—"

Her cell phone rang. It was the generic tone for an unknown number, and her insides tightened a little. Stoney, maybe? "Excuse me," she said, opening the phone and moving toward the house. "*Hola*."

"Sam?"

It was Mike Donner. "Hi," she said, wiping the frown from her face before anyone could see it. Money exchanging hands or not, she'd agreed to do a job for Olivia Donner. A job with a deadline. "What can I do for you?"

"I can't rat out my friends, or they'd never talk to me again. They know you're looking for the . . . the thing, and they know that I know you."

"How do they feel about doing the right thing and telling me who they sold it off to?"

"Sold it? Who'd want that thing?"

Samantha paused for a heartbeat. They still had it. Okay, why? "What about returning it, then?"

"I mentioned it, but they blew me off. I don't want them to think I'm a wimp or something, you know?"

She supposed a responsible adult would give him some advice about not succumbing to peer pressure and knowing right from wrong. She wasn't exactly the embodiment of responsibility, though. "The class wants it back," she said, careful not to use Mike's name in case Rick could hear her end of the conversation. "I'm going to find it; that's what I do. Are you going to see it this afternoon?"

"Yeah. Right after school."

"Okay. I'll see what I can do for you, but I'm not making any promises. Deal?"

He sighed. "Deal. The bell just rang; I have to go. Do you want to know where—"

"I'm good," she interrupted. "Get going."

"Thanks, Sam. This is not going to happen again. I promise."

If she'd been Martin Jellicoe, her advice would have been just to avoid getting caught next time. "I'll hold you to that. Bye."

"Bye."

She checked the time on the phone before she closed it. The bell must have been for the last class of the day, which gave her about fifty minutes to change into something better for snooping, get the incognito car, and drive to Leonard High School.

"Anything important?" Rick asked from behind her.

Shit. She needed to add finalizing the pool area negotiations to her schedule. She'd never make it. But she'd given her word to Rick that she would do this today. Making promises to people was stupid, she decided. "Um, no. Just an update on Clark."

Rick lifted an eyebrow. "You've located him?"

"Maybe."

He glanced from her to the landscape designers. "You know, if you have to go meet Clark, I can sign these papers. As long as you're happy with the arrangements."

Samantha grinned. "Just make sure Benjamin here is doing the grotto pool and not the resurfacing."

Rick inclined his head, every inch the British nobleman that he actually was. "Of course."

She grabbed his shoulder, lifted up on her toes, and kissed him soundly on the lips. "You rock," she whispered.

"So I've been told." He kissed her back. "Be careful."

"I will be." As careful as she could be, anyway.

Samantha reached the side street across from Leonard High School just as kids began pouring out of the buildings like rats fleeing a sinking ship. Katie Donner was already there, her Lexus parked in one of the three or four prime spots in front of the school.

Mike and his two friends—David and the unnamed

one—dove into Katie's Lexus, and she took off in the direction of the park again. Baseball practice looked like it was a good cover for mischief. Anything mundane usually was, though. She was pretty sure where the boys would be heading next, but she stayed a couple of car lengths behind them just in case she was wrong.

They did exactly the same thing as they had earlier in the week, down to the other two kids who arrived at the park about two minutes after they did. Hm. Five fifteen-year-old boys. Unless they hormoned her to death she didn't think she'd have much trouble rescuing Clark.

The question of what a group of teenage boys might be doing with a neutral-gender anatomical dummy if it wasn't for money, though, did give her a case of the heebie-jeebies. Hopefully enough of Anatomy Man remained . . . salvageable that she could return him to Miss Barlow's class.

As soon as the Lexus drove off, the kids bagged up their bats and gloves and headed across the park just as they had before. She kept parallel to them, and turned into the far end of the strip mall to keep an eye on what they were doing. She waited until they passed by the burger place and went behind the row of stores, and then she climbed out of the Explorer and locked it behind her.

Even though she was matching herself against kids ten years younger than she was in age and about a hundred years behind her in life experience, any gig was good for getting the old heart pumping. This one was no exception.

She stopped just short of the corner of the long strip of shops, listened for a second, and then took a quick look down the length of the narrow alley. The last of the boys disappeared over a fence on the opposite side. Well, this was getting interesting. Apparently they were actually doing something clandestine.

Stuffing the car keys deep into her pants pocket, she took a short run at the fence and grabbed the top of it. Using her toes for leverage, she hiked her head over the top. No sign of the kids, so she heaved herself up and over, landing on her feet amid some tall weeds and rusted rolls of spare fencing. Two empty-looking warehouses filled the rest of the yard.

After a second of listening she heard the squeaky rattle of a roller door closing, and headed for the building just to her left. Whatever the hell they were doing with Clark, if Anatomy Man was actually there, she was really starting to get creeped out.

It didn't help when she found a window to look through. Inside two of the kids were pulling off their clothes, while one of the others dragged a heavy-looking roll of tarp into the center of the warehouse. With Mike's help he pulled Anatomy Man free, put a long, blonde wig over the dummy's head, and spent a couple of minutes pulling bikini bottoms and a top onto Clark and then arranging arms and legs.

"What the fuck?" she murmured, shifting to a window closer to the middle of the wall to get a better view. She'd seen some pretty sick things in the course of her life—one instance of mummy necrophilia came to mind—but these were upper middle-class teenagers who played baseball, for cripes' sake.

The two boys put clothes back on, thank God, but not the ones they'd worn to school. Ratty, ripped, and splattered with red, they went over to Mike, who held a tray of what looked like paint. As he spread black around their eyes and streaked more red into their hair and on their faces and hands, it dawned on her. Makeup. And costumes. And Clark was a prop of some kind.

Then David pulled a camcorder out of his backpack and set it on a tripod they'd evidently stashed in the old warehouse. A movie. They were making a horror movie—or at least she assumed it wasn't a romance. Relieved, she kept watching as Mike and another boy put on black T-shirts with POLICE printed in white across the back. Then they went through a scene, zombies versus cops, with Clark as an unfortunate female victim being ripped open. Blood and internal organs flew everywhere, with blood packs and fake guns going off to complete the mayhem.

She laughed silently. Of all the scenarios she'd envisioned for Clark, seeing him turned into a movie star hadn't been one of them. It was a pretty clever idea, really.

It probably would have been simple if she wanted to go and retrieve Anatomy Man right then, but since the kids knew that she was acquainted with Mike, he would get the blame for ratting them out and ruining the movie. And she'd kind of given her word to him that she wouldn't wreck his reputation with his friends.

Quietly she backed off. From the look of things, Clark wasn't going anywhere. For one thing, according to the paperwork from Miss Barlow, he weighed seventy-five pounds. For another, the boys had obviously been keeping him there for the last couple of days, anyway. Clark's removal could wait until the Spielbergs were finished for the day.

Before she climbed the fence again she took a quick, quiet walk around the perimeter. She could haul Anatomy Man back over the fence, but she didn't want to rip his latex skin or clock herself with him if he fell. At the front of the warehouse a rolling chain-link gate opened onto a cul-de-sac. Or it would, if not for the heavy chain and padlock keeping it closed.

That would be her way in, then. It would be much easier to pull Clark out to the back of a car than to get him over an eight-foot fence. With a last glance into the warehouse to make sure the guys hadn't seen her, she climbed the back fence again, landing in the alley on the far side.

Samantha dusted off her pants and then went around to the Explorer again. One caper almost down, and one more very big one on hold until she heard from Castillo or Stoney, or until the Mallorey party tomorrow when she could check out Wild Bill Toombs's closed-off room for herself.

When she put the Explorer into reverse and backed out of her parking spot, she caught sight of a black Miata on the far side of the burger place. Okay, Palm Beach might be a small, insular community like Rick said, but it wasn't that small.

"Okay, buddy," she muttered, hauling the wheel around, "let's find out who you are."

As she turned the Explorer in the Miata's direction, the black car accelerated and merged into the street. Without hesitation, Samantha pulled out after it. If the Miata had been tailing her while she'd been following the kids, then she was losing her touch. Getting followed under any circumstances was very, very bad.

The sports car accelerated down the street, weaving through slower afternoon traffic. With the Explorer she wasn't sure she could catch up—and especially not without drawing a lot of attention to herself. That could spook the boys, and she'd lose track of Clark again. And Clark needed to be back home in Miss Barlow's classroom by the beginning of school on Monday.

"Shit." Slowing down to the legal limit, she made a left and headed back in the direction of the island. The Miata would have to wait, but she wasn't going to forget about it. Not until she figured out what was going on.

Chapter 17

Friday, 5:19 p.m.

Richard sat out by the pool, a beer at his elbow, and looked over the revised incorporation documents for the local television station he'd bought last year. "Why am I even looking at this?" he asked.

"Because you said you wanted me to run it by you before I filed it," Tom Donner answered, working on his own beer. "All we changed were the fiscal report dates."

Taking a breath, Richard picked up his pen and signed off on the affected pages. "Next time I do this, remind me that I'm too important to be wasting my time with fiscal reports."

"You got it."

Tom leaned over the table and pulled Samantha's sketches for the pool around to face him. "Did the nursery guys leave these? You must be throwing a lot of money around to earn the Monet treatment. Don't tell Jellicoe I said so, but this is going to look nice."

"Actually, Samantha drew those."

"Jellicoe?"

"Mm hm."

Tom looked through the half dozen drawings of the planned pool, landscaping, and plants. "Jellicoe drew these? Really?"

"She did."

"What the hell's she doing being a cat burglar when she could be Picasso?"

"Put that in the past tense, if you please. The cat burglar bit, anyway."

"I hate to say it, but she's good. In my amateurish opinion, of course."

That was his Samantha, modern-day Renaissance woman. Richard wondered from time to time if there was anything she couldn't do. Except become ordinary. She could pretend that on occasion, but for her, "ordinary" was only a mask. "I'll pass your opinion along, shall I?"

"I wouldn't."

"Hi, fellas," Samantha said from the balcony of the master suite above and behind him.

Richard twisted to glance up at her. All in one piece, thank God. "How is Clark?"

She came up behind him, sliding her hands down his shoulders and leaning around to kiss his cheek. "How did the garden negotiations go?"

"You'll—"

"Clark?" Tom repeated, breaking in on the conversation. "Livia's dummy? You found it?"

Samantha shrugged. "I have some leads," she said, swiping Richard's beer and taking a drink.

"You'll find it," Richard said, hoping he sounded encouraging. "And to answer your question, the garden negotiations went swimmingly. You'll have enough left on your gift certificate for several beds of flowers and a wheelbarrow."

"Excellent. I've been wanting a wheelbarrow."

He grinned, despite the abrupt realization that her relaxed, easy demeanor probably meant that she'd satisfied her adrenaline craving for the day. And that generally entailed her doing something illegal—or dangerous, at the least. "By the by," he said coolly, "Detective Castillo called the house." He glanced at his watch. "He'll be here in about twenty minutes."

She nodded, dropping into the chair between him and Tom. "I hope that means he's got something for me."

It would be nice if whatever information Castillo had would encourage her to change her mind about breaking into Toombs's house tomorrow night. "He didn't say."

Tom pushed to his feet. "Well, before the discussions about illegal activities start, I should get going. Katie's making enchiladas."

"Much as I'd like to hurry you on your way," Samantha put in, "there's a cop coming to the house. Should you be drinking and driving now, Yale?"

"I had a third of a beer, Jellicoe. Rick?" He shook hands with Richard, then headed into the house toward the front door.

"That was nice of you to worry about him," Richard said.

"It was beer from your house. I was worried about you."

"Ah." Richard accepted his bottle of beer back and took another swallow. *He* wasn't driving anywhere tonight. "So, anything interesting in your life today?"

"Maybe."

"Your lead about Clark didn't pan out?"

Her mouth twisted briefly. "I know something about somebody you consider a friend," she said, her green eyes alert and serious. "I think I can fix things, make it all come out okay, so my question is, do you want me to name names, or keep somebody's secret for them?"

She'd said all that without giving him a clue even about whether this someone was male or female. "Does keeping this secret endanger you in any way?"

"No. It will hurt this person's reputation if it should get out. And I'm not sure that's deserved."

"Would it change my opinion of this person?"

"It might. And it would put you in the middle of something that you'd probably prefer to avoid."

He wanted to know. He hadn't built his empire by being satisfied with ignorance on his part or anyone else's. But Samantha excelled at reading both him and everyone else, and if she seriously thought he wouldn't want to know, he probably didn't. Otherwise she would have told him outright. "Unless you need my help, I'll consider this to be your business," he said slowly. "But if you do need my help, you will tell me. Fair?"

She nodded, squeezing his fingers briefly. "Fair."

He eyed her for a second. "This is about Clark, isn't it?"

"Yep."

"Just clarifying." Richard cleared his throat. "Any news from Walter?"

"No. The ads will show up in the papers tomorrow."

She started for his beer again, then put her hands back in her lap. If he hadn't made the study of Samantha Jellicoe his primary concern over the past year, he wouldn't have known anything troubled her. "Is there a Plan B, if he doesn't respond to the ads?"

"I've never had to figure out a Plan B." Her lips tightened. "There are a couple of old hangouts I could try, and a couple of old acquaintances I could hit up. And if he doesn't get hold of me tomorrow, I'll call Delroy in New York. He might have an idea or two."

"What about the police?" he asked, even though he was fairly certain he already knew the answer to that one. "A missing persons report?"

"No way," she returned, as he'd expected. "I don't want the cops digging into Walter Barstone's life any more than I want them digging into mine."

He turned his hand over, and she placed her fingers into his palm. "And there are things you could do before to find him that you can't do now," he said quietly. And Walter had never gone missing for this long when she'd been crooked. Would she blame him or her new life for Barstone's absence? God, he hoped not.

She shrugged. "If he got into something, I don't know what it is. But I'm going to break his neck if he doesn't have a really good reason for bailing on me like this."

"Hi, kids," Detective Castillo said, coming through the same set of double doors that Tom had used.

"Hi, Frank," Samantha answered, freeing her hand.

In the past, Richard had been much more familiar with police chiefs and mayors than with their subordinates. And when a homicide detective they'd met in the course of his job could refer to him, one of the wealthiest men in the world, as "kid," life had taken a turn for the quirky. And Richard rather liked it that way. "Frank," he said. "May I get you a beer or a soda or something?"

"A Diet Coke would be great."

While Castillo sat at their table, putting a folder down on top of Samantha's sketches, Richard went to the soon-to-be-redesigned barbecue and pulled a soda from the small refrigerator there. "Samantha?"

"I'm good, but somebody's almost finished off your beer."

Chuckling, he pulled out another beer with his free hand and closed the fridge with his bare foot. Samantha was witty and sharp under the worst of circumstances, but after a nice, satisfying, relaxing adrenaline rush—or an orgasm, which he preferred for her safety's sake, if nothing else—she surpassed herself. And, he realized abruptly, he'd just freely agreed not to ask her what she'd been up to. That clever little minx. Richard hesitated, then handed over the drinks and took his seat again.

Castillo popped the tab on his soda and drank. "Okay. I went to my guys in Robbery, and I turned up nothing except what I already told you."

Samantha glared at him. "I waited four days for that? Give back that soda."

"Hey, let me finish! Because you mentioned Japanese antiques, I compiled a list of people from around here who've had any of that stuff stolen from them." He opened the folder. "This is what I came up with."

"Can I see it?" Samantha asked, reaching.

"No. I'm not even here, okay?"

"Jeez. So tell me, then."

"First, I have a question. Why Gabriel Toombs and the Picaults?"

Richard sat forward. "They have the largest Japanese collections on the entire East Coast."

"That's it?"

Not looking at Samantha, Richard nodded. "That's it." Confessing that she'd stolen something on Toombs's behalf and that the Picaults felt hinky and that she'd logically eliminated all other credible suspects wouldn't benefit anybody except maybe Castillo's guys in Robbery.

The detective blew out his breath. "One of these days I'm going to explain the meaning of 'cooperation' to you. Like I said before, the Picaults were robbed once, about four years ago, in New York. They lost mostly electronics, jewelry, and cash, plus a small jade statue of a guy on a horse." He glanced in Samantha's direction, then went back to the folder. "Toombs has never been hit," he continued, "not that I can find, anyway. About a half-dozen other robberies in the area were Japanese antiquities."

"He's *never* been robbed?" Samantha repeated, making the statement a question.

"He's never reported a robbery. Why, do you know something I don't?"

"So many things, I have no idea where to start."

"Mm hm. Well, I know a thing or two, too. Guys with samurai sword collections and the training to use them probably don't get hit. Not successfully, anyway."

Samantha paused, Richard's new beer halfway to her lips. "Frank, Mr. Homicide Detective, did you ever happen across a D.B. with big old sword cuts?"

"D.B.?" Richard interrupted.

"Dead body, officially," Castillo supplied. "Or dirt bag,

unofficially. And yes, I did. Two and a half years ago. The guy was a hood, a gang member, and honestly we had too many suspects and no way to narrow it down. Decapitation, though, isn't really street gang style."

"So you suspected Gabriel Toombs?"

"He has kind of a reputation for having a very rigid sense of justice. Like I said, though, no proof. And honestly, there were other guys with more motive. Toombs never reported a break-in or anything. And I could be totally off base with this."

Christ. "If you thought you were so off base, as you say, you wouldn't have mentioned it."

Castillo collected his folder and his soda and stood. "I just like to give people a heads up. Because I believe in cooperation and everything. So is there anything you want to tell me about any of this?"

"Sure," Samantha said, turning in her chair to face the detective. "I've got a black Miata following me around. Any ideas?"

"Yeah. I'll run black Miatas. There's probably only a hundred or so of them in Palm Beach County."

"The first three numbers or letters or whatever on the plates are 3J3, if that helps."

"It might. I'll take a look. Bye, Rick, Sam."

"Thank you, Detective."

Fiddling with the beer bottle, Richard waited until Castillo was gone before he cocked his head at Samantha. "You saw the Miata again, I presume?"

"I did. And when I started after it, it went into warp drive and disappeared. Since it wouldn't know I was following it unless it was following me first, I'm pretty sure it was. Following me, I mean."

"You lost it, then?" he asked, surprised.

"Traffic, kids, me in your incognito car—going all Darth Vader on the Miata didn't seem like a very smart thing to do."

"Speaking of smart things to do," he began, "how about not breaking into Toombs's house?"

"Don't start that again, Rick," she said, her voice calmer than he expected. "He can't hack me to pieces if he doesn't know I'm there. And he won't. I just need a look into one room."

"Unless the swords and armor are in there."

She blew out her breath. "I used to do this kind of thing—exactly this kind of thin—for a living, Brit. I'm good at it. And I know what I'm doing."

"I'm going with you."

"Rick, you are not going with m—"

"Will you carry a gun?" he interrupted.

"No. Guns are for guys who can't get in and out without being seen."

"Guns are to keep you alive when someone goes after you with a samurai sword," he insisted. "I'm going to carry one, and I'm going with you. Now if you think you can win this argument, go ahead and try. Otherwise, I think we should go and get some picanha."

"Hans is cooking top sirloin? We must have been good today."

"Don't change the subject. Do I tail you and ruin your B and E, or do we go in together?"

She muttered something that didn't sound very flattering. "Fine. *If* you agree to do what I say."

"I agree," he said easily.

Samantha didn't know whether he meant it or not, but

she supposed she'd have to take him at his word. Having him along would help resolve the problem of toting out sixty pounds of fragile armor and two valuable swords, but it could create a whole new set of problems.

"I've gone into places with you before," he stated, standing and holding her chair for her.

"Yes, when nobody was home and where security sucked."

"Toombs will be at the party, and you'll take care of security. And I will follow your lead."

A successful break-in was more than a matter of willingness to go in and follow instructions. On the other hand, keeping him from getting involved would be pretty much impossible. "I guess after dinner we'll have to pick out our matching B and E outfits."

Rick took her hand as they headed inside. "Men don't wear outfits."

"Studly man clothes, then." Okay, he wanted to keep it light. That was better than more yelling and threats and trying to order her around.

So far she'd avoided telling anyone about Mike Donner's involvement with Anatomy Man. All she needed to do was take a quick trip to the old warehouse tonight to rescue Clark, and then another jaunt to Miss Barlow's classroom to drop him off. Then at least that would be finished.

After a moment she realized he was steering her toward the stairs rather than the dining room. "Where are we going?"

"To eat top sirloin. Picanha, remember?"

"In bed? Won't that be messy with the steak sauce and everything?"

"Not in bed. In the Keys."

She hauled on his hand until all six-foot-two of him stopped on the landing. "Don't make me hit you on the head and call Dr. Klemm."

He grinned at her. "I liked having the helicopter in England, so I bought one for Florida."

Now it made sense. "When did this happen?"

"Yesterday."

She snorted, shaking her head at him. "Boys and their toys."

"That's right. So I need shoes and a jacket, and you need a wrap or something, and we're flying to Islamorada. I made seven o'clock reservations at Braza Leña."

If she didn't know better, she would be ready to swear that Rick knew she had B and E plans for the night and he was trying to disrupt them. What a way to do it, though. Dinner at the edge of the Caribbean. Of course to get there and back she would have to ride in a helicopter, but what the hell. "Just don't expect to get lucky in the air tonight," she said, separating from him just inside the bedroom suite.

"I can wait until we get back home," he returned with a slow, sexy smile.

"Oh, you're so sure of yourself, aren't you?"

"I am." He sat on the couch to pull on his brown loafers, sans socks. "And the next time you figure out that a car is tailing you, please don't wait twenty minutes before you tell me."

Wow. He'd actually said the *P* word. "The Miata was probably the paparazzi, or Nancy O'Dell from *Access Hollywood*. I think she has a thing for you, Brit."

"I'm taken. And so is she, if I recall." He stood again. "And not to change the subject, but did you get a look at Castillo's list of thefts?"

"I did." While she decided how much she wanted to say about Frank's file, Samantha ducked into her dressing closet and changed out of her sneaking-around T-shirt and into a black and red striped Donna Karan blouse, then slipped a thin black jacket off a hanger. Honest as she tried to be with him, there were some things he would be both better off and safer not knowing.

"And?" he prompted, stopping in the doorway and leaning against the frame.

"And that's one of those things where I have to ask if you really want to know the answer." There. Now the decision could be on his head.

"Unbelt. And I know you know what that means, so don't try to change the subject again."

"Fine. Since you asked so nicely, I'm responsible for three of those pieces from Castillo's list. Feel better?"

"Do you know where any of them ended up?"

"Just the bridle. Stoney would know about the rest, but I seem to have misplaced him." Blowing out her breath, she forced a smile and strolled up to wrap her hands into his lapels. "So are you sure you want to ride in a helicopter with me? I'm kind of mad, bad, and dangerous to know."

He kissed her softly. "You and Lord Byron," he murmured. "And you're not mad. You're . . . unique. And I thank God for that every day."

"Good save," she said, noting that he hadn't argued with the "bad" or "dangerous" bit. She tugged on his hand, pulling him toward the hallway. "That first part didn't quite sound like a compliment, but then you pulled it off."

Rick came to a sudden stop, nearly jerking her off her feet.

"Ow."

"I was serious," he said, frowning.

She let him keep his grip on her hand. "I know that," she retorted. "It scares me a little that you're thanking God for me, so I made a joke. Okay?"

He met her gaze. "Okay. But I still can't help that I love you."

"That's not as scary as it used to be. And I love you, too." She pulled on his hand. "Can we go get our picanha now?" The sooner they went, the sooner she'd be able to get back, and the sooner she'd be able to rescue Clark the Anatomy Man.

Chapter 18

Saturday, 2:08 a.m.

"I didn't ask to fly the helicopter until we were out over the water and away from any civilians," Samantha said, climbing out of the back of the stretched Mercedes S600.

"That didn't make me feel any better. The Atlantic Ocean is rather substantial. And deep."

She laughed. "The pilot was right there. And we had flotation devices in the back."

Ben closed the rear door behind them. "Would you like some assistance getting into the house?" he asked.

Samantha patted him on the shoulder. "We're good. If

you come out in the morning and find us on the driveway, though, I give you permission to drag us inside."

With a quick, stifled smile Ben nodded. "With pleasure. Good night, Miss Sam, Mr. Addison."

"I think the lad believes we're pissed," Rick observed as the car pulled around the side of the house to the garage.

"You're pissed," Sam amended. "I'm a little tipsy. What the hell are mango mojitos, anyway?"

"Mango rum and mint leaves," he answered, "among a few other things."

"I'm glad I only had two of them." She glanced at her wristwatch. Damn. Her buzz wasn't too bad, but she was not going to try a B and E unless she was one hundred percent sober. Clark's rescue would have to wait until tomorrow.

"Do you have somewhere to go?" Rick asked, pushing open the front door and stepping aside to let her enter first.

He was obviously more sober than she'd given him credit for. "I was going to go on a dummy rescue," she said, deciding she'd give that honesty thing a try again, "but it can wait until tomorrow."

"Good." Rick snagged her arm, tugging her up against him as he backed into the closed door.

She leaned up along his hard chest, kissing him open-mouthed, their tongues dancing. With his free hand he unzipped her jeans and slid his fingers beneath her panties. The pleasant warmth already running through her spiraled into intense, insistent heat.

"I'm sorry," she said, her voice a little ragged, "does this mean you'd like to make an appointment with me?"

He curled a finger, pressing into her. "Clear your calendar," he murmured, taking her mouth again.

Holy smokes. She'd gotten to fly—or hover, actually—a helicopter for a couple of minutes tonight. It had been thrilling and exciting, but this was better. Much better. Rick's arms, his skin, his warmth and the way she knew she was safe in his company—he stirred her up more than a boatload of mango mojitos.

Withdrawing his hand from her pants, he went to work unbuttoning her blouse, trailing his fingers across her breasts as he did so. She hissed in a breath. During the day the foyer would have been busy, crisscrossed with maids, housekeepers, and security. At this time of night the only people she had to look out for were the three security guards who patrolled the inside of the house.

Whether she had the power to hire and fire them or not, she still didn't want anybody stumbling over her while Rick had his hands in her bra or underwear. "Let's go upstairs," she rasped, as his fingers closed over her right nipple.

"Right here on the floor," he said, pulling her blouse and bra aside and replacing his fingers with his mouth.

Samantha put a hand against the door to brace herself as her knees went wobbly. She knew it wasn't from the rum. Christ, he felt good. But her brain hadn't totally shut down. Not yet, anyway. "Pick a room, sailor," she insisted, grabbing his hair and pulling him away from her chest.

"You're a tease; that's what you are," he panted, and grabbed her hand, towing her into the downstairs sitting room and slamming the door behind them. "There."

"Lock it. You just made a lot of noise."

"Bloody . . . Fine." Rick strode back to the door and twisted the lock.

As he came back to where she stood beside the old Georgian cabinets, he pulled his jacket and shirt off, tossing them onto the floor. Even if she'd come up with another thing to protest she wouldn't have, not when he had that look on his face.

"Anything else?" he asked.

"Just you."

Samantha pulled off her own blouse, knowing that if he had to mess with it much longer he would just rip it off, which would suck because she happened to like it. She let him unfasten her bra, since *he* liked that. Sinking onto the floor to lean back against a leather-covered chair, she tilted her head back as his mouth closed over her left tit. *Mm.* With his mouth occupied, he pulled off her shoes and then tugged down her jeans, dropping them somewhere close to his shirt.

Her panties followed; she'd lost a handful of them over the past year, and wondered on occasion what the housekeepers must think, discovering them tossed behind bookshelves or hanging off lamps or burning in the fireplace or something. Rick, of course, thought it was some kind of mark of his virility when he could make her underwear vanish. Like he needed anything other than himself for that.

Rick took her by the hips and tugged her forward away from the chair. When she was flat on her back he sank down, wrapping his hands around her thighs and leaning in to tease between her legs with his lips and tongue.

Samantha gasped, her eyes practically rolling back in her head at the sensation of his mouth on her. Pretty much from the time their clothes started to come off she was ready to go, but Rick liked to drive her right to the edge—or past it—before he got down to serious sex.

"Get your damn pants off," she demanded, writhing and making pitiful moaning sounds.

He lifted his head to meet her gaze. "You do it," he said.

Tightening her legs around his shoulders, she rolled them both over, putting herself on her stomach and him on his back. She didn't stay in shape for nothing. She sat up, straddling his bare chest. "Are you ordering me around?" she asked with a slow smile.

Rick nodded. "I am."

She bent down and kissed him again. "In that case," she murmured, having trouble breathing as his hands cupped her breasts again, "I guess I'll make an exception and take care of that."

With a laugh he rose up on his elbows to watch as she slid off him and went to work on the fastening of his jeans. "I'm glad you're feeling cooperative."

"Yeah, well, that's your fault. You have quite the incentive package."

"Don't you mean packet?"

"Nope." She opened his pants and pulled them down as he lifted his hips to help her. "Package."

He kicked off his loafers, and she tossed his jeans and boxers over the chair. Sedentary as his life could be, he still managed to keep in shape—a living, breathing, sexy-as-hell work of art. And he was all hers, apparently.

"Come up here," he said, taking her hand and drawing her up along his body again.

"You revved me up," Samantha breathed, reaching down to close her hand around his cock. "Now it's your turn."

"I'm always revved up around you." He kissed her, slow and deep, rolling them at the same time so she was underneath him. "The second you walk into a room, every time you smile," he continued, pushing his hips forward and sliding inside her, "your laugh, your frown, your—"

Samantha covered his mouth with her fingers. "I get it,"

she managed, locking her ankles around his thighs as he started a slow, deep thrust, "I'm very cool."

"You're more than cool. You're . . . amazing."

Blue eyes held her gaze as he moved inside her. Tonight he looked so . . . soulful, almost like she could drown in those deep blue eyes of his. All the arguments lately, the destruction of her emergency backpack, the insistence that she get going on the garden, lunch with Katie and all the talk about kids, and she still couldn't imagine anything better than this.

It all spun together in her mind, mixing with arousal and pleasure and memory—her memory of that weird conversation with Donner and his saying Rick was dancing around giving her something . . .

"Oh, my God!" she gasped, her body shuddering with release even as her brain seized up.

"That's what I like," Rick breathed, speeding his pace until he shuddered and lowered himself on her.

Samantha didn't feel nearly as relaxed as he obviously did, or as she usually did after a very nice orgasm. He was thinking about proposing to her. About marriage. What the hell was she supposed to make of that? *Holy crap*. She pushed at his shoulder. "Off," she demanded.

He lifted his head to look down at her. "What's wrong?" he asked, his breathing still hard and fast.

She felt even less ready for conversation. "You're heavy," she improvised, shoving again.

Rick lifted off of her, sitting as she scrambled to her feet. "Did I hurt you?" He ran a hand gently down her calf, his voice husky.

"No! Of course not." His shirt would do a better job of covering her than her own, so she snatched it up and pulled it on, buttoning up the front despite her shaking fingers.

"Something just occurred to me, and I need to take care of it."

"You thought of something else you needed to take care of right in the middle of us making love?" he asked darkly.

"'Making love' sounds lame. We were having sex. And I wasn't doing my taxes or anything, so don't get your testosterone all in an uproar. Something just popped into my head. Don't get all bent out of shape." She hurried over to the door and unlocked it. Air. She needed some air. A lot of air.

Rick pulled on his jeans and stood, striding over to close the door again when she started to pull it open. "I am bent out of shape," he snapped. "So tell me what thought popped into your head, Samantha."

"It's my thought, not yours. Get out of the way."

"No."

She let go of the door handle. "Fine. I'll go out the window."

He grabbed her shoulder, pushing her back against the door. "What the devil's got you so frightened all of a sudden that you're trying to run away?"

"I am not fucking running away. Quit screwing with the way things are before you totally ruin everything! Now let go!"

Richard let her go. She scrambled out the door and for the stairs, which relieved him a little bit. At least she wasn't running out the front door. Yet. He squatted down to gather up the rest of their scattered clothes, then sat in the old leather chair, the shoes and garments in his arms.

She'd figured out that he meant to propose. That was the only reason he could think of for her to make the "quit screwing with the way things are" statement. Not quite the reaction he'd hoped for. And he had a ring to pick up tomorrow. "Shit," he muttered.

How could he do what he did, successfully managing several billion dollars' worth of business concerns, and not be able to figure out one woman? What was the difference, anyway, between staying together and staying together with rings on their left hands? Okay, kids, roots—he understood all of that. But they were so alike. How could he want it so badly and her not at all?

It wasn't possible. Whatever she might say, she was just scared. She'd lived day to day for so long that of course the idea of committing to a future terrified her. "You stupid git," he said to himself, standing again. He couldn't leave it like this. If he did, she might very well vanish before he had a chance to convince her otherwise.

The bedroom door was closed and locked. Bloody wonderful. He maneuvered the clothes and shoes around until he had two knuckles free. "Samantha?" he called, knocking.

Nothing.

Since he'd wrecked her backpack, and thank God for that, she couldn't have gotten her things together and left already. He knocked again. "Sam?"

At the far end of the hall he heard a low cough, and jumped.

"Problem, Mr. Addison?" Pablo Esqueda, one of Solano Dorado's night security guards, asked as he walked closer. "I have a master key, if you—"

The door clicked and opened a couple of inches. "I'm good," he said, using one of Samantha's expressions and elbowing the door open far enough for him to get through it. He closed it behind him with one bare foot and dumped the clothes onto the couch. "Why do the security guards have master keys?" he asked, spying Samantha's backside as she disappeared into her dressing closet.

"Because if there's a problem inside a locked room, they should be able to get in," her muffled voice came.

"Into our bedroom?" Yes, he was avoiding the subject, but just talking with her might get him some of the information he very badly needed.

"I just wanted some breathing room, Rick."

Of course she *wouldn't* want to avoid the subject, but he still needed to tread a little more carefully. "What happened to the thing you needed to take care of?"

She stepped outside the closet as he approached it. Putting her hands on her hips, wearing nothing other than his gray shirt, she gazed at him steadily with her chin up. Scared, but defiant. His Samantha. "Are you going to bust my chops?" she asked. "Or are you going to step back and let me catch my damned breath?"

God, she was sharp. And lethal. And she'd just put this entire business squarely on his shoulders—which at the moment was precisely where it belonged. It was bloody tricky, when his action would depend on her reaction, and yet he had to make his move first. "I have never done anything with the intention of restricting your breathing," he said slowly. "And I never mean to do anything to cause you hurt or distress, now or in the future. I hope the way I feel about you isn't what's distressing you."

"I like the way you feel about me. Don't screw with it. With this." She gestured between the two of them.

"Take your breathing room, Samantha. But neither one of us is much for standing still. Sooner or later I'm going to want to walk forward, and I'm going to ask you to take that next step with me."

She shivered; he could see her hands shaking. Despite the abrupt urge to wrap his arms around her, he stayed where he was and waited.

"That is not the thing to say if you want me not to pass out."

"Apologies."

Her lips quirked. "I can't think about this while I'm looking for Stoney and Minamoto's armor and Anatomy Man," she finally said. "I've loved this last year. And I love you. Bu—"

He held up his hand. "Breathe," he said, hopefully hiding his own abrupt alarm. He was *not* going to let her finish that sentence. "I love you. Relax. Let's get some sleep."

Samantha tilted her head. "You're not going to push . . . anything?"

"Not tonight." That was for bloody certain. As for after, he was already fighting against the ego and pride that were demanding to know why *any* woman would hesitate to marry him. He and Samantha *would* marry; he just needed to find a way to make certain that would happen.

Luckily at the last second Richard decided to take his cell phone into the bathroom with him, because it rang the second before he stepped into the shower a little after nine o'clock in the morning. He grabbed for it, hoping the echoing ring hadn't awakened Samantha, and checked the caller ID.

"Tom," he said in a low voice.

"Are you in a cave?"

"The bathroom. What do you want?"

"I'm returning your message from yesterday."

Richard blinked, trying to remember what he'd been doing yesterday before the helicopter ride to Islamorada. He definitely remembered what had happened after they'd returned. "Oh. Right."

"So do you still want me to go with you to you-know-where in an hour?"

"Why are *you* speaking in code?"

"Because Jellicoe's sneaky."

He couldn't dispute that. Did he want Tom to go with him to Harry Winston? This was his decision, his and Samantha's. Tom didn't approve, and while Katie liked Samantha, he knew she hesitated as well. And after last night, he didn't want that around him. Not while he was picking up the engagement ring. Unable to help a quick glance toward the closed bathroom door, he lowered his voice still further. "No. I've got it covered. Thanks for returning my call."

"Um, okay. I'll see you later."

"Ta."

Slowly Richard closed the phone and set it back on the counter. Then he silently unlocked the bathroom door and opened it. Leaning out, he peered around the sitting room. Nothing. That didn't mean she wasn't there, though. He wanted to be certain that Samantha hadn't overheard any of that conversation. As Tom had so eloquently put it, she was sneaky.

Naked, he crept through the dark sitting room and leaned around the half-closed bedroom door. She lay in bed, her eyes closed and her breathing slow and steady. He tried to feel relieved, but in truth he *still* couldn't be certain that she hadn't been on the other side of the bathroom door, drawn her own conclusions, and then fled back to the bed before he'd been able to move.

"Samantha?" he whispered.

She stirred, throwing an arm across her face. "What?" she grumbled.

"Did my phone call wake you up?"

"No, you woke me up just now," she said, sitting up to look at him. "Is something wrong?"

Git, git, git. He straightened, since creeping obviously wasn't necessary any longer. "No. I was trying to let you sleep in, and apparently I'm an idiot."

Samantha actually smiled. "You're a good-looking naked guy, so that excuses a lot. What were you doing?"

"I was about to jump in the shower."

"That's good, because otherwise this would be scary."

"Like you've ever been scared of anything," he returned. Except for last night, but he wasn't going to mention that this morning. He doubted that she would, either.

For a second she looked at him. Then she flopped back onto the bed and lifted the covers over her head. "Thanks, Brit," she murmured.

"You're welcome, Yank. Care to join me in the shower?"

"I'm going back to sleep. Go away."

"Going away." He slipped back out and shut the door the rest of the way, just in case someone else called him about something he didn't want her to overhear.

Chapter 19

Saturday, 9:49 a.m

Samantha looked out Rick's office window as the Jaguar headed down the front drive of Solana Dorado. He'd been friendly and kept things as light as a feather, then slipped out of the house without a word. That sucked.

Even when they fought, she always felt comfortable with him, and now they were both on eggshells. He'd told her to breathe, but he hadn't said anything about forgetting what she suspected, and he hadn't told her she was wrong.

Of course neither of them had actually said the *M* word, but once the thought had crossed her mind, a lot of things over the past weeks suddenly made more sense. Panic welled up through her chest again, raw and cold, and she took a quick stride around the room to push it back down. This was crazy. There'd never been a husband in her daydreams of retiring in Milan with cabana boys waving palm fronds over her. She'd never even really been able to picture herself getting old. She'd wanted to, though, obviously, or she wouldn't have retired at the top of her game.

"Fuck," she muttered, striding around the room again. She pulled her phone out of her pocket and dialed. "Pick up the damn phone, Stoney!"

After one ring the automated message about the moron who owned the phone not having a voice mail system set up came on, and she snapped it closed again. She and Stoney joked about him being her Yoda, her source of spiritual and moral advice, but it was true. She'd grown up with Martin and Stoney, and Stoney had been the one to buy her first bra, her first box of tampons—and whether his moral compass pointed a little less true than that of other people or not, she relied on him. And now he was missing.

It was coming close to the point where she was debating asking Detective Castillo to try to track down Stoney's car. Frank would be mad, Stoney would be really mad, and she was already pretty pissed at herself for letting this happen.

In the meantime she supposed she could talk to Aubrey about what Rick was up to, but he was less crotchety and more Obi-Wan Kenobi–like than Stoney—he would only tell her to follow her feelings and do what she knew was right. Well, fuck that. She was a thief. Obviously she didn't know what was right.

So there she was again, waiting to see if someone else was going to make a move. She didn't like working that way; it felt like standing on a freeway with her back turned and waiting for a truck to hit her from behind. After last night she already felt like she'd been run over and dragged.

The phone on Rick's desk buzzed. The house intercom. Samantha walked over and hit the speaker button. "Jellicoe."

"Miss Sam, this is Mourson down in security. I have a tractor, a flatbed, and about twelve guys at the front gate. They say they're with Piskford Nurseries and they have an appointment."

Crash, boom. "Let them in, Louie. Have one of your guys meet them in the pool area to supervise."

"Acknowledged."

She probably should have checked for a start date on the contract Rick had signed on her behalf. Man, they moved fast. If she'd been trying to impress a very wealthy client with a couple of acres that might one day need to be re-landscaped, though, she would probably be on her most impressive behavior, too.

After she grabbed her shoes from her closet, she headed down the outside stairs to the pool. Three days ago she'd been terrified about the idea of being responsible for creating a garden. Now, though, it seemed like a pretty good distraction.

Her phone rang out the theme from *S.W.A.T.* as she reached the bottom step. Waving at the nursery team to go ahead and set up, she flipped it open. "Hi, Frank."

"Hey. I thought you should know, I ran your black Miata. There are three of them with license plates starting in 3J3, but only one of them belongs to Gabriel Toombs."

"Toombs?" she repeated, deeply surprised. Wild Bill Toombs had been following her around? Why?

"Yes, Toombs. So whatever you're looking into, he seems to know about it."

"Gosh, Frank, you didn't even come over for breakfast and tell me in person."

"I'm not joking around, Sam," the detective said in a sharp voice. "You remember me mentioning that Toombs is a dangerous guy?"

"I remember. I'm not a kid, Frank. But thank you for the heads up. I appreciate it. Really."

"It's not going to change the way you're doing anything though, is it?"

"Probably not. But it changes the way I think about it."

"If I get called out for a homicide and it's you, Sam, I'm gonna be really pissed off."

"You and me both. Thanks, Frank. Bye."

"Bye."

She sat at one of the pool-side tables as the Piskford crew started hooking up hoses and a pump to drain the pool. To Frank, Toombs tailing her meant that Wild Bill somehow knew about her investigation. To her, it meant that Toombs had suspected something about her, probably before they'd ever met in person, and now he was trying to verify it. Since there were a limited number of things he could be suspicious about, talking to Stoney right now would have been very handy, damn it all.

Since she couldn't talk to Stoney, now she really did need to talk to Aubrey. She dialed his cell number.

"A very good Saturday morning to you, Miss Samantha," his low drawl came.

"Hey, Aubrey. I take it I didn't wake you up."

"I am on hole number seven of a very good golf game, my dear."

Hm. "Who's out there with you?"

"Dr. Randall Harkley, Wild Bill Toombs, and Alfonse Soroyan. Is something amiss?"

Adrenaline jolted through her system, heating her up again. "Did Toombs hear you say my name?" she asked carefully.

"He's in the other cart with Alfonse. Why?"

"Are you golfing nine or eighteen holes?" she asked, instead of answering him.

"Eighteen. Which will take another two and a half hours including lunch," he said, his voice sharper.

He got it, then. "So I'm going . . . jogging." She stood, going to the stairs that led up to the bedroom suite. "If you find yourself companionless, why don't you give me a call?"

"I don't like to argue with a lady," Aubrey returned, "but maybe you shouldn't . . . go jogging alone. Is your gentleman there?"

"What are you now, a personal trainer?" another male voice, Dr. Harkley's no doubt, came a little more distantly.

"I am a man of many talents," Aubrey drawled.

"Rick went out," Samantha said as the other conversation stopped. "I can be there and back in an hour, Aubrey. Maybe less. Just call me if he leaves."

"Very well. Watch out for . . . dogs and sidewalk cracks and such."

"I'll be careful. Thanks. I'll call you when I get back home."

"Oh, you do that, my dear."

In the bedroom she headed for her closet, shedding her pink T-shirt in exchange for a white one. She snatched up a black Florida Marlins baseball cap and pulled on her white socks and athletic shoes.

At the sight of herself in the mirror on the back of the dressing closet door, she stopped. Yeah, she was ready to go—Florida golf clothes, hat ready to shade her eyes and cover her hair, her face a little flushed and her eyes wide and sharp. All systems at the ready. "Shit," she muttered, and pulled out her phone again.

"Hello, my love," Rick's cool voice came a moment later.

In the background she could hear a voice paging somebody to a gate. "Are you at the airport?"

"I took the helicopter to Miami and back," he said.

This would have been easier if he'd still been in Miami. "I'm about to do something that's going to piss you off, but I'm telling you first so I get points for that, right?"

"That depends," he returned carefully. "What are you about to do?"

"I just called Aubrey about something else, and he's on hole seven of eighteen, golfing with our friend."

"Samantha, no."

"It's the best opportunity I'm going to have. If we go missing during the party tonight, he'll notice."

"And how do you know he'll notice our absence?"

She hesitated. Telling Rick about who'd been trailing her could be pretty unwise, but he needed to understand that she wasn't trying to be a hard ass about this. "He owns a black Miata. Frank just called and told me."

"He . . . Sam, you do not go near that house. Do you hear me?"

"He's occupied now, Rick. Viscanti needs his answer in four days. I'm going. I'll call you as soon as I get back in the car."

"Shit. Sam—"

She hit the end button, switched it to vibrate, and pocketed it again. "Not good, not good," she muttered at her reflection, and reached for her tools backpack, the one Rick hadn't destroyed, and then scooted downstairs for the garage.

Her phone vibrated. She checked the caller ID as she

grabbed the SLK keys off their hook, just to make sure it wasn't Aubrey warning her off already. Nope. It was Rick, and so she stuffed it back in her pocket and slid behind the wheel of the banana yellow Mercedes.

Normally she favored a more nondescript car—and one that wasn't hers to start with—but the SLK fit Toombs's neighborhood pretty well. And this was a good-guy B and E, so no lawbreaking other than what was strictly necessary.

Her phone rang four more times as she drove to Wild Bill's house and parked the car half a block away. All the calls were from Rick, and she could practically see the smoke rising up from the display. If they hadn't explored the depths of unpleasantness yet, they probably would when she got home. She would have turned off the phone, because it was damned distracting, but she couldn't risk missing a call from Aubrey.

Before she climbed out of the car she went through her black backpack—lock picks, wire and glass cutters, duct tape, copper wire, a can of aerosol hair spray, and her very nice black leather gloves, along with a couple of paper clips and rubber bands. All a girl needed for a day or evening out on the sly. She had more sophisticated equipment stashed around Solano Dorado, but she'd kept a pretty close eye on Wild Bill's security arrangements when she and Aubrey had gone on the house tour, and she didn't think she'd need any of it.

She rubber-banded her hair and stuffed it up under the Marlins baseball hat, then reached into the tiny back-seat area for the spare pair of Rick's golfing gloves she'd snagged and pulled them on before she got out. Echoing the beep of the car lock engaging, tires screeched down the street behind her. She flinched, automatically ducking her shoulders as she glanced over.

A green Jaguar shot up parallel to the curb right behind the SLK and stopped about an inch short of her bumper. *Dammit.*

Rick shoved open the door and then slammed it shut behind him. "Get back in that car," he ordered, in the don't-fuck-with-me voice he used during business negotiations.

"No. You get back in *that* car before you jack everything up."

"I'll throw you in there if I have to."

"You know, my second instinct was right. I shouldn't have called you. I could have . . . done my shopping and been back at the house without you ever knowing it."

"I'm not debating with you, and I'm not arguing. Get back in the fucking car, Samantha."

She lifted her chin, hefting the backpack in her right hand in case she needed to swing it at him. With the tools inside, it might just drop him. On the other hand, he was bigger than she was, and he fought dirty. "I am not Lucy Ricardo, and you're Rick—not Ricky. I don't have to'splain things to you, and I don't need your permission to do my job. Back off. Back the hell off."

For a long moment he glared at her, his muscles held so tightly that he actually shook. Then he turned on his heel and yanked open the Jaguar door again. Before she could even resume breathing, he popped the trunk and went around to the back of the car. Then he pulled out a tan baseball cap and grabbed a pair of matching gloves, part of his regular golf attire.

"Let's go, then," he snapped, shutting the trunk again.

"What do you think you're doing?"

"I'm being Ethel, apparently. Move."

Samantha put her hand on his chest, stopping him. "Just a minute. The same rules apply. You do what I say in there."

"I haven't forgotten my side of the agreement."

He was still being angry and British, but she couldn't fault him for either one of those. Instead she wrapped her fingers into his light blue polo shirt and leaned up to kiss him. His rigid mouth softened, and he pursued her a little when she backed off.

"Okay?" she asked, taking his cap and setting it low over his eyes. He was still pretty recognizable, so she would have to make sure that he didn't get seen at all.

Rick pulled on his gloves. "Okay."

Well, this was going to be interesting. Going in during the day would have been easier if she'd been alone, and if she hadn't been photographed in Rick's company enough that somebody on the street might actually just recognize them together. At least they were dressed fairly normally, though it would have been better if they'd been right on the golf course instead of a block away from it. Any delays were bad news.

"Come on."

They walked hand in hand along the street until they drew even with Toombs's property. As soon as traffic cleared she set her toes into the block fence and swarmed over it. Rick followed a moment later. "No outside sensors?" he asked in a low voice.

"Just motion-activated lights. That doesn't much matter during the day."

He was probably still angry, but at least he had the experience to know that everything had its place and that this was not the time to snipe or argue. Instead he stood silently at the corner of the house and kept watch while she hoisted up the nearest bathroom window in what would have been the servants' quarters nearly a century earlier.

Climbing into the small guest bathroom was easy, and

it took her only a minute to creep down the short corridor and open the back door for him. On her own she probably could have been upstairs and in the room by now, locked or not, but since she had a second pair of eyes—and somebody to help lift the armor—she wasn't going to leave him standing outside in the open.

As soon as he stepped inside she closed and locked the door again. No sense in leaving any trail to follow. "Today," she whispered against his ear, "is one of the days the two housekeepers come in to clean. Keep your eyes and ears open."

He nodded.

"Let's get a move on. This way."

They went up the stairs, Rick two paces behind her. She stopped three steps from the top and sank down onto her hands and knees, creeping up to look down the long hallway in front of them. With the housekeepers there the door and window alarms were off, but she didn't want to stumble across anyone. And just because she knew of two employees didn't mean there weren't five or six others around. Rick had over a dozen just at Solano Dorado.

The hallway stood empty except for the glass-encased kimonos and Kabuki costumes. There were plenty of places to hide, but hopefully she and Rick were the only ones being stealthy today.

"These are nice," Rick breathed.

"Stop sightseeing." She'd known he would like the displays, though; if they decided on a costume exhibit for the Rawley Park gallery, she would recommend a similar method of presentation.

"Apologies."

A door opened halfway down the hallway. Moving fast, Samantha shoved Rick between two of the displays while she ducked behind one on the opposite side of the wide hall. A maid emerged, vacuum cleaner and dust cloths with her. She closed the door behind her, moved one room closer to where they hid, and went through that door.

With a half grin, her heart beating hard and fast in her chest, Samantha moved back to the middle of the hallway and padded forward toward the two turret rooms at the far end. So far the B and E had been simple, and it wouldn't have been that much more challenging at night, except for the additional task of circumventing the perimeter alarms. Maybe Mr. Samurai relied on his reputation to keep people out of the house. She couldn't come up with any other good reason why this house had never been hit.

Then again, from what Frank had said, maybe it *had* been hit, and Toombs had taken care of the intruder or intruders himself. Well, Toombs was out playing golf, and the only pointy swords she wanted to see were the ones belonging to Minamoto Yoritomo.

As they reached the turret rooms, she grabbed Rick's arm. "If that door opens," she said, indicating the one from which vacuuming sounds currently emanated, "get into the room behind us as fast as you can."

"And you?" he whispered.

"If I can't get this door in time, I'll be right behind you. Watch my back."

"Always." Rick positioned himself between her and the hallway—her knight in shining armor even when they were being the semi-bad guys. Just in case their luck was still holding, she tried the door latch. Locked.

Samantha freed a paper clip from her pocket and stuck the end into the lower of the two locks. Generally only one of a pair of locks ever got used, but these both seemed to be engaged. She could open a lock within ten or fifteen seconds. After twenty-five, though, she'd shifted only one of the cylinders into place.

"Sam?"

"Shh." Not only was this a double key lock, but it was a nice one. A very nice one. With a frown she pulled out her wallet of lock picks and unzipped it. "Hold this and keep it steady," she whispered, inserting a thin rod into the upper lock.

Rick half turned, holding the rod in place for her. At least he wasn't commenting that she'd lost her edge, though that would probably come later. But a tough lock was good, she reflected as she squatted down to twist the tiny internal cylinders. It meant there was something worth protecting behind it.

With the heavy-duty tools put to use, the lock clicked open in another twelve seconds. That was nothing to brag about, but she'd worry about buying one of the locks to practice on later. Taking a breath, she pushed down on the latch and squeezed through the door, Rick right behind her.

"What the f—"

"Shh," she warned him again, gingerly closing and locking the door before she turned around. And froze. "What the fuck?" she muttered.

Chapter 20

Saturday, 12:13 p.m.

She was everywhere. A row of pedestals, four of them, stood in the middle of the room, each of them topped with a rare piece of Japanese antiquity. But all the rest was her. Samantha Jellicoe. Everywhere.

"Christ," she said, her voice unsteady and her face pale.

Richard looked from her to the half circle of wall joined to the outer semicircle of shuttered windows. A light switch was set into the wall just behind her, and he reached back and flipped it on.

Recessed lights illuminated the artifacts and softly lit the orderly framed photos, newspaper articles, website grabs, and magazine pages. He moved closer, still stunned first at seeing them, and second at seeing so many of them. Some of the magazine captions weren't even in English.

"There have to be a hundred of them," Samantha muttered, still not moving from where she'd stopped just inside the turret room door.

"More than that," he returned shortly, moving along the wall.

It made him feel ill, deep in the pit of his stomach. Gabriel Toombs was apparently quite a fan of Samantha. Some of the newspaper articles were about thefts, in Australia, Morocco, Vancouver, Tokyo, Paris, Munich . . .

"Are these all jobs you've pulled?" he asked.

"What?"

"These articles. Are they your work?"

"*That's* what caught your attention? What about the photo of us eating ice cream from last week? Or the one of me jogging? Or—"

"Are these just robberies," he interrupted sharply, "or are they *your* robberies? Because I'd like to know if he knows for certain who you are, and how long he's known and has been tracking your career."

Her green eyes widened. "God," she whispered. "He *knows*. He knew about me when we had lunch at the Sailfish Club, and when he gave me a tour of this house." Visibly shaking, she joined him by the wall.

He wanted to hold her, but they needed answers. And they needed them now. "Take a look."

Inhaling deeply, she studied the glass-framed articles. "They're not all mine," she finally said, "but more than half of them are."

"He's a good guesser, then." Keeping his emotions shoved out of the way, Richard tore his gaze from the candid photos to look at the items on the pedestals. An old, delicate-looking tea set, a stunning, intricate fan, a silver-decorated bridle . . . "What about these?" he asked, still trying bloody hard to keep his focus. Both of them falling apart would only serve Toombs. "Are these your work?"

Samantha cleared her throat. "Yes. All four of them are. When I took them, I didn't know they were for Toombs, except for the war br—"

"The war bridle," he finished, going back to the wall with the framed candid photographs. He was in some of them, at the periphery, cut off, clearly not the focus of the photographer.

"I don't get it, Rick," she said shakily. "The armor and the swords aren't here. But this . . . this is crazy."

He'd forgotten that they'd come for the Yoritomo items. As soon as he'd seen this, everything else had ceased to matter. "Some of these articles are nearly a decade old," he said quietly, trying to put the pieces together while his surprise began to spin into something else. "The photos are all since we met. The past year only."

"He could have suspected or realized something, some mistake I made, and backtracked me from there. Old papers aren't hard to get."

"The police haven't been able to track you backward or forward."

"The cops need proof. Some of these grabs aren't mine, so he doesn't know everything." She made a slow circle. "Nearly everything, sure. He knows I like peppermint ice cream."

Richard took a slow breath and held it. "The pictures are all from here in Palm Beach. He hasn't followed us around the world, the smug bastard."

"Rick?"

There were times when he was with Samantha that he didn't know how to describe his feelings. He just didn't have the words. Today, though, seeing this, he knew exactly what to call the emotion searing into his muscles and his bones. Rage. Simple, pure, red-tinted rage.

Toombs had violated her—her privacy, her past, her freedom that she held dearer than anything else. And Toombs had smiled and invited her into his home. They thought he'd stolen something, and he had. Just not what they'd expected.

"Rick?"

Samantha touched his arm, and he jumped. "When's he supposed to get back here?" he forced out, his jaw clenched so hard it ached.

"We came for the armor, and it's not here. Let's go."

"I'm not going anywhere." *Except down to the Jaguar to get the Glock out of the glove box.* However proficient Toombs claimed to be with a samurai sword, a bullet between the eyes was even more efficient.

"Rick, we have to go."

"No. I'm sorry, but this trumps your lost armor. I will not—"

"I want to leave," she said more loudly, her voice catching.

He blinked. "Sam—"

"I am freaked out, and I want to leave. Now."

It went against every baser instinct he had, but Richard nodded. "I'm taking all of this with me."

"You can't."

"Why the fuck not? I don't want him setting eyes on you ever again. Even in photos."

"He'll know I was here. If he doesn't have the armor, then the Picaults do. I won't tip them off."

"This is not about—"

"It's about what I say it is, dammit."

The vacuum cleaner down the hall shut off. Immediately Samantha went back to the door and shut off the lights.

"It's not just the armor," she said in a lower voice. "We can't get caught here."

At the tense worry on her face, he realized she was correct—they needed to go, and without leaving any sign that they'd ever been there. If the maid called the police, if the police came into this room looking for an intruder, they would see all of this. And proof or not, the police would connect the articles with the pictures, and they would start hounding her like never before. Hounding them. If the police actually found the two of them in the room . . .

"Okay." Richard took her hand, and she clenched his fingers hard. "Let's get out of here. I'll follow your lead."

Her expression calmed as she released his hand and leaned her ear against the door. Good. This was what she knew, what she was better at than anyone else he'd ever heard of. They both needed to calm down—at least until they were out of this bloody house.

The vacuum started again, closer. "She's in the other turret room," Samantha whispered. "When I say, you head down the hallway and stay to the far side. That'll make it harder for her to see you."

"And you?"

"This is dead-bolted. I'll have to lock it again from the outside. Wait for me at the top of the stairs, under cover."

"Sam—"

She slowly pushed down the latch, then pulled the door open an inch. Peering through the narrow opening, she reached back with her free hand to touch his chest. "Ready?" she breathed. "Go."

Smoothly she stepped back and opened the door at the same time. Richard slipped through as quickly and quietly as he could and made for the nearest cover, between two of the glass-encased kimonos. As he looked back, she'd already closed the door again. She was in there with all that . . . shit, all by herself.

And all he could do was wait. And watch.

Because he was looking for it, he saw the door inch open again. She slipped out, closed the door again, and squatted in front of it. She had her lock picks in her teeth, and a small compact-sized mirror strapped to her forearm with what looked like a rubber band.

Adjusting the mirror, she went to work on the lock. He'd wondered how she would keep track of the maid and relock the door at the same time. Christ. No wonder that no one had ever caught her. Except for him that one night, and more than ever he realized that that had been pure luck—good on his part, and bad on hers.

Abruptly she moved, keeping low and aiming directly for him. *Shit.* He was supposed to be waiting by the stairs. "Go," she mouthed, glaring at him, and he went.

Down the stairs, through the old servants' corridor, and out the back door. She pushed him back against the wall while she relocked that door, then led the way to the side wall. With a small, audible breath she hit the wall and scrambled up it like Jackie Chan, while he followed more like a slow, lumbering rhinoceros.

She grabbed his feet to guide him down, then let him go and changed her grip to his hand as they walked around the corner to where they'd left the cars. Her movements were spare and tight, too abrupt to match the ease with which he was accustomed to seeing her move. He unlocked the Jag and pulled open the passenger door, sliding in from that side and tugging her in after him. Samantha sat there, still, for a moment while he leaned across her and closed the door again.

There behind the lightly tinted windows they were fairly well invisible unless someone walked right up to the car and pressed his head against the glass. Samantha continued to grip his hand tightly, and slowly he pulled her against him until he could bring his right arm around her shoulder and hold her.

"People aren't supposed to notice me," she said abruptly.

"He noticed you because of me," he commented, ready to accept all of the responsibility for this one if it would help restore her to her usual spirits.

"No, he didn't." She pulled free of him to slam both of her clenched fists into her thighs. "He might have *seen* me because I'm with you, but he already knew about me."

"What makes you—"

"I stole that fan in Paris nearly three years ago, the tea set three months after that, and the jade lion a year after that. And the bridle—"

"The bridle was a year and a half ago," he finished. "He's known about you for at least the last thirty-six months. But he didn't take a photo of you until after you and I met."

"Not that we saw, anyway. I didn't check his underwear drawer or his fucking night stand." She shuddered. "Why didn't I know about this?"

Her muscles shivered, and he took off her silly Marlins cap and pulled her into a tight, hard embrace. He'd made it his crusade, his most important thing in life, to protect her. Clearly he'd failed. Miserably. As her hands clutched into the back of his shirt she gave a single, gasping sob.

Why hadn't she known that someone had been trailing

her every time they stayed in Palm Beach? The times they were together in public, she'd come to expect that someone would be snapping their picture. That could account for some of the photos. But the rest . . . She'd been stalked, was still being stalked, and hadn't known it.

"You know how to recognize undercover police, FBI, Interpol," he said slowly, speaking into her tousled hair. "They have certain patterns they follow. You can't expect to see something trackable in an insane person."

"Is he crazy?" She lifted her head to look up at him. "Because I've spent a couple of hours in his company on two different occasions, and I thought he was kind of weird, but otherwise pretty together. When he showed up for lunch, Aubrey hadn't told him that I was the female guest who'd be there, but he didn't start foaming at the mouth or anything when he saw me."

"He knows Aubrey works for you."

"Aubrey works for a lot of women."

"I don't know, Samantha, but I mean to find out. And I mean to stop it. If I don't hear the answers I want, I'll burn that house to the ground with him in it."

"Not if I beat you to it."

Slowly she relaxed in his arms, while he worked at shoving his fury into a corner where he could deal with it. Where he could smile and shake Gabriel Toombs's hand tonight at the Malloreys' dinner party and tomorrow at the house of the apparent real crooks. As far as he was concerned the Picaults could steal every piece ever shown at the Met—Toombs had tried to steal a piece of Samantha, and that would never be forgiven, or forgotten. Even without the ring he currently had stuffed in his pocket, no one got between him and Samantha. No one.

* * *

Rick actually got out of the Jag and walked her to the SLK. If she needed another clue that everything had veered out of control, the way he'd decided that she couldn't walk five feet on her own provided it. She pulled out the keys and hit the door unlock.

"Do you need to work on whatever you were doing in Miami?" she asked.

"No. It's taken care of. I think we should go home and confer about this."

Truthfully, she wanted to forget the whole thing, but she knew she'd be having nightmares about seeing her image frozen jogging in Wild Bill Toombs's private, double-locked turret room. She hadn't suspected anything of the kind. As little as she liked to make excuses for herself, Rick had a point—she had no reason to expect that something like this was going on. She could think of one person who might know, though, that she'd worked for Toombs on four different occasions. And he was missing.

"I need to find Stoney," she muttered, clenching the keys in her fist.

"Walter? I know you miss him, but I think we have . . ." His voice trailed off. "You think he knew something," Rick said grimly, in that tight voice he'd been using since they'd entered the turret room.

"I know he knew something. I'm just not sure what. But he'd better have a fucking good explanation for bailing on me if he *did* suspect Toombs of being a freakazoid."

"I'd like to see Walter again myself, then."

"Back off, King Kong. Stoney's mine to pound, not yours."

"That's something else we can debate back at home, then."

"No, it's—"

Her cell phone rang. "Somewhere Over the Rainbow." Frowning and unable to cover another shiver, she opened it. "Aubrey."

"Sorry, my honey flower. He skipped lunch. So I hate to sound like one of those clichéd horror movies, but get out of the house."

"I'm out." She looked at Rick. "Where are you heading now, Aubrey?"

"Home for a nap. I've got a party to attend tonight."

"The Malloreys. Right. Me, too. Would you stop by Solano Dorado on your way? I need to talk to you for a minute."

"I'd be honored."

She hung up. "Okay, let's go."

"Why is Aubrey coming over?" Rick asked, not moving, one hand still holding the SLK door open.

"Because he's better acquainted with Wild Bill than we are, and because he's a pretty observant guy. And because he's going with us to the Picaults tomorrow, and we're pretty sure now that they have my armor and swords. Any other questions?"

"Don't take it out on me," he said more evenly. "And forgive me if I'm feeling a little protective at the moment."

She leaned up and kissed him. "Thanks."

"Mm hm. I'll follow you. And Toombs had better hope he's not driving his black Miata in this direction right now."

Samantha almost told him to calm down and rein it in, but he knew the score. They both did. The only difference was that he seemed to have all of his testosterone-fueled attention on beating Toombs to death, and she still wanted to recover the Yoritomo stuff before she took any other action.

"Just stay close," she said, half to keep him from running suspicious people over, and half because she'd never been so glad to have a partner as when she'd walked into that room.

"I will." He kissed her again and closed the door for her, then went back to the Jaguar.

She took a deep breath and then started the car and headed for home. Despite the ickiness of how she felt seeing that . . . Samantha shrine or whatever it was, it would have been worse if she'd taken Rick's initial advice and not gone in at all. How long would it have continued, the black Miata or whatever car he'd driven previously tailing her while he took his slimy photos?

Her phone rang again—the James Bond theme. "I'm okay," she said, trying to sound irritated and not sure she was succeeding.

"I know you are, but what about me?" he said in his cultured British accent. "That was quite the shock."

"You don't have to go all Monty Python for me," she returned with a half smile. "I'm okay. Really. We do need to go over some strategy, though. You're right about that. I want a plan before I have to look at him again."

"How do you check to see if Walter's tried to contact you?"

"First should be a phone call. If not to my cell, then I'll check the office phone and the house machine. After that, an answer in the paper, but that wouldn't be out until Monday at the earliest." After that, she didn't know, but thankfully he didn't ask.

"He'll contact you," Rick said after a moment.

It sounded comforting on the surface, but she had the distinct feeling that he wanted to let Stoney know just how irritating being blindsided like that was. Her two guys fighting. Great. Except she wasn't too happy with her surrogate father at the moment herself. He had his own agenda, sure, but he'd never left her hanging before.

"Are you going to stay on the phone with me all the way back to the estate?"

"That's the plan."

"No. I need to concentrate on driving. I'm wigging out enough without adding holding your hand to the mix. Save your minutes, Brit."

"Okay. Just wave frantically if you need me."

She glanced in the rearview mirror to see the Jaguar a car length or so behind her. "Will do," she said, and hung up.

None of the photos had been of her on the estate; apparently Peeping Tom was okay only when she was in public. Either that or he didn't think he could beat the estate security. Anyway, she'd never felt more . . . safe than when those gates opened and the SLK and the Jaguar traveled through them and onto the palm-shrouded drive. Rick was absolutely right; Toombs needed to be prevented from ever taking another picture of her. How to go about that without opening herself to blackmail or arrest or something, though, could be a little stickier.

Chapter 21

Saturday, 1:32 p.m.

Samantha stood with her arms folded, looking through the window of the Solano Dorado library down at the chaos on the pool deck. It was way too early to see anything resembling the plans she'd put together for the area, but it didn't look the way it had this morning, either.

"They certainly seem enthusiastic, don't they?" Rick observed, coming up to lean against the window frame beside her.

"What exactly did you say to them when you signed the contract?"

"Only something about how much value I place on people adhering to the schedule they agree on."

"You didn't bare your teeth or anything?"

"Only in a smile."

"Nice."

He was taking the Toombs room of ick better than she expected, at least on the outside, though that was probably for her sake. She knew him well enough to recognize that he'd put on his calm, business face and hadn't taken it off since they'd left that turret room. Whatever he felt, he wasn't going to let anybody, even her, see. Not until he was ready, or he'd done whatever it was he thought he needed to do to correct the situation—which since he'd said would include burning Wild Bill's house down, it just might.

The intercom buzzed, and Rick went to see to it. At his query she heard Reinaldo announcing that Mr. Aubrey Pendleton had arrived. "Do you want to meet him in here?" Rick asked, muting the intercom.

"Here's good."

"Bring him up to the library, if you please."

"Right away, Mr. Rick."

"How well did you say Aubrey knows Toombs?" Rick asked as he returned to her side.

She recognized that tone, too. "I know you want to punch somebody," she said, turning from the view to watch the door, "but keep a lid on it. Aubrey's on our side."

He caught her arm, turning her to face him. "You have no idea what I want to do, Samantha."

The glimpse of pure rage in his eyes before he let her go and went to greet Aubrey startled her. She knew he was angry and that Toombs's actions had messed with his male ego, but oh, boy. Her Sir Galahad was armored up and ready to rumble.

Quickly she pushed past him and took Aubrey's hand. "Thanks for coming," she said, maneuvering him around Rick to the big work table in the middle of the room.

"My pleasure," Aubrey drawled. "Did you find the armor and swords?"

"No. Not exactly."

Rick took the seat opposite him. "How well do you know Toombs?" he asked, his tone clipped.

Aubrey looked from him to Samantha, his tanned brow furrowing. "Is something amiss?"

"I asked you a question."

"Rick, stop it." Samantha sat down beside Aubrey, as much to protect him as to show that they were all friends here, whatever Rick might be thinking. "Has Toombs ever been married?"

"Once, I believe," Aubrey answered, looking from one of them to the other. "I'm beginning to feel rather alarmed."

"What happened to her?"

"They divorced, according to rumor. It was before I met him, so at least twelve years ago. Why?"

"Does he date?"

"On occasion he'll attend an event with some young thing, but I don't think I've ever seen him with the same lady more than once. He talks about women a great deal, and likes pretty, young ones."

"Okay." Samantha glanced at Rick, but he was still bottled up tight. "Has he ever . . . talked about me? Before we all met for lunch at the Sailfish Club, I mean."

Aubrey sat back. "I'd like to know what's going on. I think you know by now that I'll tell you anything that might help, but obviously something serious has happened." He looked directly at Rick. "But I will not be bullied or threatened."

Rick placed his palms flat on the table. The two men started a stare-down, and Samantha rolled her eyes. *Men.* In a way this typical male behavior was actually a little comforting. At least she could predict and understand this.

"Rick went into the house with me," she said, noting both that a couple of months ago she would never have willingly confessed to anything, and that neither man seemed willing to give her credit for her honesty. "We got into the locked room."

"So I assumed," Aubrey said, his attention still obviously on Rick. "You said you didn't find the shogun armor."

"We found a room covered with framed pictures of me. Candid photos, magazine prints, everything." She intentionally left out the theft articles; Aubrey knew some things about her past, but confessing for no reason just wasn't her style.

Pendleton turned from his staring contest to look at her. "I beg your pardon?"

"It was a fucking shrine," Rick finally contributed.

At least he was speaking again. "I'm trying to figure out if it's a crush, or something creepier or scarier," she added on to that.

"Holy Hannah," Aubrey muttered.

"Instead of commiserating," Rick put in again, his voice still hard, "how about some of that assistance you volunteered?"

"That must have been quite a room," Aubrey said quietly. "I recall that Wild Bill knew I had taken at job at your security firm; I don't have your memory so I don't recollect the exact words we exchanged, but he definitely knew we'd begun working together."

"He'd already started taking photos of me by then," Samantha commented, beginning to wish that Rick would leave the room if all he was going to do was threaten and glower. "Did he ask to meet me or anything?"

"He did mention that he might be interested in consulting with you on some security matters. I gave him your business card, but didn't press anything."

"Why not?" Rick asked.

"I socialize with Wild Bill, play golf, attend banquets and parties, and he's one of the few year-round residents here. I have never referred to our relationship as a friendship, though, and I never will. Especially now."

"You told me to be careful around Toombs," Samantha pressed. "Was that just a general warning, or did you mean because of those possible mob connections you mentioned?"

"'Mob connections'?" Rick snapped, coming to attention again. "What the bloody—"

"Rumored connections," she broke in before he could start a tirade. "And Aubrey's the one who told me about it."

"How long has he been . . . pursuing you?" Aubrey asked.

"At least the last three years." She didn't say how she knew that, and thankfully Aubrey didn't ask. The statute of limitations for those four items in Toombs's possession was still valid.

"Three years," he repeated. "You know, about three years ago, Wild Bill left town for about three months. I believe he went to Europe on an extended vacation. I don't know if there's any connection to you or not, but it's the only thing that comes to mind."

It might, but she had the feeling she would have to ask Toombs if she wanted any more answers. At the moment she wasn't sure she was ready for that. "Thanks, Aubrey."

"If I'd known about the contents of that room, Miss Samantha, I would not have kept it from you."

"I know that. I just wanted to know if you had any inside information that maybe might not have seemed like anything at the time."

"Samantha still wants to attend the Mallorey party tonight, and the Picault dinner tomorrow." Rick pushed away from the table and stalked over to the window again.

"Are you sure that's wise? Wild Bill will be at both events."

"I'm not hiding under the bed, guys. I have a job to do. *And*, and, the armor's either with the Picaults or my whole theory falls apart and I fail at this retrieval crap. So I'm going to dinner. To both dinners. You two can do what you want."

It sounded good, anyway. In truth she wanted both of them there with her just so she wouldn't have to talk to Toombs on her own. That was scaredy-cat thinking, though, reserved for people with dull, normal lives. If she'd ever hesitated to do something because she was scared, she probably would have been in jail or dead a long time ago.

"Nonsense, my dear," Aubrey drawled in his best antebellum accent yet. "I, at the least, intend to remain close by until this is resolved."

"I'm not even replying to that, Samantha." Rick kept his back to them, his shoulders straight and rigid.

"In that case, I'm going to sketch the layout of the Picaults' house. Will you two help me with that?"

"I'm not finished discussing Toombs," Rick said succinctly.

"Then you and I can do that later. Aubrey, have you been to visit August and Yvette?"

"Once."

"Rick?"

He shifted a little. "No."

This was her fault. She'd focused her attention on Toombs because of the one known theft he'd commissioned. So now she was left with a short time frame and only her quick top-floor jaunt into the Picaults' house to go by. Walking over to the supply cabinet, she pulled out a pencil and a large sheet of graph paper.

"You actually want to plan another break-in? Right now?"

"That is exactly what I want to do right now." It was better than sitting around and thinking about what Toombs might be doing alone with her pictures in that locked room.

For the next hour she and Aubrey put together a layout of the Picaults' house. There were more holes than she felt comfortable with—under normal circumstances she would have obtained city-approved blueprints and done some surveillance to get detailed information about alarms and locks and the schedule of the occupants.

Under those circumstances, going in with a gimmick rather than by stealth would be easier, but she had no idea how to pull that off in four days. Not without Stoney to help her set it up.

Rick disappeared somewhere twenty minutes in. Fine. This was her gig, her job, her call, and those were her pictures on Toombs's damned wall. When the layout was as good as she and Aubrey could make it, she walked him out to the drive where his '62 El Dorado waited for him. "Thanks again. And I'm sorry Rick tried to pummel you."

"He's protective," Aubrey answered, sliding behind the wheel. "I can't fault him for that."

"I guess in this case I can't, either," she said grudgingly. "I'll see you tonight. And I forgot to ask—who's the lucky gal?"

"Mrs. Agnes Pendaway. Her husband's at Betty Ford, and she hates to attend parties alone."

She leaned down and kissed him on the cheek. "Be careful there, Aubrey. For a minute your accent almost slipped."

He smiled. "You do make me forget myself sometimes, Miss Samantha," he drawled easily, and started the car.

As he set off down the drive, she felt Rick come up beside her before she saw him. "Hey."

"I told you he's not gay," he observed, taking her hand as they returned to the house.

"Yes, he is. He's just not as flamboyant as he lets on."

She wanted to wind down for an hour or so before she had to put on her game face, but she had no intention of relaxing if Rick was still on the warpath. Tentatively she tucked herself against his shoulder, and he shifted to wrap his arm around her waist. Ah. This was good.

"I love you," he said into her hair.

"I love you back. Do you have it under control now?"

"If you do, then I do."

"Mm hm. Why don't I believe you?"

He turned them toward the stairs. "Just because I *want* to beat Toombs into paste doesn't mean I'll do it," he said in a low voice. "Not tonight. Unless he gives me a reason."

"And what would that reason be—blinking?"

"Perhaps."

She wrapped the fingers of her free hand into the front of his shirt. "I have a job to do. Don't screw it up for me because he's a creep. He'll still be a creep tomorrow, and the day after. The only difference will be that I won't have to pretend to like him anymore."

"Except that that's not quite true, is it?" he countered. "The bit of him that makes him dangerous is in his head—what he knows, and thinks he knows."

"So what do you propose, an assassination?"

He didn't answer.

That didn't bode well. She'd seen him nearly shoot a man's ear off for threatening her life, and he'd thrown more than one punch. She'd thrown a few herself, but there was a difference between self-defense and defending someone else. Maybe. Every time she thought about what she would do when she saw Toombs tonight, she just wanted to grab Rick and climb under the bedcovers and listen to his heartbeat.

And she didn't approach trouble that way. She faced it straight on. "I'll tell you what," she said as they reached the master bedroom suite. "You play it cool with him for the next two nights, stick with our plan, and we'll go back in and sanitize his playroom. Then he'll know that we know, and that we have proof that he has stolen items in his house."

"I like punching better."

"Rick—"

"We'll try it that way. No promises."

She probably wouldn't get anything better than that out of him. "I'm not used to being the reasonable one, you know," she said aloud. "You think I don't want to kick him in the face the next time I see him?"

"I'm glad to hear that. I know it shook you up to see that, Samantha. You don't have to pretend otherwise."

He took her arms and drew her up against his chest, then leaned down and kissed her. She slipped her arms around his shoulders, kissing him back, slow and deep. "Thanks," she whispered against his mouth.

"For anything in particular?"

"No. And yes."

* * *

The Mallorey soiree was an annual event, a charity for the homeless with none of the homeless invited. Richard doubted Lewis or Gwyneth Mallorey saw the irony in that, especially since the invitees were the fairly small number of the year-round upper-crust residents of Palm Beach. Less expense for entertaining fewer people, and less competition for media attention.

If Samantha hadn't done the security upgrades for the Malloreys' residence, Casa Palomas, he probably wouldn't have bothered to attend. Not only was he generally out of town at this time of year, but he preferred to choose his charities based on their works rather than the quality of the filet mignon served by their honorary chairpersons.

He felt especially conflicted tonight; on the one hand, he would rather have kept Samantha at home where no sick wankers could take photos of her for their own private use. And on the other hand, he wanted to look Gabriel Toombs squarely in the eyes before he throttled the bastard.

The stretched Mercedes stopped at the curb, and Ben climbed out to come around and open the door for them. Beyond the wall of paparazzi lining the sidewalk the windows of the three-story Casa Palomas were all thrown open, lights and music spewing forth into the deepening twilight. "Ready?" he asked, offering his hand to Samantha.

She'd chosen to wear deep purple and black tonight, offset by the diamond triad necklace and matching earrings he'd given to her three months earlier in England. And she looked stunning, every inch a member of the world's upper crust—hair upswept and held in place by gold pins, her chin high, her green eyes glinting. If she felt any trepidation about coming face-to-face with Toombs, she didn't show it.

"Ready," she said, and wrapped her fingers around his.

Cameras flashed as he helped her out of the car. Usually he barely noticed them; he'd long ago become used to being photographed at every public event he attended. This evening, though, he felt hyper-aware of every click, every jostling movement in the crowd.

Samantha tilted her head toward him, and the flashes increased in intensity. "You're going to break my hand," she murmured.

Immediately he loosened his grip a little. "Apologies," he returned in the same low tone.

"You were the one who used to tease *me* about being skittish in front of the press." To his surprise she flashed her quicksilver grin. The paparazzi started a supernova.

"That was before I realized that some people might use the photos in their private collections."

"I bet your pictures are in some bedrooms, Bond."

"Do not tell me that." He ignored the Bond bit for once; she called him that every time he wore a tuxedo. Tonight he had a little more in common with James Bond than she probably realized, since he carried a Glock .44 in his inside pocket.

Upscale events like this generally didn't use metal detectors; the sheer volume of gold and silver and platinum being worn by the guests made it both rude and impractical. The security guards on either side of the drive and the wide doorway were most likely there to keep the press at bay.

"Rick, welcome," Gwyneth Mallorey said, greeting him with a warm smile, her neck, ears, and wrists so encrusted with glittering gems that he wondered how she could stay on her feet. If she'd wanted to, Samantha could have her stripped bare in about five seconds, and it would be another two minutes before Mrs. Mallorey even realized it.

"Gwyneth, Lewis," he returned aloud, shifting to shake

hands with her scarecrow of a husband. "Thank you for inviting us."

"My pleasure," Gwyneth gushed, her smile widening further. "While you're here, Sam will have to give you a tour of the security equipment she installed."

Samantha stirred, and Richard tightened his grip. Sometimes it would be nice to be surprised by people. He put on his business-friendly smile. "I do love to see her work," he said. "And when we're finished, perhaps you or your husband could help me with my refrigerator thermostat question."

"Oh. Of course." Gwyneth's smile became all teeth. "For now, why don't you join our other guests on the terrace? And I hope you brought your checkbook, Rick."

"Ouch," Samantha murmured as they left their host and hostess and headed through the large, open foyer to the back of the house.

"You're the one who suggested that comeback. And I'm just reminding her to be sure of her footing before she swings her bat."

"Baseball bat?"

"Cricket bat, naturally. I'm not a savage."

"Keep that in mind, please."

Outside on the stone terrace and spilling onto the well-manicured lawn, forty or so other guests stood around in small groups, drinking and chatting. Aubrey Pendleton was there already, in the company of a tiny, yellow-haired lady who had a claw firmly dug into his forearm. The walker nodded at them, then angled his chin in the direction of the lit fire pit.

Gabriel Toombs stood on the far side of the fire in the company of Dr. and Mrs. Harkley and the Picaults. He wore all black as he generally did, his dark hair slicked back on his head and his hands folded behind his back. That smug son of a b—

Samantha pulled free of Richard's hand and strode forward, the click of her two-inch black Ferragamo heels sharp on the gray stone as she approached the fire pit. *Bloody hell.* Swiftly he lifted two glasses of wine off a passing server's tray and caught up to her. "Here you are, my dear," he said smoothly, stepping between her and her view of Toombs and handing her one of the glasses.

She blinked, lifting her gaze to meet his. "I changed my mind," she murmured very softly. "I'm going to kick that sick fuck's ass."

Chapter 22

Saturday, 8:28 p.m.

"Not tonight, you're not," Richard said just as quietly, keeping himself between Samantha and Gabriel Toombs. He didn't try to touch her, to steer her away, because that might just set off the explosion he was trying to avoid. "No ass kicking."

"Why the hell not?"

"Because you have something more important to do, and he'll keep for a couple of days. Hurting him now will get you on the front page of the *Post*, but it won't find you that armor." He refrained from rehashing the finer points of the argument; she knew them already.

"I thought I'd be sick, seeing him," she whispered, slowly taking a sip of the wine. "Instead I just want to—"

"I know what you want to do, Samantha. And I'm afraid you'll have to get in line. They might have been your photos, but they were pictures of the woman I love."

She closed her eyes for a heartbeat, her shoulders lifting and falling with the deep breath she took. "You're right. This is a gig; I can pull this off for a gig."

Under normal circumstances that would have bothered him, but tonight he only nodded. "Good."

He moved out of the way, tapping his glass against hers. "Now you can worry about holding me back."

She did tend to attack her problems head on, and she'd been remarkably restrained up until now. When he considered it, in fact, her trepidation about seeing Toombs was more out of character than her charge across the terrace. And he'd nearly missed it, because he was consumed with his own vengeful imaginings.

August Picault waved them over. Apparently Richard was going to have to restrain himself. And if he didn't, he was fairly certain he'd have backup for the fight.

"Good evening, Rick, Samantha," August said with a smile.

"Good evening," Richard returned, and faced Toombs. "Samantha tells me that your collection is magnificent," he said so smoothly that he nearly startled himself. "I wish I'd been able to see it."

Toombs inclined his head, his black eyes shifting to Samantha. "I'm leaving for New York to see to some business in a few days, but when I return I'd be honored to have both of you over for a tour and for dinner."

"That's very kind of you, Wild Bill," Samantha said, smiling.

"It would be my pleasure."

"In the meantime," Yvette Picault said, wrapping an arm around Samantha's free one, "you will come to see our home tomorrow, yes? We have some very lovely pieces, if I say so myself."

"I'm looking forward to seeing everything," Samantha agreed, all charm. "What time do you want us there?"

"We always go for a bike ride along the beach at sunset on nice Sunday evenings," Yvette answered. "Is eight o'clock acceptable? I know we eat later than most Americans, but it is the tradition in France."

"That sounds wonderful to me. Rick? Wild Bill?"

Richard and Toombs both agreed, and they all seemed to assume that Aubrey Pendleton would be amenable to anything. Since the plan Samantha had discussed in the Solano Dorado library earlier had involved taping down sensors and window locks during the dinner and breaking in shortly after they supposedly left for the night, they would be in for a long evening. He might have an early meeting on Monday, but Samantha was half nocturnal. At least she hadn't argued with him about accompanying her on yet another B and E. Pendleton had seemed fairly adamant about joining in, as well.

One of the servers came out to the terrace to bang on an absurdly dainty-looking gong, and all of the guests trooped into the house to take seats at the multitude of round tables in the formal dining room. As he'd expected, the dinner was filet mignon, followed by speeches from Gwyneth Mallorey about how gracious she was, and from the director of the homeless project who actually ran the program.

"How much are you going to give?" Samantha asked, leaning against his arm as he wrote out the check.

"I figured five thousand would get us out of here without any dirty looks," he returned in a low voice, most of his attention still on Toombs halfway across the room. He wished the bastard would make some kind of move, pull out a camera and aim it at Samantha. Then the gloves would come off.

"We're leaving *after* dessert, right?"

He snorted. "You amaze me," he whispered, lifting her hand to kiss her fingers.

"Hey, it's strawberry cheesecake with chocolate drizzles. The—" The small purse Samantha had over the back of her chair hummed, making her seat vibrate. "Excuse me," she said to the other guests at the table, and lifted it free, standing and moving to the side of the room as she flipped it open. She didn't recognize the number. "*Hola*," she said in a low voice.

"Honey pie. How the hell are you?"

Her heart clenched and then began hammering. "Stoney? Where the f—where have you been?" she hissed, taking a self-conscious look around and moving farther from the tables.

"Oh, here and there. The—"

"Are you drunk?"

"You betcha."

"Where?"

"Felipe's on Third."

"You stay right there. Do you hear me?"

"I can't pay my tab," he said in a loud, slurred whisper. "I have to stay. Why do you think I called?"

"Do not move, Stoney. Promise me."

"I promise."

She hung up and returned to the table. "I have to go," she whispered in Rick's ear, slinging her purse over her shoulder.

He grabbed her wrist. "What is it?"

Dammit, she wanted to go. Now. Taking a breath, she leaned closer again. "Stoney," she murmured.

Rick took his napkin from his lap and set it on the table. "Excuse us," he said, much as she had. "Don, will you see that this check gets to Gwyneth?"

The lawyer-looking guy on his left nodded. "Of course. I hope nothing's wrong?"

"No. A bit of a time zone complication," he said with his trademark smile. "Good evening."

"Good night, Rick, Samantha."

As they left the room, Samantha couldn't help a surreptitious glance past his shoulder. Toombs sat with his back half to them, but she wouldn't have bet a nickel that he didn't know she'd left. If they spied a black Miata on the way to Felipe's Bar, it was getting run off the road.

Rick took out his phone and dialed Ben as they left the house. A minute later the stretched Mercedes pulled up to the center of the drive. "Ben, please take us to Felipe's Bar on Third Street," she said, sitting back despite the wish to climb into the front seat and take the wheel herself.

"That's not a very nice part of town, Miss Sam," the driver said over his shoulder as he pulled onto the street.

"I know."

She dug into her purse. Small as it was, after she'd dumped in some paper clips, a pair of wire cutters, and her lipstick and phone, there hadn't been room for much else. She pulled out two twenty-dollar bills. "Do you have cash?" she asked Rick.

"A couple hundred," he returned, his eyes studying her face.

"Stoney's drunk, and he said that he called because he couldn't pay his bar tab. He doesn't drink very often, but when he does—I'm not sure my forty will cover it."

"No worries," he said, at least reading her well enough to not start in about Stoney being a bad influence on her. Stoney was family. Period.

She fidgeted in her seat. Nerves of steel during a robbery were one thing; seeing her surrogate father after he'd been missing for a week was evidently enough to make her all squishy inside. Even when she was ready to be furious at him.

"Did he say where he'd been?" Rick asked, looking far calmer than she probably did.

"I didn't ask."

"You—"

"Oh, don't worry; I will. I just want to make sure he's somewhere he can't vanish when I do."

"That sounds familiar," he muttered under his breath.

She heard it, anyway. And she really couldn't dispute it. "I get it," she said stiffly. "The walking a mile in your moccasins. But at least my leaving had a logical reason behind it."

"I'm not going to argue with you right now. I'm more interested in Walter's very bad timing for making himself scarce."

"So am I, but I'm hoping it was just a coincidence."

"I am as well, believe it or not."

Twenty minutes later Ben stopped the Mercedes half a block from Felipe's. A scattering of Harleys and some very shiny muscle cars lined the street right in front of the bar, and Rick moved closer to her as they walked. As for her, this was like home. She'd grown up in seedy bars where Martin could charm information about prime robberies out of his fellow low lifes. She'd learned to blend in anywhere, but sometimes places like this were the easiest for her.

"Follow my lead, okay?" she asked, stopping just outside the open door. It was loud and warm and stinky inside, almost like a physical presence.

"To a point."

Squaring her shoulders, she strolled into Felipe's.

Somebody whistled. "Look what just came in!"

"High society has arrived. Get out the champagne, Felipe!"

All eyes seemed to be aimed at her and Rick—okay, at her, since the vast majority of the bar's inhabitants were men. She flashed a calm smile. "Get me a beer, will you, honey?" she asked, sliding a finger along Rick's lapel.

Clearly he didn't want to leave her side, but with a swift, stifled glare he headed for the bar. At nearly eleven o'clock some of these guys had been drinking for five or six hours, though a number of them had just gotten started. Given a choice, she preferred the less-sauced, more reasonable ones, but neither would have been even better. At a bar, though, nice sober gentlemen would be hard to come by—except for the guy at the bar buying her a beer.

"Here, honey!"

She turned, facing the far corner of the place closest to the emergency exit. Lit by the blinky glare of an old jukebox, Walter Barstone sat at one of the peanut shell–covered tables and waved a bottle of beer in her direction. Even after hearing his voice on the phone, seeing him there and knowing—*knowing*—he was alive sent a rush of relief all the way down to her toes.

"Hey, over here!" one of the bikers echoed.

"No, me! I got somethin' for you, darlin'!"

She ignored it all, moving around the tables until her forward progress was blocked by a very large slab of a man. Big guys and biker dives. It was like Oreo cookies and cream filling, except a lot louder and less pleasant. "Hi," she said, looking up and up at him.

His grizzled red beard split in a smile. "Hi yourself. You lost and lookin' for some Southern comfort?"

"No," she returned, settling her weight onto her left foot. "Are you lookin' to become a soprano, tiny?"

"Ooh, a smart-mouth bitch. Why don't you give me a kiss with that smart mouth, bitch?"

Samantha puckered her lips, then sent the spiked two-inch heel of her right shoe as hard as she could into his crotch. As he went down with a wumph of escaping wind she smacked her lips together in an air kiss. "Sorry," she said as she stepped around him. "I don't play well with others."

Nobody else got in her way. She reached Stoney's table, stopping herself from giving her former fence a hug. Instead she sat down on his left while he gazed from her to the moaning Gigantor. "Nice kick."

"Thanks. Where the fuck have you been?"

Rick set a beer bottle down in front of her and sat opposite, on Stoney's right. "Perhaps we should have this discussion elsewhere," he suggested.

"Nah. Sam took down the biggest guy in the bar. No one'll give us trouble, now."

"Is that from the bar fight handbook?" he asked skeptically.

"Why'd you bring the English muffin here, baby?" Stony drained his bottle and went for hers, which she slid out of his reach. "I knew you would," he went on before she could answer. "He's in everything now."

"You didn't take off because of Rick," Samantha countered. "So what's going on? Were you working a deal? Did it go south?"

"A deal." Stoney gave a guttural, too loud laugh. "There have to be people willing to hire you if you want to work a deal."

"So this is because you're losing touch with the scum of the earth? Give me a break."

"No, Sam, *we're* the scum of the earth. You just figured out how to pretend you're not for a little while."

"That's enough of that," Rick put in. "Let's get him back to the car."

"It's okay. He's always been a depressed, bad-tempered drunk. No matter how well things were going."

"Well, things aren't going well now, are they?"

"I don't know. You tell me, Stoney."

He slapped the flat of his beefy hand on the table. "Ya know, you try to get along with people, set up the jobs they ask you to for the money they give you, and everybody's a professional. Then"—and he jabbed a finger at Samantha—"then you realize that the job they hired you for isn't what you thought it was, and you've been had. And your people have been had."

Abruptly alarmed, Samantha leaned closer. "Are the cops looking for you?" she whispered, unable to keep from glancing over at Rick's serious, annoyed expression. "Are they after us?"

"Oh, pshaw," Stoney grunted, nearly flattening her with his breath. "Can't a guy even have a drink and consider his future in peace?"

"I think there's a lot of stuff going on in your brain right now, Stoney," she answered. "And I think you're not going to be able to tell me what the hell it is until you sober up. So let's get out of here."

"You can't make me."

Great. "Do you want me to pay your tab?"

He giggled. "I don't have any more moola on me," he whispered loudly.

"Then let's go before you wipe me out, too."

He pushed to his feet, none of his usual Hulk-Hogan-meets-Diana-Ross grace in the motion. She grabbed him under one arm and started him toward the door, Rick on his other side. Gigantor had gotten off the floor to sit in a chair with his knees tucked up to his chin. She knew she liked those shoes of hers for a reason.

"Hey, he's not leaving until somebody pays his tab," the Cuban-looking guy behind the bar, Felipe, she assumed, called out.

"I'll take care of it." Rick helped shift most of Stoney's clumsy bulk onto her shoulder, then headed for the bar again.

"Fuck," Stoney grumbled. "Now I'll owe the muffin."

"Pay him back tomorrow. Just stay on your feet until we get outside."

"Why can't I be a fence anymore?" he asked abruptly. "I don't want to do security. It sucks."

"You're preaching to the choir, pal."

They made it outside to the accompaniment of some whistles and a couple of catcalls, but no physical blockage. And hopefully nothing to send Rick charging after anyone. At least these guys were honest instead of going home and whacking off to her picture.

Ben and Rick reached them at about the same time, and together the three of them managed to stuff Stoney's rather large bulk into the back of the Mercedes. She and Rick climbed in behind him, and they headed for Solano Dorado.

"This is not the way to my house," Stoney announced.

"Tonight it is," she returned. "You're not leaving my sight until I know what's going on."

"What's going on is that I have to be good because you want to be good, and I'm old enough to be your damn daddy. Who made you the boss?"

"You—"

Rick put a hand on her arm. "You love her, Walter. That's why you chose to retire."

"You stay out of it, muffin," the fence rumbled. "English muffin."

Rick took a deep breath. "Perhaps you should tell him what we discovered about Gabriel Toombs."

"Not while he's like this," she answered. She didn't want to talk about it again at all, but as Rick had said, Stoney was family, and he had her back—usually—when no one else did. Except for the past week.

"Gabriel Toombs is a sneak," Stoney muttered.

"You're telling me." Okay, maybe this would be a good time to talk about Toombs, if Stoney wasn't playing it as close to the vest as he generally did. "How many times did I work for him?"

"Four times."

"Four?" she repeated, even though she knew the answer already. "Why did I only know about one?"

"Because I didn't tell you about the other three. He liked your style, he said, and offered extra if I agreed to have you, specifically, pull the other jobs for him." He snorted unpleasantly. "And I took it, because I'm scum."

"He knew my name?"

"Nah. I wouldn't tell him that. Toombs said you were

worthy, like you were the next King Arthur or Queen Guinevere or something. The freak. But hey, ten grand extra is ten grand extra."

He'd sold her out cheap. "Did it occur to you that he might be setting me up with the cops or Interpol or something?"

"No way. I told him that if either of us got double-crossed on these jobs I would send the cops the recording I'd made of our conversations."

"Why do you think he wanted my services specifically?" she asked, having to stifle her gag reflex to say the words.

"He thinks he's a shogun or something," Stoney slurred, digging under the seat until he found the cooler and pulled out a bottled water. "You're like his personal samurai or ronin or something."

"A ronin doesn't have a master."

"You know what I mean, Sam."

"Has he gotten hold of you since we started Jellicoe Security?"

Stoney didn't answer. Instead he sat back and crossed his arms, glaring out the window. To Samantha that was a big fat yes, but she wanted to hear the details. Considering what they'd found in Toombs's turret room, it could be important.

"It's an important question, Walter," Rick said, echoing her thoughts.

"Maybe you should butt out of Sam's and my business." Stoney sent a glare over his shoulder, then faced the window again. "You think you're such a hot shot, but you're the one who wrecked everything. I bet you don't have any idea what kind of income Sam gave up to stay with you. Millions. And that's all I'm saying. Millions."

"Thanks, Stoney." Samantha frowned at his profile. "Any

other shit you want to gab about? My bank account number? Where you keep your job files?"

"Fine," he grunted. "Eight months ago Toombs called me, and he says he's got it figured out, that you're the cat who pulled the other jobs for him."

"And what did you say?" Rick asked, his voice dipping into the deep monotone he only used when he was really mad or really worried.

"I said he was crazy! What do you think I said?"

"I think Rick means how did you explain your working with me in the security biz," Samantha said more gently.

Diplomatic and restrained as Rick was being—especially when she knew how explosive he could be—she was beginning to wish that she and Stoney had been able to have this conversation in private. They had their own shorthand, things they knew about each other and their world with its skewed code that Rick still had to ask.

"I said I helped raise you when Martin was working, and that I promised Martin I'd take care of you if anything ever happened to him."

She kissed his dark cheek. "And you didn't even have to lie."

He thumped his chest. "That's because I know what I'm doing."

"So he let it drop, then?" she prompted, before Rick could ruffle Stoney's feathers again. "His theory about me?"

"Well, first he tried to commission your services to steal something from a neighbor of his, but I told him again that you weren't a thief, and that I was retired."

"What did he want me to steal?"

"I don't know. Something for his collection."

"That narrows it down," Samantha said, sitting back again.

"Hm. Something Japanese and from someone close by," Rick mused. "Wouldn't it be interesting if—"

"No," she interrupted. "Because that would mean that he's known all along about the Picaults' theft, and it's too weird if he wanted to hire me to steal exactly what I'm planning to steal tomorrow."

"And nothing else in our lives has been strange and coincidental."

She sent him a brief smile. Yep. Life was strange and coincidental. With babysitting Stoney tonight she would miss her second chance at wrangling Clark the Anatomy Man, which meant she had to get it done tomorrow or explain why she hadn't to a ten-year-old.

At least she had all of her family back together and safe for the moment. Until tomorrow, anyway, when it would start all over again.

Chapter 23

Sunday, 10:48 a.m.

Richard rose from his computer and headed toward the back of the house. Somehow in his determination to convince Samantha to do something about the garden, he hadn't anticipated how loud the results would be.

"Christ," he muttered, as he walked into the library. Yes, the house was nearly a hundred years old in places, but the walls and windows should have somewhat cushioned the sound.

"How do you think I feel?" Walter Barstone muttered from in front of the window. He clutched a cup of coffee in his hands, his chocolate-colored skin tinged with gray.

"Walter. I didn't know you were still here."

"Sam wants to talk to me. Which I assume means yell at me." He took a sip of coffee. "And I can't remember where I left my truck."

"Somewhere down by Felipe's, I would guess." Rick made his way over to stand at a neighboring window. Where his pristine blue-bottomed pool had been, a brown morass of mud and half-removed concrete lay obscured by a tractor and a backhoe and some other construction lorry he couldn't recall the name of. "Shall I send my driver to look for it?"

"No. I'll take a cab down there once I get paroled from here."

"Samantha said you were a gloomy Gus when you drank. That extends to the hangover, I see."

Walter eyed him. "You're lovin' this, aren't you?"

"Excessively. And you owe me eighty-five dollars."

"Eighty-five bucks? I didn't drink that much."

"No, you drank fifty dollars' worth. The rest was a tip and to convince Felipe not to contact *Entertainment Tonight* to tell them that Samantha and I visited his establishment."

"Felipe sold out cheap."

"He also thought I was someone named Brad Hillier, apparently the star of a soap opera."

Walter snorted, then pressed his free hand against his temple. "So it sucks to be famous, but it sucks even more when they don't recognize you."

"It's quite the quandary." Richard waited for a moment until the noise from the thing breaking his concrete in the remaining corner of his pool subsided. "Did Samantha tell you why we were questioning you about Toombs?"

"Because you figure him for the armor heist."

"Because we went into his house yesterday morning and found a locked room plastered with articles and photographs of Samantha."

The cup dropped out of the fence's hands. "*What?*"

"Yes. Apparently Mr. Toombs has been stalking her for most of the past year, and following what he presumes to be her career for approximately the last three years. The four items you arranged for her to steal for him are on granite pedestals in the middle of the room."

"That sick fuck," Walter whispered, his already ill-looking countenance turning chalkier. "That son of a bitch."

"My thoughts precisely."

Barstone faced him. "You seem pretty cool about it, actually, Addison," he said, his voice shaking.

"Yes, well, I've had nearly a day to dwell on what I intend to do to Wild Bill Toombs." He kept his own tone crisp, but he couldn't help the growl as he said Toombs's name. Dwelling, imagining, anticipating, whatever he chose to call it, when he finished with Gabriel Toombs the bastard would not look at another female, much less Samantha, ever again with anything more than a sad regret. At least he surmised that the removal of Toombs's genitalia would have that effect.

"I'll kill him," Walter was muttering, his sightless gaze on the deconstructed pool area.

"Not if I get to him first." Rick walked over to the work table and buzzed the intercom for Reinaldo. "We've had a slight coffee spill in the library," he informed the head housekeeper. "And could you bring a fresh cup for Mr. Barstone?"

"Mr. Stoney? Right away, sir."

"Sorry about that," the ex-fence returned.

"No worries."

"Where's Sam, anyway?" Walter asked.

"In the shower."

Taking a breath, Rick rejoined him at the window. He needed to take this step sometime. Now, when they were partially on the same side, would probably be the best moment he would find. "I'm a traditional fellow," he began.

"Are we still talking about Toombs?" Walter asked.

"No."

"Then save it until my head stops trying to explode. We can fight then."

"Traditionally, I would approach a lady's father for this."

Barstone turned around to face him full on. "Huh?"

"Under the circumstances—under any circumstances, actually," Richard continued, ignoring the protests and the suspicion and surprise, "I know she considers you to be more of a father than Martin is. I do, as well."

"What are you talking about?"

"I'm asking for your blessing, because I intend to ask Samantha to marry me."

Walter sat down rather hard on the deep window sill. "Holy cow."

That was better than *no fucking way*, Richard supposed, though an immediate agreement and a warm handshake would have been ideal.

"Does she know?"

"She knows I want to marry her, yes." Did she know that he still intended to propose? That was a horse of a different color.

"What if I say no fucking way?"

Ah, there it was. "I didn't ask for your permission," Richard said more evenly than he felt. "I asked for your blessing."

"So why bother to ask me, if my answer doesn't matter?"

"It matters."

"What matters?" Samantha said, strolling into the room with two cups of coffee and a Diet Coke on a tray in her arms.

"I asked Reinaldo—"

"I snagged the refreshments from him, and sent him off for some of Hans's fresh-baked brownies."

"I thought you preferred the brownies from New York," Rick murmured, taking the tray from her and kissing her at the same time.

"We don't talk about that where Hans might overhear," she whispered back, removing a coffee from the tray and handing it to Walter. "And both kinds are very fine, anyway."

"You're in a good mood," Walter observed, looking from Richard to Samantha.

"Why shouldn't I be? My guys are both here and safe, and *I* don't have a hangover."

"Very funny, smarty pants." Barstone kept his gaze on her as she took the soda off the tray and popped the tab. "Rick told me about Toombs's house."

"Yeah? Great. I wanted to tell you, to make sure you know that I don't think you or I did anything wrong. We've had clients request my specific services before."

"Maybe, but I should have told you when he showed up at the office and wanted to hire you for a break-in."

"Yes, you should have," she agreed. "Why didn't you?"

"You were in Paris with the English muffin, and I thought

I'd handled it. If I'd had any idea that he was taking photos of you, honey, I would have—"

"I know."

"What did you do with the pictures?"

Samantha frowned. "We left them there. I'm looking for stolen armor, and I didn't want Toombs talking about how his house was broken into. And I didn't want him to call the cops and have them take a look at my photos and those articles on thefts sitting all nice and cozy next to each other"

"What if you'd still been a thief? What would you have done then?"

For a long minute she looked at her former fence. "If I was still in the game and I didn't have a reason to keep my B and E a secret from him, I would have burned his house down, starting with that room."

The calm certainty with which she said it startled Richard, even though he'd said the same thing himself yesterday. She'd put on a white hat, as she liked to say, but he doubted that dark, dangerous side of her, the one that knew she needed to look over her shoulder or she'd get jumped from behind, would ever go away. Like last night when the behemoth biker had confronted her, and he'd been ready to rush to her rescue. Instead she'd dropped the fellow before he could take more than a single step.

"That's my girl," Walter said with a grim nod.

Bloody wonderful. Good old Walter was back to remind her how much easier things had been during the good old days. "Samantha," Richard said aloud, "Walter and I were just in the middle of discussing something. Will you give us another moment?"

"Sure. But don't go anywhere, Stoney. I need to talk to you, too."

"Lucky me," the fence grumbled.

Once Samantha left the room again, Richard went over and quietly closed the door behind her. "I wish you wouldn't do that," he said.

"Do what? Drink your gourmet coffee?"

"Encourage her to do things like burn people's houses down. There are other ways of . . . seeing to things that don't lead to arrest for arson." For the moment he ignored the fact that he wanted to castrate Gabriel Toombs. He hadn't said that out loud, at least.

"I told you before. I support Sam in whatever she wants to do. Unlike you."

"Yes, well, that's because I want her to have a long, happy, free life of the not-in-prison variety."

"With you."

"With me."

"Why not just leave things like they are, then? I'll admit, she's been pretty happy since she met you." Barstone took a sip of his coffee. "Except for the time she got shot and that time she got arrested. Gosh, that all happened after she moved in with you."

"And the git following her career and pasting it on his wall started before she met me. And the files with Interpol and the FBI just waiting for a photograph or a fingerprint to go with all the evidence they've been compiling since her career began. I had nothing to do with that. Are we really going to compare lives, Walter?"

"Marrying her won't turn her into Lady Addison."

"Lady Rawley, actually. And I think that's between Samantha and me. I just wanted you to know."

"I thought you wanted my blessing."

"That, too, but I can live without—"

"Okay."

Richard closed his mouth again. "Okay?" he repeated, lifting an eyebrow.

"Okay. I give you my blessing." Walter twirled his hand in the air, a very poor imitation of a royal salaam.

Deeply surprised, Richard took a drink of coffee to give himself a moment to mentally reposition himself. "Why the abrupt turnaround?"

Barstone lifted a thick eyebrow. "I gave you a thumbs up. Do you really want to know why?"

"Yes. I do."

"Fine. She started talking about retiring a couple of months before she met you. But pulling another job or two was still more interesting for her than anything legit she was doing. She could get away with that for another couple of years, but ultimately she'd end up like Martin. I think you're the only thing she'll stay retired for." He hesitated. "And you love her more than anybody else who's ever been in her life. Except me, of course."

Given some of the fence's actions, Richard could dispute that, but he didn't say so aloud. "Thank you, then."

"Yeah. I don't think she'll be as easy to convince as I was." Barstone walked to the door. "Now if you'll excuse me, I have to go get chewed out and then get a cab and go find my car."

Richard waited until he was alone in the library before he took a seat at the work table. Down below the Piskford workers continued demolishing his pool, the sound of breaking concrete and the broken chunks being loaded into the rotating dump trucks reverberating through the house. And to think, talking to Walter had probably been the easiest thing he would encounter today.

Even so, he gave a slight smile. He'd convinced Tom and

Walter—mostly—and now he had only one person left to go. The most important one.

Samantha lounged against the railing at the top of the stairs and drank her soda. Whatever Rick and Stoney were talking about, and she presumed it was her, at least they weren't yelling. She considered listening at the door, partly out of curiosity, but mostly because with her life as it was, secrets flying around her could be dangerous.

Just as she straightened, though, Stoney emerged from the library and shut the door behind him. "You okay?"she asked.

"I feel like he's the principal who just gave me detention, and you're the kid I was out spray-painting the walls with. Yes, I'm fine."

"Did you remember where your truck is?"

"In general."

"Let's go get it."

"I'm not going to tell you what he said to me. It's a guy thing."

Dammit. "Well, I don't want him to hear what I say to you."

"Oh, this is a fun day."

Still grumbling, he followed her through the foyer, where she snagged a brownie off the plate Reinaldo carried in the direction of the library. "Which car should we take?" she asked as they walked into the garage.

"You make pretty free with Addison's stuff, don't you?"

She glanced sideways at him as she freed the keys to the Barracuda. "It's my way."

"Oh, I know that."

Whatever he was thinking, he didn't say anything else as she started the car and they headed out the front gates back toward Felipe's. At about the halfway point she pulled into a grocery store parking lot and turned off the engine. "Okay."

"Okay, what?"

"Why did you take off? That's what."

He frowned, his eyebrows almost joining. "I told you last night."

"That shit about Toombs? Or the part where you said you didn't want to do security work anymore?"

Stoney looked out his passenger window for a long moment. "You know I love you, honey. So when you retired from the biz, I retired, too. Fewer split loyalties for you, I guess. But it's been a year."

"You didn't think I would last this long going straight?" she asked, her chest tightening. She knew he'd done it for her, and she knew he hadn't been universally happy about it, but did he resent it? Did he resent her for it?

"Actually, no, I didn't. I thought when you took the job restoring art at the Norton that that was as straight as you could go. And even then every couple of months you'd start asking about the requests I was getting for items, hunting around for something that interested you."

"That's *my* problem," she retorted. "Don't change the subject. You disappeared. And you owe me an explanation."

"Why do I owe you an explanation?"

"Because you're my damn family, Stoney. You don't get to take off without letting me know you're safe."

He took a deep breath and blew it out again. "I needed to think, okay?"

"Think about what?"

"About whether I'm willing to keep hitting up my old contacts for information so you can take down somebody they work with. It kind of shuts the door on my ass, too."

"Oh." She gazed at the steering wheel. "Have they been threatening you?"

"Everybody threatens everybody, Sam. You know that. It's part of the game. But eventually, and probably sooner rather than later, I won't have anybody left who'll talk to me."

"I'll still talk to you."

"Oh, gee, thanks." He gave a brief smile. "This acquisitions retrieval thing you're doing. You really like it."

"So far. Except for seeing the creepy Toombs room."

"Tell me about that, will you?"

"I don't want to talk about it right now. I want to talk about how you're the only person I can say anything to. I missed you this week. You have no idea what's been going on here. I had to take Aubrey with me to scope out Toombs's house."

"I couldn't have gone in there with you legitimately, anyway. Aubrey's a good guy."

"So are you. So don't go around thinking that you're leaving me to face all this crazy shit alone."

"What happens when I run out of contacts? Then I'll just be the incredibly handsome black guy working in your security office."

"And my partner. If you get bored down the line, we'll find something else for you to do. Maybe open an antiques shop. You like that stuff, and you're good at it."

"You're working pretty hard at finding reasons for me to stick around."

"Well, you spent a couple of days figuring out that same thing, didn't you?"

"I did. I went down to Miami, talked with a couple of

people, got some job offers for acquisitions, and tried to figure out what it would be like without you pulling those tricky jobs and earning us the really big bucks."

"Stoney, you—"

"I couldn't imagine it," he interrupted. "I don't like doing security installations, but I'd like working acquisitions without you around even less. And then I got mad at myself, because I figured you're like the butterfly out of the cocoon thing, and I need to let you go to make your life easier."

"You don't make my life harder," she retorted, her voice, and her emotions, a little unsteady. "You keep me from going crazy about all the law abiding."

"I'm glad you said that. Because last night—and this morning—I figured out that you do some things you don't like so you can hang around the English muffin, so I can do some things I don't like so I can hang around you. Of course I was buzzed at least part of the time, so it probably doesn't make any sense."

She leaned over and hugged him. "Thank you,"she said, a tear running down her face.

"No, thank you, honey. Now tell me about the creepy room."

Samantha told him as she started the car again and headed back out onto the street. Jeez, for a minute there she'd thought she was going to lose him to the dark side again. She had Rick as an incentive to stay good, but he wasn't the only reason. Good luck lasted only so long, and she'd had a very long streak of it. Stoney's only incentive for staying legit seemed to be her.

"So he's been tracking your career for the last three years, and stalking you for one year."

"That's what it looks like. I can't even describe what . . . It was the creepiest thing I've ever come across. And I don't even want to think about what he does in there." She shuddered.

"And he just walked into Jellicoe Security and wanted to hire you for a job. He probably would've been waiting in the bushes to take more pictures of you while you did your thing. He could have landed you in prison, Sam."

"Your own hire setting you up is pretty low," she agreed. "It's a good thing I retired."

She felt Stoney looking at her, and kept her gaze on the road. Yes, she still felt sick knowing her candid moments were in a locked room, but she had a break-in tonight where she would be accompanied by two novices. She needed to focus on that. She was actually glad to be able to focus on that.

"Anything else happen while I was gone?" Stoney asked.

Samantha cleared her throat. B and E's were so much easier to talk about than personal stuff. "Rick's been hinting around—or trying not to hint around—at something," she admitted reluctantly. "I think he wants to get married."

"'Get married'?" Stoney repeated. "To you?"

"Donner's already taken," she said dryly. "Yes, to me."

"Huh."

He didn't sound all that surprised, considering that she broke into a cold sweat just saying it out loud. "That's all you have to say? 'Huh'?"

"Does he need a tax write-off or a publicity photo opportunity or something?"

"No."

"Then why'd he ask you?"

"He hasn't asked me. Not yet." She frowned, edging on being annoyed.

"Okay, why *would* he ask you, *if* he asked you?"

Her brow lowered further. "Whose side are you on?"

"Is there a side?"

"What? Step away from that body and bring me the real Stoney."

"The real Stoney's probably got my truck," he muttered.

"That is not helpful."

"What do you want? My advice? Honey, I was married once for about six weeks, thirty years ago. You have to figure this out for yourself. You definitely have some baggage, but if he's doing the asking, then I would have to say that he's probably figured out how this will—would—affect him. So you worry about what's best for you." He shrugged. "Either you're planning on staying, or you're thinking of leaving. I'm with you, whatever you decide on."

"Thanks. I think." Stoney was right, but that didn't make it any easier to figure out. What was better for her? How the hell did she know? She knew what she liked and what made her happy, but chocolate did that, too—and that went straight to her hips.

"That's *if* he even asks you. You're kind of high maintenance."

She snorted. "Look who's talking, Mr. I Have No Money and I Can't Find My Truck."

He abruptly sat forward, pointing. "Ha. My truck's right th—"

Her cell phone rang to *The Partridge Family* theme. Donner's house. She hit talk as she pulled the car over. "Jellicoe here."

"Hi, Aunt Sam."

Oh, crap. How did somebody with a nearly photographic memory forget a six-foot-tall, gender-neutral dummy? She knew she needed to get it today. Or she'd known last night. *Crud*. "Hi, Livia. I'm glad you called. Clark will be back in your classroom tomorrow."

The ten-year-old shrieked happily. "Really? You found it?"

"I did."

"You're the bomb. Who took it?"

Samantha refrained from clearing her throat. "That's confidential, I'm afraid."

"Okay. Thank you so much, Aunt Sam."

"You're welcome."

"I love you. Bye."

"I love you too, sweetie."

As she closed the phone, Stoney was looking at her.

"What?" she asked.

"Livia. Donner's kid?"

"One of them. She hired me. I'm helping her out."

"Boy, you're just going all marshmallow, aren't you?"

"Go get your damn truck."

With a grin, Stoney opened the passenger door. "You're sure you want to go after the armor tonight? I can get you blueprints for the house by the end of the week."

"Viscanti needs the stuff by Wednesday. And if I'm wrong, I'll have a couple of days to figure out where the hell the pieces are."

"What's your feeling about the Picaults?"

"I think they've got the stuff. But then again I thought Toombs had it."

"Well, your odds are getting better." He held out his fist, and she knocked hers against it. "Call me if you need anything."

"I already do. I stuck a list in your pocket earlier." At his glare, she shrugged. "I'm keeping up on practicing my mad skills."

"Mm hm. What do you need?"

"You'll see. Just get it to me this afternoon. And call

Kim," she continued. "Aubrey and I are tired of telling her you had a family emergency."

"Okay, okay."

Samantha watched until he got the truck started and waved at her. Then she turned around to head back to Solano Dorado. Putting a blood-and-guts-covered Anatomy Man in the 'Cuda would be a very bad idea. She needed the incognito car—and maybe a partner who wouldn't mind helping her tote around a lifeless body for a little while. Or Rick, if she couldn't find that other guy.

Chapter 24

Sunday, 3:18 p.m.

"What is the tarp in the back for?" Richard asked. "And the car rags and the five gallons of water?"

Samantha grinned. "Make a left at the light."

"I'm going to find out eventually."

"Yep."

So they were apparently doing two burglaries today. It was definitely a record for him, especially after the break-in yesterday, though he wasn't certain it would be for her. "Will you at least tell me how you found Clark?"

"Trade secret. Pull in over there."

He did as she asked, stopping in front of a locked chain-link fence that surrounded a pair of empty-looking warehouses. How in hell had she found the model here? "No one's in there, are they?" he asked as she hopped out of the SUV.

"Not today."

Closing the Explorer's door, she strode up to the fence like she owned the property. Almost faster than a normal human would be able to use a key, she had the lock open. Then she unwrapped the chain. Shoving the gate open, she motioned him in. Richard followed her to the warehouse on the right, waited again as she pulled up on the rolled door that didn't seem to be locked at all, and drove inside.

An old desk and a battered chair stood in one corner, a phone and a computer monitor and keyboard—but no CPU—on the desk. What looked like a makeshift hospital bed, complete with a coat rack filling in as an IV stand, rested in the opposite corner. "What the bloody hell is this?" he asked, leaving the driver's door open and joining Samantha in front of a rolled black tarp.

"It's a movie set," she answered, taking one end of the tarp. "Help me move this away from the wall, will you?"

Richard took the other end of the heavy, six-foot roll. Red liquid flowed out over his fingers and he let go, startled. "Sam, what the—"

"It's okay."

"Are you certain about that?"He showed her his red-slicked fingers. Neither of them wore gloves. If they were caught dragging a corpse around, they'd both end up in jail and featured on *Celebrity Justice*.

She flashed a grin at him. "Trust me."

Blowing out his breath, he bent down and grabbed the tarp again. They scooted it toward the middle of the warehouse. When it was clear of the worst of the clutter, Samantha quickly unwrapped it.

"Say hello to Anatomy Man,"she said, flipping back the last layer of tarp.

Richard looked down. Clark lay in a jumble of red stained wigs and clothes, most of them female undergarments, and sticky red organs. "Good God," he muttered.

"Just be glad he's anatomically neutral," Samantha said calmly, picking up the liver and a kidney and heading for the car. "Let's get these cleaned off."

Gingerly Richard retrieved the heart and a lung. "Why are we cleaning them?" he asked.

"Because we can't put Clark back in Miss Barlow's room looking like this. All the kids would need therapy."

"I think *I* need therapy after seeing that. He is very accurate, isn't he?"

"Except for where he's missing the good parts."

Richard gave a short laugh. "Saucy minx."

"Go get the brain, Igor. I'll start on these."

He went back and collected more internal organs. "I assume this was a horror movie?"

"That's my guess."

Richard watched her rinsing off the heart for a moment. "This was kids, wasn't it?"

She paused in her washing. "You can keep asking, and I'll tell you what I know. But you asked to be left ignorant, remember?"

"I remember." Whatever she didn't tell him, he could still make assumptions and draw conclusions. Did he want to know, though? And did the parents of this kid—these kids—want to know? Should they know? "What about the movie?"

"I guess it's going to be a cliffhanger, or they'll have to finish without their victim."

"I mean, where is the film? If you're keeping the identities of the filmmakers a secret, no one can see the results."

"Clark is kind of a standout," she said after a moment. "You're right; somebody might recognize him. I'll take care of it."

"How many break-ins are you doing this weekend?"

"I'm good with this one, the school, and the Picaults for today," she said briskly. "I'll leave a note."

"'A note,'" he repeated.

"Yes. Now let's get a move on. I don't know what time exactly August and Yvette will get back from their bike ride."

This time Richard frowned. "Did I miss something?"

"Very rarely."

He put a hand on her arm, making her look at him. "We're going to search the Picaults' house after the dinner party."

"I've been thinking about that. If we go in when they're not home, and then show up for dinner later, they really won't have a clue about what happened and who did it. If we go in after, they'll have better odds of figuring out you—we—had something to do with it."

"You've been connected with forged artworks and the failed theft of the jewel exhibit at my house in Devonshire, my love. I wouldn't say they won't have a clue."

"Well, they won't have anything they can prove. And you, Lord Rawley, are the kind of person that people don't accuse of much without proof."

"So you're using me as a shield for your misdeeds."

"My good deeds. I could use another kidney here."

Shaking his head, he retrieved the last of the internal organs, then went back for the bones that had been extracted.

Clark really was a font of information—and body parts. "How are you going to clean out his . . . body cavities?"

"I'll just have to flush him with water and then towel him out. I'm not aiming for perfection. just passable."

In half an hour they had Clark fairly well cleaned and lying on the tarp in the back of the Explorer, his body parts bagged and resting beside him. Samantha covered the pseudo-corpse with the end of the tarp, then dug around until she found a piece of paper in her jacket pocket and a pen in the glove box.

"What are you going to say?"

"'We've recovered your prop and returned it to the school,'" she said, writing as she went. "'If you want to avoid criminal charges, destroy the movie, as it is the only remaining evidence of your crime.'" She looked up at him. "Think that'll work?"

"I think so."

She set the note under the edge of the computer keyboard, then paused. "Aren't we missing a femur?"

He looked at Clark's leg and then went back through the bag. "Yes."

"Great. Check the old tarp again, will you?"

Of course he got the messy job. He searched through the folds of the faux-blood–spattered tarp while she went through the desk and the cardboard boxes of other props—fake handguns, plastic handcuffs, police badges and shirts, everything a good horror movie might need.

"Oh, cool," she said, lifting a small red-filled bag about the size of a candy bar.

"What is that?"

"A blood pack. Stuntmen put them under their shirts with a small explosive charge and whammo, you've been shot. A squib."

"You're very Hollywood, all of a sudden."

She laughed. "I like gadgets. No B and E use, but it's still fun."

Something white caught his eye under the edge of a broken pallet in front of him. "Got it. Either that, or there's a real body in here."

He put the second femur into the bag. Then they climbed into the SUV and Samantha directed him to J. C. Thomas Elementary School. Before he'd met Samantha he'd never spent a day like this in his life. Now, though, while he wouldn't precisely call it routine, it wasn't all that surprising. And he enjoyed it immensely.

Generally he discovered her about to do something dangerous and had to threaten or argue her into including him. This time she'd actually returned home to recruit his assistance. Yes, life was good. He glanced sideways at her. Her green eyes were unfocused, looking in the direction of the sky and probably seeing the layout of the Picaults' house, running through the robbery, gauging how much trouble she would have finding the armor, and whether it was even actually there.

"Do you think this is a wild goose chase?" she asked abruptly.

He considered her question for a moment. "If you had, say, six months instead of six days to decipher who your main suspects were, how would you go about it?"

"Well,"she began, sliding down in the seat to prop her knees against the dashboard, "I would work on tracking the thief, even though for a job pulled ten years ago it probably wouldn't make much difference who did it."

"Even so, walk me through it."

"It would have to be an A list guy with a crew, to get in and out carrying two crates—the exact two crates and nothing else—out from under the noses of Met security, Japanese exhibit officials, and the U.S. contingent."

"How many A list guys with a crew are we talking about?"

"From ten years ago? Three." She pointed. "Make a right here."

"You're pretty certain."

"I was fifteen, just going out on big jobs solo." She shrugged. "I'd been learning everything I could, from anybody I could."

"Which three could have pulled it off, then?"

"Gabrielle de Souza, Mick McClane, and Martin."

Richard nearly overshot the turn. "Your father, Martin?"

"Yep."

Okay. This was about Yoritomo's armor, not about her colorful family history. "Who did the Met job?"

She drew a breath. "My guess would be Mick. Gabrielle mostly worked Europe, and when Martin pulled me into the Met fiasco this past spring, he was going over the blueprints as closely as everybody else. He'd never worked the Met before. I'm sure of it."

"Very well, now we have Mick McClane. Where do we go from there?"

"Not to Mick, because he's in a German prison for the next thirty-seven years. But like I said before, this had to be a commissioned job. Somebody would have had to specifically put in an order for Yoritomo's armor and swords. And both they and Mick would be really expensive."

"Someone with a very large interest in Japanese antiquities, a weak moral compass, and a very large pocketbook."

"Exactly. And I would still guess they were East Coast–based, or Mick would have done the job in London."

"Who are your top three candidates, then?" he pressed,

turning into the elementary school's parking lot. "From ten years ago, of course."

"Since I did those four jobs for Toombs, he still makes the list. If not for the moral compass thing, I'd add you, just because of the quality of your collection. And—"

"Thank you, I think."

"You're welcome. Park up there. That's the closest entrance to Miss Barlow's classroom."

He turned up the row she indicated. "Who else?"

"The Picaults are still there. I've heard their names mentioned a couple of times, so they're not exactly straight arrows."

"So there's your top three."

"Well, if we exclude you, I'd bet on Leland Spicer. But ten years ago I don't think he had the spare change to afford it. I've gone through a list of about ten other potential buyers, but I can verify they never saw the samurai exhibit."

He put the car in park. "Considering, then, that we've eliminated me, and Spicer, and Toombs, I'd say the Picaults have that armor."

Samantha smiled, reaching over to touch his cheek. "You're sweet to say so."

Richard pulled her closer by her jacket collar and kissed her. "I'm betting that you know what you're doing. I know you don't want to go back to only security installations."

"No, I don't."

He opened his door, unwilling to break the mood by considering that tonight he intended to help her find a foothold in a career undoubtedly full of danger and mayhem, and only marginally legal, if that. Keeping her wrapped in security work, though, would probably kill her—figuratively if not literally—faster than an angry homeowner.

"The parking lot's empty," she noted, "so no security guys. Probably not, anyway."

"That's reassuring."

"Mm hm. You get Clark ready, and I'll shut off the alarms."

And to think, he reflected as he lifted the back gate of the Explorer, this was the easy part of the day.

"Remember," Samantha said, keeping her voice calm and even despite the rush of adrenaline beginning to pump through her muscles, "just because August and Yvette are out biking doesn't mean the household staff is gone. Especially with a dinner party set for three and a half hours from now."

"Hence the mustache, I assume," Aubrey commented, adjusting the bristles of the red handlebars and goatee she'd pasted on him.

"Don't touch; the spirit gum's not set yet."

She stuck the last bobby pin in her own hair and then bent double to pull the long black wig on over her head. As she straightened to look in the mirror she felt like Cher, but more importantly she definitely didn't look like Sam Jellicoe. Especially with the glasses on. Pulling the hair back, she tied it into a ponytail.

"I don't think I've ever worn coveralls before," Rick noted, emerging from his dressing closet.

"You look good," she decided, stifling a grin. "I can see a future for you in the carpet-and-curtain-cleaning industry."

"As long as we don't actually have to do any cleaning."

"And watch the accent. You're a Florida native this afternoon."

"Right, y'all," he tried.

It wasn't bad. Not great, but not bad. As Stoney walked over to hand him his black curly wig, she studied the body language between the two of them. No, they weren't friends, but they didn't hate each other, either. That was something, she supposed.

"Why can't Aubrey have the Shirley Temple hair, and I'll be the redhead?"

"Because curly hair looks just dreadful on me," Aubrey drawled.

"May I point out that this isn't a fashion show?" Stoney said, tugging the front of Rick's wig forward another quarter inch. "You guys are just lucky I had three sets of coveralls and wigs handy. Sam didn't give me much notice."

"And hats. Don't forget those." She looked down at the name tag embroidered on her chest. "A. Ramirez. I'm Alice, I think."

"P. Humphreys? I don't suppose I could be Pierre." Aubrey angled his hat a little to the left.

"Paul," she decided.

"And what is the C in C. Daltrey?" Rick asked. "And please don't say Chuck."

"No, I don't think you could pull off a Chuck," she agreed. "Charles, though. You could be a Charles if you had to, couldn't you?"

"A British Charles, yes. A Florida Charles, I'm not so certain."

"Try it again, Charles."

"Bloody hell," he muttered. "Hey, call me Charles, y'all."

"Is that how I sound?" Aubrey asked. "Because it's not very suave, which is how I've been picturing myself all these years."

They were both being laid back, or pretending to be, but

she could hear the tension in both of their voices. Aubrey's especially. He'd done himself proud during the lunch with Toombs and then the house tour, though, so she wasn't too worried. He'd carry his weight.

"Be a little less suave right now, if you can, Aubrey. Your voice is pretty recognizable."

"Heck, little darlin', I'll hick it up if y'all want me to."

Stoney rubbed his hand across his eyes. "We're doomed."

She walked over and kissed him on the cheek. "I'm glad you came back yesterday, so you could help me with this. It would have been a lot harder to pull off without your gear and the van."

"Yeah, well, I wish I'd come back two days ago, so I could have talked you out of this."

Two days ago they'd thought the break-in at Toombs's would have been the end of this. She pushed away the image of that creepy room again, and of the idea that she'd be sharing a rather intimate dinner with Wild Bill in just a couple of hours.

She needed to focus now, and not just for her sake; Rick had done this kind of thing a couple of times, but not a straight-up fake out. Aubrey was a total newbie, and he would follow her lead. So for now it was loose so he wouldn't get overstressed. In the van she'd sober them up and go over the details again.

"Everybody ready?" she asked, settling the Wayne's C & F Cleaners hat so it rode low over her eyes. The glasses obstructed her peripheral vision a little, but since this wasn't a stealth job, it didn't matter. The disguise was more important today—for all of them.

Rick nodded, while Aubrey gave her an overly enthusiastic thumbs up. Stoney rolled his eyes, but followed them out to where he'd parked the Wayne's van on the front drive. Since there was no Wayne's C & F Cleaners in actuality, she could only hope that none of his contacts had used the same ruse to break any major laws. He'd said they were clean, from an old movie prop place, but that didn't mean somebody else hadn't had the same idea first.

While Aubrey climbed into the back of the van, Rick caught her elbow. "You're certain about this?" he murmured. "We can still call Frank."

"For what? Castillo can't do anything. They've had the armor long enough now that it's legal. Going in and getting it is technically against the law. So are *you* certain you want to be involved with this? You have a lot to lose if it goes south."

"I have a lot more to lose if I don't go in."

She shook her head. "No, you don't," she whispered. "Maybe I'm crazy, but I wouldn't think any less of you if you decided you didn't want to break the law with me today."

He tilted her chin up and kissed her. "This might be breaking the law, but it's for a good cause. And in for a penny, in for a pound, as they say."

Mm. Kisses before a B and E were so . . . intoxicating. Samantha gazed at him for a moment in his unglamourous costume and dopey hair, then shook herself. *Focus, dammit.* "You're driving, curly," she said, tossing him the key as she climbed into the passenger side.

As they headed out, she picked up the clipboard of work orders she and Stoney had put together. A couple of adjustments to the Picault job, and she would have figured it was legitimate herself, if she hadn't had an exceptionally paranoid and suspicious nature.

She glanced back at Aubrey to see him fiddling with his

goatee. Total weirdness. In her entire cat burglary career she'd worked with a crew maybe half a dozen times, and here she was, leading two amateurs right through the front door, letting everyone in the house see them, and coming out with stolen goods. Hopefully.

"Okay, guys. Let's go over this one more time,"she said, mentally crossing her fingers, her toes, her eyes, anything that could be crossed. For somebody who'd never had much use for luck, she was definitely counting on it today.

Chapter 25

Sunday, 5:33 p.m.

"How did you do that?" Richard asked, a half-dozen hoses over his shoulder as he followed Aubrey and Samantha into the Picaults' dining room. "You got us in here faster than you can pick a lock."

"I can pick a lock much faster than that,"Samantha returned in a low voice, still using the light Cuban accent she'd adopted for the afternoon. She sounded remarkably like Reinaldo, but then that was probably where she'd picked it up. "I just did the usual. Had Stoney call here fifteen minutes ago and tell them we were on the way, running ahead of schedule, then threatened to just go on to the next job if they didn't let us in. We are working on a damn Sunday to catch up on appointments, after all."

"The parlor's just across the hallway," the frazzled housekeeper said, gesturing. "And you promised to be out of here by seven. We need to set the room for a dinner party."

"No problem, ma'am," Aubrey returned in a more restrained drawl than he generally used. "We'll set out the driers while we do the parlor."

"Thank you. Just hurry."

"Poor thing," Samantha murmured, following the woman to the door and shutting it behind her. "This is not going to be a good day for her."

Richard glanced at Samantha as she pulled the small vacuum cleaner out of the larger canister and plugged it in. The housekeeper would probably lose her employment, and Samantha knew that just as well as he did. She might not like killing bugs, but some of the things she was comfortable with made him uneasy.

"Ready?" she mouthed, looking from Aubrey to him.

He nodded, and she turned on the vacuum. For something so small it was surprisingly loud, but he supposed that was the point. She'd decided the armor was either in the ground floor conservatory, or in the basement where she figured they kept the rest of their larger pieces, though how she'd eliminated the rest of the house he had no idea. A thief thing, most likely. Even if she had a good idea where the armor was, however, getting to it was another issue.

"Okay," she said, motioning them closer. "You guys keep up the conversation in here. Football, or something. I'll be back in a minute."

"Even if you find it, how are you going to get sixty pounds of armor and two swords back in here?" Richard asked.

"Piece by piece." With a swift grin she returned to the door, cracked it open, then slipped through and shut it again.

"Amazing," Aubrey said, pushing the vacuum around. According to Samantha, clean vacuum marks did wonders for making people believe you'd done what you said you were going to.

Bloody fearless, she was. And he was inside somebody else's dining room, cleaning. He had people do that for him at his own house, and yet there he was, dusting curtains. "Who's playing tonight?"

"Uh, Oakland and somebody. The Bills, maybe."

"So you don't follow the sport, either."

"I've tried." Pendleton grinned. "You'd think a fellow like me would enjoy watching sweaty men crash into each other and slap each other's bottoms."

"Not necessarily," Richard muttered, most of his attention attuned to any sounds beyond that door—as if he could hear anything over that bloody vacuum cleaner.

"No?"

"I happen to think that you're not precisely what you imply you are."

The door cracked open. "There's no way the Raiders can rely on their running game,"Pendleton contributed, shifting a chair for effect.

The housekeeper stuck her head in. "Where's the other one? Alice?"

"At the truck," Richard answered in the drawl he'd been practicing.

The door shut again. "Speaking of not being what we say we are, *Charles*, you should unlatch the big canister," Aubrey said.

"Right." He mentally shook himself. Just because he was

nervous about the woman who'd vanished somewhere into a strange house probably owned by thieves didn't mean he needed to start a discussion about pretenses and motivations. Aubrey was sticking his neck out today, too, and for less reason than he or Samantha had. "Thanks, *Paul*."

"My pleasure."

He knew the drill; whatever else might be going on, they needed to keep up the pretense that they'd started out with. And so he had to stay right there. Dammit, he wanted to be where Samantha was, to watch her back if nothing else.

The door opened again. "How did Madden even coach without a monitor to scribble on?" he ventured.

"Good one, curly," Samantha said, slipping back into the dining room and once again shutting the door.

"Did you find it?"

Her smile could light up all of darkness. "Oh, yeah," she said softly. "But I could use your help."

Why did it feel like he lived to hear her say things like that? "Where to?"

"Paul, can you handle it in here for a minute? Charles's schedule tomorrow is messed up, and dispatch wants to clear it up with him."

"I'm good, Alice. This room is surprisingly not clean."

"All the better for us."

Richard fell in behind her as she ducked back out of the room and into the hallway. Putting a hand to her lips, she gestured toward the stairs, where she could hear a female conversation about an episode of *Grey's Anatomy*. They continued toward the rear of the house, then through a door and down a narrow, shabbier staircase. The old servants' section of the house, no doubt.

At the bottom of the stairs she stopped him again and listened for a minute with her ear against a plain white door.

Then she turned the latch and pushed it open. "Ta da," she said softly.

Seven full pieces of samurai armor stood at attention in front of him, arranged on metal frames in various battle stances. They were all magnificent, even to his jaded and experienced eyes.

"This was just sitting down here?"

"Well, if you call something that's double padlocked and secured in an alarmed, temperature-controlled room just sitting, then yes."

And she'd gotten through all that in about five minutes. "How did you know it was down here? You couldn't have spent much time searching."

"Come on. How many flimsy old doors at the bottom of plaster-peeling staircases are double padlocked and alarmed?"

She was leaving something out, but they didn't have time to debate her considerable skills at the moment. He took only a brief look around before he walked up to the armor in the center. It looked just like the photos Samantha had gotten from Viscanti.

Along the back wall a small but period-appropriate collection of swords, shoes, knives, bridles, and saddles were grouped behind each of the samurai. "Wow," he said quietly.

"Now *these* people know how to display their ill-gotten gains," Samantha agreed. "I wonder if all of them are stolen."

"Does it matter?"

She shrugged. "No. Just curious."

It probably *didn't* matter to her; for her entire life she'd seen the dark side of wealth and what it could buy. He was probably one of the few people she knew who didn't steal items to enhance his own collection or ego. "What do you need me to do?"

"The *keiko* cuirass is fastened. I can open it, but it's pretty delicate. If you can keep it from falling off the frame, then we can get it back upstairs."

Yoritomo Morimoto's armor was stunning. The *sana* scales that made up the plated armor were hardened leather, coated with orange and yellow lacquer, the colors still bright even after a thousand years. Gently he grasped the cuirass, holding it in place while Samantha undid the leather fastenings on the right side of the armor.

"Ready?"

"Ready."

She untied the last fastening, and the cuirass came loose from the frame. Forty pounds of metal and leather settled into his arms. As he adjusted his grip, being as careful as he could, Samantha lifted the helmet, the *ikabashi kabuto* and the underlying *eboshi*-style cap, off the stand. "I'll come back for the thigh protectors and the swords," she whispered, moving back to the door.

Now if they got caught, they couldn't claim they'd just gotten lost in the house. Now they were the carpet cleaners who'd made it through that door without setting off the alarm. His heart beating faster, he kept close to her as they returned up the stairs and crept through the main part of the house.

With a party only a few hours away, the staff would be moving in to prepare any minute now. The delay she'd created by pretending to clean the dining room wouldn't last much longer. And their luck wouldn't last much longer, either.

They made it back into the dining room. As soon as the door closed, Pendleton gave a low whistle, barely audible above the noise of the vacuum. "Amazing."

"Open the canister, will you?" Samantha instructed, all business now.

He did so, pulling out the cloth they'd stored in there and helping Richard wrap it gently around the cuirass before they set it inside the metal container, the wrapped helmet going in after it.

Richard checked his watch. "We should move on to the parlor," he said. "I'd hate to have to stay and clean it after we already have what we came here for."

"You guys haul the canister. Don't make it look any heavier than you did before." Samantha hoisted the hoses over her shoulder, took the three metal hose tubes in her hands, and waited while Richard opened the door with his free hand.

As he did so, the housekeeper appeared in front of him, so close to the doorway it almost made him jump. "How much longer?" she asked brusquely.

"Give the dining room about another ten minutes, and then it's all yours," Pendleton said.

Ten minutes. That meant ten minutes until the staff started bringing in utensils and plates and otherwise filling up the hallway in front of the parlor. Ten minutes for Samantha to finish removing Yoritomo's armor and accouterments from the cellar and get them back upstairs.

"Fine." The housekeeper stalked back toward the front of the house.

"You might have given us more than ten minutes," Richard snapped, keeping his voice low.

"Sorry," Pendleton returned, frowning. "I just thought we were getting a little close to sunset."

Richard looked out the window. Aubrey was correct. They weren't just fighting the household staff. The Picaults biked until sunset. Ten minutes might even be pushing it. He gave a tight nod.

They quickly set up everything in the parlor again, and Samantha headed for the door. "I'm going with you," Richard decided abruptly.

"No, you stay—"

"It'll go faster."

From her glare she wanted to dispute that, but she knew just as well as he did that they didn't have time to argue. "Let's go then, Chuck," she snapped.

Ignoring the moniker, he followed her back into the hallway and down the narrow stairs. At this point he wasn't certain whether this house and Toombs's were just underprotected, or if Samantha was so good at what she did that she made it appear that way.

No wonder regular security installations bored her. Back in the cellar room they detached the thigh and shin guards, and Samantha pulled the tanto and daitu swords off their rack. Reverently she half pulled the blade of the longer daitu sword out of its scabbard and examined it. "This is amazing," she breathed. "Over thirty-two thousand layers of steel, and less than a millimeter at the edge. The hilt's made of stingray skin."

He gazed at her for a moment. Was that why she'd wanted to come down here alone—to enjoy what she was taking? He knew she studied the provenance of every item she contracted for. "We need to go," he said softly.

Samantha sighed. "I know."

"At least this will go back to Japan for display. You can see it again."

"But not touch it." She visibly shook herself. "Okay, I

get it. No playing with the priceless artifacts. Let's go."

Outside the door she took a minute to relock the padlocks and reattach the door sensors, and then they returned to the main floor.

Upstairs they placed the rest of the armor in the canister, and Samantha carefully wrapped the swords and pushed them into the metal vacuum tubes. They helped Pendleton clean the curtains and the rest of the floor, then headed out just as the staff started to decorate the dining room.

"Thanks for letting us get this done today," Samantha said, offering the work order for the maid's signature. "I can't believe we're so backed up at this time of year. We'll be here before ten on Tuesday to do the rest of the house."

They loaded the canister, hoses, and tubes back into the van, and headed down the drive. And just like that, they'd done it.

Samantha dialed her cell phone, her gaze still on the suit of armor currently laid out on the library work table. Even Rick had seemed a little disappointed that they had to return Yoritomo's armor. It would look so nice in his warriors' gallery. Technically, though, it was stealing from a museum, and she didn't steal from museums. Ever.

"Hello?"

"Dr. Viscanti?" she returned. "It's Sam Jel—"

"Jellicoe," Viscanti finished, his voice sharpening. "Do you have any news for me?"

"I do. Arrange to be at work by ten o'clock tomorrow morning, and I'll have a crate delivered to you."

"Oh, thank God. Thank God," the curator muttered. "You have no idea—"

"I think I do," she interrupted, uncomfortable with and unused to gratitude from a client or a mark. When she relocated something it was always a monetary transaction. And besides, Stoney was usually the one who dealt with the contractor. Half the time she didn't know who she was working for, though after what she'd seen at Toombs's house, that had clearly been a mistake. "My finder's fee for this job is sixty grand."

"I'll get a check out to you as soon as I see the armor tomorrow morning."

"It's nice doing business with you, Joseph," she said, sitting back.

Viscanti laughed, giddiness and relief in the sound. "Oh, you'll be doing business with me again, Sam. And not just me. We curators are small in number, but you'd be surprised how many people try to liberate items from museums."

Not really. "Okay," she said aloud, grinning. "Call me when it gets there, will you? I feel kind of protective of the old shogun."

"You and me both. Thank you so much, Sam."

"You're welcome. I'll talk to you on Monday."

She flipped the phone closed, blowing out her breath. That was the score she'd needed, the one to start her art retrieval going. She'd done it.

"So does it feel good to be a good guy?" Rick asked from the doorway.

He'd put on gray dress slacks and a lighter gray shirt, his gray and rose silk tie hanging untied around his neck. "Yes, it does," she answered truthfully, standing and making her way around the table toward him. "Being bad pays better, but I think I could get used to this."

"Speaking on behalf of property owners everywhere, I am glad to hear you say that." He held out his hand. "Come here."

Grinning, Samantha walked up to him, relishing the way

he twisted his fist into her shirt and pulled her up against him, the passion in his kiss and the way it made her toes curl.

"You know," she murmured, when he gave her a second to breathe, "I think you have all the makings of an adrenaline junkie. You're having a little trouble coming down from our little job, aren't you?"

Rick shook his head. "I'm having a big problem. And I know just how to solve it." Kissing her again, he shifted his grip to slide his hands up under her shirt, up beneath her bra, to caress her breasts. "You feel good."

"So do you." She closed her eyes, enjoying the sensation of his very capable hands on her bare skin. "Rick, stop."

"No."

"Yes, stop." She pushed his hands down. "We have a dinner date that we can't be late for."

"Oh, yes. That." He kissed her again, trailing his mouth down her throat.

Christ. "Did you clear Stoney to get in here so he can pack the armor up?"

"Yes, I did. Louie and Reinaldo both know he's coming. They'll even feed him if he wants to eat. And I let my pilot know he'll be flying a crate to New York. All the details are worked out."

"Cool."

"So can we fool around now?"

She snorted, shoving at his shoulders again. "Later. I have to get dressed."

He kissed her once more. "I'm going to hold you to that. Three B and E's in two days, and no sex. I could be damaged."

Abruptly she realized what he was doing. "I'm okay about dinner with Toombs, you know," she said, taking the ends of his tie and knotting it for him. "You don't have to distract me. I'm a big girl."

"Maybe I'm distracting me," he commented, running a finger down her arm. "John Stillwell will be back here at the end of the week. I'm going to put him to work doing a little research."

"Your chief assistant doing research. Could it be on Toombs's businesses? He might have mob connections, you know."

"What I know is that he won't be taking any more photos of you." His voice lowered, shaking a little at the end. "You have your things you need to take care of, and I have mine."

"Rick—"

"You'd best hurry," he said, backing out of the doorway and checking his watch. "We need to leave in about twenty minutes."

For the moment she let it go. Truthfully, the idea of Toombs continuing to stalk her didn't sit well at all. Especially when he'd been doing it for nearly a year on and off, and she'd only realized it over the past week or two. Having Rick destroy him because he'd taken photos of her . . . She'd have to think about that one.

She decided to wear pants, just in case somebody recognized them and they needed to run for it, undignified as that would be for Rick and Aubrey. If she'd figured it right, the housekeeper would no longer be employed there, and she was the only one who'd gotten a good look at them. Tough for the housekeeper, yeah, but it also served her right for letting strangers into a house that didn't belong to her without any outside verification that they had actual business there.

Rick drove the Jaguar. She must not have looked as collected as she was aiming for, because he actually reached over to take her hand for part of the drive. She would have shrugged him off, except it was kind of endearing.

As they reached the Picaults' house and climbed out of the car, Samantha took his arm. "Just remember that you've never been in here before," she murmured, noting that Aubrey and Toombs—driving his damn black Miata—had already arrived. She smiled as Yvette pulled open the front door herself. No housekeeper, apparently.

"Good evening, Rick, Samantha," she said.

"Good evening," Rick returned. "How was your bike ride?"

"Very nice. Thank you for asking. Please come in. I'm afraid we're a little ragged tonight; August had to fire our housekeeper."

Yep, they knew the armor was missing. "I'm sorry to hear that," she replied, as they walked through the foyer and down the hallway to the parlor. "It seems like so many people come here for the sun, and not to do the work they hire out for."

"Yes, exactly."

Aubrey and Wild Bill both stood as they entered the parlor. "Hello gentlemen," Rick said, moving between her and Toombs to shake hands, while she settled for nodding.

Their demeanor clearly unsettled, August and Yvette conducted a tour of the house, showing off their collection of Japanese antiquities. By now Samantha had already seen most of it, but nobody knew she'd been on the second floor except maybe for Katie Donner—and neither of them was talking about that.

She pretended to be interested in the Hina dolls, and pretended that she didn't notice every time Toombs looked over at her, which seemed to be at least twice a minute.

Rick never left her side, and with Aubrey guarding the rear she felt kind of like Fort Knox. Amazingly enough, the basement wasn't part of the tour, which made her think that the other six sets of armor were probably there illegally, too. They weren't her concern, though, unless some other institution hired her to recover them.

Except for creepy Tombs and Rick nearly suffocating her, the evening was . . . dull. Boring. Normal. Yes, the Picaults were obviously frazzled, but they'd stated it was because they'd had to fire the housekeeper, and none of the rest of them were going to contradict that. So they all made small talk and ate dinner and said admiring things about the collection, and called it a night.

"I never thought thieves would be so dull," Rick said once they were back in the Jag and heading home. "Especially after meeting you."

"Yeah, well, you met me first, and I've just spoiled you for everything else. It's like having Claim Jumper eclairs. Nobody else's ever measure up after you've had one."

"You're an odd bird, Sam."

She grinned. "Well, this odd bird is sleeping in tomorrow. I am done for the week."

"After the sex, you can sleep in. I wasn't kidding about that."

"Sex with you is my eclair. I'm not passing that up."

Chapter 26

Monday, 9:44 a.m.

"Oh, for crying out loud!" Samantha grumbled, burying her head under her pillow.

It didn't keep her from hearing Rick laughing at her. "You didn't really think that whole sleeping-in thing through, did you?" The bed settled as he sat down on the edge of it.

"You're the one who made me start work on the damn garden." The table saw started up again down below. "What the hell are they doing?"

"I believe they're making the forms so they can pour the concrete garden borders."

"Make them stop."

"I might, if you hadn't given me the curly wig yesterday." His hand grasped her ankle through the blanket.

"You are an evil, evil man."

She heard him sigh. "Fine. I'll go have Reinaldo offer them some muffins and coffee. That should give you another half hour or so. I'll be in the office."

The bedroom door closed, and a couple of minutes later the saw whined to a stop. *Finally.* Readjusting her pillow, she snuggled into the blankets again.

The cell phone on her night stand rang. Growling, she threw off the covers and grabbed the phone. "Jellicoe," she snapped.

"Sam, it's here," Viscanti's happy voice came.

Rick was right. She hadn't thought the sleeping-late thing through, since she'd asked people to call her this morning. *Stupid.* "Good,"she said aloud. "Everything intact?"

"Yes. I've already called Dr. Naruko with the new exhibit, and he's flying up from D.C. I think you may have put the Met over the top."

"I'm glad. You invite me for the opening, okay?"

"I certainly will. Bye."

"Bye."

Before she even set the phone back, it rang again. This time she looked at the caller ID. J. C. Thomas Elementary School. As she hit the talk button, she decided to put this entry into her things-she-never-thought-would-happen journal. "Hello?"

"Miss Jellicoe?"

She recognized the voice. "Miss Barlow. Good morning."

"Good morning to you. I'm not even going to ask how you did it, but thank you so much for bringing Clark back here. The kids are just so excited. It's like . . . the good guys won one."

Wow. "My pleasure. I'm glad I could help."

"I hope you'll come on the day we present our science projects. You'd be our special guest."

"I'll see what I can do," she hedged, that panicky feeling welling up in her gut again. "Have Livia let me know when it is."

"I will. Have a good day, Miss Jellicoe."

Well, she wasn't going back to sleep now. Humming, she headed for the shower and then threw on a T-shirt and jeans and found the jacket she'd worn yesterday. Rick was in his office working on the computer when she knocked at the half-open door and walked in.

"You've cheered up quite a bit," he commented.

"Viscanti called to thank me, and then Livia's teacher called to thank me. I rule the world."

He grinned. "Well, Miss Ruler of the World, how would you like to go get some breakfast before the hammering and sawing starts again?"

"International House of Pancakes?"

"Just let me get my shoes."

While she waited for him, she wandered through part of his warrior hallway and over into the library to look down at the chaos she'd instigated. A dozen guys and half that many construction trucks were out there, scooping mounds of dirt out of the ground to reshape the pool, carefully potting the plants that needed to be removed for their relocation, cutting forms for the first concrete pour, doing the man thing with their thumbs in their belts as they surveyed the—

"Miss Sam, the—"

She turned around as Reinaldo tumbled into the room. Behind him, Wild Bill Toombs walked into the library and closed the door behind him, jamming a chair beneath the latch.

"Good morning," he said, bowing.

Her heart lurched. "What the hell do you think you're doing?" she snapped, striding over to check Reinaldo. He was out cold, but at least he was breathing. "And how did you get in here?"

The questions didn't matter all that much, especially when he produced a sheathed daitu sword from behind his back. They might slow him down a little, though, give her time to figure out what he intended to do, and give Rick time to realize Toombs was in the house.

"Your gate was open. You seem to be doing some garden landscaping."

"Yes, it was time for an upgrade. And hey, I know dinner last night was a little dull, but that wasn't my fault."

He nodded. "I think it was. I talked to August and Yvette last night, after you left. You wouldn't steal it for me, so who convinced you to take it?"

"What?"

"The Minamoto Yoritomo armor and swords. The first shogun. The statute of limitations expired three years ago. The same time I discovered you."

Toombs stepped farther into the room, and she backed away from Reinaldo. "I have no idea what you're talking about."

"Of course you do. Don't insult me. You know I've been . . . studying you, because you pursued my car. I let you see it last night."

"Your car?"

"As I said, I've been studying you, Samantha Elizabeth Jellicoe. In our modern world, *you* are a samurai. You were a ronin, until I took the reins. Do you even know how many items I had you steal for me? I controlled where you went and what you did. And now when we finally meet face-to-face, I find that you've betrayed me."

Why were all the raving lunatics attracted to her? "I think you have the wrong gal," she said, holding out her hands, letting him know that she figured he was crazy. "Three years ago I was working for the Norton, doing art restoration work. And now I do security. You know that, Wild Bill."

"I could accept that you retired. I kept watch, just in case, and I knew that you'd been keeping up your warrior's regimen."

"Wild Bill, I don't know what's going on, but you're—"

"Don't lie to me," he hissed. "Samurai don't lie. Especially not to their masters."

"Okay, what do you want me to say, then?"

"I want you to tell me who you stole that armor for after you refused to deliver it to me."

"I didn't refuse to do anything, because you've never asked me to do anything—except visit your house for a tour, which I did."

He drew the daitu out of its scabbard and whirled it slowly in the air, letting the sun through the windows catch the razor-sharp blade. "After disappointing his shogun, a true, virtuous samurai would take his own life. Since your crime is betrayal, I assume I will have to assist you in committing *sepiku*."

"I am not fucking killing myself. And stay away from me with that."

Toombs lunged. Whipping backward, she avoided the blade. Samantha grabbed a stepstool, holding it in front of her like a shield. He tapped it with the blade, testing her for weaknesses. Dammit. With hand-to-hand and even the occasional knife fight she could hold her own, but where swordplay was concerned, she had a lot of weaknesses.

The door latch turned. "Samantha?"

"Rick! Toombs is in here with a sword!" she shrieked, diving sideways as he came at her again.

The solid oak thudded and inched forward, caught by the chair. It thudded again, harder.

"I'll slice him in half," Toombs warned. "This is about us."

Samantha reached over for a book and threw it at his head. He ducked it. While he was off balance, she hurled the stepstool at his legs. Toombs went down onto one knee. Immediately she swept around, catching him in the side of the face with her foot.

He moved, too, twisting her ankle and shoving her down hard on her bottom. The blade sliced out, catching her across the thigh. She kicked out again, recoiling and scrambling backward. Fuck, that hurt, but she didn't take the time to see how badly she'd been cut.

The door and the chair splintered into the room. Richard dropped the thirty-pound iron mace he'd liberated from a German knight display and charged into the room, lifting one of his own swords as he did so. Reinaldo lay sprawled half beneath the work table. Across the room Samantha limped toward the window, throwing books at Toombs as she retreated. Blood trickled from a slice midway up her right thigh.

Toombs had hurt her. The fury that had been simmering inside him for the last two days erupted. Richard roared. "Toombs!" He swept forward.

Wild Bill swung around to meet him, Japanese daitu sword clanging against English saber. "This isn't about you," Toombs said, shoving out with his shoulder. "Stay out of it."

"You threaten her, it's about me," Richard shot back, elbowing him in the face and twisting out of the way as the daitu sliced through air. He hadn't dueled with a sword since his days at Oxford, but he didn't mean for this to be a fair fight. "Sam, get out!" he growled, slicing at Toombs's chest. Cut, parry, kick, punch—anything to move Toombs away from her.

The second she had the room to move, Samantha rushed forward and slammed a book across the back of Wild Bill's head. Toombs staggered, and she did it again. "You sick fuck," she yelled, swinging again.

"Back off!"

Toombs went down onto his face. Samantha swept in again—and Toombs twisted, shoving the sword up. Red erupted from Samantha's side.

Richard's heart stopped. Time stopped. Everything went white and ice cold. Shoving with all his strength, Richard propelled his sword through Toombs's shoulder and into the bookcase behind him. With a high-pitched squeal, Wild Bill dropped the daitu and clutched at the pommel of the saber.

Richard ignored him. "God," he muttered over and over, falling onto his knees beside Samantha. "Sam, don't move. Don't move."

She pushed at him, gasping as she ran her own palms down her blood-soaked side. "It's not me," she rasped. "He missed."

"You're in shock. Don't—"

"No." Samantha grabbed his searching hands. "I'm okay."

"There's blood everywhere." His voice caught.

"Look." Freeing one of her red-streaked hands, she held up her jacket pocket. The sliver of a hole pierced it, and blood seeped through the opening to drip onto the floor. "It's that blood pack from yesterday. I'm okay. Really. I'm okay."

It took him a minute to absorb what she was saying. And then he grabbed her shoulders, pulling her against him. "Thank God," he breathed, holding her tightly to his chest and rocking. "You scared me to death."

"Me, too."

"What the hell were you thinking, charging a man holding a sword?"

"I was thinking he might hurt you," she returned, gripping his shoulders hard.

Toombs's whimpering began to sink back into his hearing, and Richard stood, lifting Samantha up in his arms and setting her on the work table to look at her leg. "Its not too bad," he said, relief now making his voice shake. "You'll need some stitches, I think."

"How's Reinaldo?"

"Ay," the housekeeper mumbled, rolling over and gripping the back of his head. "Ay ay ay, that hurt."

Richard pulled the phone out of his pocket and dialed Frank Castillo's number.

"Castillo."

"Frank. It's Rick Addison."

"Funny you should call. I was just about to—"

"Frank, Gabriel Toombs is in my library, stuck to a bookcase with a sword. He tried to kill Samantha, and knocked out one of my people. I suggest you send someone to come and get him."

"Christ," the homicide detective muttered. "Is he alive?"

"For now. I need an ambulance for Samantha. He stabbed her."

"Holy—Is *she* alive?"

"If she wasn't, Toombs wouldn't be, either."

"I'll get some units rolling. Rick, where were you this morning?"

Richard frowned. "Samantha and I slept in. Why?"

"Because I've been listening in to some calls. The fire department's at Gabriel Toombs's house right now. Something about a second-story room going up. Since you and Sam were so interested in him, I can't help wondering if you know anything about it."

Richard glanced at Samantha, but she'd been in bed for longer than he had. "I can't say I'm sorry to hear it, but we had nothing to do with it."

"No, you're more the sword and bullet type. Don't kill anybody until I get there."

"Hurry."

Reinaldo staggered to his feet, and Richard helped him into a chair. Then he buzzed security on the intercom. A minute later two guards were in the library, looking from the door to Toombs to the wreck of the room. Wherever the hell they'd been earlier, he'd worry about later. "Watch him," he said, and picked up Samantha again.

"I can walk," she protested as they left the library.

"I know. I'm feeling gallant." He brought her into one of the upstairs sitting rooms and lowered her onto the couch. Then he ripped off his shirt and wound it around her thigh. "Better?"

"You just wanted an excuse to let me see your bare chest

again," she returned, sounding as cool as she always did—except for the hand she kept wrapped around his arm.

"Frank said he was about to call us," he said, kissing her forehead. "Toombs is experiencing a second-story house fire at this very moment."

"What?"

"Mm hm." Very few people knew what covered the walls of that turret room, which narrowed down the list of suspects to four. He and Samantha were accounted for, which left Aubrey, or Walter. "Walter?" he said aloud.

"That's not his usual style, but he was pretty mad about me being trailed around." She rested her head against his shoulder. "Wow. Wild Bill's going to lose a lot of really nice stuff."

"You won't catch me weeping about that," he returned. That was Samantha, though, sympathizing with the treasures she spent so much time studying and passing from owner to owner. "Did he find out that we broke into his house?"

"No. He's here because I apparently refused to steal Yoritomo's armor for him, but I did it for someone else. I'm his samurai, and I betrayed him."

"I think when Frank gets here we'll just go with the he's-nutty-as-a-fruitcake story," Richard decided.

"It's pretty much the truth."

He sank back on the couch, settling her against his side. Last night he'd thought they'd gotten through this fairly unscathed. The passions Samantha engendered in people continued to amaze him. And he couldn't bear the thought of ever letting her get away from him. His heart accelerating all over again, he took a deep breath.

"I have a question for you," he said quietly.

"I didn't set the fire. I was busy getting sliced up."

Richard smiled a little. "Different question."

"Okay."

"A statement too, I suppose." *Quit stalling, Rick.* "I think I fell in love with you the moment you dropped through my skylight last year. But that was mostly physical. Now, it's . . . everything. We just fit. Our faults, our virtues, whatever it is, I love you. All of you. And I always will. So, now comes the question part." He reached into his pants pocket and pulled out the Harry Winston box, then slowly opened the lid. The blue diamond in the center caught the light from the window, splintering it into rainbows and dancing across the smaller diamonds encrusting the platinum band. "Will you marry me, Samantha Elizabeth Jellicoe?"

She didn't answer. He tilted his head to look more closely at her expression, and a tear ran down her cheek. At that moment he felt the stark terror and devastation of knowing he'd made a mistake, that he'd just slammed the door on his own happiness. He should have left it the way it was. Now he'd ruined it, because she wouldn't stay after she refused him.

"Yes," she whispered.

His heart stopped. "Yes?" he repeated shakily.

"Yes, Richard William Addison. I just . . . I just hope you know what you're getting into."

"That's the fun," he said unsteadily, slipping the ring onto her finger and then kissing her softly, over and over. "Not knowing."

Epilogue

Monday, 10:20 a.m.

A figure dressed in golf clothes stood with the other onlookers who gazed at the fire blazing through the roof of the house just down the block from the green. A half dozen fire trucks were stopped around the perimeter, hoses turning fire and smoke to steam. They'd have it out in a few minutes, but the turret room would never be salvaged.

"You're up, Aubrey," Dr. Harkley's voice came from farther out on the green.

Aubrey Pendleton swung his five iron up over his shoulder and rejoined the rest of his foursome. "I have the sudden urge," he drawled with a smile, "for a nice, cool glass of lemonade. Care to join me in the clubhouse when we're finished here, gentlemen?"

Bad girls who can be so good . . .

Admit it. Women have known since they were teenagers that a sultry look, some flirtatious banter and perhaps a quick coat of lip gloss is often all the arsenal they need to get what they want. It's really quite unfair . . . But there's nothing more dangerously seductive than a bad girl who knows exactly what she wants and how to get it. Our heroes don't stand a chance!

In these thrilling Romance Superleaders, meet four sexy and unstoppable heroines who are determined—by any means, legal or otherwise—to get the man of her dreams.

Love Letters From a Duke

Elizabeth Boyle
September 2007

Felicity Langley had set her sights on being the next Duchess of Hollindrake. But then she hires a mysterious footman and finds herself reluctantly drawn to him. Whatever is a girl to do when all she ever wanted was to marry a duke and suddenly finds herself falling in love with the unlikely man at her side?

As the bell jangled again, Tally groaned at the clamor. "Sounds as presumptuous as a duke, doesn't it? Should I check the window for a coach and four before you answer it?"

Felicity shook her head. "That could hardly be Hollindrake." She nodded toward the bracket clock their father had sent them the year before. "It's too early for callers. Besides, he'd send around his card or a note before he just arrived at our doorstep. Not even a duke would be so presumptuous to call without sending word."

Sweeping her hands over her skirt and then patting her hair to make sure it was in place, Felicity was actually relieved it couldn't be her duke calling—for she still hadn't managed a way to gain them new wardrobes, let alone more coal. But she had a good week to solve those problems, at least until the House of Lords reconvened . . . for then Hollindrake would have to come to Town to formally claim his title and take his oath of allegiance.

"So who do you think it is?" Tally was asking as she clung to a squirming Brutus.

Taking another quick glance at the clock, Felicity let out a big sigh. "How could I have forgotten? The agency sent around a note yesterday that they had found us a footman who met our requirements."

Tally snorted. "What? He doesn't need a wage and won't rob us blind?"

Felicity glanced toward the ceiling and shook her head. "Of course I plan on paying him—eventually—and since we have nothing worth stealing, that shouldn't be an issue."

The bell jangled again, and this time Brutus squirmed free of his mistress's grasp, racing in anxious circles around the hem of Tally's gown and barking furiously.

Well, if there was any consolation, Felicity mused as she crossed the foyer and caught hold of the latch, whoever was being so insistent was about to have his boots ruined.

Taking a deep breath, she tugged the door open and found herself staring into a dark green greatcoat, which her gaze dismissively sped over for it sported only one poor cape. The owner stood hunched forward, the brim of his hat tipped down to shield him from the wintry chill.

"May I help you?" Felicity asked, trying to tamp down the shiver that rose up her spine. It wasn't that she'd been struck by a chill, for this mountain of a man was blocking the razor cold wind. No, rather, it was something she didn't quite understand.

And then she did.

As this stranger slowly straightened, the brim of his hat rose, revealing a solid masculine jaw—covered in a hint of dark stubble that did little to obscure the strong cleft in his chin, nor hide a pair of firm lips.

From there sat a Roman nose, set into his features with a noble sort of craggy fortitude. But it was his eyes that finally let loose that odd shiver through her limbs with an abandon that not even she could tamp down.

His gaze was as dark as night, a pair of eyes the color of Russian sable, mysterious and deep, rich and full of secrets.

Felicity found herself mesmerized, for all she could think about was something Pippin had once confessed—that from the very moment she'd looked into Captain Dashwell's eyes, she'd just known he was going to kiss her.

A ridiculous notion, Felicity had declared at the time. But suddenly she understood what her cousin had been saying. For right now she knew there was no way on earth she was going to go to her grave without having once had her lips plundered, thoroughly and spectacularly, by this man, until her toes curled up in her slippers and she couldn't breathe.

She didn't know how she knew such a thing, but she just did.

"I'm here to see Miss Langley," he said. His deep voice echoed with a craggy, smoky quality. From the authority in his taut stance, to the arch of his brow as he looked down at her—clearly as surprised to find a lady answering her own door as she was to find him standing on her steps—he left her staggering with one unbelievable thought.

And her shiver immediately turned to panic.

This is him, her heart sang. *Please let this be him.*

Hollindrake!

She struggled to find the words to answer him, but for the first time in her life, Felicity Langley found herself speechless. She moved her lips, tried to talk, tried to be sensible, but it was impossible under this imposing man's scrutinizing gaze.

Yet how could this be? What was *he* doing here, calling on her? And at such an unfashionable hour?

And no wonder he was staring at her, for her hair wasn't properly fixed, her dress fours years out of fashion, and her feet—dear God, she'd answered the door wearing red wool socks!

Tally nudged her from behind. "Felicity, say something."

Reluctantly wrenching her gaze away from his mesmerizing countenance, composing herself, she focused on what it was one said to their nearly betrothed.

But in those few moments, Felicity's dazzled gaze took in the coat once again—with its shockingly worn cuffs. *Worn cuffs?* Oh no, that wasn't right. And where there should be a pair of perfectly cut breeches, were a pair of patched trousers. *Patched?* But the final evidence that cooled her wayward thoughts more thoroughly than the icy floor that each morning met her toes was the pair of well-worn and thoroughly scuffed boots, one of which now sported the added accessory of a firmly attached small, black affenpinscher dog.

Boots that looked like they'd marched across Spain and back, boots that had never seen the tender care of a valet. Boots that belonged to a man of service, not a duke.

And certainly not the Duke of Hollindrake.

She took another tentative glance back at his face, and found that his noble and arrogant features still left her heart trembling, but this time in embarrassed disappointment.

To think that she would even consider kissing such a fellow . . . well, it wasn't done. Well, she conceded, it was. But only in all those fairy tales and French novels Tally and Pippin adored.

And that was exactly where such mad passions and notions of "love at first sight" belonged—between the covers of a book.

"You must be the man we've been expecting," Tally was saying, casting a dubious glance in Felicity's direction. Obviously unaffected by this man's handsome countenance, she bustled around and caught up Brutus by his hind legs, tugging at the little tyrant. "Sorry about that. He loves a good pair of boots. Hope these aren't your only pair."

A Touch of Minx

Suzanne Enoch
October 2007

Samantha Jellicoe and Richard Addison are at it again! Sam knows Rick wants more of a commitment from her—it's just so hard for a barely reformed thief to resist a golden opportunity to test her skills. But is she willing to risk losing her sexy billionaire lover?

For a second she hung in the air before she smacked into the palm's trunk and wrapped her arms and legs around it. That would have hurt if she hadn't worn jeans and a long-sleeved shirt. Black, of course; not only was the dark color slimming, but it was the clothing of choice for disappearing into shadows. Sucking in another breath, she shimmied up the rough trunk until she was about four feet above the house's roof.

The roof here at the back of the house was flat and had a very nice skylight set into the ceiling of the room she needed to get into. Glancing over her shoulder to make sure she was lined up, she pushed off backward, twisting in midair to land on her hands and knees on the rooftop. Keeping her forward momentum going, she somersaulted and came up onto her feet.

Normally speed wasn't as important as stealth, but tonight she needed to get into Richard Addison's office before he tracked her down. And for an amateur, he had a pretty good nose for larceny. Of course she was a damned bloodhound, if she said so herself.

With another smile she crouched in front of the skylight and leaned over to peer into the dark office space below. Just because he'd announced that he would wait for her to show up outside the door didn't mean that he'd done so. The padlock he'd put on the skylight stopped her for about twelve seconds, most of that taken up by the time it took her to dig the paper clip out of her pocket.

Setting the lock aside, she unlatched the skylight and carefully shoved it open, gripping the edge to lean in headfirst. The large room with its conference table, desk, and sitting area at one end looked empty, and her Spider-Man senses weren't wigging out.

Pushing off with her feet, she flipped head over hands and landed in the middle of the room, bending her knees to cushion her landing and cut down on any sound. A small black box topped by a red bow sat on the desk, but after a glance and a quick wrestling match with her curiosity, she walked past it to the refrigerator set into the credenza and pulled out a Diet Coke. Deliberately she walked to the office door, leaned against the frame, and popped the soda tab.

A second later she heard the distinctive sound of a key sliding into a lock, and the door handle flipped down. "Surprise," she said, taking a swallow of soda.

The tall, black-haired Englishman stopped just inside the doorway and glared at her. Blue eyes darkened to black in the dimness, but she didn't need light to read his expression. *Annoyed.* Rick Addison didn't like to be bested.

"You used the skylight, didn't you?" he said, making the sentence a statement rather than a question.

"Yep."

"I padlocked it an hour ago."

"Hello," she returned, handing him the Diet Coke. "Thief. Remember?"

"Retired thief." He took a drink and gave it back to her before he continued past her to the desk. "You didn't peek?"

"Nope. The thought never crossed my mind." Well, it had, but she hadn't given in, so that counted. "I wouldn't ruin your surprise."

When he faced her again, his mouth relaxed into a slight smile. "I was certain you'd attempt to get around me in the gallery hall."

"I went out through the library window. If I'da been a bomb, you would have been blowed up, slick."

Grabbing her by the front of the shirt, he yanked her up against him, bent his face down, and kissed her. Adrenaline flowed into arousal, and she kissed him back, pulling off her black leather gloves to tangle her bare fingers into his dark hair. A successful B and E was a lot like sex, and when she could actually combine the two, hoo baby.

"You smell like palm tree," he muttered, sweeping her legs out from under her and lowering her onto the gray carpeted floor.

"How do you think I got in here?"

Rick's hands paused on their trek up under her shirt. "You climbed up the palm tree?"

"It's the fastest way to go." She pulled his face down over hers again, yanking open the fly of his jeans with her free hand. She loved his body, the feel of his skin against hers. It amazed her that a guy who spent his days sitting at conference tables and computers and arguing over pieces of paper could have the body of a professional soccer player, but he did. And he knew how to use it, too.

He backed off a little again. "This was supposed to be fun, Samantha. Not you climbing up a tree and jumping onto a roof thirty feet in the air."

"That *is* fun, Brit. Quit stalling. I want my present." She shoved her hand down the front of his pants. "Mm, feels like you want to give it to me, too."

Halfway to the Grave

Jeaniene Frost
November 2007

Catherine Crawfield has more than a few skeletons in her closet. She's a vampire slayer with a big attitude, who makes an unlikely alliance with a vampire named Bones to track down an even more menacing evil. Though their chemistry is sizzling hot, how long can their dangerous association last?

"Beautiful ladies should never drink alone," a voice said next to me.

Turning to give a rebuff, I stopped short when I saw my admirer was as dead as Elvis. Blond hair about four shades darker than the other one's, with turquoise-colored eyes. Hell's bells, it was my lucky night.

"I hate to drink alone, in fact."

He smiled, showing lovely squared teeth. *All the better to bite you with, my dear.*

"Are you here by yourself?"

"Do you want me to be?" Coyly, I fluttered my lashes at him. This one wasn't going to get away, by God.

"I very much want you to be." His voice was lower now, his smile deeper. God, but they had great intonation. Most of them could double as phone-sex operators.

"Well, then I was. Except now I'm with you."

I let my head tilt to the side in a flirtatious manner that also bared my neck. His eyes followed the movement, and he licked his lips. *Oh good, a hungry one.*

"What's your name, lovely lady?"

"Cat Raven." An abbreviation of Catherine and the hair color of the first man who tried to kill me. See? Sentimental.

His smile broadened. "Such an unusual name."

His name was Kevin. He was twenty-eight and an architect, or so he claimed. Kevin was recently engaged, but his fiancée had dumped him and now he just wanted to find a nice girl and settle down. Listening to this, I managed not to choke on my drink in amusement. What a load of crap. Next he'd be pulling out pictures of a house with a white picket fence. Of course, he couldn't let me call a cab, and how inconsiderate that my fictitious friends left without me. How kind of him to drive me home, and oh, by the way, he had something to show me. Well, that made two of us.

Experience had taught me it was much easier to dispose of a car that hadn't been the scene of a killing. Therefore, I managed to open the passenger door of his Volkswagen and run screaming out of it with feigned horror when he made his move. He'd picked a deserted area, most of them did, so I didn't worry about a Good Samaritan hearing my cries.

He followed me with measured steps, delighted with my sloppy staggering. Pretending to trip, I whimpered for effect as he loomed over me. His face had transformed to reflect his true nature. A sinister smile revealed upper fangs where none had been before, and his previously blue eyes now glowed with a terrible green light.

I scrabbled around, concealing my hand slipping into my pocket. "Don't hurt me!"

He knelt, grasping the back of my neck.

"It will only hurt for a moment."

Just then, I struck. My hand whipped out in a practiced movement and the weapon it held pierced his heart. I twisted repeatedly until his mouth went slack and the light faded from his eyes. With a last wrenching shove, I pushed him off and wiped my bloody hands on my pants.

"You were right." I was out of breath from my exertions. "It only hurt for a moment."

Much later when I arrived home, I was whistling. The night hadn't been a total waste after all. One had gotten away, but one would be prowling the dark no more. My mother was asleep in the room we shared. I'd tell her about it in the morning. It was the first question she asked on the weekends. *Did you get one of those things, Catherine?* Well, yes, I did! All without me getting battered or pulled over. Who could ask for more?

I was in such a good mood, in fact, that I decided to try the same club the next night. After all, there was a dangerous bloodsucker in the area and I had to stop him, right? So I went about my usual household chores with impatience. My mother and I lived with my grandparents. They owned a modest two-story home that had actually once been a barn. Turned out the isolated property, with its acres of land, was coming in handy. By nine o'clock, I was out the door.

It was crowded again, this being a Saturday night. The music was just as loud and the faces just as blank. My initial sweep of the place turned up nothing, deflating my mood a little. I headed toward the bar and didn't notice the crackle in the air before I heard his voice.

"I'm ready to fuck now."

"What?"

I whirled around, prepared to indignantly scald the ears of the unknown creep, when I stopped. It was *him*. A blush came to my face when I remembered what I'd said last night. Apparently he'd remembered as well.

"Ah yes, well . . ." Exactly how did one respond to that? "Umm, drink first? Beer or . . . ?"

"Don't bother." He interrupted my hail of the bartender and traced a finger along my jaw. "Let's go."

"Now?" I looked around, thrown off guard.

"Yeah, now. Changed your mind, luv?"

There was a challenge in his eyes and a gleam I couldn't decipher. Not wanting to risk losing him again, I grabbed my purse and gestured to the door.

"Lead the way."

Lord of Scoundrels

Loretta Chase
December 2007

Jessica Trent wants only to free her nitwit brother from the destructive influence of Sebastian Ballister, the notorious Marquess of Dain—she never expects to desire the arrogant cad. But when they are caught in a scandalously compromising position, will Jessica submit to her passion or will she have no choice but to seek satisfaction?

Lord Dain did not look up when the shop bell tinkled. He did not care who the new customer might be, and Champtois, purveyor of antiques and artistic curiosities, could not possibly care, because the most important customer in Paris had already entered his shop. Being the most important, Dain expected and received the shopkeeper's exclusive attention. Champtois not only did not glance toward the door, but gave no sign to seeing, hearing, or thinking anything unrelated to the marquess of Dain.

Indifference, unfortunately, is not the same as deafness. The bell had no sooner ceased tinkling than Dain heard a familiar male voice muttering in English accents, and an unfamiliar, feminine one murmuring in response. He could not make out the words. For once, Bertie Trent managed to keep his voice below the alleged "whisper" that could be heard across a football field.

Still, it was Bertie Trent, the greatest nitwit in the Northern Hemisphere, which meant that Lord Dain must postpone his own transaction. He had no intention of conducting a bargaining session while Trent was by, saying, doing, and looking everything calculated to drive the price up while under the delirious delusion he was shrewdly helping to drive it down.

"I say," came the rugby-field voice. "Isn't that—Well, by Jupiter, it *is*."

Thud. Thud. Thud. Heavy approaching footsteps.

Lord Dain suppressed a sigh, turned, and directed a hard stare at his accoster.

Trent stopped short. "That is to say, don't mean to interrupt, I'm sure, especially when a chap's dickering with Champtois," he said, jerking his head in the proprietor's direction. "Like I was telling Jess a moment ago, a cove's got to keep his wits about him and mind he don't offer more than half what he's willing to pay. Not to mention keeping track of what's 'half' and what's 'twice' when it's all in confounded francs and sous and what you call 'em other gibberishy coins and multiplying and dividing again to tally it up in proper pounds, shillings, and pence—which I don't know why they don't do it proper in the first place except maybe to aggravate a fellow."

"I believe I've remarked before, Trent, that you might experience less aggravation if you did not upset the balance of your delicate consitution by attempting to *count*," said Dain.

He heard a rustle of movement and a muffled sound somewhere ahead and to his left. His gaze shifted thither. The female whose murmurs he'd heard was bent over a display case of jewelry. The shop was exceedingly ill lit—on purpose, to increase customers' difficulty in properly evaluating what they were looking at. All Dain could ascertain was that the female wore a blue overgarment of some sort and one of the hideously overdecorated bonnets currently in fashion.

"I particularly recommend," he went on, his eyes upon the female, "that you resist the temptation to count if you are contemplating a gift for your *chère amie*. Women deal in a higher mathematical realm than men, expecially when it comes to gifts."

"That, Bertie, is a consequence of the feminine brain having reached a more advanced state of development," said the female without looking up. "She recognizes that the selection of a gift requires the balancing of a profoundly complicated moral, psychological, aesthetic, and sentimental equation. I should not recommend that a mere male attempt to involve himself in the delicate process of balancing it, especially by the primitive method of *counting*."

For one unsettling moment, it seemed to Lord Dain that someone had just shoved his head into a privy. His heart began to pound, and his skin broke out in clammy gooseflesh, much as it had on one unforgettable day at Eton five and twenty years ago.

He told himself that his breakfast has not agreed with him. The butter must have been rancid.

It was utterly unthinkable that the contemptuous feminine retort had overset him. He could not possibly be disconcerted by the discovery that this sharp-tongued female was not, as he'd assumed, a trollop Bertie had attached himself to the previous night.

Her accents proclaimed her a *lady*. Worse—if there could be a worse species of humanity—she was, by the sounds of it, a bluestocking. Lord Dain had never before in his life met a female who'd even heard of an equation, let alone was aware that one balanced them.

Bertie approached, and in his playing-field confidential whisper asked, "Any idea what she said, Dain?"

"Yes."

"What was it?"

"Men are ignorant brutes."

"You sure?"

"Quite."

Bertie let out a sigh and turned to the female, who still appeared fascinated with the contents of the display case. "You promised you wouldn't insult my friends, Jess."

"I don't see how I could, when I haven't met any."

She seemed to be fixed on something. The beribboned and beflowered bonnet tilted this way and that as she studied the object of her interest from various angles.

"Well, do you want to meet one?" Trent asked impatiently. "Or do you mean to stand there gaping at that rubbish all day?"

She straightened, but did not turn around.

Bertie cleared his throat. "Jessica," he said determinedly, "Dain. Dain—Drat you, Jess, can't you take your eyes off that trash for one minute?"

She turned.

"Dain—m' sister."

She looked up.

And a swift, fierce heat swept Lord Dain from the crown of his head to the toes in his champagne-buffed boots. The heat was immediately succeeded by a cold sweat.

"My Lord," she said with a curt nod.

"Miss Trent," he said. Then he could not for the life of him produce another syllable.

Under the monstrous bonnet was a perfect oval of a porcelain white, flawless countenance. Thick, sooty lashes framed silver-grey eyes with an upward slant that neatly harmonized with the slant of her high cheekbones. He nose was straight and delicately slender, her mouth soft and pink and just a fraction overfull.

She was not classic English perfection, but she was some sort of perfection and, being neither blind nor ignorant, Lord Dain generally recognized quality when he saw it.

If she had been a piece of Sevres china or an oil painting or a tapestry, he would have bought her on the spot and not quibbled about the price.

For one deranged instant, while he contemplated licking her from the top of her alabaster brow to the tips of her dainty toes, he wondered what her price was.

But out of the corner of his eye, he glimpsed his reflection in the glass.

His dark face was harsh and hard, the face of Beelzebub himself. In Dain's case, the book could be judged accurately by the cover, for he was dark and hard inside as well. His was a Dartmoor soul, where the wind blew fierce and the rain beat down upon grim, grey rocks, and where the pretty green patches of ground turned out to be mires that could suck down an ox.

Anyone with half a brain could see the signs posted. "ABANDON ALL HOPE, YE WHO ENTER HERE" or, more to the point, "DANGER. QUICKSAND."